TURNING HEARTS

SHORT STORIES ON FAMILY LIFE

EDITED BY

ORSON SCOTT CARD
& DAVID DOLLAHITE

BOOKCRAFT
Salt Lake City, Utah

These stories are works of fiction,
and any resemblance to actual persons,
living or dead, is purely coincidental.

Library of Congress Catalog Card Number: 94-79640
ISBN 0-88494-948-6

Second Printing, 1995

Printed in the United States of America

TURNING HEARTS

SHORT STORIES ON FAMILY LIFE

Christmas 1998 –
Anne, here's a book to
remind you of our Young Women's
theme this year. Cuddle up in your
soft blanket and read some stories!
Love you, Aunt Karen

Dollahite:

To my parents, Elizabeth and Mel Dollahite,
for life and love

Card:

For Richard Cracroft,
shepherd of mantic fiction among the Mormon people

Contents

Families in Fiction

ORSON SCOTT CARD

Most literature is adolescent literature. Oh, the heroes are in their twenties or thirties or forties—they certainly *look* like grown-ups. But when you examine the story, you realize that the hero of story after story is actually a functional adolescent. He has cut himself loose from family and the community of his childhood. Like the Lone Ranger, he wanders in search of wrongs to right, great deeds to accomplish; when he has accomplished his noble deed, he wanders on, rootless, leaving people to ask, Who *was* that masked man?

Masked man indeed! The adolescent hero is grandly poetic. His nobility excites all our youthful yearnings for greatness. But tomorrow he won't be there. And even when he's among us, we have no idea who he is.

His awful secret is that he has no idea who he is, either. He *is* the mask. Without it (without the Superman suit, without the license to kill, without the shining armor) he's just a bag of throbbing tissues like everyone else. Unbearable ordinariness. O let me not be plain, cries the adolescent. Let me not be predictable.

Or, in other words (the words the adolescent's parents hear, alas): Let me not be responsible for anything. Let me do such good as appeals to me, and move on. Don't expect me to be reliable. That's Dad's job.

Perhaps it was predictable that feminist literature, instead of replacing the adolescent with grownup heroes, merely created mythic female wanderers. Nor has academic-literary fiction improved the situation. Disguised in the trappings of the contemporary world, their stories are still largely about men and women cutting themselves loose from family ties, abandoning job responsibilities, and going out to find themselves.

There's nothing intrinsically wrong with adolescent heroes; indeed, the prevalence of these stories suggests that there is a near-universal hunger for stories of the noble deeds of the Rootless Stranger. But the truth is that adolescence is, or should be, only a stage in our lives. Beowulf was a wanderer, it is true, when he slew the monster Grendel and its mother; but then he settled down and ruled a kingdom in peace and justice and safety for many years, before, in his old age, he died saving his people from a dragon. It was not an unknown adolescent who died for his people. It was the king, a father. They knew him.

The present American obsession with the adolescent hero is more a symptom than a cause of the national malaise. Many divorces are mere retreats into adolescence, the stage in life during which commitments do not matter; most children born out of wedlock are the product of adolescent visions of manliness, the overwhelming stranger who is never there when the seeds he planted germinate and need tending. Certainties have become tentative, not because we have learned some ancient truth about the transience of all things, but rather because we have forgotten that we have it in our power to make some things permanent: marriage, parenthood, family. The adolescent is incapable of these commitments; American fiction generally reflects and, I fear, glorifies that incapability.

The situation is not universally bleak. There are still many solid marriages and stable families. And there are writers telling stories about the grownups who create them. I think at once of Anne Tyler, but she's not alone. Walter Mosley's hard-boiled detective is struggling to put down roots and hold firm as a grownup; so is James Lee Burke's. All three of these writers explore the lives of people who choose not to escape even from painful and difficult relationships, who cannot or will not flee from the consequences of their own mistakes.

As with so many other aspects of Mormon culture, we seem to resemble America far more than is healthy for us. My literary friends who sneer at childishly romantic LDS popular fiction seem oblivious to the fact that their own heroes are, often, just as adolescent, and their stories just as escapist. Only the settings and style are different.

But we Latter-day Saints *do* know something about families. We have not lost our commitment to permanence. We aspire to be grownups, to be responsible, reliable, predictable . . . and, the world's myths to the contrary notwithstanding, people who make these commitments are not dull. Tolstoy was wrong: Good people (or, at least, people trying to be good) are infinitely varied in their struggles; it is the unreliable, rootless, soon-to-be-gone adolescent heroes who, ultimately, are all the same.

I am far from being the only (or even the primary) LDS writer who has tried to buck the trend and write fiction about adult heroes. But it never crossed my mind to try to gather stories by many of these writers within the covers of the same book, not until my good friend, family therapist and researcher David Dollahite, proposed to me that we coedit an anthology that would try to fulfil the prophecy and turn the hearts of the fathers to the children and the children to the fathers.

It is well known in the book business that anthologies don't sell. Readers these days want novels. And yet I couldn't help but believe that this book might be different. There is an audience hungry for stories about people who have made the commitment to life that creating a family represents. If we print it, surely they will find it.

My editor and publisher at Bookcraft, Garry Garff and Cory Maxwell, surprised me (but I shouldn't have been surprised) by agreeing to the project, risky as it was, almost immediately. Then came the most nerve-wracking step: inviting established Mormon authors to take part in the project. What if no one wanted to take part? Or, worse yet, what if they wanted to, but their stories simply didn't deal with family relationships as we hoped?

We need not have feared. We had so many excellent submissions that we had the luxury of picking and choosing so that the anthology would cover all aspects of family life. We also received stories across the whole spectrum of contemporary literary technique, from polished "slick" fiction to somewhat challenging literary fiction, from humor to high drama, from harsh realism to visionlike spirituality.

Who are the writers we are publishing here? Some are full-time professionals whose names you are probably familiar with; some are appearing in print for the first time, or at least for the first time with fiction. The two editors felt confident enough of each other's judgment that we have dared to include two of our own stories here. My own work has been before the public for many years; I am proud that this volume also introduces the first published fiction of my coeditor, David Dollahite. A convert to the Church in his late teens, when injury ruined his hopes of a career in professional tennis he turned his extraordinary intelligence and energy to family studies. He has a gift for compassion and healing, and through his long experience with research and family therapy, he has deep reservoirs of knowledge about family life. He also is awake to things of the Spirit and to the nuances of the art of storytelling, and so I was not surprised when his story "Possum Funeral" turned out to exemplify all that I hoped for in the fiction of commitment.

When you dig into the pages of this book, you will discover many voices, but, at root, they all sing the same deep song. Time after time, as I read these stories, I found myself weeping—or laughing aloud—but always at the same realization: This is true. This matters, and it's true.

Possum Funeral

DAVID DOLLAHITE

In the middle of the chapel, Jared Lawson sat with one arm around his wife Ann and the other around his oldest son Bryan. Tara sat next to Ann and Daniel was on Ann's lap. Jared had been away on business the past Sunday and felt happy to be back in his home ward with his family. Having lived all his life in Arizona until a year ago, it was a little funny for him to realize that he now considered North Carolina home.

Jared thought about the Sunday School lesson he was going to teach on the Atonement. He knew he still needed to think of an experience from his life to illustrate the main point.

Bishop Dennick announced, "We appreciate those who helped at the cannery last week. And, Bryan Lawson turns eight next Saturday and will be baptized and confirmed by his father on Sunday at four P.M. We hope you will all attend. The opening song will be hymn number 292, 'O My Father,' after which Sister Lewis will offer the invocation."

Ann took Jared's hand and squeezed. Bryan looked up at Jared and smiled and Jared hugged his son close to him. Along with the congregation, Jared opened the hymnbook to what, for him, had always been a bittersweet hymn, since it was sung at his father's funeral. Then it hit him: Jared was now the same age that his father had been when he died—and Bryan was the same age that Jared was then. He had been so involved with family, church, and work that he hadn't seen it coming.

Suddenly, waves of pain and loneliness washed over him and he felt hot tears run down his face. He tried to do what he always did when thoughts of his father came: think about other things. But when he sang, "O my Father, thou that dwellest in the high and glorious place, when shall I regain thy presence and again behold thy face?" he knew he was not singing to his living God, but to his deceased father. He noticed other people looking at him and realized they must think he was weeping with joy at Bryan's approaching baptism. He wiped the tears away and forced himself to think about his lesson. He made it through the meeting, taught a thoughtful, if sterile, lesson on the Atonement, then sat in priesthood meeting fighting the pain.

On the drive home from church, Jared listened to the kids telling Ann about what they learned in Primary. He watched the brown and orange leaves, some dancing in swirls in the road, pushed high in the air by the wind from passing cars; most wet and flattened to the pavement under spinning wheels. He thought about the letter he just received from his mother, who lived back in Tucson. She said that she wished she could be there for Bryan's baptism, but that because of her failing health, North Carolina was just too far to come. He wondered how long she would live.

Jared slowed the car to make the turn onto Shady Lane. As he turned onto their street he saw, lying on its back at the bottom of their driveway, a gray-white, cat-size animal with a curled, hairless tail and a tooth-filled mouth gaping open, its purple tongue hanging out. Somehow the sight of the dead animal triggered Jared's memory of his father lying in the casket, his strong hands folded unnaturally across his chest, his face covered with makeup that tried to hide the burns.

Daniel, their rambunctious four-year-old, asked, "What's that, Mom?"

"It looks like a cat," six-year-old Tara answered.

"It looks like a giant rat to me!" Bryan added.

"It's a possum," Ann said.

Jared pulled into the driveway. Everyone else got out of the car and gazed down at the possum. Inexplicably, Jared felt both fear and anger rise within him.

Tara leaned into the car. "Daddy, what are you going to do with it?"

"I'm not doing anything with it. I'm not getting near it!" Jared got out of the car and headed for the front door. "I'm going to have someone get that disgusting creature out of here." Jared knew he was overreacting, but he didn't want to see or even think about that creature and the memories it stirred. In the kitchen Jared took out the phone book and called the Humane Society and the Sanitation Department. All he got were answering machines telling him to call Monday.

Bryan came in the kitchen and asked, "Dad, can we bury him like we buried that bird last year?"

Jared remembered how serious Bryan had been when they dug a little hole, put the bird in it and filled it up. He thought fleetingly about burying the animal, pictured again its long, hairless tail and sharp little teeth, then dismissed the thought in disgust. "No, that was a cute little robin and this is a disgusting cat-sized rat."

"What are you going to do with it?" Ann asked.

"I guess I'll get rid of it myself. I'll get a shovel and throw it as far back into the woods behind the house as I can."

Jared went out the back door to the old shed in the back yard. He got the shovel and walked toward the front yard. Their neighbor, Ogden, who was in his garden, waved and said hello. Jared explained to him what had happened.

Ogden leaned on his rake and looked at Jared. "Yeah, I hear possums in your back yard quite often at night. Your persimmon tree there probably feeds half the possums in town—it's one of their favorite foods."

Jared smiled. "Well, I'm going to throw this one back in the woods so maybe the others will think twice about coming into my back yard. But they're welcome to eat all the persimmons they want; it makes fewer for me to clean up."

"Yeah, they're pretty messy," Ogden said.

"If they tasted good, that would be tolerable, but I tasted a persimmon once and I don't plan to repeat that experience!" Jared remembered the year before, when he had picked one of the little golden-purple fruits and bitten into it, expecting it to taste sweet. Instead, it had been the most soul-souring thing he had ever tasted, and his mouth dried so rapidly and so completely he thought he would die of thirst. He had run into the house and drunk three glasses of water, but his mouth still felt like a bowl of old dust.

"Yeah, they're pretty sour till after a couple of frosts. Even then, you kind of have to develop a taste for them. My Libby makes a great persimmon pie, though."

"You know, Ogden, I've thought more than once about chopping down that tree. Now that I know persimmons attract possums I'm tempted even more."

"Get yourself a good chainsaw. Persimmon wood is used to make golf club heads. It's really hard stuff."

"Thanks, I'll remember that," Jared replied. "Well, I'd better get rid of that creature."

As he walked down the wet driveway, he saw Bryan standing in the street, reaching down toward the possum.

Jared cried out, "Bryan! Get away from that thing! It's probably got some disease!" Bryan backed away and Jared hurried down, scooped the possum onto the shovel and made his way back up the steep driveway, with Bryan following behind. Jared was surprised at how heavy the possum was, and he wondered how far he would be able to throw it into the woods. He rammed his shoulder against the gate to the back yard, but it was latched and didn't give. The possum fell off the shovel and landed on its back, its paws curled up, its mouth full of teeth and its black eyes staring at Jared, who cringed at the sight and had a surprisingly strong urge to smash the creature's face with the shovel. He saw Bryan staring at the possum, so instead of maiming the lifeless animal, he turned and kicked the gate open, breaking the latch. He scooped up the possum again and went through the gate, picking up momentum as he moved toward the short wire fence that separated the yard from the five-acre wooded lot that sheltered his house from the four-lane street beyond.

As Jared reached the fence, he drew back the shovel smoothly and flung the possum into the forest, its lifeless body bouncing past an old bottle and up against a fallen tree—an

almost picture-perfect toss. Had it not been for the layer of rotting persimmons and wet leaves on the ground, along with the
fact that he still had his Sunday shoes on, he would probably
have kept his balance.

He plopped down on his rear and felt the cold, wet muck
seep through his suit pants. Bryan had come through the gate
just in time to see Jared fall, and he laughed and pointed at his
father sitting there in the slop trying to get up. Jared glared at
Bryan in shame and rage, picked up a persimmon, and threw it
at his son. It fell short, and Jared sent Bryan into the house with
a shout. Bryan ran into the house crying, and told his mom what
had happened. Ann and the kids came to the window to watch.

As Jared got up he envisioned dozens of possums feasting
on rotting, putrid persimmons every night in his back yard,
their sharp little teeth dripping with juice and their long rat tails
curled around each other. He said out loud to the tree, "That's
it! You're firewood!" He strode to the shed and grabbed the old
rusty axe that had been his father's. As he turned and faced the
tree, he felt a surge of rage rise up within him and walked, teeth
clenched, his eyes zeroing in on the kill.

The first whack of the old dull axe against the hard bark of
the stately tree sent a sharp sliver of pain up his arm to his
shoulder. But his shame and rage drove him to continue attacking with all he had. Over and over he whacked at the trunk, and
at the loneliness and the humiliation he felt. The axe had little
effect on the tree and no effect on his pain. Jared realized that
he needed a sharper tool and dry pants. He thought of the fact
that his father could have cut this tree down in ten minutes,
and would never have thrown anything at his son in a fit of
anger.

Jared remembered something his father had said to him a
couple of times in the weeks before his eighth birthday: "Son,
after your baptism, I will lay my hands on your head to confirm
you a member of the Church, just like when I was a boy and
your grandfather laid his hands on my head, and just like when
my father was a boy and his father laid his hands on his head.
And when you're twelve, I'll lay my hands on your head and or-
dain you to the priesthood, just like my father did, and his father, and his father."

But three days before Jared turned eight, his father was killed fighting a fire. So Jared didn't feel his father's hands on his head that day. When he turned twelve, it was not his father's hands that conferred the Aaronic priesthood, nor at eighteen when he was made an elder. With each ordinance, Jared had longed to have his father's large, strong hands on his head and to hear his father's voice call him by name and bless him.

Now his yearning for his father overwhelmed him. He realized that he was completely on his own as a father. He felt sure that he would never be the kind of father to his son that his dad had been to him. Jared felt himself going into one of his dazes—the ones that only came when he thought about his father.

He shook his head and tried to stop the clouds in his mind. He tried jamming the axe into the trunk, but it fell and landed in a pile of persimmons. Jared just left it there, and as he walked toward the house he vowed that on Saturday he would finish the job.

After Jared showered and changed his clothes, he went into Bryan's room and sat down on the bed. "Son, I'm sorry I got angry and yelled at you. I don't know what got into me. And you had every right to laugh. It must have been pretty funny to see me plop on my rear in a big squishy pile of muck! And I'm *really* sorry I threw a persimmon at you. I never should've done that. Lucky for you I'm not as good a pitcher as I used to be."

Bryan answered wryly, "That's because you don't play catch with me enough."

"You're right, I don't. I'll try to do better. But now, let's go throw some food in our mouths, okay?"

Bryan came along to dinner, but Jared could tell he still felt hurt.

After the blessing on the food, Tara pleaded, "Daddy, please don't chop the tree down, because Libby told me and Bryan she would make us pudding if we collected one hundred persimmons."

"Yeah, Dad, and I want to climb that tree someday," Bryan added. "Remember you told me you would teach me to climb it when I got older. Well, could you teach me today?"

"Not today, but maybe another day," Jared answered.

Bryan's face told Jared that he was disappointed, but not

surprised. "But Dad, you promised! You never let me do *any-thing* fun."

Jared remembered having made the promise months before. "I don't let you do anything dangerous. Maybe in a couple of months, but not today."

"Kids, Dad's had a hard day and he's tired," Ann said. "Let's talk about what we're going to do for family home evening tomorrow night, okay?" The conversation shifted to who would give the lesson and what they would have for refreshments, and Bryan mentioned he wanted to practice the baptism, but Jared, not really hearing, looked out the window, daydreaming about his father.

* * *

That night Jared had the dream about his father again. Jared was on the pitcher's mound of the Little League baseball field he had played on as a youth back in Tucson. The red dirt of the infield and the mound was newly raked and soft, the sun shining without a cloud in sight. Jared was pitching, about to throw his best curveball and strike out the batter. His father was in the stands cheering for his son—all the world was right. Then a howling fire alarm went off, and the boy in the batter's box transformed into Jared's father, dressed in his firefighter's uniform, holding an axe. Suddenly, huge rectangular black clouds that looked like burning houses swooped in over the field, throwing coffin-like shadows on the grass. Crimson sparks burst from the clouds and Jared's father ran to the mound and covered him with his large yellow-orange coat. Jared felt safe, even though he could see hot sparks flying around his head and burning the green grass all around him. Suddenly Jared heard his father cry out in agony and saw him fall backward onto the pitcher's mound. He burst into flames before Jared's eyes. Jared tried to find water to throw on his father, but there was none to be found. It was too late; his father was utterly consumed. Only the axe lay on the mound of dirt, blackened with smoldering ashes.

* * *

At breakfast the next day, before the kids were up, Ann said to Jared, "Bryan sleepwalked again last night. This morning I found him in the front room. I feel a lot safer since we added the deadbolts, but maybe we should take him to that sleep clinic in Raleigh." Ann didn't say it, but they both knew that Bryan often sleepwalked after his father got angry with him. Jared knew that Ann was trying not to blame him, but he could see the concern in her eyes. Bryan occasionally hurt himself banging into a door or tripping over something. He had even walked outside a couple times, and once he woke up in the car. That was when they had installed the deadbolts, which Jared was responsible to lock each night.

* * *

Monday evening, the family gathered in the living room for family home evening. Although last night's dream still lingered, Jared had promised himself that in spite of yesterday's craziness, tonight he would be involved and happy.

After the song and prayer, Tara asked, "Dad, can I tell you what I learned about possums today?"

"Sure, honey. Tell me everything you learned."

Tara perked up. "Well, we went to the library and I got a book about possums, so I know all about them. When they're born, they're only as big as a bee, and then they climb all the way up into their mama's pouch because they are *marsupials*." When she said *marsupials* she cocked her head a little and smiled at her mother.

Then she went on. "They stay in their mama's pouch until they're about two months old, and about the size of a mouse. Then they can come out. And when a possum is really scared, like if a big dog attacks them, they fall down and their heart slows down and they stick their tongue out and the dog thinks they're dead. They don't know they're doing it, they just get so scared they almost die, but they're really just sleeping. Then after a while, when it's safe, they open up their eyes, get up, and go home."

Daniel asked, "Mom, was that possum really dead or just pretending?"

"It was really dead, sweetheart," Ann said as she stroked Tara's hair.

Tara continued, "And the reason possums get hit by cars is that they go out to the road to eat dead animals. But do you know what possums love to eat more than anything, Daddy?"

"Big Macs and fries?"

"No, silly! Persimmons! That's why you can't cut down the persimmon tree. Because then they would be hungry, and then they might have to go out into the street to try to eat dead animals, and then they could get hit by a car, and then you would have to throw it in the back with the shovel and probably slip on the persimmons and get your pants wet, so you just can't cut it down, Dad." Bryan and Daniel nodded and Ann smiled.

"Tara, you'll make a great missionary," said Jared.

Ann explained, "I think the kids are also thinking about Libby's promise to make persimmon pudding." She looked at the children and said, "Now I think it's time for a performance by the Lawson children."

The kids sang, and the rest of home evening went on with the usual activities, except that Jared's mind wandered. Ann gave the lesson on baptism, and after the lesson she said, "Bryan, wasn't there something you wanted to ask Dad?"

Bryan said excitedly, "Dad, can we practice the baptism?"

Jared remembered practicing the baptism with his father the week before he was to be baptized. Suddenly he felt terribly sad. He choked up and his eyes watered.

He knew that he really should practice with Bryan. But he felt that if he did he would fall apart and make a scene. He heard himself say, "Let's do it Sunday after church so it will be fresh for the real baptism, okay?"

"Okay, Dad," Bryan said, disappointment in his voice.

* * *

Later, Jared and Ann were lying in bed, and Ann said, "What's going on? Yesterday it was almost as if you were attacking the persimmon tree, not to mention Bryan. Tonight you wouldn't even help your own son prepare for his baptism! This just isn't like you. What's wrong?"

"I don't know. I can't get Dad out of my mind. I feel like I'm all alone and lost in a cold, dark mist, with no way out."

"Honey, we're all here for you. I know this must be a hard time for you, but, Bryan is really, really excited about his baptism and I don't think it's fair for you to ruin it for him."

"I know. I'll try to snap out of it." Jared rolled over and stared into the darkness. He fell asleep telling himself to get a grip and give his son more attention. But his dreams were still about fires and funerals and death.

The next few days were filled with sadness and confusion for Jared. He couldn't concentrate and felt a nagging sense of fear and loss but he couldn't seem to do anything about it. On Tuesday morning, driving to work, he ran a red light and drifted into other lanes without realizing it. Wednesday he sat through two meetings and a marketing presentation without really hearing what anyone said. Thursday night he had the recurring dream about his father driving his truck to the fire that killed him. In the dream, Jared tried everything he could to stop the truck, but it kept speeding toward the flaming death trap that took his father away from him.

* * *

On Friday morning as he drove to work, Jared saw a large, black hearse several cars ahead in the other lane. He tried not to look at it, but felt drawn to watch it. The large rear door seemed to beckon him. A couple of cars made turns and he found himself pulling up next to it at a stoplight. He avoided looking at the driver, but because the light remained red for what seemed to be minutes, he finally took a quick peek. The driver looked over at him at the same time. He wore dark sunglasses, and Jared was sure he saw a slight smirk, as if the driver were thinking, "You'll end up in one of these, too, buddy."

The rest of the day, Jared wasn't able to concentrate on his work at all. He kept thinking of the hearse, the dead possum, and his father in the casket.

The buzzer on the phone startled him from his thoughts. He picked up the receiver.

"Mr. Lawson, your wife is on line three," the secretary said.

"Oh . . . yes . . . thank you." He pushed on the button. "Ann. What's wrong? What happened?"

"Nothing's wrong. Just called to remind you to stop and get ice cream and whipping cream for Bryan's party tomorrow." Ann's familiar voice helped bring Jared back to reality.

After work he stopped and got a bucket of strawberry ice cream and can of whipped cream. Ann would complain about his wasting money on the canned stuff, since she preferred to whip up cream herself, but the kids loved the way Jared squirted out their names in big letters on their birthday cakes.

That night in bed Ann asked, "Jared, would you dig those two stumps out of the front lawn tomorrow? I'd really like to plant a tree in that spot before winter." She had been trying to get him to do it ever since they had moved into the house. Jared wondered whether she wanted to get him out of the house the next day so she could prepare for the party without him, or whether she just wanted him to work off some tension.

* * *

Saturday morning Jared got up around 10:00 and puttered around the house trying to find things to do. He blew up some balloons and taped up a sign that said, "Happy Birthday Bryan." He knew that Ann was trying not to remind him about the stumps, and he knew that she knew he remembered and was trying to act as if he didn't. They had played this game many times before. He wondered if he really did expend more energy trying to avoid doing yardwork than it would take just to do it. Ann liked to say that he did.

About 11:00, Bryan came into the kitchen and said, "Dad, can we play catch for a while before the party?" He had both of their gloves and was tossing a ball in the air.

"Sure, son. It's your birthday after all!" Jared figured that playing catch with his son on his birthday was as good an ex-cuse as any to avoid yardwork. And it would get him out of the house. Jared and Bryan went into the back yard and tossed the ball back and forth for a while. Jared's shoulder was still a little sore from ramming it into the gate the week before.

"Dad, let's play the game when you pitched the no-hitter,"

Bryan said. He then adopted a serious pitching stance and looked to Jared for the sign. This was part of their baseball ritual, but Jared knew Bryan was also trying to cheer him up. They would take turns being the pitcher and the announcer. One would pitch while the other would catch and call the play-by-play action.

Jared held one hand to his mouth like a microphone and said in his best baseball announcer voice, "It's the bottom of the seventh with two outs. Lawson's no-hitter is still intact. He walked the last batter and the count is full. Lawson's looking for the sign."

Jared then assumed a catcher's crouch and gave the sign for a fastball. Bryan shook off the sign, as Jared knew he would; he always went to the sinker with two strikes. Jared gave the sign for a sinker. Bryan nodded, checked the runner at first, and delivered the pitch.

Jared was always amused when Bryan tried to throw a sinker, because it never curved and usually sailed high. This pitch was different. The ball came straight at Jared's glove. Jared was glad he wouldn't have to chase the ball, but then the ball took a dive, went under his glove and through his legs and rolled over into the area of the yard under the persimmon tree.

Jared called out, "A swing and a miss! Strike three! The game is over! Bryan Lawson has thrown a no-hitter!"

Bryan raised his arms in victory and shouted, "Did you see that pitch? That ball dropped like a rock!"

Jared was proud of his son's pitch, but a little embarrassed he hadn't caught it. They walked over to get the ball, and it had persimmon juice on it. Jared picked it up with his thumb and middle finger and said, "Boy, you really put some stuff on that pitch! You'd better wipe it off before the ump sees it!"

Bryan laughed and said, "Yeah, and now that I can throw a *real* sinker, I'll be able to pitch a real no-hitter some day!"

"I'm sure you will," Jared said. "Wade Boggs couldn't have hit that pitch! Let's go in and get some lemonade before your friends get here."

"Yeah, I can't wait to tell Mom about my pitch!" Bryan ran toward the back door.

Jared watched his son and smiled. He remembered how

much he had wanted to make his mother proud of him. At least *she* had been at the game when Jared pitched the no-hitter three years after his father had died. He remembered his mother's words to him after the game: "Your father would have been so proud of you!" In the flash of that memory, Jared went from feeling warm and proud to feeling desolate. His chest started to hurt a bit and he felt a little out of breath. He suddenly pictured Bryan pitching a great game and then looking into the stands in vain for his dead father.

Jared tried to put this out of mind and told himself he had to compose himself for the party. As Ann said, he had no right to let his pain ruin Bryan's birthday.

Several boys had arrived and were playing in the living room. Jared tried to enjoy the party and be happy. He was able to act silly and tell the boys some jokes, which raised his spirits a little. It went pretty well for a while. Then Ann brought the cake out, and Jared wrote Bryan's name on with the whipped cream. The boys were impressed with his artistry. Ann took a picture as Bryan blew out the candles.

Then it happened. The flash from the camera triggered Jared's memory, and things went into slow motion. Jared flashed back to his seventh birthday party—the last one with his father. His dad had written *Jared* with whipped cream so thick it started to lean. He got down near the cake on the opposite side from Jared and said, "Okay, blow out the candles and I'll get your picture." When Jared took in the biggest breath in his life and blew out the candles, whipped cream flew onto his dad's face and camera. Jared saw in his mind the way his dad reared back his head and laughed. "Attack of the killer whipped cream!" his dad had cried. Jared tried to fight the emotion but he felt his throat tighten and his eyes burn. He wanted to get up and leave so he wouldn't embarrass himself and Bryan, but he seemed paralyzed. He felt weak and hopeless. The others were laughing at something Tara had said, but Jared didn't really hear them.

Ann saw Jared's tears and quickly got the kids involved in a game in the other room. A minute later Ann came in, stood behind him with her arms around him, and whispered, "Please don't do this at Bryan's party."

Jared took a couple of deep breaths and whispered, "I'll go and get some fresh air and try to get a grip. I don't know why I can't get control of myself."

Ann said, "Honey, you've done the most important things for Bryan today. I can do the rest of the party. Please go and do something that will make you happy—*anything*."

Jared went outside and looked at the yard. He thought about going to a movie or to the driving range. He wanted to be alone but he felt guilty about doing anything really fun by himself on Bryan's birthday. Then he wondered what his father would have done in his situation. He would probably have worked in the yard. Jared remembered his vow about cutting down the persimmon tree. But he knew he'd have to borrow a chain saw and the noise would disturb Bryan's party. Jared decided he could at least dig out those stumps for Ann.

He went and got the shovel and the axe. He thought of going to the hardware store to get a new axe, but decided instead to use his father's. He pulled the axe from the persimmon mush and wiped it off on his sweatshirt. He got the pumice stone and sharpened the old axe. He walked around to the front yard and surveyed the two stumps, about a yard apart. It looked as if he would have to dig two separate holes, but then he decided to begin by digging a large hole between them. He dug down about two feet until the shovel hit a large root connecting the stumps. It was a hot, humid day, and Jared quickly became soaked with sweat.

Jared picked up the axe and began chopping at the root. He thought of all the stumps he had seen his father remove from the yard and the way his father would let him help and make Jared feel he needed him. He loved to work in the yard then. But then Jared thought of all the things he never had the chance to do with his father: all the work in the yard alone, or with his older brother making fun of his smallness and weakness—*chop;* all the baseball games he played with only his mother watching—*chop;* all the father/son camp-outs and general priesthood meetings he had to go to with uncles or home teachers—*chop, chop;* and all those touching letters his missionary companions received from their fathers, telling their missionary sons how proud they were—*chop, chop, chop.* He began to feel intense anger for his father's being taken away from him—*chop, chop.*

He was angry at the fire that took him, *chop,* angry at God for allowing it to happen, *chop,* and angry at himself for not being there to stop it, *chop, chop*—and then he experienced a deeper, darker anger at his father for deserting him, *chop, chop, chop, chop, chop.* He hacked at the old, gnarled root until exhaustion brought him to his knees. Every muscle in his body was weak, and sweat dropped off his face into the hole.

The pain of the sadness, the pain of the loneliness, the pain of the grief flowed over him. Jared leaned over the open hole and sobbed freely. The tears rolled off his face, and he cried into the hole, "I can't do it alone! It's too hard for me! Dad, I need you. Dad, I miss you."

After a few minutes, he took off his glasses, wiped them with his shirt, wiped his eyes, and put his glasses back on. Then he stood and, with one swing of the axe, he chopped the final strand of root in two and pulled one stump free. He tossed it on the pile of dirt made from the hole. He chopped at the other stump until he was able to pull it loose. Then he looked into the hole and made a decision. However difficult it was, he would no longer allow the pain he felt over his father's loss to prevent him from being the kind of father his children needed.

Jared brought the axe into the back yard and laid it up against the persimmon tree. He looked at the tree and, with a new sense of strength and purpose, thought, You're next!

Jared went in the house and showered. When he came out refreshed, the party was over and the boys had gone home. Ann came over, gave Jared a big hug, and said, "Thanks for taking out those stumps."

Jared smiled at Ann, then asked Bryan, "Would you like the family to go on a drive, and maybe a short picnic?"

Bryan said, "Yeah, that would be great!"

"Where would you like to go?"

"I don't know," Bryan said.

Ann looked out the window. "The trees are really pretty with the fall colors now. Barbara said that Forest Lawn Cemetery is one of the prettiest places in Greensboro. We could go there."

Bryan piped in, "Yeah, that sounds fun. I've never been to a graveyard. My friend at school said they're really not that scary—during the day."

"Yeah, then I can collect some pretty leaves!" Tara said.

"Isn't there somewhere else beside a *cemetery* we can go to see pretty trees?" Jared protested. He had not been to a cemetery since his father's burial. He had never liked even driving by a cemetery.

"Dad, can we *please* go?" Bryan pleaded. "Maybe there'll be a good tree there I could climb." The kids all moved toward Jared with excitement on their faces.

Ann glanced at Jared and said, "I thought the bright colors might cheer you up a little after your battle with those stumps. It was probably a bad idea."

Jared looked at each of his kids, who seemed ready for disappointment. He reminded himself that his father was buried 2,000 miles away, and of the decision he had just made. "No, it was a great idea. Let's go to the cemetery."

The kids cheered. Ann and Jared put together a few things to eat, got everyone into the car and drove up Battleground Avenue and turned right onto Pisgah Church Road. They passed several new housing developments with large ornate signs bearing names like "Hickory Farms," "Yester Oaks," and "Pinewood Estates."

Jared, trying to avoid thinking about the cemetery, said, "Can't they come up with anything besides the name of the trees they cut down to build these places? Why don't they call them what they really are, 'Treeless Forest,' or 'Deforestation Village'?"

Ann smiled and responded, "And, when did you become such an environmentalist? You want to cut down a tree in your own back yard, remember?"

"I *am* an environmentalist! All that persimmon tree does is pollute the air with its smell, and the ground with its hazardous waste droppings. I'll be doing the environment a favor by sending that persimmon tree to the big lumberyard in the sky. Besides, then we can rename our property 'Persimmon Plantation' and add ten thousand dollars to the resale value of the house!"

"There's the rec center. Turn in here," Ann said. They got on a wide curving road with tall maples and ginkgoes, their leaves shining like millions of gold and bronze medallions in the sky. Jared tried to be as lighthearted as he could, making jokes about overweight joggers, but when he saw the first group of grave markers on the right he became silent.

Ann met his eyes. "Kids, let's just drive around and look at the leaves for a few minutes, and then we'll go back to the park lawn for our picnic."

"Please, can we get out and walk around?" Tara suggested. I want to get some of those pretty leaves on the ground."

"Yeah, then we can climb on those rocks!" Daniel cried.

"Those are not rocks and they're not for climbing," Ann said. "They're grave markers to tell you the name of the person buried there. A cemetery is like a church, and we should be reverent."

Bryan asked, "Can we go see what the stones say? I can't read them from the car."

Jared remembered seeing his father's name and the dates of his birth and death on a new marker in Arizona. Fighting sadness, he glanced at Ann with a mock worried expression and said, "They're not going to let us out of here alive if we don't let them out of the car!"

Ann whispered to Jared, "Will you be all right?"

"Sure. Okay, kids, you win. We'll have the picnic here. It must be a good place to be; after all, people are just dying to get here!"

When the road divided, Jared drove around to the left and parked under a large maple. They got out of the car, and Ann said, "Under this tree seems like a good place for a picnic."

As Jared and Bryan got the food out of the car, Tara and Daniel darted toward the grave markers. Jared volunteered, "I'll go down and try to keep Daniel off the stones. Bryan, would you help Mom set up the picnic?" He hurried down the grassy hill, speckled with yellow and red leaves, toward the graves. Ann and Bryan watched Jared go and then spread the blanket out and set the food on it.

When it was all set up, Bryan asked, "Mom, can we find a small tree for me to climb so I can surprise Dad?"

"Sure."

Jared had been explaining things to Tara and Daniel and reading names off the stones for them. He turned and looked toward the car and saw the picnic spread out on the grass, but did not see Ann or Bryan. As he began scanning the cemetery, he heard Bryan call out, "Dad! Look, I'm climbing a huge tree!"

Jared looked toward the sound, and saw Ann helping Bryan into a large, golden-yellow persimmon tree. Bryan got settled on a branch, looked at Jared, smiled widely, and waved. Though his first instinct was to rush over and "rescue" him from the danger, Jared just waved and smiled back.

As he watched his son pick persimmons and toss them down to Ann, then climb out of the tree, Jared felt shame and guilt. How often had Bryan asked him to teach him to climb large trees! How often had Jared denied his children the normal fun of childhood because of his excessive anxiety? Jared had always understood that his overprotectiveness toward his children came from having lost his father. But the joy in Bryan's face as he ran toward Jared made painfully clear the high price Bryan had paid for that overprotectiveness. Clouds of sadness began moving in over Jared, but he shook his head, took a deep breath, and remembered his promise.

Bryan ran up and showed Jared, Tara, and Daniel the persimmons he had picked. "Here, try one. It's really good!" Tara and Daniel each took one of the wrinkled, yellow and purple fruits and ate it.

"Oh, no! Not the dreaded-smelly-sour-dusty-prune things!" Jared feigned horror, holding his hands up to protect his mouth.

Bryan held out one to Jared. "Come on Dad, have one. They're really sweet."

"Thanks, but I'll pass."

Ann took a bite of one, and said enthusiastically, "Jared, it doesn't have the sour taste you described! It's really sweet! You'll like it."

"Not a chance." Jared watched as his family ate the persimmons and licked the juice off their fingers. "Well, let's go eat some real food. How about a picnic?"

As they walked back to the maple tree, they came to a large grave stone. Bryan read aloud, "'James Birchwood. 1927-1963. I have passed the bar . . .' What does that mean, Dad?"

"It means he was a lawyer but the North Carolina bar exam must be a real killer," Jared said, smiling at Ann.

Ann smiled and said to Bryan, "It's a phrase from a poem,

honey. It means that he has crossed over from this life into another life." Ann looked at Jared and teased, "You're sure having
a good time!"

"Well, it's pretty here, and quiet. It's a nice place to visit, but
I wouldn't want to *live* here! Let's go eat so we don't starve to
death!"

As they all ate, they looked around at the stones and grass
and leaves. Then the silence of the cemetery was suddenly broken by a loud grinding sound. On the top of a little hill a yellow
backhoe raised its arm while a man dressed in overalls stood by
and gave directions to the operator.

The backhoe's yellow claw began its descent, and Jared said,
"Why do they dig graves during the day? Can't they do it in the
evening after the visitors leave?" He got up from the blanket
and, out of curiosity, walked over to them. When he got a little
closer, he realized that the men were only uprooting a small
lilac bush. He approached the man giving directions to the operator and asked him why they were digging it up, yelling over
the Bobcat's motor.

The man yelled back, "The guy who owns this plot said to
take it out. They do it all the time. They complain if you don't
put something near the grave. And they tell you to clear the
things out if you put them there."

Jared said, "What are you going to do with it?"

"We're just gonna chuck it. Too much trouble to replant
them. Nobody wants someone else's bush."

"You're just going to throw it away? Is it healthy?"

"Sure. If you want it, take it. It'll save us a trip to the landfill."

"Just a minute. Let me talk to my wife." Jared went over to
Ann and said, "They're going to throw away that bush. Why
don't we take it and put it in the yard?"

"It's pretty, but it may not do well in our clay soil. We don't
have any fertilizer, either."

"At least we can try. I can borrow some fertilizer from
Ogden. I know it seems strange, but for some reason I really
want to plant this bush today. It won't take long. I've already
dug the hole!"

Ann smiled at Jared. "Well, if you insist. But we do need to
get home so I can give my piano lesson at four o'clock."

Jared turned and motioned to the driver, indicating that he wanted the bush. He went and backed the station wagon up to where the Bobcat was and put down the middle seat.

"Thanks for the bush. I hope it lives," Jared called out as he grabbed the trunk of the lilac.

"It will—if you protect the roots from losing the dirt by wrapping it with a towel or something," the driver said.

"Let's see if I have something." Jared looked in the wagon and found an old towel. The two men picked up the lilac, and Jared put the towel on the ground. They wrapped the roots and Jared lifted the bush to the car.

On the way home, Jared decided that the next time he was in the west he would go to Tucson and plant a bush by his father's grave.

*   *   *

They turned onto their street and saw Barbara Winters and her twelve-year-old Nathan waiting at their front door for Nathan's piano lesson. As they got out of the car, Nathan looked at the lilac and asked, "Did you get your Christmas tree *already?*"

"No, that's our new car air freshener," Jared said. "It's a little larger than most, but then it smells better, too."

"Sister Lawson, you don't know how lucky you are to have a husband who is always so happy and funny," Barbara said in her warm Southern way.

"Yes, it's only when he's sleeping that my face gets a rest from laughing," Ann said wryly.

"Not always," Jared said as he closed his eyes, cocked his head, and let out a loud snore.

They all laughed. Jason and Bryan stayed behind while the rest went in the house.

"Dad, can I help you plant the bush?"

"Sure. I'm going to see if I can borrow some fertilizer from next door. You guard the lilac, okay?"

Jared went next door and knocked. Ogden opened the door, and Jared said, "Hey, how are you, Ogden? We got a bush from the cemetery that we want to plant tonight. Could you loan me some fertilizer and give me some quick advice on planting a lilac in this clay soil?"

"Sure, come on out to the shed. Where did you say you got the bush—a lilac, you said?"

"Yeah, a small lilac. At the cemetery. We were there to see the leaves, and they were going to throw it out. So we asked for it."

Ogden opened the shed and handed Jared the can of fertilizer. They spoke for a few minutes about planting things in clay soil.

"Thanks very much, Ogden. Well, guess I've got some planting to do."

Ogden volunteered, "I'll come on over and help." They walked over and Ogden looked at the hole. "Now that's a serious hole! You better fill it in with some mulch. There should be plenty in the compost pile in your back yard."

"I don't think we have any mulch in our yard," Jared said.

"Over in the corner of your yard by our garden there's a big pile. That ivy has taken it over, though. We'll have to pull some up to get at it. Ivy is pretty, but it chokes out everything else. We're going to need all the strong arms we can get." Ogden looked at Bryan.

Jared put his arm around Bryan, and the three of them walked into the back yard and up to the huge patch of ivy that had been one of the attractions of the yard when Ann and Jared had first thought about buying the house the year before. Ogden climbed into the patch of ivy that rose about six inches from the ground and cleared out a spot while Jared went to the shed and got a shovel, some gloves, and the old wheelbarrow. He came back over to the ivy mound in time to see Ogden scoop out a load of dark, soft mulch with his hands.

"There it is. Been under there a few years now, so it'll be just what you need." Ogden and Jared filled up the wheelbarrow, with Bryan helping, and they took it to the front yard. Ogden poured the mulch from the barrow into the hole, and Jared put some dirt back in.

Jared said, "I guess we need to mix it up now." He and Ogden knelt by the hole, and Jared began to reach in when the front door opened. Nathan came out from his piano lesson, a relieved expression on his face.

"What are you doing now?" Nathan asked.

"Mixing some dirt from the hole with some mulch—leaves and stuff—and some fertilizer. It'll give the bush some more nutrients," Jared said, as if he had worked at a nursery all his life.

"Can I help?" Nathan asked. He knelt down and dug his hands right in, and Jared tossed his gloves down and joined him. Bryan came over, too, and before Jared could say anything he had lain down by the hole and stuck his arms in up past his elbows.

Ogden added more mulch from his supply and poured in fertilizer. "Oh, good, a little sugar for the bread dough!" Nathan said. Jared and Ogden smiled.

Jared put his hands in the mulch bread dough, and asked, "Are we making sour dough or wheat bread?"

Bryan said, "Cinnamon bread! That's my favorite!"

Barbara, Ann, Tara and Daniel came out of the house to see the four bakers kneeling around the hole, laughing. Ann inquired, "Are you boys having fun playing in the mud?"

Bryan replied very seriously, "We're not playing in the mud. We're making cinnamon bread for supper tonight."

"Come on kids, let's get supper on while Dad finishes planting the lilac," Ann suggested.

Bryan pleaded, "Can I please stay? It's my birthday."

Ann looked at Jared, who said, "Sure, son, we could use your help." The other kids went in with Ann, though not without complaints.

Jared waved to Barbara and Nathan as they drove away, then turned to Ogden and asked, "Okay, boss, what do we do now?"

"Put the bush in the hole, pack some more mulch and dirt around it, stomp it down, add some more mulch around the top, water it heavily, and then pray for rain," Ogden said. They took the towel off the roots and put the lilac in the hole. Ogden and Jared held it up while Bryan filled in the hole. They all stomped on the dirt to pack it tightly.

Then Ogden concluded, "That's it. Now give her a good watering and spread some pine needles around it to hold the moisture in."

Jared said, "Thanks for the fertilizer. I really appreciate your helping me like this. And thanks for showing me the mulch pile; that'll really help our garden next spring."

"Happy to help anytime," Ogden said, as he turned to walk home. "Oh, by the way, Bryan, Libby told me to tell you that she would still love to make some persimmon pie for you. Just get about a hundred persimmons from your tree and bring them to her. Then we'll have your family over."

Bryan smiled and nodded his head.

"That sounds great," Jared said, as he thought of how much sugar would have to be added for him to be able to eat a piece of persimmon pie and the amount of water he would have to drink afterward to get the dryness out of his mouth. They waved goodbye, and Ogden went home. Jared let Bryan water the lilac for several minutes. After the bush had its fill, they themselves took a couple of long drinks from the hose.

Jared put his arm around Bryan. "Thanks for helping, son. It's getting dark, and I just need to put the stuff away. Get cleaned up and eat some supper, okay?" Bryan took off his shoes and went into the house. Jared went around to the back yard, raked up a barrow full of pine needles, and put them around the lilac. It was getting dark now.

Jared loaded up the wheelbarrow with the shovel and axe and threw the towel on the stairs, so he would remember to bring it into the laundry room. He walked over to the persimmon tree, leaned the axe up against the trunk, and stood there for a minute looking at the tree, sizing it up. Then he heard a rustling in the woods just a few feet away, and grabbed the axe instinctively. He realized it was only a rabbit or a bird, or possibly a possum foraging for dinner. Standing there alone he realized how afraid of the dark he really was, but holding his father's axe gave some comfort. He wondered how often his father had used this axe to cut firewood. Jared remembered an old picture of him and his father cutting down a Christmas tree with an axe and he realized it was probably this very one.

He decided to do something he hadn't done in many years.

He went up into the attic and found his old cardboard box of photographs. It was caked with dust and smelled musty and old. He brushed off the dust, brought the box down to the living room and placed it on the floor.

Ann and the kids came in and watched as Jared opened the box and looked in. They came over and sat on the floor facing him. Bryan asked, "What's in the box?"

"Pictures of me and my dad," Jared answered, as he hunted for the picture he had remembered. He found it, showed it to the children, and told them about how he and his father had gone into the hills to cut down the Christmas tree. Jared looked down at the picture and tried to remember all he could about his father's last Christmas with them.

Bryan asked, reaching into the box, "Can we see more pictures?" Jared nodded, still looking at the picture, and Bryan rummaged around and pulled out a yellowed newspaper clipping, folded several times. He unfolded it, looked at it, gave it to Jared and asked, "Is this Grandpa?"

Jared took the clipping and looked at the picture and nodded to Bryan. It was a photo of a firefighter lying on his back on the ground outside a burning home. Two other firemen were reaching into the coat of the fallen man and taking out a little girl who looked unconscious. Tara and Daniel came around behind Bryan and looked at the picture, eyes wide.

Jared realized that he had never really told his children the whole story of how his father died. They knew it was fighting a fire, but they didn't know all that happened. "My dad was watching me pitch in a Little League game when two firetrucks came by with their sirens on. Dad and a couple of other volunteer firemen drove off right away. When they got to the burning house, a mother and father were outside screaming that their baby girl was somewhere inside. My dad quickly grabbed his axe, put on a fireman's coat, and ran into the house. They said he was in there for almost five minutes. He finally staggered out the front door, then turned and fell on his back, unconscious. But his charred hands still held onto the two-year-old girl inside the coat. The girl lived but my dad didn't. He died from severe burns and from all the smoke he inhaled. After the fire was out, another firefighter found the axe by the house. They gave it to me. I never liked to use it because it brought back the memories of his death. I'm not really sure why I hung on to it all these years."

"Grandpa was a real *hero!*" Bryan said, reverently.

"Yes, he was," Jared said.

"Grandpa died to save the little girl," Tara added, "just like Jesus died to save me."

Through his tears, Jared looked into Tara's eyes and saw love and gratitude. All these years Jared had focused on the losses *he* had suffered because of his father's death. "Yes, I guess he did," he managed to whisper. For the first time Jared felt something other than grief and pain at the thought of his father's death. Tara came over and squeezed Jared's neck and Daniel came and sat on his lap.

Bryan still held onto the picture and said, "I wish Grandpa was still alive."

"Me too," said Jared. "He's with Heavenly Father now, but if we love each other, and try to be like Jesus, we will be with Grandpa forever." He hugged Daniel. "Well, it's time to hit the sack. Tomorrow's a big day!"

The kids complained and said they wanted to see more pictures, but relented when Jared said, "I'll show you some more for family home evening." Jared and Ann got the kids bathed and ready for bed. After the kids were in bed, Ann and Jared talked about Bryan's baptism the next day. Jared went over the baptismal prayer in his mind and thought about what he might say in the confirmation blessing. What if Bryan did not feel the spirit? What if Jared did not say the words his son needed to hear in the blessing? If only he could know what his father would have said to him.

* * *

The screech of tires braking on wet asphalt and a muffled thump woke Jared from a peaceful, dreamless sleep. He looked over at Ann. As usual, she had not even stirred from the sound. He wasn't quite sure what the sound was, but he sat up in bed, and his first thought was of Bryan sleepwalking. Jared heard a car speeding away and suddenly realized he had forgotten to lock the doors. His heart raced as he dashed out of bed and grabbed his robe. Without putting on his glasses, he rushed into Bryan's room. Jared's heart sank: As he had feared, Bryan was not in his bed. He quickly looked in vain in the bathroom and the living room. He dashed to the kitchen and grabbed the flashlight from the cupboard and ran out the front door. He hurried down the two stairs to the driveway, but on the second stair he stepped on something soft and wet. Startled, he drew back and shined the light on the towel he had forgotten to bring in.

He shined the light around on the street in front of the house and, although without his glasses his vision was blurred, his light reflected two bright eyes at the bottom of the drive. His spirit sank and he cried, "No, please God, no!" He sprinted down the driveway, his bare feet slapping the wet pavement. Jared shined the light again and, instead of the body of his son, he saw the body of a possum lying on the pavement, still and lifeless.

Then he heard Bryan call out from the house, "Dad, what happened?" Jared turned around quickly and saw the silhouette of his son standing in the door frame. He bowed his head, thanked God, and promised himself to take Bryan to a sleep clinic that week and never to forget the locks again. Bryan walked down to where Jared and the possum were, and Jared pulled his son close to him.

"Where were you, son? I searched all over the house for you."

"I heard a loud sound, and then the door opened and when I woke up I was in the big chair in your office. Why did you come outside, Dad?"

"I heard a noise, and I was afraid that you had come outside and got hit." Jared was still quite shaken.

It had been sprinkling in the night, but a strong wind was breaking up the storm clouds. Lightning split the night sky to the rumble of distant thunder, and moonlight slid through the gaps between dark clouds. Rainwater glistened on the road. It was a warm, Indian summer night. A large cloud sailed from in front of the full moon, and Bryan could clearly see the body of the possum. "Is she dead? What happened?"

"I think so. It was hit by a car that just drove off," Jared said.

"Can we bury her under the persimmon tree? I think she'd like that."

"What makes you think it's a she?"

"She's prettier than that last one," Bryan said.

Jared thought the animal did look almost cute, lying there in the moonlight. Bryan said, "Dad, we really should bury her under the persimmon tree. It'll make the tree happy and help things grow."

Jared decided to treat this animal the way Bryan wanted. "Okay. We'll need something to carry her in. Bryan, get that towel on the stairs? Here's the flashlight." Bryan got the towel and gave it to Jared. Jared spread it over the possum and rolled her up in it. "Son, you have the light. You lead the way to the tree." Jared knelt down and gathered the lifeless possum into his arms. He followed Bryan to the persimmon tree, walking over the smooth, grassy ground, covered with soggy leaves and soft pine needles.

There were periodic thunderclaps and some lightning to the southeast. The moon came out from behind a cloud again and bathed the persimmon in a yellow glow. Jared laid the possum down next to the trunk of the tree, silhouetted against the moonlight, then gazed at the leaves and the fruit of the tree. He could barely make out the fruit. Most of it must be on the ground. Why would a tree produce so much fruit just to have it drop on the ground? To feed possums? He moved his feet around a little and thought this must be what it felt like in a wine press. He wondered what persimmon wine would taste like. He figured that when you drank it you would get very thirsty, and the more you drank, the thirstier you would get. These thoughts made him realize just how thirsty he was.

Bryan asked softly, "Dad, you've been sad all week. Why aren't you happy that I'm being baptized?"

Jared was startled to learn that his son had made the connection. "I'm really happy that you're being baptized. It's just that the dead possum last week got me thinking about things that I'd tried to forget. And I've had a lot of nightmares this week about things that make me very sad."

"Dad, were you sad when you were baptized?"

Jared knelt down next to Bryan and put his arm around him. "Yes, I was, son. When I was a little boy growing up, I always knew my dad would be in the water with me, say the prayer, lay me under the water, and lift me out again. He talked about it a lot during the months before I turned eight. We practiced it together during the last family home evening he had with us. In the years after Dad died, I often remembered that night. I kept trying to put that practice baptism and my real baptism together so my dad was the one who baptized me. Sometimes it almost worked. I also knew that after I was baptized, Dad would lay his hands on my head and bless me like he used to when I was sick. I always felt safe and happy when my dad blessed me. Sometimes I felt a kind of warm glowing all over."

"That's how I feel when you give me a blessing—warm and happy," Bryan said.

"I'm so glad you do, son." Jared stared at the trunk of the persimmon tree. "But when my dad died, all that changed. My baptism was one of the hardest days of my life. I felt so alone. The gift of the Holy Ghost has given me comfort many times, but sometimes when I needed my dad, he wasn't there. It was raining on the day of my baptism, and it was like the rain clouds were inside my head. Sometimes, like this last week, I feel like the rain has never stopped."

Bryan wrapped his arms around Jared tightly, held him, and said, "I'm glad you're going to baptize me, Dad. Even though you're sad."

Jared couldn't speak for a few minutes. He looked at the shrouded body of the possum and thought he saw some faint movement. When he could speak he said, "You know, this tree really is pretty." Then, with a bit of invitation in his voice, he added, "I just wish it weren't so messy."

"Me and Tara could pick up the persimmons when they fall and give them to Libby so she could make persimmon pie," Bryan said hopefully.

"I suppose you could do that." While Bryan was talking, Jared had been staring at the towel wrapped around the dead possum and was sure he had seen movement.

Bryan said, "Look, the possum is moving! It's alive!"

Jared removed the towel, and the possum's stomach area was definitely moving. Jared expected the possum to get up, but instead, a tiny mouse-size possum emerged from the stomach area and climbed up toward the face of the mother possum.

"I knew it was a girl! It's a mom, and that's her baby!" Bryan said. Then they saw another emerge.

"Those poor babies," Jared said, realizing they were probably now orphans, if the possum killed last week was the father.

Bryan said excitedly, "Can we keep them for pets, Dad? If we don't, they'll die. We can feed them from a bottle like those lambs on TV. Tara said they eat almost anything! We'll take good care of them, I promise!"

"Okay, let's see if they'll come to us." Jared and Bryan reached out toward the possums when a flash of lightning lit up the woods like mid-day. Jared and Bryan both drew back, startled. Then a gust of wind sent several persimmons dropping to the ground around the tree. Bryan gathered some and gave one to each baby possum. They nibbled at the fruit hungrily and then crawled through the wire fence into the woods. They seemed to know they were on their own now.

Jared was surprised they could eat more than their mother's milk. He said, "Son, I think the persimmon tree and the other possums in the woods will take care of the baby possums better than we can, don't you?"

Bryan nodded. Then Bryan handed Jared a small, wrinkled persimmon that Jared thought resembled nothing more than a small, overripe prune. It had lost its golden sheen and was a dark purple. It was much smaller and softer than the one he had eaten last September. Bryan said, "Dad, here's one for you, too."

Jared remembered last Sunday when he had thrown a persimmon at his son, and yesterday when he had refused to eat the one Bryan had offered him at the cemetery. The expression on Bryan's face was so trusting and hopeful that he took the persimmon from Bryan's hand, put it to his lips and nibbled. He was surprised to taste the sweetest fruit he had ever eaten.

Jared ate the persimmon and said, "Thanks, son, you were right yesterday. This does taste sweet." He placed the towel back over the possum and said, "It's time to go inside now and go back to sleep. We can bury her during the day, when it's light, okay?"

"Okay, Dad."

They went back in the house. Jared tucked Bryan in bed, then made sure the locks were bolted on the outside doors.

Jared climbed into bed, looked at Ann still sleeping soundly, and wondered again how she could sleep so deeply. He thought about waking her up to tell her what happened, but decided he would tell her in the morning.

He lay in bed and thought about the baptism the next day, and still worried that he would not say the right things in the confirmation blessing. He wasn't sure he knew Bryan as a father should know his son. He knew that right now he felt closer to his son than he ever had, but he still felt some invisible barrier between himself and Bryan. He wanted to break through it, but he didn't know how. Jared drifted off to sleep praying for strength and thinking about his father, his son, and baby possums.

The next thing he knew, Jared was again standing in the back yard with Bryan and the possum babies were coming out of their dead mother's pouch. The wind was blowing and moonlight bathed the persimmon tree in a yellow glow. Bryan handed Jared the persimmon, and when he ate it, suddenly Jared's dream shifted and he was on one bank of a pure blue stream of flowing water. On the opposite bank stood a man, his back to Jared, under a bright golden tree. The man picked a piece of fruit, turned around, and beckoned for Jared to come to him and eat. As the man called out to Jared and smiled, Jared saw that it was his father.

Jared's heart began pounding, and he felt great love and longing. As Jared went down into the stream, his father came down the other bank and joined him in the middle. His father gave him the piece of fruit, and he took it and ate it. Then his father took Jared's right hand in his left. Jared grasped his father's left wrist with his left hand, just as they had practiced at home. His father raised his hand to heaven, prayed, and then immersed Jared in the cool, crystal stream. When Jared came up from the water his father embraced him, then placed his hands on Jared's head and said softly, "My dear son, I love you. I'm proud of what you've done with your life. You shall come and be with me, forever." A rush of the Spirit filled Jared and blew the clouds from his soul. For the first time he could remember, Jared felt completely filled with joy.

Jared awoke from the dream, startled to both see and feel his father's spirit next to his bed, and the lingering touch of hands on his head. He wondered why, after so many years, his father had come to him now. He seemed to feel the whispered answer, "To turn the heart of a father to his son, and a son to his father."

Jared reached out for his father, but as the vision faded, Jared saw Bryan walk through the spirit of his father into Jared's open arms. As Jared gathered his son to him, Bryan said, "Dad, I just dreamed there was a man in my room who looked like Grandpa. He smiled at me."

"I know, son." Jared held him tightly, his tears dropping on to Bryan's head, and felt his son's little heart beating as quickly as his own.

"Are you *still* sad?" Bryan asked, hearing his father's soft weeping. "Last night I prayed you'd be happy for my baptism today."

Jared whispered softly in his ear, "No, son, I'm crying *because* I'm so happy. Today I'll baptize you and lay my hands on your head and bless you. This will be one of the happiest days of my life. I love you so much, and I'm so proud of you for wanting to be baptized."

After a minute, Bryan asked, "After my baptism, can we bury the possum under the persimmon tree? Next Saturday we can plant a bush over it to help us remember."

"Sure."

"And maybe for our family night activity, I could climb the tree and throw persimmons down to all of you for some pie," Bryan suggested.

Jared looked into Bryan's hopeful eyes, smiled, and said, "You bet. As long as you don't throw me any of your sinkers!"

They held each other, talking quietly about the baptism and the burial, about climbing trees and playing baseball, and about pictures and stories of Grandpa as Jared felt the first bright rays of the morning's sunlight pour through the window to embrace them.

Tim

KRISTEN D. RANDLE

"The tooth fairy's here."

This is Jessi, the night wanderer—voice of semi-reality, hooking me slowly up out of a dream I already can't remember.

"Ginny—"

Conspiratorial whisper. I am only barely getting any of this. Actually, it's probably the twelfth time she's said whatever it is she's saying. I am asleep. I deserve to be asleep. I have a *right* to be asleep. And I am no light sleeper, perhaps due to the fact that I've spent the last seven years of my life sleeping through Jessi. When I move into the basement, this won't be a problem.

"The tooth fairy is here *right* now, Gin. *Will you wake up?*"

But I am not about to wake up. Not even to walk her to the bathroom. I spent all day taking orders from Dad the Project Man and Mother the Master Gardener, lifting barges and toting bales and taking down storm windows, and now I am tired to death and sore all over and *nobody's* going to tell me what to do in the middle of the night—I don't care if this tooth fairy of Jessi's is wearing spangled tights and dancing on Jessi's head.

"*Ginny*—" she's whispering still, and I sigh and turn over so all she's getting is my back.

"Ginny," Jessi says, not whispering now, but using this kind of low, intense voice. "Will you just please *look* at least? Because I don't think this guy in the window is really the tooth fairy."

36

"Jessieee," I hiss between my teeth, and I turn over and throw the covers off and I sit up, ready to kill her. And then I freeze, because something in this room is wrong. There is definitely somebody sitting on our windowsill. You can see the shape, darker than the sky, a shadow biting into the light line of the curtains. I left the window open tonight—I don't know, maybe dreaming of spring lilacs and highwaymen. But we didn't put the screens up today because they still need scraping and now there's somebody sitting in my window, crushing the curtains. And I turn around and squint at the clock, like that has anything to do with anything.

The person sitting in the window does not move. Or else, time is suddenly going very slowly. Maybe that's it, because I can feel blood beating in my ears and my face has gone all hot. I've read about stuff like this, but never in a million years like it was something that could really happen in my own nice little middle-class world.

But here we are, not breathing. Waiting.

"What is it, Ginny?" Jess is asking, sounding a little wet in the throat. Still, nothing moves. Only later does it strike me that what I should have done is I should have started screaming my head off. Now, all I do is turn on the light so I can see, the little lamp on the table by my bed. I squint at the window, one hand up against the light. There is a pale face there that I know should be familiar, floating above a letter jacket that is not from my school. I am not sure this is not part of a dream.

"This is a *boy*," Jessi says, glaring at the face accusingly.

I am feeling very odd, the way I would if my wallpaper had just come walking down the stairs and sat down to breakfast. There's a dog barking down the street. "It's three o'clock in the *morning*," I say, as though everything would have been fine if he'd just shown up at two.

But he doesn't speak. I am seeing more clearly, now. No wonder I hadn't recognized him. His eyes are lost in darkness and there is a discolored place by his mouth that may or may not be shadow. He is all over disheveled. "What happened?" I ask him.

My bedroom door opens. "What's going on in here?" my mother asks, rumpled up with sleep, squinting against my little

light. She peers across the room to check on Jessi, but ends up
staring at the tooth fairy. "What's going *on* in here?" she asks
again, and it comes out like this time she *means* it. And then she
looks at *me*.

"How should I know?" I say. "I just woke up myself."

"Is this some friend of yours?" she asks, glaring at him.

"No," I say, and he winces, like I slapped him. "Well, you're
not," I say, feeling stung. What I don't say is, "not that I haven't
tried," which would have been true, but very ill-timed. "This is
Timothy Sainsbury," I tell my mother, and it sounds weirdly for-
mal, considering the circumstances. "He used to play tenor
with me in the jazz band."

"I still do," Timothy snaps, the first words to come out of his
mouth. "I was there today."

"Yeah, and it's a good thing you were," I snap back.

"Do you *mind?*" my mother says, staring at me. She shifts
the look to him. "Why are you sitting in my daughter's window?" she asks.

He doesn't answer. There seems to be a terrible misery in
his face. My mother stiffens.

My father is standing behind her now, his hair all sleepy and
upended, listening. Jessi has gone back to sleep.

"Do your folks know you're out this late?" my mother asks,
more gently.

Timothy's face blanks out.

My mother frowns, and glances at me for enlightenment.
"He only moved here last fall," I tell her. "He lives with his
uncle or something. That place out by the hatchery where Dad
gets the ice cream, I think."

"Sainsbury's," my father says, his voice surprisingly deep.
He has his eyes on Timothy. "I do the books for the dairy. The
taxes," he says quietly. He is nodding slowly, like he's just understanding something. "I've always found Emmott Sainsbury
to be a very principled man." He looks down at my mom as
though he's reminding her of something. "Some people find
him stiff."

"Yes, sir," Timothy says softly, his eyes down.

"Where're your parents?" my mom asks.

He closes his eyes.

"That's okay," my mother says. "Forget it."

I keep expecting somebody to get yelled at. I am a little amazed at the way my parents are carrying on this polite, civilized conversation. It's all a little surreal, and I am beginning to yawn.

"Why did you climb in Ginny's window?" my mother asks, now. "What were you after?"

"Nothing," he says sharply. He understands exactly what she's getting at, and so do I. I am suddenly feeling very alert. "I just . . ." he says, but he is having trouble with his answer. So we all wait.

Finally, he presses a hand over his chest, and he says, "We used to have a house a lot like this. Not big. Just nice. Yard and a dog. We had trees, too." He is staring at the floor. "I just needed to be inside . . . this house."

Nobody says anything.

"You don't know," he goes on, "but sometimes, on my way home, I watch you. In the garden, sometimes. You yell at each other and it sounds familiar to me. I just . . ." Now, he is whispering to the floor. "I guess I'm homesick." He swallows and he looks at me. "I'm sorry," he says lamely, and he is staring at the floor again. And we are still waiting.

"My parents," he says, finally, "took the little car, and they went to the mall." You have the distinct impression at this moment that he is made of nothing but glass. "My brother and my parents." His mouth tightens. "They didn't come back." He shrugs, and his face is tired. "There was an accident. It wasn't their fault. It was almost a year ago."

My mother sighs.

"That's why you came to stay with your uncle," she says after a minute.

"I stayed with a friend for a while. After. There was a funeral and the family came, but I stayed with this friend. I thought maybe I could just keep on staying there. But Uncle Emmott said he wanted to take me out for lunch, but he ended up taking me to the airport instead. He wouldn't let me go back to the house first. Not for my sax. Or pictures." He sighs and leans his head against the window frame. "He said it was best to just start over. Maybe . . . I don't know." Now he shakes himself and looks up with this horrible little fake smile.

"Who hit you, Timothy?" my father asks, softly.

Timothy's hand goes straight to the dark place by his mouth. He opens his mouth, but then he doesn't say anything, and he closes it again. He just sits there stiffly.

"What happened?" my father asks.

"I went to jazz band," Timothy says at last, still very stiff. "I was supposed to be mucking out. But I didn't do it. And I went to jazz band, instead. And then I gave him lip over it." He stops there and stares down at the rug, and this flush comes over his cheeks.

"He had to be there today," I say after a moment. I seem to be responsible for explaining this to my parents. "Mr. Pratt told him, if he didn't make it to jazz band today, he was going to lose the horn to somebody who was serious about playing both bands."

"The thing is," Timothy says with a certain desperate energy, "I have to have a scholarship. It's the only way I'm ever going to get into college. I'm good enough to get one. But if he won't let me go to band—"

"Couldn't you explain this to your uncle?" my mother asks. It's like she hasn't been listening.

"My uncle," he says, bitterly, "thinks that music is a waste. He thinks that college is a waste. He says I already have a place in a good business. He means the dairy. He says, if I ever decide to grow up, he'll leave the dairy to me. See, he doesn't have any kids to leave it to."

"It's a good business," my father says, slowly.

"I hate it," Timothy hisses, but then he immediately pulls himself back inside. "My parents always wanted me to go to college," he says, very calmly. "My father was a securities analyst. My uncle says that wasn't a real job. He says that people with college degrees are just playing a game with economics. He says they don't really produce anything, they just suck up the resources. Does he have the right to say that to me?" Now, he's looking straight at my dad. "Do I have to believe him because he took me in?"

"He's trying to do his best for you," my mother says, softly. But I don't believe her heart is in the words.

"Did your parents leave you any money of your own?" my father asks.

"I don't know," Timothy says, kind of sagging against the windowsill. I suddenly realize that we haven't asked him to come any further into the room. Maybe he hasn't wanted to come in any further. "I asked once, but my uncle was offended. He says a man should have to work for what he has. He says hard work makes an honest man. He says my father was always trying to get something for nothing, and he doesn't want me to be my dad." Timothy grimaces and then he sighs. "I work for him every day. And I don't mind that, really. It's just, they never talk. Not to me. Not to each other. Nobody ever laughs over there. I'm just not doing very well. Not in school. Not—" He shrugs, and then everything seems to go out of him.

"You can call the police," he suggests wearily, "because this is definitely breaking and entering. I don't really care. But they would just send me back there"—and now I see that his hands are shaking—"and I don't want to go. And I just really don't know what to do. So—" He gives this vague little wave of his hand that evidently means *so here I am.*

My mother is staring into space. Suddenly, she blinks and hunches her shoulders, like she's got a chill, and then she seems to rouse herself. "Well," she says, "it's kind of too late for you to be wandering the streets now. Maybe you better stay here tonight, eh?" She cups one hand over the other and breathes warmth into them. "We'll call your uncle and let him know you're safe."

"No," Timothy says quickly. My mother looks at him like she hadn't heard right. "He'll come and get me," he says, panic edging his voice. "Look," he says, obviously trying to be reasonable, "he doesn't even know I'm gone."

"You sure about that?" my father asks. Timothy nods, eyes pleading. "Okay," my dad says, finally. "We'll work it out in the morning. Come on." He jerks his head toward the hall. Timothy slides off the windowsill hesitantly, glancing at me. Then he follows my father out into the hall.

"Strange night," my mother says, after we've heard them go down the stairs. "What do you think about him?" she asks me, nodding her head after them. "You think he could be an ax murderer?"

"He's a good sax player," I tell her. This is an understatement. "And I always thought he was kind of cute. Not that he ever cared. He never says a word to me. He never says a word to anybody."

"You still think he's cute?" my mother asks. I can tell that this is a searching question.

"Mom," I say through a yawn, "I've got a crush on Scott Saltmarsh, remember? I've only been talking about it for about two months, now." My mother is nodding. "Yeah," she says. "That's right. Well, okay. Well, go back to sleep." She smiles at me and goes over and tucks Jessi in. "Turn off the light," she snaps at me, like it's the fifth time she's had to say it.

"Fine," I say, feeling very cross all of a sudden, and I turn off the light and lie down. And then she kisses me, of course, and says "I love you." I hear her go to the linen closet and then downstairs.

I lie there awake, thinking about all this stuff. I finally get up and close the window. An hour later, I'm still hearing my parents' voices, hushed, in the kitchen.

The next morning, Timothy is at the breakfast table, and Jessi and my brothers, Caleb and Cameron, are staring at him. He looks worse than last night, actually—big circles under his eyes, and that bruise on his face. My mother hustles the little kids through their oatmeal and out the door.

"Look," my mom says. "Timothy, why don't you come on back here after school today, okay?"

He looks up at her, his eyes very guarded.

"I don't want you to stay for jazz band. I just want you to come back here right after." He opens his mouth, but she holds up her hand and makes silence. "We're going to try to straighten some things out today, talk to some people, and find out what's going on with your situation—but I don't think it would be real swell if your uncle shows up at school looking for you and there you are at jazz band, got it?"

Timothy nods. I can tell he's biting the inside of his cheek, like he's trying to keep his mouth shut on things he might ask.

"And you, too," she says to me.

"Me?" I say, surprised.

"Yeah. I want you home right after also."

"After jazz band. I can't miss jazz band," I tell her, not believing that's what she meant.

"One day, you can miss," she says.

"We have playing tests today."

She shrugs with her hands, and suddenly, I am outraged.

"Look, this is not my problem. This is *his* problem," I am saying, probably too loudly. "Look, just because . . . Mom—I *have* to be there—"

My mother gives me this absolutely chilling look. "You heard what I said." And I hear what she didn't say—*you want to stop a minute and maybe think of somebody besides yourself?* And suddenly, it's like I'm seeing myself from the outside. I look over at Tim. His cheeks are flaming, and he is staring hard at the table. So, why didn't I just spit in his face? Suddenly I hate him for letting me do that to him. I now feel like a complete jerk, and my own cheeks are incredibly hot.

"Fine," I say, and I slam myself away from the table and pick up my books and slam my way out of the door. I don't even realize I left my flute case in the kitchen until he finally gets to the bus stop and hands it to me without a word. I don't look at him then—not even during band, later. All day, I hate myself. I can't stop seeing myself from the outside, and I hate hearing how trivial and stupid I keep sounding.

My mother just shows up and pulls me out in the middle of sixth period, so I not only miss jazz, but I miss a bio quiz, too.

"What is wrong with you?" my mother says to me on the way home.

"Why did you get me out of class?" I demand, fuming, which doesn't make any sense at all, since normally I would *love* to have to miss class—

"Because we need to talk about something," she says. "Because I need your advice, and I need to talk to you before school is out, okay?" I slouch down in the seat and stare out of the window. I have the weirdest parents in the world. You have to get mad at my mother because she's standing there making Groucho eyebrows at you, dangling a shovel like she's trying to entice you with it, even though she *knows* you've already spent the whole morning slaving your behind off for Dad, and by now you're nearly claustrophobic. Real compassionate. So you grab the shovel, and you turn your back on her—pointedly—and then she says, "Ginny, Ginny, *look* at me." You do not, at this point, want to look at her. Not if you have any sense at all. But she keeps after you until you do.

So you give up, and you turn with great dignity. And there

she is with her eyes crossed and two fingers stuck up her nose so you have to look up her nostrils. She has absolutely *no* dignity. Not that she cares. And what are you supposed to do when you see your mother like that? It's horrible; she *always* ends up making me laugh, and I never, never, never get to be deeply, righteously angry. At least she doesn't do this in front of my friends, but then, she hardly ever makes me that mad in front of my friends. At this moment, though, I happen to know I'm acting like a jerk, and the worst thing is, I know she's not going to be asking me to look at her.

"Ginny," she says now. "Why are you acting like this?"

The thing is, I don't know why. It's just I know she hates me now, after this morning, and I feel horrible.

"Are you mad at me?" she asks.

"Right," I say. I practically spit the word.

"Yeah, right," she says.

"Why would I be mad at you?" I say. I'm close to crying, but I'm not going to do it. I don't know what she expects. I'm supposed to act like nothing happened? Like I don't know she has utterly no respect for me anymore?

My mother takes a quick look at me. "Did something awful happen today?" she asks. "Did you find out Scott Saltmarsh is actually married or something?"

"No," I say, but she has surprised me into a kind of a laugh.

"So you had static electricity in your pants and they were sticking to your legs all day?"

I give her a disgusted look. "I'm wearing jeans," I point out.

"Okay, so you ate school lunch, and then you went around all day with creamed spinach stuck between your teeth, and you didn't notice it until after you found out that Scott Saltmarsh had been planning to kiss you, but he didn't do it because of the spinach?"

"That's it," I say. Now I'm smiling.

"Do you really hate Timothy?" she asks me.

"No," I say, and the smile goes away.

She lets a beat go by and then she says, "Are you sure? Because you were—"

I turn my face to the window.

"—not real kind to him this morning." She is not looking at me, but I feel the listening.

"I know," I say, finally.

"You want to tell me why?" she asks, flicking on her turn signal.

"Mom, I don't want to talk about it," I say. "I feel stupid enough about it already. I was just—I don't know. I wasn't thinking, I guess."

My mother nods and turns right. "So you don't hate him," she says again, like that's the whole issue.

"No," I say.

"Because—" she says, and I look at her because it strikes me that there is something strange going on here. There is definitely something going on behind what she's saying. "Timothy has a lot of family—your dad did some calling around this morning. Everybody seems to really like him—but nobody seems to be able to do anything about him."

"Did they leave him some money?" I ask.

She laughs and glances at me. "Ever practical," she says. "Yeah. The house and a car and a little money. Anyway, that's beside the point. A kid with money is still just a kid. How would you like it if suddenly one day we were gone, and you find yourself living with some stranger who doesn't love you, and who tries to make you over into something you don't want to be?" Her voice goes very quiet. "Somebody who thinks they have to hit you to get through to you."

Suddenly, I think I understand what it is that they were talking about all last night.

"So?" I say, cautiously.

"So," she says. "We have that room downstairs."

"I want that room," I say. "You know I want that room."

She glances at me again and turns down our street. "You have a room. A good room."

"I have no privacy," I point out.

"So, I should say to Tim—go back to your uncle. Or go live in the street. The room Ginny already has isn't good enough for her. She needs privacy."

I am angry because she's left me no dignified out. There is no safe answer to this. No answer but the one she wants.

"We have space in our house," she says, and then a bell rings in my head—this talk my parents have been having for the last two years: should we have another baby or not? Pregnancy is not easy on my mother; it pretty much tears her body apart, so it seems to me there should be no question, even though I think babies are sweet and all. But my parents can't let it alone. It always comes down to this: we have space in our house. But then my mother always asks—do we have space in our life? Tim would certainly take up less of her life than a baby would.

She stops the car in our driveway, and I am finding myself very disturbed. I gather up my stuff, and she gets out and we walk up the stairs to the back door and go in through the kitchen. The house smells like cookies. My mother never makes cookies.

She goes through into the den and I can hear her purse drop onto her desk. I lose my stuff and follow her into the den.

"So, do you really *want* him to live with us?" I ask her.

"I don't know," she says. "I know I don't want to send him back to his uncle's. I went out there once when your dad had to pick up some papers. Emmott Sainsbury is a dour, abrupt man. And his wife. They just aren't warm at all. I can imagine they don't know anything about kids at all. Course, they wouldn't *know* they didn't know anything." She makes a funny little noise out the corner of her mouth and flips the strap of her purse. "It would only be for a year. Till he graduates. Problem is," she says, shrugging and looking just a little wet-eyed, "it's kind of our last year together as a family. You'll be going off to school—" She shrugs again. "I just don't want to ruin this last year. I don't want you to feel pushed aside, you know? Because you're more important to us than Timothy, Gin. You honestly are."

I drop into a chair.

"This is why I wanted you home early. Because your dad already decided. But I need to know how you feel about it. And we need it settled before Tim gets home today. It's just—I think he might be a really nice kid. And I'm afraid he's really been needing his mother." She smiles sadly at me, puts her hand on my shoulder, and leaves me alone in the room.

I glance at the clock. Middle of seventh period. Forty-five minutes until my life changes. Because I don't see how I could ever say no to this. I try to think about Timothy, everything I ever knew about him. But that's not much, because he has always been so totally transparent. And then I think, anybody that transparent couldn't be that much of a strain on our family. And then I wonder what he'd be like if I could just get him to open up a little. The idea is not without its charm. I go and find my mother and tell her, okay—we should give it a try, anyway.

We are sitting in the kitchen when he gets home. He comes to the kitchen door as my mother must have told him to do, and we have left it open. By the way, my mother *has* made cookies. They are sitting on a plate in the middle of the table, and there are glasses ready for milk and I am not believing how much this looks like some Norman Rockwell painting. *Home from School,* they would call it, or something like that, and it would go down in history as The Way Real Families Do Things. When the boys and Jessi get home, they will faint dead away with shock.

Anyway, Timothy is standing in the doorway, speaking of fainting dead away—white-faced and very uncertain. Most uncertain when he looks at me. My fault, of course.

"It's not like you have to knock on the door," I say after he's been standing there for about twenty seconds. He blinks at me. "It's already open," I point out. My mother is glaring at me. She gets up from her chair and says "Come on in, hon," and holds out her hand as if she's drawing him in by force of sheer hospitality. Immediately, I flash on another little interchange between my parents—"Don't say 'hon' to guys," my father says to her—this is in reference to the way she talks to my brothers' friends. "'Hon' is *not* a guy word." And she says back to him. "I'm a mother. I can say 'hon' whenever I want."

Timothy takes a step into the room. I don't smile at him. I think he would be most uncomfortable if I suddenly started smiling at him.

"Sit down," my mother says. "Let me get you some milk," she says, like it's the most natural thing in the world. Timothy lowers himself into a chair and takes another nervous look at me.

"I'm sorry about this morning," I say to him, finally—I still can't seem to sound nice, but at least I'm trying. "Somebody got me up in the middle of the night, and I think maybe I was a little cranky this morning. I apologize."

He only nods, but now he is looking a little less like an anxiety case and more like a tired boy.

My mother pours milk for us, and pushes the plate of cookies toward Tim. But he doesn't touch anything.

"Look . . ." he says, and then he starts moving his thumbs over the condensation on his glass, making lines through it, and he doesn't say more.

"We need to have a talk," my mother says, sitting down at the table.

He looks up at her, miserable again. "I need to apologize. I'm—" embarrassed, I could have filled in for him, as it's all over his face. "I don't know what got into me last night. I don't know what I was doing in your window, and I never should have dumped on you—"

My mother holds up her hand.

"It's not something I've ever talked about," he says, almost to himself. "It was a mistake."

"Actually," she says, "I think it was probably high time you did talk about it. And I think you probably oughta talk about it some more—" he starts to look a little scared again "—but only when you're ready. Now, I need to tell you. My husband called around a little bit today. He talked to your uncle in West-chester, and your aunt in Philadelphia. Your uncle here isn't ac-tually your legal guardian, Tim. The rest of your family isn't all that happy about the way things are—but they don't know what else to do with you. Your parents did leave you some money—and the house and the other car. Nothing's been sold. They just don't know what they should do with any of it, yet."

Timothy is rubbing his hand over his face and then he heaves this tremendous sigh.

"But this is what we would like to do," my mother goes on. "One option is that maybe you could stay with your friend's family for the next year. Or you could stay here. With us. You can have the basement room for your own place, and you'd be very welcome here. Anyway, you don't have to go back to your uncle. Unless that's what you want."

Timothy's face is blank, his elbow on the table, and his hand, resting over his mouth.

"We'd like you to stay here," she says, gently. "We want you to. If it would make you happy."

He takes a nice, careful breath, staring at his milk glass. He laughs once, not like he thinks anything's funny, and looks at my mother. "You don't know me," he says.

"We've been learning a lot today," my mother says. "We feel like we know enough."

He shifts his weight, nesting the milk glass in both hands. I notice that his hands are shaking. He's staring at the glass again.

"You can think about it," my mother says. "We'll talk about what to do with the house. My husband—probably you should call him Doug—Doug can take you up there sometime soon, so you can go over your stuff and decide what you want to keep. But you know, it's up to you."

My mother is looking at him like she's afraid he's going to just suddenly shatter into a million pieces and blow away, and she moves away from the table—meaning to give him space, I think. But then he starts a slow nod. Still staring at the milk, he says, "Are you sure."

She looks at me. She thinks it's me he's worried about. Or maybe she thinks he'll believe me because we're the same age.

"She already asked me about it," I tell him. "She wouldn't have asked you if I'd pitched a fit about it, okay? And she wouldn't have asked you if she wasn't sure herself." I look at my mother. "She's not that nice a person. Anyway, they're probably just after your money."

He gives me a quick look, his eyes dark, and then I have to grin at him, and he has to grin back at me. "I don't believe you," he says to me.

"I know," I say. "They seem so nice, don't they? But my father gambles and drinks, see—and my mother—didn't you see the washing downstairs? She has to take in washing." I shake my head. "They're in debt up to the eyebrows."

My mother is poised outside of this, watching. Timothy looks at her. "I could help you iron," he offers, drawing her in.

"Done," she says, and that's that. I've lost the basement room forever, and I'll never be able to come downstairs in my pajamas again.

"The only thing is," I say to him, warning. "From now on you're going to have to talk to me."

He looks offended. "I talk to you," he says. "I always talked to you."

"You never did. And if you're going to be here, and you're going to be one of my brothers, you're going to have to talk to me, and you're going to have to keep your hands off my stuff." I make an extremely snotty face at him, and he lets his mouth drop open.

"Drink your milk," my mother orders, "and stop bickering." Timothy's eyes go big, but then he sees she's smiling, and suddenly, all the stiffness seems to fall away from him. He says, "Yes, ma'am," and he drinks it, and he has a cookie. "More?" my mother asks, and seeing his hesitant face, she decides for herself, "More." And she pours him another glass.

My mother explains things to Jessi and my brothers, who immediately begin using Tim as a jungle gym. And then my father and mother take Dad's little truck over to Sainbury's Dairy to collect Tim's stuff. Tim doesn't go. Nobody even asks him if he wants to go, and he's not offended by that. Then we move his stuff—there is not very much of it—down into his room. After dinner, we listen to an hour's worth of sax practice that keeps stabbing up through the floorboards even when you close the basement door. All through that hour, my mother keeps darting these glances at me. Finally, she says, "Don't *you* play the sax?" and I'm groaning to myself, because it's like a bad omen.

"I'm going to be an astrophysicist," I remind her, hoping to nip this off right now. "*I'm* not going for a jazz scholarship." Which line of reasoning, of course, she doesn't buy.

But this was only the beginning.

At first, Tim was like a ghost. He'd come up for dinner, eat, and then disappear downstairs. He played his horn a lot those first weeks. He is incredibly good—but you can only take so much mournful sax before it starts totally depressing you.

But then my mom starts sending the boys downstairs—the girls are now pretty effectively banned from the basement—knowing that five minutes down there with those little boys is pretty effectively going to flush Tim out. She devotes herself to figuring out Family Activities so that Tim will have to be part of them. She always has these little snacks ready after school so he has to sit there and talk to her. I guess she's never felt like she had to pry anything out of me with bribes.

And she makes him set the table. That used to be Jessi's job—not that she misses it. My mom makes a game out of this; she stands at the top of the stairs and calls down in this fluting voice, "Oh, Timothy, dear—could you trundle up here and set the table?" So now, he uses the same kind of fruity voice and calls back, "Certainly, Mother dear."

I guess her strategy is working, because this afternoon, he comes looking for her, and he says, out of the clear, blue sky, "Mother dear, could you come explain the laundry room to me?" And she says, "Certainly, Timothy dear," and they head down the stairs, and the upshot of this is he's down there now, doing his own laundry.

This is very admirable. Admirable that she's so diligent about him. Admirable of him for doing his own laundry. Except now, of course, do I dare say anything to my mother like, "Haven't you washed my green jeans yet?" Only if I'm stupid would I say such a thing, thanks to Tim. Although you do have to suspect that this laundry business is not really so much a display of mature personal responsibility as it is he's embarrassed to have somebody messing around with his dirty underwear.

And the more comfortable he is being upstairs, the worse it gets. Like he not only sets the table, but he clears. I mean, I clear, too—it's not like I don't. But sometimes I have things on my mind, and I forget. He never forgets. And he washes pans sometimes. Nobody asks him; he just starts doing it. Like he doesn't have any homework? Like he hasn't already been working hard all day? And every time he does it, I can feel my mother looking at *me*.

He calls my father Doug. He finally asked my mother if he could call her "mom." I think it was hard for him to ask. I think it's hard for him to say. But he adores my mother, anybody could tell that. I think, if she ever yelled at him, he'd just go downstairs and slit his wrists. That isn't healthy. Not that my mother's been yelling at anybody much lately, which we all find extremely unnerving.

Jessi says to me the other day, "He's really kind of . . . perfect, isn't he?" She's noticing because Tim is now getting the little boys to do unnatural things, like cleaning up their Legos and hanging towels up after their bath. But I *know* all of this is not quite right; his eyes are too sad, and he still doesn't really talk. I challenged Alvin, who was second tenor, and I beat him, so Tim and I share a stand, now. And, I mean, he does, like, talk—but he's so, I don't know—*civil*. You know the way you can just *feel* a summer storm before you even see the clouds? That's Tim.

Sometimes I ask him about how things were at home. I asked him once if he had a girlfriend back there, because he's evidently kind of immune to the girls around here. But he won't talk about any of that; he just kind of shrugs and says, "I don't remember."

Once I asked him what his mom looked like. "Kind of like yours," he says, and that's it. He's not bitter or rude about it or anything. He's just closed up.

If I tried to keep my mouth shut over something—over just about *anything*—I *know* I'd die of it. I talk to my mother about everything. It's not like I'm asking for answers or comments, or anything. Actually, I really don't *want* answers or comments or anything. I just need to turn myself inside out every so often. I have to. But Tim won't. He just gives you a short answer that has this big, fat period at the end, and you can't ask him anything else without embarrassing yourself. So, he's not really keeping our deal. He'll talk to me about teachers, or about class stuff, or about music—or even about my own family, as long as it has nothing to do with how he actually feels about any of those things. Which means he's not really talking to me.

The rest of my junior year is nearly gone. In the spring when it's warm, we eat lunch outside, seniors and everybody, all together. We have a good senior class this year, a lot of people I really like, and all of a sudden, I realize that two weeks from now these people will graduate, and I won't see them like this anymore—just sitting out on the lawn and being funny. I've passed these people in the hall every day for three years, and only now do I realize how much a part of me they are. It's a very awful and sweet feeling, knowing I'm going to be losing something I'm only just realizing I had.

Tim never comes outside for lunch.

In some ways, Tim seems older than I am. Maybe next to him, I just sort of feel immature and silly. Like, there's really not that much to smile about, so why am I laughing all the time? Like dreams are dangerous because they're never going to come true, and then you've wasted all this time spinning images in your head. Highwaymen and lilacs. Wild countries stuffed into the backs of old wardrobes. Summer nights and Phil Collins and waiting.

Tim doesn't wait. He just does things.

It's summer, and he goes out in the morning and he weeds the flowers my mom has planted under my window. The footprints he left there a month and a half ago are gone. My mother has not asked him to do this. She has a whole list of spring cleaning junk we're going to have to do today, anyway. But here he is, on his knees in the dirt, weeding, and I can't stand it anymore.

I kneel down beside him in the grass. You can smell the dirt, and the sun is already very warm. "Tim," I say, "we need to talk."

"Get that little bit of clover over there," he says.

I look around, trying to figure out what he's talking about.

"Under the meter," he says.

"Tim," I say again. "I need to talk to you."

He doesn't answer. He just combs through the dirt with my mother's garden claw weeding thing.

"You're doing too much," I say to him, because I don't know how else to start. "And it's not like I'm sorry you're here or anything. Because I'm not sorry. Even though it's a little different than I thought it would be. But it's cool, and my parents really like you and everything. But the thing is—you're really kind of making it hard for the rest of us."

He's still combing. "Yeah?" he says, after a moment.

"You jump up and do the dishes. You iron your own shirts. And why are you doing this?" I ask, pointing at the dirt with my whole open hand. "This is the kind of thing I'm talking about."

He rocks back and sits on his heels, looking at the flower bed.

"It needed weeding," he says.

"That's not the point," I say, exasperated with him.

He shrugs. And then he goes back to work.

"Tim," I say. "You're *supposed* to be a kid. You're supposed to be *enjoying* your life. You're supposed to be trying to get *out* of doing stuff like this. Not volunteering. Now my mother expects us all to volunteer. And I had things to *do* this afternoon."

He changes tools and now he's jabbing at something I don't know how he can tell it's not supposed to be a flower.

I watch him for a minute, and then I give up. Except I'm really mad. Except I feel more like crying than I do yelling at him, which is what I would do if Jessi was acting this way.

Just before I stand up, he starts talking. "Every month," he says, still digging at this big weed, "my uncle would sit down with the bills and compare them to the last year's, to find out how much money I was costing them. Then he'd give me an itemized bill. So much for water, so much for electricity, so much for gas. And food. And gasoline. And sewer." He shoves the digger down into the root of the weed, and I hear it tear.

"Why?" I ask him.

"It's what I cost," he says, and he pulls the weed out of the ground. There's this huge, gross white root hanging underneath it. Tim scowls at the hole. "I didn't get it all," he says.

"So?" I ask.

"So, I had to pay the bill." He tosses the weed on the pile he's started.

"You're kidding," I say, glancing at my parents' window.

"He had a list of jobs. Anything that was a result of my being there, like laundry, he just expected me to do. He said I had no right to make extra work for my aunt. And he was right; that was fair—it wasn't like I was doing them any favors, living there. He said, actually, one more adult around the house should mean less work for everybody. Except I wasn't used to doing anything, so it wouldn't seem like less to me, because for once in my life, I was taking some responsibility."

There's just the tiniest edge of bitterness in his voice now. But he sighs, like he's releasing it, and he runs his fingers through the loose dirt.

"The other jobs, things he'd have to pay somebody to do— like mucking out—he'd list how much each job was worth to him, and whatever I cost him, I had to work off. I had to keep my accounts balanced. If I worked any extra, he counted that as investing in the business."

Now he's meticulously pulling up these tiny little shoots that are coming up around the pansies.

"It was fair," he says. "It just caught me by surprise." He tosses the little shoots onto his pile, one by one. I am hugging my knees, kind of cold even with the sun there. I am strangely empty of words.

"My parents never made me pay for anything," he says. He's holding a tool again, and he rests one dusty wrist on top of the other. "I never even knew anything cost anything."

He leans forward and starts working on the grass that's coming up against the foundation wall. "I guess I thought everything was free." The tip of the tool rests in the dirt. There's a noise behind us and I glance back. The dog is sleeping in the sun, curled up about a foot away from Tim. The dog follows him everywhere. "I can even recall a couple of times when I felt like my parents owed me something." This is very bitter.

He is quiet now. I mean, he is not talking, but the air is crackling around him and he is poised over something, the tool forgotten in his hand. "You know what I said to them that last morning? They asked me to go to the mall with them? And then they said that Chris was coming, too—my brother? And you know what I said? I said I didn't want to go if Chris was going. I said it would be boring."

We are both holding very still.

And then he turns away from me and picks up the pile of weeds. "I gotta throw these away," he says. "Get the tools, will you?" And he gets up and walks away around the corner of the house. The dog groans and starts to get up, but I grab him and make him let me use him as a pillow. I'm lying there in the sun with my head on the warm dog, and his musty hair is all around my face, and I still don't have any words. Nothing will focus into words. I just keep getting bashed by these huge washes of chill.

I lie there until my mother is calling me, and even now, I hear myself resenting the intrusion. And I am thinking I must be out of my mind.

Whatever it was Tim had made me feel disappears the second I see my mother's Saturday list. It's a *long* list of the worst kinds of jobs, and she keeps adding to it. When we clean bathrooms, she makes us empty drawers and cabinets and scrub them out.

We wash down walls and turn over mattresses, and my father has the boys scraping the old paint off the rest of the screens. We empty out all our closets and drawers and cull out everything that smacks of winter or that doesn't fit, or that we just plain hate, and then we get out all the summer storage and start all over. When we are finally finished, Dad puts hamburgers on the barbecue and the kids play, and I go to take a shower.

I am standing naked in the shower when I hear the screaming. At first, I think it's just Jessi being mad at the boys. This is not an unusual occurrence. But the screaming goes on, so I turn off the water, just in time to hear my mother yelling. "Damn it, Tim," she yells, and it scares me to death, because she doesn't talk like that. Then my father is calling her and the car doors slam, and then I hear the engine roar as the car takes off down the road.

I towel myself off in a panic, knowing that something truly horrible must have happened. I am halfway down the stairs, still zipping up my pants, when Tim comes slamming in from the front, the boys right behind him. He kind of stops in mid-step when he catches sight of me, and then looks away and realizes I'm standing there poking my shirt into totally undone pants and I whirl around, stuffing like mad. Tim's face had been dead white, all the way to the lips. "What *happened?*" I ask them.

"Jessi got a spike through her foot," Caleb declares.

"What?" I say, snapping and turning all at once. Caleb's eyes are huge.

"She was running around the side of the house, and she stepped on that weeding thing that looks like a big claw," Cameron explains. "She must have come down right on top of it because it went right through her foot, just about."

"The claw?" I ask, weakly, because I am just remembering. Tim is not looking at me. "I forgot to put it away."

"Tim had it out," Cameron says.

"It was my responsibility," Tim says, his voice husky.

"No, it wasn't," I snap at him. "You asked *me* to put them away."

"You shoulda told that to Mom," Cameron says to Tim, outraged. "*I* would've told her."

"It was *my* fault," Tim maintains angrily, and then he stalks off down the hall, and we hear him slamming his way down the basement stairs and into his room.

This is so weird; usually I'm being fierce because somebody is saying something is my fault, but suddenly I'm furious because somebody is saying something *isn't* my fault.

"They took her to the hospital," Cameron says, "and I think the hamburgers are burning out back."

So we rescue the hamburgers—which are not actually burnt—and we kind of clean up, and get buns ready. But nobody feels like eating. And nobody feels like calling Tim. So I tell Cameron to go find Caleb a video, and I sit alone on the back steps, watching the shadows grow long and trying to figure out a way *I* can believe this was Tim's fault. Or at least Jessi's, for stepping on the stupid thing.

But the sky is pretty well dark and the car comes cruising back up the street, and I still haven't been able to work that one out. All I can think of is I'm going to have to tell my mother the truth, and Tim's alone in the basement feeling heaven knows what—

I hear their voices. A car door slams and I hear Jessi, who sounds okay. They're going up the front walk, and I trot around the house to follow them. My father is carrying Jessi; I can see their silhouette against the hall light as they go in the door. I don't want to have to go in there.

As I slip inside, I hear my mother tell Caleb to go get Tim. Everybody else is in the living room. Lights come on and Jessi is installed in Mom's usual corner of the couch. I am still standing out in the hall when Caleb comes back with Tim trailing along behind.

Tim doesn't look at me, but he waits for me to go before him into the living room. And then we are there and my mother turns and faces Tim. "Jessi is all right," she says first.

"Mother," I say, because I need to get this over with.

One of my mom's eyebrows goes up. Not a good sign.

"It was my fault," I say, finally. "Tim asked me to put the tools away while he was cleaning up the weeds. And I just forgot. You called me, and I just spaced on it." My eyes start stinging. "I'm really sorry, Jessi," I say, and it sounds so stupid next to getting a spike through your foot.

"I got the tools out," Tim says. "I should have made sure they were put away."

"So you should have checked up on me?" I snap, turning on him. "Oh, that's nice. You think I'm too stupid to take care of it?" Here I am, glaring at him, and then I suddenly hear what I'm saying.

"Shrewd guess," my father says, and then Jessi starts laughing. I am too embarrassed and miserable to laugh. Mother is still too mad.

"You asked Ginny to put the tools away?" she asks Tim.

"Yes, ma'am," he says. "But I should have taken care of it myself."

"Why didn't you tell me that?" she demands, really fuming. "Why did you stand there and let me yell at you like it was all your fault when it wasn't?"

Tim is standing there with his mouth open, but with absolutely nothing coming out. He's being chewed out for not whining. My mouth is open, too.

"How old are you?" my mother demands.

He blinks at her, and he says, "Seventeen." My mother crosses the few feet of space between them and takes his face in her hands, the way she does when she really wants our attention. "When we asked you to stay here, nobody expected you to be thirty-five." She is drilling right through all his careful responsibility with her eyes. "If you're going to live here, Timothy," she says, quietly, "you've got to *live* here. You've got to let yourself be one of the children. That's what *we're* here for—to be the adults." She lets go of his face, and then she puts her arms around him and makes him hug her. He doesn't do it well at first, but then he seems to give in.

After that, she puts him away from her and she's in dress-down mode again. She levels a look and a finger at him. "Never," she says. "*Never* again do I want to hear that you've trusted Ginny to follow through with *anything*. You understand?"

Everybody else is laughing before it suddenly gets through to me what she said. "*Hey*," I say, but Jessi is laughing, too, and I figure that has to be fair. And I am relieved. Except I can pretty much guess who is going to be waiting on Jessi hand and foot till her foot heals. And it's not going to be Tim.

After that happened, Tim started thawing out. He still doesn't talk about his family, and I have never seen him grieve or cry. And he is still irritatingly personally responsible. But we are now really good friends, and he is finally taking a few things for granted.

Now, we tell people that we are fraternal twins. Sometimes it seems to us that we really are. When Tim decided he liked Rebecca Lief our senior year, I set them up—I thought she'd be good for him. When Adam Mihlman asked me out, Tim forbade me to go; he did *not* approve of Adam. Tim and I actually sort of depend on each other, now.

So often, I end up sitting alone on the back steps, surprised by what I have seen through his eyes. That first night, I had been dreaming of highwaymen. Instead I got Tim, but now it strikes me that he has indeed stolen some of my self-centered innocence from me.

It is all so strange to me now. I am draped over a chair in the living room, kind of ruefully studying the Very Nice Watch my parents have given me for graduation. I have always known that new cars and trips to Europe are not exactly my parents' style, but somehow I had looked for something more exciting than this watch. It looks so—adult. I am afraid that my thank you may have lacked some enthusiasm.

My diploma is upstairs on my desk in its little hard-cover folder. The speaker at the graduation held one up and talked about how it was the symbol of our entrance into the adult world, and the end of our childhood. This was supposed to be inspiring, but I am now a little depressed. This afternoon, we have taken pictures, and we have gone out to dinner with the entire available extended family. Now the family is alone again, just sitting around in the few hours before we leave for the Last Party. My dad and mom are reading the paper, the kids are playing Risk; everything is supposed to be different, but it is still so all the same.

And then Tim comes in.

He stands in the doorway, his diploma case in his hands, and he is looking at my mother and swallowing.

"You okay?" she asks right away, putting the paper aside. Tim takes a slow step into the room, and then another, and I see, suddenly, that his eyes are full of tears. He crosses to my mother, and then he does something I have never before seen another human being do. He goes to his knees in front of her. He puts his diploma in her lap as though it's some kind of offering. He takes a long breath, and then he looks at her, and he says, "Thank you."

That's all.

Then he puts his face against her knee, and it is suddenly very quiet.

I glance at my dad, and he signals the kids and we all get up and leave the room. Nobody says anything. We just sort of instinctively follow each other down the hall and out through the kitchen to the back steps. We stand there for a minute, looking at each other, and then I sit down. And my father sits down, too—close to me, a step above, and the kids sit. We just sort of settle there, leaning on each other. And we wait, watching the shadows grow long across the lawn.

Father, Forgive Us

RANDALL L. HALL

Virgil Nelson picked up the scriptures and sat back in the rocker-recliner he had received on his fiftieth birthday several years before. The kids were all in bed and Loretta, his wife, was visiting a sick aunt who lived in the other end of town.

The scriptures, brown leather and indexed, were a gift from his oldest, who was going to college in Seattle. Virgil liked the heft of the large-print edition. It seemed to match the weight of the scriptural message, a message that struck him squarely in the heart that evening.

"And again, believe that ye must repent of your sins and forsake them, and humble yourselves before God; and ask in sincerity of heart that he would forgive you."

He had read the passage in Mosiah many times before, but this time King Benjamin's message was as plain as stars on a cloudless night. It said "sins." Not shortcomings, not weaknesses or imperfections.

For over forty years Virgil had been praying that the Lord would help him overcome his shortcomings and imperfections with an occasional acknowledgement of his weaknesses.

It was, he realized, staring out the window toward a darkening horizon, a very safe phrase. "And help us to overcome our shortcomings and imperfections."

His parents had always used the phrase. It seemed so natural.

And comfortable. There had never been any real sinners in town, much less in his family. Just people with shortcomings and imperfections.

Even when Sheila Johnson left her family to run off with a sales representative from a computer company, Virgil hadn't seen it as sin. "Must've had a weakness in that area," he told Loretta.

But that evening, reclining in the warmth of the leather chair, he saw it for what it was.

And it struck him hard, like a blast of cold wind that robs you of breath. He too was a sinner—not a shortcomer or an imperfectioner, but a sinner.

He had squirmed a little bit and headed for the kitchen for some bread and milk. He ate mechanically, thinking all the time about how, even though he was the High Priest group leader, he still used some cuss words when the occasion warranted, he had missed a few home teaching visits in the last several months, and he hadn't accepted it very gracefully when the Vietnamese family had moved into the old Larsen place.

Sin was still on his mind several hours later when he and Loretta knelt down together for their nightly prayer. It was her turn and he listened carefully. Yes, there it was, all right. "And please help us to overcome our shortcomings and imperfections."

He coughed, masking a sudden desire to laugh.

The next night he met things head on. "And please forgive us for our sins," he prayed earnestly.

Virgil didn't look up, so he didn't see his wife's eyes shoot open, staring at him with a peculiar expression on her face.

Perhaps he should have sensed it the next morning when Loretta stayed in bed until after he had showered and shaved. He couldn't remember even three such occasions in their marriage of thirty-one years. She was always up getting breakfast and making sure he had a freshly ironed shirt. He dressed and hemmed and hawed around, but even when he casually reminded her of the time, she only mumbled something about cornflakes in the cupboard and turned over, pulling the covers tightly around her.

And so he fixed his own breakfast and made a rather feeble

attempt at ironing his shirt before heading downtown to the hardware store he owned with his brother Art.

Loretta, who had spent a miserable night, spent a miserable day. What could Virgil have meant? What could he have done?

It was 2:30 in the afternoon when it came to her. Feeling faint, she sat down in Virgil's big leather chair to collect her breath and her thoughts. The new part-time bookkeeper at the store. That was it. Clive Sorenson's cousin Rhonda, a young divorcee who had moved into town three months ago with no ring on her finger, two little girls and a smile that'd make any woman question her motives. And Virgil had hired her.

No, she thought, trying to calm herself. Virgil would never do such a thing. I've got to get ahold of myself.

She spent the rest of the afternoon cooking a roast and baking the coconut cream pie that Virgil and the judges at the county fair relished.

Then he called.

"I'll be home a bit late tonight. Got some inventory that has to be taken care of." .

"Couldn't it wait until tomorrow night?" she asked with a catch in her voice.

"Nope. Some things just can't wait."

She thought of going down to the store and having it out right then and there, confronting the two of them in their sin. But she didn't.

The roast and the pie went to the neighbors.

She was in bed when he got home and wasn't any too happy when he rousted her out to pray. Blaming a sore throat she declined to take her turn. So Virgil prayed again. And when he asked for forgiveness of sins again she felt like throwing up.

By the end of the week he was acquiring a taste for cornflakes and had made some real improvements in his shirt ironing technique.

Virgil was home the next night sitting in his leather rocker-recliner when the phone rang.

"It's for you," Loretta called from the kitchen. There was something in her voice that wasn't quite right, like she had stepped suddenly into subzero weather from a too-warm room. And she turned just a little red around the ears as she handed Virgil the phone.

"It's the bishop," she said looking away from him.

Virgil took the phone and said, "Hi, Grant, what's up?"

Virgil was a bit surprised but yes, he thought he could get away from the hardware store a little early the next day and go up the canyon for some fly fishing. Grant and Virgil were second cousins, only two years apart. They had done a lot of fishing in their grown-up years, but it had been quite a while since they had last gone together.

The next afternoon found them on the river with the sun going down and the light resting golden on the water. They had fished in silence for almost twenty minutes, waiting for the first strike.

"How's the business, Virg?" Grant asked, almost too casually.

"Good," Virgil replied softly. He could see a big brown circling, and with a practiced flick of his wrist he dropped the fly about ten feet above the fish and let the current bring it down slowly.

"How are things working out with Rhonda Howard?"

"Okay."

"She's a mighty fine-looking woman."

There was something constricted in Grant's tone, like only half the air was getting through his vocal chords. Virgil glanced up.

Grant had his head down and was looking away, playing his line. He spoke again. "Pretty enough to turn a man's head."

"I suppose," Virgil said, looking over at his friend, wondering where all this was leading. Grant was as decent a Christian as he knew. Been married to the same woman for over thirty years and had five wonderful kids. Somehow he just couldn't see Grant being tempted. But, you never knew.

Just then the brown hit, thrashing the surface of the water. Virgil jerked his rod instinctively. Too late.

He almost swore, but caught himself. "Dang." If Grant hadn't rambled on I might have had him, he thought to himself. There must be something laying heavy on his mind. Grant was usually the most reverent fisherman he knew. Maybe someone in the ward was being tempted. Maybe that temptation was Rhonda and Grant was just thinking out loud. Well, thought Virgil, I sure don't want to know anything about it. That was bishops' business.

They headed home an hour later. Virgil had caught four nice German browns. The bishop hadn't caught a thing.

"How was fishing?" Loretta asked as he came in the door. Her eyes were red.

Has she been crying? he wondered. "Fine," he said. "I caught four. Grant didn't get a thing."

"Talk about anything in particular?" she asked, looking out the window.

"No," he said, taking the creel off his shoulder. "Can't say as we did." He figured it best not to mention what Grant had said about Rhonda. Loretta was a good woman but you never knew what conclusions she might jump to with a tantalizing prod like that.

He got a glass of water from the kitchen tap. "You feeling all right?" he asked.

Loretta nodded yes, but not very convincingly, and when Virgil came upstairs after putting away his gear she was already in bed, lying in a straight line just an inch and a half from the far edge. Virgil shook his head, confused. Nobody seemed to be acting normal anymore.

Two more days of cornflakes, partially ironed shirts and suspiciously red eyes later, Virgil called from work again.

"Loretta. I'll be a little late tonight. Got some book work that can't wait."

"Fine," she replied, so calmly she surprised herself. "Take all the time you need."

She hung up the phone slowly, feeling like she was floating. She took the frying pan from the sink and with one blow of jealousy, anger and anguish she dented the new formica countertop.

Book work my eye, she said to herself. I thought that's why you hired that dreamy-eyed tramp.

Fifteen minutes later Virgil heard pounding on the side door.

What in the hell? he thought, then caught himself. I mean heck. This sin stuff just didn't go away that quickly.

He got up from his chair and walked down the hallway. The pounding continued until he opened the door. It was Loretta. There were no tears in her eyes but they were red.

"How's the book work coming?" she asked, struggling for control. "Need some help?"

"No," he said, not knowing quite what to make of it all. He knew she wasn't well. He should have paid more attention to her but the last week or so had been so busy with meetings and inventory and all.

Gently he took her elbow, guiding her toward the door.

"Why don't you go home and get some rest," he said in his kindest, most protective voice, "and I'll come home in a while and fix you some of that herbal tea Margaret sent us."

She shook his hand off her arm and looked him right in the face. Her eyes got wild. "I'm going back to that office with you," she said quietly through clenched teeth.

He shrugged and the two of them headed toward the office. She stopped at the doorway and looked around. On the hat rack was a woman's white sweater.

Loretta reached out to touch it, then jerked her hand away. "Whose is this?"

"Oh, I think that's Rhonda's."

"And where is she?" Loretta asked quietly, looking around the room. Her eyes stopped on the closed door leading to the stockroom.

"Sacramento, I think," Virgil replied. "Been down there almost two weeks taking care of some kind of legal fiddle-faddle about custody of her kids. Be nice when she gets back so I don't have to work overtime."

There was a long silence. When Loretta turned around there were tears in her eyes.

Something's out of whack, Virgil thought to himself. "Let me take you home, Loretta. I can finish this another night."

She took out a handkerchief and wiped her eyes and shook her head no. She looked at him and smiled. It had been almost two weeks since he had seen one and he was more confused than ever. She shook her head again, took a deep breath, kissed him on the cheek, and then left without saying a word.

* * *

When Virgil finally got home that night it was after ten o'-clock but he was greeted by a kiss, the smell of pot roast and the sight of two huge coconut cream pies on the counter. He noticed a dent in the formica but decided not to ask. He wasn't sure he wanted to know and he wasn't sure he would understand anyway.

And forty minutes later he glanced quickly across the bed as he heard Loretta pleading sincerely, "And Father, please forgive us for our sins."

Birthday Gift

CARROLL MORRIS

Keith Winters knew his wife Janet and their two children were planning a surprise for his thirty-first birthday. Even if Janet had bothered to mask her excitement, the giggles and whispers of seven-year-old Craig and five-year-old Annie would have alerted him. He caught them often with heads together, murmuring and giving him sideways glances. Their enthusiasm charmed him, as did Janet's conspiratorial smiles. These children were his children; this woman was his wife. He knew he was a lucky man.

As the days went by, he amused himself by ticking off the possibilities, things he wanted but didn't feel he could allow himself, what with the monthly payments on their new house and the still-unsteady situation at the chain restaurant he had been asked to nudge into the black. A new set of golf clubs. The fish finder he had been eyeing. Season tickets to the Minnesota Twins. But none of those things seemed likely, even if they had been possible. They wouldn't have put that sparkle he had been seeing into his children's eyes.

When Annie and Craig deposited a wriggling black puppy in his lap, he was caught completely off guard. He tried to cover his dismay, tried to force his face into an expression approximating pleasure, but failed. It was obvious to all of them that the last thing he wanted for his birthday was a dog.

"Don't you like your puppy, Daddy?" asked Annie, her forehead wrinkled in concern. "She's so cute!"

The puppy sniffed and nuzzled him, trying to insert her nose into the gap between two buttons of his shirt. Suddenly she stood on her hind legs, forepaws braced against his chest for balance, and began licking his face. He arched back to avoid the unwanted affection. The puppy lost her balance and slid halfway off his lap, her toenails scratching him through the cloth of his slacks.

Craig rescued her by pulling her onto his own lap. "She's a cocker spaniel," he said, his voice earnest, "just like the dog you had when you were little. The one in the pictures."

When he didn't respond, Craig continued with worried intensity, "She won't get too big to be a house dog. And she won't be any trouble. I'll feed her every day, and I'll take her for walks, too. I promise."

He could tell Craig was hoping to make this moment turn out as planned. They all were. No one moved except the puppy, who was now making Craig the object of her exuberant exploration. Then Annie started to cry. Keith reached for her, but she sought her mother's side, pressing her face into the denim of Janet's jeans. Craig joined them, the puppy in his arms.

"I don't understand," Janet said.

All he could do was shrug his shoulders and say, "I'm sorry."

Janet took the puppy from Craig with a fierce protectiveness. "Come on, kids. Let's go set up Sassy's bed."

Annie hesitated. "Isn't Daddy going to help?" she asked. "He was supposed to help." It was a plea as much as a question, and Keith understood that the scenario was supposed to include all of them setting up the puppy's new home together. A Polaroid moment. He started to rise, but Janet's look stopped him. "Daddy," she said, "is going to clean up the kitchen."

Annie and Craig went into the mud room, Janet following. Keith stopped her with a question as she was just about to go through the door. "Who named the dog Sassy?"

She turned in the doorway. "Your children picked out both the dog and the name," she said in an accusing tone. "Why?"

"Sassy is so close to Suzy, I thought . . ."

"Coincidence. But for some reason I had the idea you'd be pleased."

He knew by the way her eyes grew wide and bright that she was trying to keep from crying. "I don't understand you at all," she said. "You've always told so many stories about the fun you had with Suzy."

"I didn't tell you all of them."

"Maybe you should have."

She turned away, leaving him alone in the kitchen. The cake with its cheerful inscription sat uncut in the middle of the table, surrounded by Keith's favorite special-occasion meal: pot roast with potatoes, carrots and gravy. Although Janet was all but a vegetarian, she had made it as a special treat for him.

"Happy birthday, Keith," he said to himself. He carried the dirty dishes from the table to the sink. On the last trip, he slowed down while passing the mud-room door and craned his neck for a glimpse of what was going on. Janet was defining the dog's area with the safety gate they had used at the top of the stairs when the kids were toddlers. The kids were trying to restrain the puppy. There was a flurry and a squeal, then laughter. "Get me some paper towels," Janet called with a fleeting glance in his direction. He pulled a strip from the roll and handed them to Craig. "Sassy peed all over the floor," Craig said with a giggle. He watched them clean up the mess from the doorway, wishing he could change the moment the gift was given.

The first of the phone calls came as he was starting the dishwasher. It was from his sister Leslie. He had been expecting to hear from her; he would hear from his brother and his parents, too, before the night was over. None of them were close, geographically speaking. He and his siblings had grown up in Logan, Utah, but only his parents lived there now. Leslie and her husband were in Phoenix; Fred lived in Plattsburg, New York. The distance—and their lack of inclination, he had to admit—made shared time rare, but they always communicated on birthdays and holidays. It wasn't much, but it was something.

"Happy birthday, big brother," Leslie said. Her voice was as relentlessly cheerful as ever. The sound of it conjured up her large, almost homely face, its too-big features softened by a charming good will.

"How does it feel to be thirty-one?"

"Why do people always ask that?"

"I don't know about others, but I do because I want to know—I'll be thirty-one myself in a couple of years."

"It feels odd. I remember when Uncle Hebe was thirty and I thought, 'Gee, he's old.' Now I'm there myself, and I don't feel any smarter than I thought I was then."

"How depressing. Isn't the idea that we're supposed to improve with age? You know, 'Every day in every way I get better and better,'" she said, quoting one of their mother's self-improvement slogans.

Another volley of shrieks rolled from the mud room, sparked by shrill yapping.

"Is that a dog I hear?" asked Leslie.

"Yeah. It's my birthday present. Janet and the kids surprised me with it."

"I bet you just about croaked when you saw it was a dog."

"Close," he said.

"What kind is it?"

"Cocker spaniel. They named her Sassy."

"Cute. It's about time. I've always thought you needed a dog."

"Dogs are more trouble than they're worth, especially puppies."

"Maybe so, but you've got one now."

"I don't suppose I can take her back, can I?"

"Not after they've named her."

"That's what I was afraid of. But I really don't want our lives complicated the way it would be if she stayed. We couldn't leave for a weekend without finding someone to take her. Then there's the shots and grooming—"

"Now you sound just like Dad."

"Don't say that!"

"Well, you do."

"If I do, I'm smart enough to stop something before it gets out of hand."

"That's garbage. You want that dog, you know you do. It's just hard for you to give up your resentment about what happened to Suzy. You think by punishing yourself you can get back at Dad somehow."

"That's not it at all."

"Wanna bet?"

He smiled at her tone; he knew how she must look with her chin jutting out in a challenge. "Still feisty, are you?"

"You better believe it. Think about what I said, okay? Don't make a decision you'll regret."

"I'll try not to."

He was just hanging up the phone when Janet came into the kitchen. He told her who had called; she acknowledged him with a curt nod. "I need to find an old blanket for Sassy," she said.

He stepped in front of her, forcing her to stop. "I'm sorry I made a mess of things. I know you and the kids went to a lot of trouble to make me happy. I'm just sorry you didn't know how I felt. That's my fault. I should have told you."

"Tell me now," she said, her arms folded and her hips akimbo.

So he did, as brutally as he could. "My dad killed Suzy."

She stared at him, uncomprehending. "What do you mean, killed her?"

"He took her to the vet and had her put to sleep—just because he was ticked off."

"He wouldn't do that."

"Ask him if you don't believe me."

She shook her head, a motion slowed by shock. "There must have been a reason. Your dad isn't like that."

"You don't know what he was like back then."

"True, but I still can't believe—"

"Believe it. Because that's the way it happened."

The scuffling noise of children and dog seemed inordinately loud in the silence that followed. "Maaaa!" called Craig. "Hurry up!"

"I'm coming," Janet said over her shoulder. She gave him a bewildered look, then went to get the blanket. On her way back through the kitchen, she said, "This doesn't make sense. There must be something you're not telling me." She hesitated, waiting for an answer, even as the children's insistent voices pulled at her from the other room. When he didn't reply, she went to them.

He finished loading the dishwasher, started it, then wiped the countertops clean. Washcloth still in hand, he leaned against a cabinet, tipping his head so he could see what was going on in the other room.

Craig caught him watching. "Look, Dad. See how we've made her a little pen?"

They had positioned the gate to block off the empty space between the clothes washer and the wall to the side of it. Most of the floor was covered with newspaper. "In case she pees again," Annie explained, grinning as she said the word. A pink plastic dog dish with depressions for both water and food stood toward the front. At the back was a pile of soft old blankets molded into a nest. In the nest was a wind-up clock.

"The clock's to keep her company at night so she won't whine," Craig explained. "This is the first time she's been away from her mommy."

Janet smoothed down a tuft of the little boy's hair. "She'll be all right," she assured him. There was doubt in her voice, and Keith could read a plea for answers in her eyes, but he couldn't give her any.

"What about the other presents?" Craig asked.

Janet sat back on her heels. "It's just as well we didn't wrap them," she said. With a sigh, she stood and retrieved a small collar and retractable leash from the cupboard over the washing machine. "These were supposed to be part of your present." She held them out to him, but he made no move to take them. So she buckled the collar on the uncooperative puppy and then attached the leash. "What do you say, kids? Shall we take Sassy on a walk?"

They jumped and clapped their hands, then fell to squabbling about who would get to hold the leash first. "Girls first," said Janet. Then she asked Keith if he wanted to come. He shook his head.

"Okay, if that's the way you want it."

"It's not the way I want it!" His voice, tight and loud, brought frightened looks to the children's faces, anger to Janet's. "I'm sorry, I didn't mean to shout," he said. When their expressions didn't change, he added, "I'm sorry, okay? How many times do I have to say it?"

In answer, Janet carried Sassy out the door, herding Craig and Annie in front of her. Then she put the puppy down and handed Annie the leash. Sassy strained at it, pulling Annie down the driveway behind her. At the end of the driveway, they turned onto the street. As was the case in most nearby suburban developments, their neighborhood had no sidewalks.

If Keith had chosen their new home, his family wouldn't be walking in the street. They would be living in Minneapolis itself on a street of moderate homes not far from Lake Harriet. A street graced by some of the few remaining elms, where homes stood cheek by jowl, their neat, green lawns edged by the sidewalk that bound them into a neighborhood. But Janet's concern about schools and her desire for a large yard had held the day. She had also argued that it was closer to his restaurant, which he had to admit was important, given the long and difficult Minnesota winters.

He was still watching his family when the phone rang. His younger brother Fred: "Hi there, old man."

"Hey, yourself," he said, flopping down on the sofa. The baby of the family, Fred was a landscape architect. Keith had not seen him for three and a half years, but the intensity in his voice was still the same.

"What does it feel like to be thirty-one?" Fred asked.

"You guys aren't very original, are you?"

"Leslie called."

"Yep. Wanted a preview."

"Well, you're the trailblazer," said Fred. "Might as well give me one, too."

"If today's any indication, I'd just as soon skip to thirty-two."

"Cheery thought. You should be a happy man. It's a time to celebrate."

"I'm afraid it hasn't been much of a celebration."

"What happened?"

"The kids got me a dog."

Fred laughed. "What's so bad about a dog?"

"You should know."

"You're not still wallowing around in that Suzy thing are you?" Fred asked in disgust. "It's been twenty years."

"Right. It's been twenty years and my dog is still dead and Dad has never apologized."

"What should he apologize for? It was more our fault than his. If we had put her on her chain the way we were supposed to, she wouldn't have been chasing ducks around the pond and messing up the neighbors' yards. And the neighbors wouldn't have kept calling the pound."

"He didn't have to kill her."

"If I remember right, the city gave Dad two choices: pay a big fine and make sure she was never let loose outside, or—"

"He could have given us another chance."

"What good would that have done?"

"We would have made sure she was on her chain."

"Come off it. It never would have happened."

"What makes you say that," Keith said, his anger rising like bile.

"Because whenever you wanted to play with Suzy, she was 'your' dog. But whenever it was your turn to feed her or make sure she was on the chain, you'd say, 'I'm not going to do it. She's not my dog.'"

Keith jumped to his feet. "I did not," he yelled.

"You most certainly did," Fred yelled back.

"That's not the way it happened."

"Says you. Dad did what he had to do, and it wasn't easy. I saw him when he came home, and I can tell you, he was as affected by this thing as you were."

"Oh, yeah?"

"Yeah."

"I never saw any evidence of it."

"You didn't want to."

"Now you're really making me mad."

"That wasn't my intention," said Fred, but his voice was still brusque. "I just wanted to wish you a happy birthday."

Keith rubbed his face with his hand and exhaled, a long blowing-out of anger and resentment. "I know," he said. "I'm sorry things got out of hand."

Their goodbyes were awkward. Keith sat down on the couch again, resting his elbows on his thighs, letting his hands dangle loosely. It was getting dark; shadows gave the room a forlorn aspect. The house was quiet except for the hum of the dish-washer. He leaned back and closed his eyes.

And there on the backs of his eyelids was the image of Suzy, running around the edge of the pond and into the unmown grass in the empty lot next door. A cocker spaniel miniature poodle mix, she wasn't even a third as tall as the grass in high summer, so once she was in it, he couldn't actually see her. But he could see the wake that marked her progress. And every now and then, she popped up to take her bearings, head barely clearing the top of the grass, ears flying and mouth open in a silly grin. Suzy, hiding gifts of pancakes and chicken bones under his pillow, managing somehow to pull the bedspread back over her offering so that he was always surprised when he turned the spread back at bedtime. Sitting at attention by his side as he picked raspberries, waiting for him to give her the juiciest and ripest. And . . . Suzy, barking and whining in utter misery whenever she was put on a chain. Threatening anyone who came to the door. Chasing—and catching—ducklings and birds, then depositing them on the doorstep. Going into de-pression whenever they left her with someone else while on va-cation, refusing to eat or drink.

The images of Suzy brought him to the verge of tears, but the sound of voices coming up the walk stiffened his control. He went to the door and watched the little parade, not sure if it was the memories or the sight before him that made his heart heavy. Annie and Craig were both dragging their feet, worn out by their jaunt with the puppy. The puppy was worn out as well; she was asleep in Craig's arms, her head resting in the crook of his elbow. The leash hung over it, the end dragging along be-hind. All of them, Janet included, looked content, their faces glowing with a surfeit of joy.

Until they started up the stairs and saw him standing there. Then there was only doubt and sadness.

"Looks like everybody's worn out," Keith said, hating the hollow heartiness of his voice.

Janet nodded. "I think they're all ready for bed." She held out her hands for the puppy. Craig handed Sassy over, being careful not to wake her.

Janet looked at Keith. "Would you make sure the kids get their baths while I take care of Sassy?"

"Sure. Come on, sweetie." He swung Annie up into his arms and started down the hall. "Let's go, big boy," he said over his shoulder to Craig. "You're next."

He gave Annie a quick bath, guided her limp arms and legs into her pajamas and tucked her in. She normally insisted on stories at bedtime, but on this night, she didn't protest when he turned out the lamp on her dresser without reading from her favorite books. He kissed her goodnight and felt her warm breath on his cheek as she murmured something in reply. Closing her door softly behind him, he went to check on Craig.

Craig wasn't in the bathroom; he was sitting on the edge of his bed, still in his sweaty clothes. "Better hit the tub," he said. "Your mother won't like if it I let you go to bed without taking a bath."

"Daddy?" Craig's voice was solemn. "Are you going to let us keep Sassy?"

Keith started to answer, but his son's voice tumbled on in his eagerness. "She doesn't need to be your dog," he said. "She can be my dog. My birthday's next month—we can pretend she's my birthday present! I'll take care of her real good. And we'll get you another present tomorrow, one you'll like."

Keith sat down next to Craig and put his arm around the boy's shoulder. "You guys really surprised me, you know. I figured you had something up your sleeves, but the last thing I would have guessed was a dog."

"We thought you liked dogs."

"I do."

"Then why . . ."

He sighed heavily. "It's something I can't explain right now. It's too complicated."

"But what about Sassy? Can we keep her?"

"I have to think about it, okay?"

Craig's doubt showed in his eyes. "I guess."

"Now it's time for that bath." Keith found the sensitive spot on Craig's ribs. Giggling, Craig jumped from the bed to get away from his father's searching finger. As Keith moved toward him, he backed out of the bedroom. Several giggles and tickles later, he was in the bathroom, where Keith wanted him to be. "Call me when you're done," he said. "I'm going to go see what your mom and Sassy are up to."

"I want to come, too!"

"Nope. It's bath time. I mean it. You can look in on the puppy before you go to bed, okay?"

When he was satisfied that Craig was going to bathe, he joined Janet in the mud room. She was sitting cross-legged, her back to the wall, watching the puppy sleep.

"How're things going?" he asked.

"She's asleep, if that's what you're asking."

"Where's the clock?"

"I wrapped it up in that old towel."

Now he could see the lump of towel at Sassy's back. "I'm surprised that it works. I remember my mom using that trick to get Suzy to sleep the first night we had her, but she whined all night long. Dad was furious. He didn't want a dog in the first place."

"Like you don't want Sassy."

"No. Nothing like that. Dad told Mom outright that he didn't want a dog. He did everything but forbid her to get one—not that that would have done any good—but she was convinced we needed a dog to teach us responsibility."

"That's a lousy reason to get a dog."

"Well, that was Mom's reason. Dad was furious, but what could he do, once we kids had seen the dog? If he made Mom take the dog back, he would be the bad guy. Again." He frowned and ran his hand through his hair.

"You feel as if you're in the same spot, don't you."

He nodded.

"If you really don't want a dog in the house, I'll take her back. And I'll make it right with the kids."

"And they'll never forgive me."

"I'll make them understand," she said. Then she added, "But *I* have to understand first. What happened with Suzy? And why won't you give Sassy a chance when I know you love dogs?"

He was trying to organize his thoughts when Craig yelled for him and at the same time, the phone rang.

"Why don't I check on Craig," she suggested. "The phone's probably for you."

This time his mother was on the line. She sang "Happy Birthday" all the way through while he held the phone out from his ear. "How's my birthday boy?" she asked.

"Fine."

"I wish you lived closer. The way all you kids have scattered from coast to coast, I almost think you wanted to get too far away for us to visit."

"You can come visit anytime, Mom."

"Maybe at the end of summer. Your father and I are going to take the camper to Yellowstone, then on up to Glacier."

"Sounds fun."

"We would take you all with us if we had enough room, you know."

"Oh? I seem to remember you saying that you and Dad bought a small camper specifically to discourage tagalongs."

She laughed. "Just kidding. Here's your father. He's been waiting to talk to you."

Right, he thought.

"Congratulations! You made it to another birthday," his father said.

"It seems that way."

"Wait until you get as old as I am, then you'll be glad for every birthday you have."

"No doubt."

"I suppose you got lots of presents from the kids."

"Not lots, one big one. Janet and the kids thought they would surprise me. They gave me a puppy. She looks a lot like Suzy."

"If she acts like Suzy, you've got your work cut out for you. But you always did want another dog."

"That's right, I did—when I was younger. Now that I think back on what happened to Suzy, I begin to wonder if it's such a good idea."

"Why's that?"

"Dogs get caught in the middle, you know what I mean? People get angry and the first thing you know, the dog gets killed."

"Here we go again. We had a lot of problems with Suzy, you know that. We decided it would be for the best."

"Who is 'we'?"

"Your mother and I. We talked it over."

"The way I remember it, there wasn't any talking. You were crazy out of your gourd. All you wanted to do was get rid of her."

"It wasn't like—"

"For a long time afterward, I was afraid you would get rid of us kids if we caused too much trouble. Did you know that?"

"What crap. Your mother and I gave you kids everything we had to give. We made some mistakes, but we did our best and frankly, I'm sick of plowing the same field over and over again. I don't get to talk to you very often, and when I do, I'd like it to be pleasant. I'd like to hear how the kids are and what Janet is doing and what's going on with you."

Keith thought, What's going on with me is that I got a dog for my birthday, and it brought everything back, and I don't know what to do about it or how to get past it, and I want to get past it as much as you want to forget it.

"Come on, son. Why don't you tell me how things are at the restaurant?"

"Better, finally," he said. "I think I've got the personnel problems solved. We should be showing some progress on the books, soon."

"Great. Glad to hear it. Now, how are those grandkids of mine doing?"

Later, when children and puppy were asleep, Keith and Janet lay in their bed and he told her about Suzy.

How they had all been in the back yard that day—his dad had decided to spend his summer vacation working on needed home repairs—when the uniformed woman from the city's Animal Control Department walked around the house, clipboard in hand. How she had told them that there had been another complaint about Suzy running loose, a violation of the city ordinance.

"Was she running loose?" asked Janet.

"Yes. We could hardly tell her the neighbors were mistaken when Suzy picked exactly that moment to go splashing in the pond. She told Dad and Mom it was the third complaint, and that they had two choices: either pay a fine or have the dog put down." He was amazed that he could say the words without a quaver.

"Why didn't your folks just pay the fine?"

He shrugged. He remembered how horrifyingly large the fine had sounded to him at the time, but he didn't mention that.

Nor did he mention any part of his conversation with Fred. He knew that to be fair, the whole story would have to be told, but he didn't want to be fair. What he wanted was for Janet to understand his pain, to think that there was only his side.

"That must have been a horrible day," she said when he finished.

"No kidding. Do you know we have it memorialized? Mom decided that each of us should all have one last picture of ourselves with the dog."

She sat up, incensed. "No."

"You've seen it, it's in my photo album."

He fetched the thick photo album his mother had put together for him and climbed back into bed beside Janet.

"See? That's it."

He pointed to a square photograph of a boy and a dog, both of whom had dark curly hair flopping down over their eyes.

"Didn't your mother ever cut your hair? Or Suzy's?"

"Sure—when it got so bad she couldn't ignore it. That was the problem-solving strategy in our household. We'd lope along with everybody doing their own thing until something would go wrong. Then Mom or Dad—or both—would get a bee in their bonnet and make life hell for all of us until we straightened up. Then they'd loosen up the reins and everything would go back to the way it was before. Until the next brouhaha."

Janet's eyes were thoughtful. "That's what happened, isn't it? With Suzy, I mean? Instead of solving the problem when it would be easy to solve, everybody let it slide until there was a crisis."

"I suppose. I told my high school counselor about Suzy once. He said Suzy was a metaphor for the dysfunction in our family."

Janet ran her finger over the photo, touching the tousle-haired boy and the shaggy dog, a wistful gesture. Then she closed the album. "I meant what I said earlier, Keith. If having Sassy in the house will make you too uncomfortable, I'll take her back. The people we bought her from said we could return her if she 'didn't work out.' I don't know exactly what that means, but I'm sure it covers a situation like this."

"How long do we have?"

"A week."

"Then let's keep her for a week. Maybe I can get my head screwed on straight by then. I don't want the kids to think I'm mean."

"It would be easier if you could make up your mind now. They'll be too attached after a week."

"A couple of days, then."

*   *   *

Those days were miserable. Janet, who had been so understanding when he told her, was by turns morose and irritable. She gave him long wistful looks full of unspoken hopes. She picked on his personal habits, like the way he left his socks in a pile by his side of the bed and clanked spoon against bowl when eating cereal.

It was worse with the kids—they tried to do everything just right. For three days they did their evening chores without any fussing. They went to bed when they were supposed to—without being asked. They minded their manners and never missed a chance to give him a hug or a smile.

They were perfect, but it was all wrong. Every time he looked in their eyes, he knew what they were thinking: Don't be too noisy, it might make Dad mad, and then we won't be able to keep the dog. Don't fuss over bedtime, or we won't be able to keep the dog. Don't make too much noise, don't spill the milk, don't forget to tell Dad how much you love him. The worst was listening to their ingenuous prayers: "Please make it so that Sassy can stay. Please help Daddy so he'll love Sassy the way we do."

He had become the bad guy. If he told them the puppy had to go, none of them would ever forgive him. If he said the puppy could stay, Craig and Annie would keep up their vigilance at least a little longer—at least until the novelty of the puppy wore off—and then they would lapse into being children again. And he would start yelling at them, resentful that there was another living thing in the house that made demands on his time and affection and money. And reminded him of the most painful time of his life.

The day dawned and he still had no idea what he was going to tell them. They all watched him with expectant eyes as they ate breakfast. They hovered around him after morning prayers, hoping he would say the word. They watched him back down the driveway, their listless waves betraying their fear.

He half expected them to be waiting for him in the same place when he got home, but the front yard was empty. The house was empty, too, but he could hear the sound of children's voices coming from the back yard. He took off his suit coat, draped it over the back of a kitchen chair and loosened his tie. Then stood at the patio door, watching them.

Janet had set up a large play area for the dog with extra garden fencing from the garage. He could imagine what she had said to the kids: "Your daddy won't like it if Sassy messes up his garden."

Sassy wasn't the only one inside the large fenced circle; the children were lying on their stomachs, teasing her with blades of grass. Janet was pulling weeds in the flower border. He went out on the deck. "Hi, guys," he said, waving his hand. The children acknowledged his greeting, then turned back to the dog. Janet put down her trowel and joined him on the steps. "How was your day?" she asked.

"Rotten. I couldn't think about anything but Sassy and the kids."

"Do you know what you're going to tell them?"

"Not yet. Why does this have to be so hard?"

"It doesn't have to be," she said, resting her head against his shoulder. "I haven't thought about anything but you and Sassy and Suzy for days. And there's something I want to say before you make up your mind." She turned his face toward her and held it in her hands. "The past is just that—the past. Look at what you have right here, right now. It's everything you've ever said you wanted: A home. Children who love you. A wife who loves you. I'll go along with whatever you decide, Keith, but remember that you'll be deciding for all of us."

"Do you really trust me to make that decision?"

"Yes."

He pulled her into his arms. "Thank you. I needed to hear that." He held her for a moment, then said, "There's something I have to tell you, something Dad told me once, a long time ago. I couldn't accept it at the time, I guess. After he took Suzy to the vet's, he had to go to City Hall and verify that she had been put to sleep, or he'd still have to pay the damned fine. He said he made it through . . . the hard part, but when he got to City Hall and tried to tell the lady behind the desk, he started to cry. He couldn't help it and he couldn't stop it. The poor lady didn't know what to do. Finally she said, 'You must have loved your dog very much.'"

Janet pulled away from him. "Why didn't you say that the other night? It wasn't fair of you to let me think your father did it out of meanness."

"I know. I'm sorry."

"You need to tell *him* that."

He nodded. "There's something else." He took a deep breath and forged on. "Dad said that every night when he came home from work, Suzy would run down the driveway to greet him. He said he knew that she, at least, was glad to see him."

He stumbled over the last words. His shoulders shook and a hoarse cry escaped his lips.

Hearing it, the children looked up from their play. They were motionless for a moment, their faces suffused with fear. Then Annie cried, "Daddy! Daddy! What's wrong?" They scrambled over the fence, knocking down a section in their haste. The puppy dashed over the flattened section and up the steps. She wriggled her way between the children and onto Keith's lap. He scooped her up, one hand under her haunches, the other at the nape of her neck, and pressed her to his chest. Her soft hair rubbed against his cheek as her nose searched his neck. Out of the corner of his eye, he saw Craig give Janet a triumphant smile, pull his fisted arm down in a swift gesture and mouth the word, "Yes!"

The Color-Blind Bull

JEAN LIEBENTHAL

"I'm sorry I have to bother you this way," my mother says. "I've always been able to get myself to the dentist without any help before, but with my knee in this shape, I was afraid to drive. I wouldn't want to hurt anybody else."

Has her tone of voice always been this apologetic, or is it just that I haven't noticed before? And she seems smaller, somehow, since Dad died—smaller and cautious, as if everything in her life is tentative.

"It's okay, Mom," I say, though really I am already drowning in unaccomplished tasks. Unpaid bills that are by now probably overdue, a house that will soon defy the Department of Health; all this on the home front only. At school, a stack of ungraded papers, lesson plans—the list is endless.

"Dr. Evans usually has me take an antibiotic when he works on a bad tooth," she says. "If I need a prescription filled, do you think you could take time to stop at the drugstore afterward?"

Exasperation wells up in me, but her hesitancy, her timidity is, I suppose, what disperses the feeling. Or perhaps it is the memory of the conversation I had with my Aunt Helen yesterday.

"Sure, Mom," I answer, making the effort to keep my voice calm. "We'll get whatever you need."

We are nearing town and my mother gazes out the window

at the open fields that are thawing, getting ready for planting, as if by studying them intently enough, she can somehow soak into her veins the moisture, the newness of spring.

"Have I ever told you about the time Hank and I got cornered by that bull when we were kids?" she asks. "He always insisted it was color-blind, though how he knew that was a mystery to us all. Later on, someone told me all bulls are color-blind. Maybe he'd heard that, too."

I couldn't count the number of times I've heard the story of Mom and Uncle Hank and the color-blind bull, and I open my mouth to say so. But Aunt Helen's words echo in my mind.

* * *

"Just remember—what goes around comes around," was what she'd said.

I hadn't particularly liked her tone of voice. I liked even less the condescending smile that went with it. My reaction must have shown, because she soon added, "Well, what's the matter with you?"

"Just surprised, I guess. Cliches like that aren't normally your style."

I felt that she deserved my sarcasm and I used it to cover up my disappointment. Aunt Helen had always been my ally. At least, that's what I'd thought.

"I'd better get going," I said.

"Oh, come on, Cassie," Helen replied. "You don't have to go away mad!"

"Who's mad? Mad means insane. I don't think I'm there quite yet, but I'm working on it."

"Okay, angry, then, if we have to be so precise and pedantic."

This was not a good visit. I disliked having to be defensive with the aunt I generally feel so at ease with.

"I'm not angry, either," I said. "It's just that you usually try to help me with my problems."

Aunt Helen dusted the edge of the end table with her finger. "Look at this dust," she said, evading my statement. "I'm slipping. Used to dust every day or so."

"I tell you about a problem, Aunt Helen, and you tell me about your dusty table. The two don't correlate."

She started folding towels. "Your problems don't usually concern your mother—my sister."

This startled me. Sometimes I seem to forget, in a way, that Helen and my mother are really sisters. The youngest of a large family, she's twenty years younger than Mom, who was the oldest, and about fifteen years older than I am. I've thought of her as more of a sister, the big sister I never had. She has been my mentor and my friend. Though I am thirty-seven years old, I still go to her for support and advice. Now she seemed to be turning away from me.

I made another attempt. "I really wonder whether she doesn't have Alzheimer's. She tells me the same things over and over, and when I interrupt to say I've heard it all before, and I've heard it more than once, she gets her feelings hurt," I said. "There are other things she neglects to tell me that I need to know. She thinks she's already told me. I've been studying up on the symptoms. It really seems like the beginning of Alzheimer's disease."

Aunt Helen glanced up from her folding. "Or maybe the beginning of Old Timer's disease. That's an illness that seems to strike us all, sooner or later—usually sooner than we're ready for it. How long has it been since your mother has seen her doctor? Do you know?"

"A few weeks ago. But he wasn't looking for any particular symptoms."

"I think there's a disease that strikes your generation pretty frequently," Aunt Helen continued, still folding and smoothing. "And that's Categorizer's Disease."

I stood up and started for the door.

"Come back here," Aunt Helen said, with a wry smile. "Let's go out in the garden. I have some weeding to do. And while I weed, I want to tell you a little tale about myself. I *know* you'll stop me if you've heard it before."

She knelt down and loosened the soil around her plants with a small garden trowel. "Get those weeds in the corner while we talk, will you?" she asked.

I worked with her in silence for a few minutes, grateful for the shade.

"I'm waiting," I finally said, "for the little tale about yourself."

"Oh, yes. That," she answered. "It involves your grandmother and it was a long time ago. She was about sixty at the time, give or take a couple of years. I'd already noticed some changes in her. Seemed she did some rather odd things at times and had picked up a few peculiar characteristics.

"But I got really concerned when she started calling me about names."

"What names?"

"Oh, various names. Maybe you've heard the saying, 'The nouns are the first to go.'"

"No, I don't think I have."

"Probably not. You're not old enough, yet. But some day you will be. You'll look for a name, and it won't be there. It won't exactly be gone—just misplaced. It will emerge at a later time, when you don't need it anymore."

"Names of people or names of things?" I asked.

"Both. But primarily people, and of course that's the most troublesome, particularly when you can't escape the necessity of introducing them to one another.

"But to get back to my story," Aunt Helen continued, "Mother kept making these phone calls, at all times of the day. One morning she woke me up just before six. 'Now what's the name of that movie star?' she asked. 'You know, that handsome one who was so sophisticated. He has the same name as a stove, or a lantern or something.'

"It wasn't much of a clue, but we did finally come up with Ronald Coleman's name. I think that was about the time I told your Uncle Victor that I was afraid Mother was losing her mind. Nobody had told us about Alzheimer's, or I'm sure I'd have been even more worried. She didn't get much worse, though, so the worry stopped, but I was always rather disdainful when she would phone to enlist me in her search of names.

"Then one day, just a couple of years ago, a funny thing happened to me. I started to introduce Camilla Harper to Evelyn Petree. I'd known them both for years. I had called Camilla by name not an hour before. But now there was this terrible pause that just got longer and longer. Finally she took pity on me and produced her name herself. I spent all afternoon apologizing. That was the beginning of a humbling experience which is, it seems, ongoing."

I could feel myself blushing. Without knowing it, I'd been

criticizing Aunt Helen along with Mom. "That must have been terribly embarrassing for you," I said.

"Horribly. And I was so shocked. I had always had an unusually good memory for names. I was not only embarrassed, I was angry. And I was scared. Something must be wrong with me! Up to this time, I'd been quite good at patting myself on the back for having taken such wonderful precautions to stay sharp, quick and alert. A couple of weeks later the same sort of thing happened again, and then I found myself with the movie star problem my mother had had—the very one I had so little tolerance for. I was saying to my friend, 'Wasn't he wonderful—what was his name?—and that movie. Oh, you know, the one about the fellow who made his wife think she'd gone bonkers.' That was the first time I fully realized that Mother hadn't somehow caused or at least courted a lapse of memory. Until then I had subconsciously believed she could have had control of what was happening to her if she'd wanted to."

"Then what?" I asked.

"Then nothing," Aunt Helen said. "Not exactly nothing, I guess. I didn't talk to anyone about it until I got my next physical. Then I told Doc Hill."

"What did he say?"

Aunt Helen shook the dirt from the red roots of the weeds. Then she laughed and replied, "He said I had the symptoms of the beginning of a fatal disease—old age. He told me it was incurable, but that I had plenty of company. And he advised me that the only thing to do was to learn to live with it and laugh at it. It would never get any better."

"Won't it really?" I asked.

Aunt Helen stared at me, her face assuming an exaggerated expression of confusion.

"Who did you say you are?" she asked. "I don't think we've met before."

We both laughed. But underlying my laughter was a disquietude I could not shake off, and my smile soon faded.

"This doesn't seem at all fair," I said. "I don't like to see this happening to Mom," I said.

Aunt Helen wiped her sweating forehead with the back of her hand.

"How do you think she likes it?" she asked, softly.

* * *

I pull up between the two yellow parking lines in front of the dentist's office. I switch off the key and look hard at my mother's profile. Etched in the lines of her face I see things that, in the fast pace of my active, hurried life, I have tried not to see. I see how old she is getting. I see her reticence, her fear of being intrusive. I see, beneath the veneer of the fixed, resigned smile, a sharp loneliness that refuses to be hidden.

I repeat back to her the question she has just asked me. "Did you ever tell me the story of the color-blind bull?"

I know the words to the story practically by heart, but have I ever really grasped the meaning of it? I'm afraid the answer to that is no. I have never tried to imagine my mother as a child she once was, never tried to feel the fear she must have felt when the furious, panting bull charged her and the little boy who was in her care as they scrambled under the barbed wire fence. I have never gotten close enough to smell the wild mint growing thick on the ditch bank of her youth, nor to feel the sun, hot and dry on the black, turned soil. I know the words by heart, but I have never really listened.

I reach out and take my mother's fragile, dry hand in mine. She looks up, surprised. Her face slowly flushes with pleasure.

"I think maybe you have told me that story before, Mom," I say. "But it's one of my favorites, and I'd like to hear it again."

Me and the
Big Apple

JAROLDEEN EDWARDS

The phone call came at 10 A.M., when I was in no mood for complications. I hadn't even started the breakfast dishes yet! I had bathed the baby and put her down for her morning nap. Brad and Tara had been fed and cleaned up, and were outside getting dirty again, but everything else was behind schedule. Marsh had returned home from New York too late to take care of his suitcase last night, and unpacking it had taken me longer than expected this morning. Now the suitcase sat empty on the unmade bed. Beside it was a pile of Marsh's dress shirts for the cleaners.

As I added his shorts and stockings to the heaped laundry basket, I stared at the full diaper pail next to it and wondered if I could possibly carry everything to the basement in one load. That's when the phone rang.

I knew when I picked it up and heard Marsh's cheerful "Hello, honey!" that I was in trouble. Marsh never called from work except with bad news. And bad news was always an unexpected trip. My problem was that I was still mad from the last trip. Well, maybe *mad* wasn't exactly the word; it was more like . . . nope, *mad* was the word.

"Honey," said Marsh briskly, "I've been in meetings all morning and we've pulled together the report on the company AMBEX wants to acquire. Just finished pushing the last figures.

The secretaries are working like mad on the final copies and displays.

"I talked to Ted Farrell in New York and he says that their Big Board meets tomorrow and they want a full-dress presentation. They never thought we'd finish this soon. If we impress them with this one we'll get a contract for all their consultation work. Do you know what that could mean?"

I knew it was a rhetorical question, but I couldn't resist. "Yes," I muttered sotto voce, "dinner at Delmonico's every night."

"What?" said Marsh, puzzled, his train of thought interrupted.

"Nothing," said I. "It's an inside joke. When do you have to leave?"

There was a short pause, and when Marsh spoke his voice had lost its business edge.

"Honey, I'm really sorry." He sounded warm and real, and I relaxed my grip on the phone a little. "I have to leave on the three o'clock plane this afternoon. I'll only be gone a couple of days, and if everything goes well, then maybe I can take a few days off and get some work done on the kitchen."

Oh cruel bait! Oh milksop to a wounded heart! Oh promises! Promises! Ever since we moved into this big old house in Evanston, Marsh has been promising that he would modernize the kitchen. His new consulting business is doing well, but most of our money is tied up in it so we can't afford a contractor.

However, Marsh is handy at remodeling skills and he keeps telling me that as soon as he can take some time off he will replace the old cabinets and flooring in the kitchen and turn the big pantry into a laundry room. With new wallpaper and paint it will be grand!

But the new firm not only takes our money, it also takes most of Marsh's time and energy. So the new kitchen remains a dream. And sometimes the old kitchen gets to me.

Like two nights ago when Marsh called from New York. I was serving the children hamburgers at the kitchen table.

"It's kind of noisy in the background there, Marsh," I said, "where are you calling from?"

"Delmonico's," he replied. "Ted Farrell took me to dinner so we could finish up some work."

"Delmonico's!" I screamed excitedly. "What's it like?"

"Oh, it's nice," said Marsh in a matter-of-fact voice.

"Nice? *Nice!* Is that all you can say about *Delmonico's?*"

"Honey, I'm working so hard on these balance sheets I haven't even noticed the restaurant."

Marsh sounded a little impatient, and I wanted to say to him, "The trouble is, Marsh, that in the past six months I've stood in this kitchen and talked to you in San Francisco (Chinatown, Fisherman's Wharf), Los Angeles (Brown Derby, Century City), Dallas and Houston (money, money, money), and New York, New York (It's a Wonderful Town, the Big Apple). And somehow it doesn't seem fair, Marsh. I mean . . . this kitchen versus Delmonico's?"

Of course I didn't say any of it. We talked about the children, instead. But the thought rankled.

Then, to top it all off, when Marsh came home last night, he had been exhausted. He leaned against the doorjamb, and his suitcase thudded on the bedroom floor.

"I'm ready to drop, Joanne. You'll have to forgive me. I've been in meetings for twelve hours and that jet lag is really getting to me."

By the time I was ready for bed, Marsh was already asleep, snoring lightly from exhaustion. I lay close to his warm, solid body, wishing he would wake up and make love to me. That's when I started getting mad.

I lay in the dark, making a neat mental ledger. Marsh and I were leading totally different lives. On my side of the ledger were an ugly, inefficient kitchen, a tight budget, the endless demands of three small children, and an absent husband. On his side of the ledger were THE JOY OF TRAVEL, LUXURY HOTELS, THE BEST RESTAURANTS, and CONFERENCES WITH DYNAMIC EXECUTIVES. In fact, it seemed to me, he had the WORLD AT HIS FINGERTIPS.

So now, here I stood with the phone in my hand, the aggressions of my wakeful night still not worked out of my system, and Marsh was telling me he had to leave for New York again today.

His voice continued, apologetically, "I've got to have some clean shirts, dear. Could you possibly launder some? If not, maybe you could run out and buy a couple? I'll be out to get my bag about 12:30. I've got to run now. I came out of the meeting especially to call you."

"Calling to tell me to launder your shirts in two hours?" I said, "You don't get any points for that, Marsh. Now if you'd get out of a meeting to call and tell me that you love me—for that you'd get points!"

"I do love you," said Marsh, and his voice was sure. "See you at 12:30."

Thereupon, I smiled and decided that I could make it down to the laundry room in one load. Hooking the diaper pail over one arm, I stacked three dress shirts on top of the overflowing laundry basket and grasped it firmly in both hands. Peering over the top, I moved unsteadily down the narrow service stairs and into the kitchen. As I reached the swinging door leading to the pantry, I dropped a shirt on the floor. I put the bulky basket down, disengaged the diaper pail and reached over for the shirts. At that moment, Brad came swinging out of the pantry and hit me square in the rear with the door. I sprawled out with my stomach on the basket and one elbow in the diaper pail.

Brad came around the edge of the door and looked at me with startled innocence. "Mother," he said, "what are you doing lying down on the laundry basket?" His hands were behind him and he was slowly backing out of the kitchen.

"Brad . . ." I started, not knowing what to yell at him about first—that he obviously was snitching cookies from the pantry, or that I'd told him a million times to watch that swinging door, or that he had made another hole in the knee of his pants.

Faced with such a heap of lecturing, and stomached by such a heap of laundry, and calmed by his look of fascinated concern, I gave up.

"Brad," I said simply, "be sure to share the cookies you're hiding behind your back with Tara."

"Gee, Mom!" Brad's eyes were round with wonder. "How did you know I had cookies?"

At 12:30 when I heard the cab drive up, I felt calmer. There's something therapeutic about laundry, and my anger had dissipated in the hum of machines. Marsh's suitcase was repacked, with three freshly laundered shirts on top.

I went to the front door as Marsh was paying the driver. He turned and saw me at the top of the porch steps.

"Honey!" he called. His eyes were shining with love, and his smile warmed me. "You are just being wonderful about this!" He picked up his briefcase and bounded up the high front steps two at a time. Neither of us saw Brad's baseball bat on the top step. Marsh's foot landed on it, and the bat spun backward with the speed of a bullet. He flung his arms forward to catch himself, but his briefcase was so heavy that it bent his arm at a terrible angle. I heard a sickening crack.

"Marsh!" I screamed, desperately trying to catch him, but he was down in a second. "Honey, honey! Are you all right?"

His face was white with pain. "My arm!" he groaned, "I'm sure it's broken."

Marsh is seldom wrong, and this time he was very right. Two hours later he was lying in a bed in the Evanston hospital, sporting a neat white cast on his lower arm. He was beginning to feel groggy from the painkillers, and he was begging me, as I sat holding his good hand, to hurry home, get his precious briefcase, and take it to New York on the next plane.

"Listen," Marsh said, "I know you don't want to leave me, but it's a very simple fracture. I'll be home tomorrow. Peggy and Dan will be happy to keep the children for a couple of days.

"Joanne"—his voice was urgent—"the whole report is in my briefcase, and if Ted Farrell doesn't get it tonight he can't make the presentation tomorrow, and then we have to wait a whole other month until the next board meeting. Please, Joanne, if you leave right now you can catch the five o'clock plane. I'll take care of everything on this end, you won't have to worry about a thing. Say you'll do it, and I'll call Ted and tell him you're on your way."

So that's how I, everyday housewife et cetera, came to be in a taxi with my best clothes packed neatly in Marsh's suitcase, his ticket clutched in my hand, headed for O'Hare Airport, New York, the Berkley Hotel, Delmonico's, the Great White Way, Park Avenue, and who knows what else!

The Joy of Travel

It was strange sitting by myself in the cab. I kept worrying about Marsh and the children, and it made me feel restless, so to distract my mind, I opened Marsh's briefcase to see if there was anything to read.

Carefully I sifted through the pages of his report. Charts, figures, balance sheets, surveys, projections in stunning detail. No wonder Marsh told me how hard he had been working. He's really incredible, I thought with pride.

The taxi pulled up in front of the Eastern Airlines entrance and I scrambled out. Marsh always did the tipping, so I was uncertain what to do. Remembering vaguely something about ten percent, I figured quickly in my head ten percent of $12.70. Since I couldn't very well give the driver twenty-seven cents, I rounded it out to thirty. Handing him thirteen dollars, I said grandly, "Keep the change."

He gave me a funny look and drove away. I stood on the curb with my shoulder bag and Marsh's briefcase and suitcase. A redcap came up and asked if he could take my bags.

"What flight number, ma'am?" he asked.

"Well, you see, I don't really know. My husband broke his arm and so he missed the early flight and I'm going in his place, only I don't know if I can get on the five o'clock flight, and his ticket is for the three o'clock flight." I realized that I was going into more detail than necessary.

The redcap shook his head. "I can't take your bag if you don't have a place to take it. What do you want me to do with it?"

Just then, I glanced at the big clock in the terminal. Only twenty minutes until flight time!

"Oh, forget it!" I exclaimed. Purse and briefcase on one arm, suitcase on the other, I staggered into the terminal to the ticket desk, dropped everything in a heap and held out Marsh's ticket.

I explained the situation to the ticket clerk twice, and the clerk explained the airlines policy to me twice before we decided to call the office that handles all of Marsh's ticketing. Fortunately, Marsh had also called them and they okayed the new ticket. The clerk pointed to a sign that read "Gates 19 through 29." You board your plane at gate 29. It is now boarding."

I started off down the long ceramic-tile corridor. Marsh's heavy briefcase kept flopping against my leg, and I had to switch arms frequently. It was a long distance between gates 19 and 20. A clock in the corridor told me I had five minutes until five o'clock, so I started really hurrying. I developed a sort of jog-walk-run-slide technique. But at gate 25, I gave up all pretense of dignity and sprinted, arriving breathless at gate 29 just as the steward was about to close the door.

On the plane, I was assigned to a middle seat. I squeezed in between two men in business suits and sat down. The seat was narrow, and I didn't know what to do with my purse or the omnipresent briefcase, so I sat with them piled on my lap.

I was perspiring so much that my forehead was dripping, my blouse was sticking to my back, and my nylons felt glued to my legs. I rummaged in my purse for a hanky. All I could find was a napkin I'd used to wipe off Brad's face at McDonald's last night. I began to mop up my forehead, praying that I wasn't leaving any catsup marks on my face.

As I calmed down, I realized that the stewards had given final takeoff instructions. The roar of the engines and the velocity of the airplane increased, and so did my terror. I gripped the armrests on either side of me. The one on my right moved under my clenched fingers. Uncomprehendingly, I looked down, only to see a man's hand. I was holding it in a death grip. "Sorry," I whispered. "I'm a little nervous."

I folded my hands in my lap and hunched my shoulders forward so I wouldn't take up too much room.

The rest of the short flight was uneventful, and fortunately Ted Farrell was waiting for me at Kennedy airport. Even with his help, it took about an hour to collect my suitcase and find a cab.

With the briefcase safely delivered, I looked forward to a good visit with Ted. I settled back in the cab, ready to relax and enjoy my first visit to New York.

"Oh, Ted!" I exclaimed as we drove up onto the brilliantly lighted bridge and looked down the river to the mighty skyline of Manhattan. The river was festooned with bridges like diamond necklaces across the evening sky. "It's just like the pictures, only more beautiful! It's really New York!"

"Hmmm," said Ted, who was carefully reading Marsh's reports and making notes on a yellow legal pad. Silence.

"Listen, Joanne," he said after a few minutes, "would it be all right if I call Marsh tonight? I've got a couple of things I need to ask him."

"I think that would be fine," I replied, downcast. Those words were our total conversation until we arrived at the Berkley Hotel.

Luxurious Hotels

After fifteen minutes, Ted had straightened out the question of my taking Marsh's reserved room and had explained that he was not my husband and would not be staying.

The hotel did not seem to approve of the arrangement, but the bellboy took my bag. Ted came up to the room, too, so that he could call Marsh and let me speak to him when they were finished with their business conversation.

I had somehow imagined that all rooms in New York hotels would have huge beds, satin drapes, and luxurious carpets, like an old Ronald Coleman movie, or maybe like modern Las Vegas. I was not prepared for the impersonality of the smallish room with the practical beige carpet.

Ted put through his call. I was dying to have a shower and stretch out on the bed. Instead, I sat down on an uncomfortable side chair and waited politely for Ted and Marsh to finish their conversation. "Do you want to talk to Marsh?" Ted asked, handing me the phone.

"Honey, thanks a lot, you're just great," said Marsh on the phone, and the whole wild day was worth it. He said he was feeling well. Then he said he had another favor to ask.

"Ted needs someone to work the opaque projector and to take around the handouts and stuff like that during the meeting. If he briefs you tonight, do you think you could do that tomorrow? I was going to do it for him, and we don't have time to get anyone else. It means an extra day in New York for you, too, and I know how much you must be enjoying that."

Ted was already spreading papers and displays on the floor to show me the layout.

We worked for about an hour until I understood my part of the presentation.

"You're a good sport. I'll see you bright and early at the AMBEX Building." Ted patted my shoulder and was off down the corridor.

To get ready for my shower, I had to peel off my clothes. The bathroom was hot and steamy, so I was anxious to get back into the air-conditioned coolness of the room, but when I stepped back into the bedroom, it was hot and steamy, too. The air-conditioning had stopped working.

I couldn't fix it, the bellboy couldn't fix it, and even the engineer couldn't fix it. So, at 1:30 A.M., I repacked my suitcase and was taken to another, even smaller room, where the air-conditioning was working too well. An unfamiliar room, an alien bed, a strange city. "Is this what it's like, Marsh?" I shivered under my meager blanket.

I didn't think I slept, but when my wake-up call came at 7:30 A.M., I couldn't wake up. It dawned on me that it was only 6:30 in Evanston.

When I got down to the hotel lobby, I had 15 minutes to make it to AMBEX.

Dynamic Corporate Execs

The AMBEX Building is on Park Avenue. What I didn't know was that Park Avenue is only one block from Lexington Avenue, where the Berkley Hotel is. I got into a cab and told the driver, "AMBEX Building, please."

Two blocks later, I got out of the cab and paid him the minimum sixty cents (the meter hadn't even *moved!*).

The board meeting was at the very top of AMBEX's huge glass building. The tall windows looked over the great city, and I couldn't take my eyes off of it: the penthouse roofs with their little gardens, the great green square of Central Park, and the long avenues running parallel to the shining rivers.

Some men came hurrying in. They were all wearing dark, tailored business suits, their faces were tanned and smooth, and most of them had white hair. They were impeccable and they looked strangely alike, as though they had been turned out on the same lathe and then individual differences had been painted in.

Ted came over to me. "You're to sit in the corner chair over there until our presentation starts."

The men sat around the enormous polished walnut table. As the morning moved on, the voices, muffled in the large, deeply carpeted room, and the sun coming through the window at my back gradually did their work. I had to fight sleep—I really did! I dug my fingernails into my palms, I curled my toes inside my shoes, I bit my tongue, I took deep breaths, and I fell asleep.

Finally, the meeting was adjourned for lunch. Ted came over and told me that our presentation would be directly after lunch. The president of AMBEX had invited us to eat in the executive dining room.

I'll remember this lunch forever, I thought as I looked around the sumptuous room gleaming with silver, crystal, and fresh flowers. I told myself that I was lunching with the Giants of American Industry.

"Hear you played with Roy Lampok on Saturday, Ken," said the president to one of the men. (Apparently the general conversation does not begin until the president speaks.)

"Yes," said Ken, "I shot my best game in four months."

"How was that water hole?" another asked.

I listened to detailed descriptions of golf courses, and the worst holes to play in the Greater New York area, parts of Florida and the Caribbean. Since I couldn't contribute to the conversation, I turned to the menu.

I was ravenous, but I noticed that each item had the number of calories per serving listed next to it and the men ordered sparingly. My roast beef and baked potato were conspicuous among all those salads. No one had dessert, so I said a mental farewell to the cherry cheesecake which was listed on the menu at 450 calories per serving. After lunch, we trooped back to the board room.

The presentation was a great hit. Ted came up and told me that Marsh was a cinch to get the consulting contract.

The men congratulated me on my brilliant husband. Then

the president came over. He was very impressive. He shook my hand, and after thanking me, he said, "I'm told that this is your first visit to New York, and so to celebrate the occasion, I have asked two of our young executives to take you and Mr. Farrell to dinner and a show. I hope you will enjoy yourself. Please give my regards to Marsh, and tell him we hope he recovers rapidly."

"Oh, thank you very much!"

A night on the town in New York! What I've always wanted! But I wished that Marsh were here, and I wished that I weren't so darn tired.

The Best Restaurants
The Glamorous Life

"They've moved up curtain time on weeknights to accommodate commuters, so we won't have time to eat right now," said Bill Green, a young man with dark, styled hair, and a modest executive moustache. "We'll grab a sandwich at a delicatessen on Broadway, and then we can eat at Luchow's after the show."

There were no unoccupied cabs on Park Avenue.

"Oh, well," said Brooks Alder, a serious young man with horn-rimmed glasses. "It isn't that far, let's walk."

He didn't really mean *walk*, what he meant was *stride*. We wove our way through the dense crowds of people who were rapidly emptying the business districts of Manhattan, ignoring red lights and "Don't Walk" signs.

Brooks stopped us outside a dirty-looking place called Donovan's. He ran in and came back out with a paper sack.

"Pastrami on rye with mustard," he said, and passed the sack. We each took out a fat sandwich filled with layers of thinly sliced pastrami. We ate as we walked and it was delicious!

The theater was small and our seats very close to the front. "Just think, Joanne," I whispered to myself, "this is Broadway!"

Bill leaned over and whispered as the curtain opened, "This is a brand-new play. The reviews aren't even out yet, but I've heard that it's excellent."

That was the last word anyone directed to me during the rest of the performance. The play was some kind of avant-garde social satire, without a real plot but with a lot of really dirty jokes and unclothed people. When you're from Evanston and you're not with your husband, that kind of thing is definitely embarrassing.

"Well," said Brooks as we left the theater, "you can't win 'em all." Which was about the best any of us could think to say.

But Luchow's was everything I had ever dreamed. I even thought I saw Brian Keith at one of the tables! When I saw the prices, I gasped, and I ordered venison with all the trimmings.

By now, it was nearly 11:00 P.M., and we were all drooping a little. I sensed that Bill and Brooks did this sort of thing so often that it wasn't all that fun for them, and I could tell that Ted was wishing he were home in bed. I wasn't sleepy, but I was beginning to feel alien and uncomfortable—too full, too tired, and too far from home.

After dinner they took me in a cab back to the Berkley. Ted wanted to get out and go in with me, but I couldn't face explaining him to the night clerk again. So I thanked all three of them and, since they were enlightened males, they let me go into the hotel alone.

When I went to the desk for my key, the hotel clerk looked in the slot. It was gone.

"Are you sure you are registered in that room, madam?" he inquired.

"Yes, I'm positive."

"Let me check," he replied. "What is your name?"

"Mrs. Marshall Stevens," I said emphatically.

He looked in his files. "Mrs. Stevens, you told us last night that you only wanted the room for one night. We assumed you were checking out today. Your bags have been brought downstairs."

I stood quietly for a minute.

"Could you please call the airlines and find when the next plane leaves for Chicago?" I asked.

The cab dropped me off at Kennedy airport at 2:30 A.M., and I dozed on a waiting bench until 4:30. Then I bought myself two magazines, drank a 7-Up, and caught the 5:00 A.M. commuter flight to Chicago.

At 8:30 A.M. I wearily climbed out of the cab in front of our home in Evanston, Illinois. In the early morning light I looked at the dear old house with unabashed affection. No matter that the paint was peeling and our renovations were still nothing but dreams—I suddenly saw the soul of the house and knew that it was "home." Inside waited my own bed, my own kitchen, my children and a husband who loved and needed me.

My heart pounded with joy and I grabbed my bags and raced up the back steps to the kitchen door and pulled it open eagerly.

Marsh was sitting in his bathrobe by the breakfast table. The surface of the table was littered with boxes, milk cartons, spilled cereal, and juice glasses. There was a broken jar of peanut butter on the floor in front of the stove. Brad and Tara were playing with their food, still in their pajamas. Brad's elbow was sticking out of a hole in his sleeve.

Baby Sarah was in her jumper chair and Marsh was trying to feed her strained apricots. She had yellow baby food in her hair, on her nightgown, and all over her face.

Dirty dishes were stacked in the sink, and Marsh had a two-day growth of beard. He looked bedraggled and bewildered, like a man lost in the midst of a foreign land where he understood neither the customs nor the language, but was trying very hard to fraternize with the natives.

Everybody looked up in surprise as I walked through the door, and then pandemonium broke loose. The children shouted, the baby gurgled and jumped up and down in her jumper. Best of all, Marsh strode over to me, hugged me with his good arm, and kissed me like he never wanted to stop. He hadn't been *that* glad to see me in a long time!

"Hey!" I gasped. "That's some welcome."

"Joanne," Marsh said, with absolute conviction, "I've never been so glad to see anyone in my entire life!"

The children were tugging at my skirts. "What did you bring me, Mother?" Brad asked. Tara hugged my knees as though she wanted to hold me so tightly that I would never get away from her again, and the baby giggled and spit strained apricots all over her nightgown.

It was absolutely wonderful. Marsh grinned at me over the

noise and confusion. "You know, honey," he said, a little ruefully, picking up Sarah with his unbroken arm and handing her
to me while I grabbed a towel to wipe off the worst of the apricots, "I used to kind of envy you—you know, on cold, snowy
mornings when you could lie in a warm bed while I had to go
out in the blizzard, scrape off the car and fight my way downtown. Or on days when I didn't feel like working but some big
account was falling apart and I knew it was going to be a
wretched day at the office and there you were—planning a picnic for the kids." He shook his head apologetically.

. "On days like that, I used to think you had it made," he
went on. "What a terrific, fun, easy life you had! Well, believe
me, after two days of trying to handle all this . . ." He waved his
good hand to indicate the children and the house. "I tell you—I
had no idea how hard this was—or how much it takes to keep it
going."

I had tears in my eyes and Marsh asked with concern,
"What's wrong?"

"Nothing," I answered, smiling through the tears. "Nothing!
It's so funny, Marsh, because I've envied everything about your
life—and thought you had all the exciting, wonderful things . . ."

Marsh looked so puzzled and tired that I figured we could
talk it all out some other time. But I did want him to understand how I was feeling. I wanted him to know how good I felt
about being home.

"I've learned so much in these past two days, Marsh—about
you, about myself, about what really matters." I stumbled for
words. "You see, dear, we both thought the other one had the
apple—but the fact is, neither one of us does! We both had half
an apple, though. It takes both of us, working, sacrificing in our
own way, and it's all for moments like this when we're all together. That's the only time the apple is whole."

Marsh shook his head and grinned. "I think you've got a
touch of jet lag."

"Maybe," I said. He hugged me again and the children
pressed around us while the morning sun streamed through the
windows into our old, homely kitchen.

But I was determined to make him see how much I had
changed so I tried one last time. "Oh Marsh!" I said. "It feels so

good to be home that I am going to say something which I know I'll regret. If you ever quote me once I've said it, I will deny it!"

Marsh looked at me expectantly and I said solemnly, as though I were making some kind of pledge to him and myself, "Just for this moment—mind you, for this one brief moment—just for right now—"

"Yes," Marsh said impatiently, urging me to finish. "Go on."

"What I would like to say," I continued, "is that somewhere along the way I had forgotten how much I love all of you, and how lucky and happy I am, and right now"—I took a deep breath and then plunged on—"for this one wonderful moment, I think that this very room—this kitchen that I have hated since the day we moved in—is probably the most beautiful room in the world!"

Mallwalker

JERRY M. YOUNG

When Bill woke up, Janet was not there beside him—again. It had been 221 days since her funeral. And still he was not used to being alone. He covered the dormant pain in his soul with a sigh and flexed his mind with thoughts for the day.

Round about him in the darkened room were things they had put there together. Even in the predawn shadows he could have described every picture, every decoration, Janet's brush and comb set on the dresser where she also kept several stylish bottles filled with sweet smelling things, and all the other possessions that had become so ordinary and natural to his world.

But he dared not think of such things. Get up and get going had been his strategy all these months. Even that was getting harder to keep up. Work had lost much of its meaning and purpose without her. Without it there would have been too many unfilled moments and debilitating memories. At the very least it gave him something to do.

So he began this day, slipping carefully from his place on his side of the bed as if he still might disturb her.

* * *

Morning chill made him shiver and he tightened his muscles as if that would keep him warm. His ritual routed him through the hall where he turned up the thermostat, and then on to the kitchen where he started heating a pan of milk for his hot chocolate. In the bathroom he took time to brush his teeth. Funny, he thought, no matter how hard she tried, Janet could never get him to brush his teeth after breakfast instead of before. But breakfast tasted better in a fresh mouth, he would tell her. And she would laugh. And they would kiss. And that tasted better too with fresh breath.

At breakfast he read what he wanted of the paper. He still had time. The mall wouldn't open for nearly 20 minutes. There would not be time again to read for himself until after he finished Barclay's books. They were a mess. They always were. But this month was worse than normal. Bill knew it could take as many as 15 to 20 hours to put everything right. Barclay expected them back by noon tomorrow.

For a moment Bill wondered if he should forego his morning walk. That would give him an extra hour on the books.

No.

He needed the exercise. His heart needed the exercise. He'd make up for whatever time he took this morning by working into the evening—night—maybe even early morning.

He washed his dishes—one cup, one spoon, one knife and one saucepan—setting each onto the plastic rack that sat on the drainboard beside the sink.

The doorbell rang while he was drying his hands. Before he could put down the towel he heard the front door open and a familiar voice call to him.

"Hi! It's me."

And then another familiar voice skipped into his life.

"Grampa!"

Bill stepped from the kitchen and positioned himself to welcome his visitors. He leaned down and felt the arms of his granddaughter wrap around his neck. And he raised up to receive the embrace of his daughter.

"You working today?"

"Just on my way, and Kirstie wanted to stop by and see her Grampa."

Bill gave Kirstie a tighter squeeze, turning in place—back and forth.

"Well, you can stop by and see me any time you want."

Kirstie leaned back in his arms, adding weight to her four-year-old body. And she placed her hands on his cheeks. Her tiny face turned serious and she looked deeply into his eyes.

"Grampa—you know what?"

"What?"

"I miss Grammie."

She meant only to express her love for her grandmother. But the soft, innocent voice brought all those memories back into his heart and mind. And he could feel the tears rising within him.

He drew her close to him and tightened his hold on her, using the extra effort to disguise his faltering voice.

"I miss Grammie too, sweetheart."

Jeanette's head dipped in disbelief. It was the last thing she expected her daughter to say. But all too often Kirstie would say the unexpected. Very embarrassing.

"Kirstie," she chided. "Sorry, Dad."

"No," Bill sniffed quickly. "It's all right. She just loves her grandmother."

"I know. But this girl's going to be the death of me."

"Serves you right. That's how your mother and I felt about you."

"What goes around," Jeanette said, satisfied that her father had not been affected too much by what her daughter had said.

"So, you really going to work? Or did you just want to come by and chat?"

"No. We're on our way to the babysitter's. I'm working the day shift."

"That's better than the night shift."

"Tell me about it. We have something of a normal life when I work days. We even get to have dinner together. So why don't you come to dinner tonight?"

"Sounds great. But I have to work."

"Barclay's again?"

"You guessed it."

"Come on over anyway. If you have to do his account you won't take time to eat a decent meal."

He tilted his head in preparation to turn her down.

But she insisted.

"Six-thirty. Come as you are. And you can leave as soon as we're done."

"You sure?"

"Positive."

"Okay. That'll be nice. Real nice. Thanks."

"Okay," she said. "Now for the real reason I came by."

She took from the deep pocket on the side of her smock a stethoscope which she slipped in place about her neck.

"Oh, Nettie, how come you do this to me all the time?"

"Kirstie, honey, let Grampa put you down now. Mommy has to listen to his heart."

"Can I listen too?"

"Maybe. But let Mommy take a turn first."

She listened carefully to his heart and lungs, asking him to cough at the appropriate time.

"What'd you have for breakfast?" she asked while she was standing behind him.

"Toast . . ."

"And probably hot chocolate, too. Right?" The tone of her voice carried her disapproval.

He shrugged. "Boy. Good thing you're only a nurse."

"Only?" she questioned as if she'd been offended. At the same time she pounded him on the back.

"And a good one at that," he added with a smile.

"The best," she said, waving the loose end of her stethoscope at his nose. "And don't you forget it."

"But it's still good that you're not my doctor."

"Dad, you need to take better care of yourself. That's not a good breakfast. One day that kind of thing will kill you."

"So? Everything's going to kill me. At my age I should worry about such things?"

"You bet. Then the rest of us wouldn't have to worry about you so much."

"I'm all right."

"No you're not," she said in a scolding way.

He took her in his arms and whispered, "Yes I am. And you know it. My heart's doing all right, isn't it?"

"The damage is never going away, Dad. And if you keep on abusing yourself it's going to turn on you."

"Come on, admit it. Sounds good, doesn't it?"

She tightened her face, doing her best to scowl. But it didn't work. And she began to chuckle. "Okay. I have to admit, it sounds pretty good. You still walking every day?"

"On my way right now." They moved to the door together and while he put on his jacket there came to his mind a thought. "By the way, Nettie, you weren't thinking of inviting someone else over tonight, were you?"

She gave him another scowl and a laugh. But she didn't give him a straight answer.

He knew what that meant. That made him even more grateful for his work.

*   *   *

Bill placed his jacket on the low, decorative brick wall that set aside one of the sunken rest areas in the court outside the entrance to the Penney's department store in the University Mall. Assessing the twinge in his ankle, he felt the need to stretch and warm up. So he stepped into the rest area and began stretching his leg muscles—leaning against the retainer and pushing back against his heels. The mild arthritic pain in his ankle flared and he closed his eyes against the stress. After a few months he realized it would only feel better when he built up the circulation in his joints. It was time to stop stretching and start walking. He angled across the main concourse level to the outer wall and began his hike.

*   *   *

From the very beginning, management of the University Mall in Orem, Utah, opened around 6:30 A.M. so people could walk around inside before the stores opened at 10 A.M. It became a cheap place for some gentle exercise. Many who walked there were trying to stay alive—walking being the common therapy for heart patients of one kind or another.

There's no mandatory way to walk the mall. Some walk in the center, round and round, cutting as close as they can to the decorations, planters, and booths. Others walk along the walls and out into the wings of the mall, taking full advantage of the spacious quality of the building, extending their walk as far as they can. Some people walk laps. Others walk time.

Bill's course carried him into the wings. But he timed himself so he could measure how fit he was. Long ago he'd abandoned the practice of taking his pulse—counting beats for 10 seconds and multiplying by six. He'd been told not to let his heart rate rise above 120. At first he meticulously counted every few minutes. Now he hardly counted at all. He could feel how well he was doing.

At the end of his 45 minutes he wanted to have walked the mall at least three times—with a good deal to spare. On his best days he could reach past the halfway point of the fourth lap.

He wouldn't be doing that well today, he thought. And consciously he tried to compensate for his sore ankle. He took extra long strides and kept them up from where he started, all along the concourse leading to Mervyn's. He was nearly there when he heard someone speak to him from behind.

"Looks like you've got a hitch in your giddyup this morning."

He knew who it was. So he turned only slightly toward the voice allowing him to keep his stride.

"Morning."

"You okay?" she inquired, slowing slightly to stay with him.

"Just a little stiff in the ankle. I'll be all right. How about you?"

"Oh, I've seen better days." She smiled warmly.

"Hey! That's a classy outfit." Bill reacted to a new jacket she was wearing. Mostly white, the stylish, loose-fitting "Umbro" warmup jacket had a block of tiny black checks running across the yoke and partially down the long sleeves.

She turned so she could face him—walking backwards. She pulled at the fabric at the waist.

"Thank you," she said with a nod and a smile. "My kids gave it to me for my birthday."

"They have good taste," he said watching her smile at him again before turning to continue her pace. Bill thought about adding something more. But he thought better of it and let her go—again.

* * *

They'd become friends of sorts, the two of them walking every morning. One day several weeks ago, when they'd reached a crowd going slower than either of them, he'd gestured for her to go first through the small opening in the group. She smiled at him and mouthed the word "Thanks." Later that week she passed him on one of the corners, her arms pumping with vigor and her legs striding with great strength.

"And there she goes," he said, shaping his voice with the twang of a race announcer.

She laughed. And the next day she initiated what had become their ongoing, albeit distant, conversation.

And neither of them knew the other's name.

Still, they'd come to sense each other's moods and feelings. He knew when she was having a bad day. And she could tell when the stiffness in his legs held him back. Once he even told her about his heart attack. And she'd mentioned that her husband had died of a heart attack three years before.

On this particular day they both finished their walks at the same time. Actually, she was stretching when he reached the area where she was—and where he'd left his coat.

"You still don't look too happy," she probed with a smile.

"Got a lot of work to do," he admitted.

She accepted that with a nod.

"And right in the middle of it all, my daughter's invited me over to dinner."

"What's so bad about that?"

"I'm pretty certain she's trying to match me up with one of her friends."

The woman burst into a laugh.

"I'm sorry," she explained before she regained her composure. "I don't mean to—it's just that I know exactly what you're going through. My kids and my friends are doing that to me all the time."

He shrugged. "At least I won't have to spend much time over there. Everyone knows I can't stay—that I have a lot of work to get out tonight. I get to leave when we finish eating."

She nodded. "Well, good luck. And be careful."

"What do you mean?"

She took into her expression the quality of a tease. "Be careful. They might ask you to drive her home."

He smiled with raised eyebrows, wondering what she meant.

"I'm not joking," she said. "Happens to me all the time. It goes something like this—I get an invitation for dinner and my host arranges to pick me up. So I end up over there without my car. But sometime during the evening something always comes up and the other guest is asked to drive me home."

"You're kidding. Well, it won't happen to me. I'm driving."

She tilted her head slightly and held a wide grin on her face as if she'd just proven her point.

* * *

The next morning, by the time Bill's "friend"—wearing her white "Umbro" warmup—reached the mall, she found him sitting on a bench, leaning against the retaining wall of the rest area outside the entrance to Penney's. At first she was going to kid him about being a loafer. Then she noticed how pale he looked and how he labored with his breathing.

All the memories of seeing her husband in the early stages of his heart attack flooded into her mind stirring a sense of panic within her. She took a position in front of him, sitting back on her haunches, looking into his face.

"Are you all right?" she asked, fearful of an obvious answer.

The quiet voice reached into Bill's mind and he opened his eyes to find his friend right there in front of him, her face filled with deep concern.

"I'm fine," he said with as much of a smile as he could generate. "Just tired—very tired."

The woman could see his problem was not as bad as her husband's had been that horrible day three years before. She raised herself from the crouched position and took a seat beside him. Automatically she took hold of his wrist to test his pulse. What she felt frightened her.

"You should be in the hospital."

He shook his head. "No thanks. I've been there before. Too many people die there." He smiled at this woman who somehow had taken on a completely new dimension to her beauty.

"Then you need to see your doctor. Come on, I'll take you there."

"No thanks. I've seen him before. He's getting rich telling me what I already know. Over and over he tells me."

"Then why don't you take his advice?"

"I am. I'm here, aren't I? He says walk every day. So here I am—walking."

She shook her head. "Men! You're all alike."

For the first time he leaned forward, taking his weight from the wall.

"No, it's just that I stayed up late last night to finish all that work I had to do. And by the time I got to bed I couldn't sleep. And then I felt short of breath. That's normally a signal my heart's acting up. So I took a nitro and later on I took another. Everything calmed down and I fell asleep. But when I woke up I had this horrible headache. Nitroglycerin pills do that, you know. And I thought I'd work it out of my system with a walk. You just caught me resting for a minute. I'll be all right."

"You sure?"

"Positive. I'm an old hand at this routine. I just need some rest. I'll be fine."

She sensed the unlikelihood of forcing this man to do something against his will—even though it might be for his own good. Also, it wasn't her place to do such a thing. So she changed directions.

"How was your dinner date last night?"

He smiled, pleased that she would remember.

"Fine."

"Was it a date?"

He laughed. "I can't believe how close you described my evening. I got there and sure enough, my daughter had invited a nice lady from her work. She's a nurse—my daughter, that is. Did I ever tell you I have a nurse for a daughter?"

The woman shook her head.

"And her friend works at the hospital in the billing department. Just my age. You know. Nice lady. Kinda pushy though. No. A lot pushy."

The woman enjoyed the description of his blind date.

"Well, they'd picked her up. And just like you said, Nettie's husband suddenly had this emergency he had to take care of in his car. So guess who had to drive the other guest home?"

Bill's friend chuckled with some satisfaction.

"All things considered, it was quite a pleasant evening. And do you know why?"

She shook her head again.

"Well, I kept thinking about you and how you'd called the shot so closely. And do you know something else?"

She smiled this time.

"There was only one thing that bothered me. All night long it bothered me. I kept thinking, I don't even know her name—your name."

"Carolyn," the friend said with a smile. "Carolyn Andrews."

"Carolyn," he repeated. "I've always like the name Carolyn. In fact we were going to name our second child Carolyn. But she turned out to be a Brian."

Carolyn smiled and nodded.

"Andrews," he said thoughtfully. "Are you any relation to Nick Andrews? From Boise?"

"My husband's brother."

"No kidding? Nick and I were missionary companions a hundred years ago."

"Is that right? That's interesting. Nick's been wonderful to me. He and Al were very close."

"Al was your husband?"

"Yes."

"What'd he do?"

"He was a general contractor."

Bill nodded.

"You miss him?"

"Oh, yes. We did everything together. He even had me doing his books. So I kept right in there with him in everything."

"You know accounting?"

"Oh, yes."

"You doing anything now?"

"No. Just some crafts and artwork."

"Want a job?"

"What kind of job?"

"I've got some books to finish up by noon and I don't think I can make it—not without help."

She studied him carefully. Should she? No question about it, this man needed help. And not necessarily with his accounts. There was no way he should be doing much of anything until he recovered from his problem. Okay. Why not? *He looks safe enough.*

"Okay. I'll be happy to help."

"That's great!" Bill reacted by smacking his hands together. "There's only one problem."

"What's that?"

"I've never had an assistant before. I have no idea what to pay you."

She thought for a moment. "You can take me to lunch. Only just one thing."

"What's that?"

"Well, just exactly who is it that I'll be working for?"

He laughed and color blotched onto his pale face.

"Bill Mason. Not William, just plain old Bill."

* * *

She followed his car out of the mall parking lot onto the BYU diagonal. They headed east into the river bottoms and up past Cougar Stadium to a street leading into a residential area just north of the huge Marriott Center. He wound around a couple of turns and pulled into a double carport. She simply pulled in beside him.

It was a ranch-style bungalow with a basement showing from window wells hidden by some shrubbery. Inside she could tell that a lot of loving care had gone into the decor—and then had been left to be taken care of by a man. It was dust mostly that gave him away. But also there were newspapers and magazines stuffed in holders and stacked in places that detracted from the pictures and vases and figurines that once had broken up the space all by themselves.

He gave a brief and unnecessary tour of the working part of his quarters: the living room, dining room—converted to his office—and the kitchen. It impressed her to see a spotless kitchen in contrast to his messy desk and a semi-cluttered living room. Not bad marks though—for a bachelor.

Bill went right to work bringing her up-to-date on the account.

"Barclay owns and manages property."

"Barclay? Wayne Barclay?"

"You know him?"

Cynicism filled her laugh.

"My husband did business with him—once—a long time ago."

"Sounds like you know about him and his idiosyncrasies."

"Idiosyncrasies? Are you kidding? The man's a jerk. He drove us nuts—always trying to get something for nothing." The intensity of her emotions increased with every phrase. She made no attempt to hold back her feelings. "Right at first he insisted that all he wanted was a limited contract. And we obliged. But then, when we got into the job, he kept throwing all these other things he expected us to do for the same price as the original contract. When we objected he threatened to not pay us."

"Yeh. That's the same Wayne Barclay I work for. What'd you do? How'd you come out?"

"We didn't. We finished our work, lost money, cut our losses and went on to a legitimate project."

Bill shook his head. He'd never thought that Barclay might be dealing with others as he'd been dealing with him. But it figured.

"Well, this is what we still have to do here," he said, turning his attention to the task.

And he explained how he'd managed to get all the rental receipts entered into their proper ledgers. That had taken him the most time. And he'd run the totals. Somehow they defied all attempts to balance and reconcile.

"After we do that we have to run his expenses."

"I suppose his expenses are all these receipts in this cigar box?"

Bill nodded.

She smiled at him. She wanted to ask him how he put up with Barclay. But that wasn't her business—at least not yet.

Now what made her think such a thing?

She gave a slight shake of her head. Then she looked over at Bill to see if he'd noticed anything. He hadn't. Good.

"Tell you what, Bill," she began, placing her hand on his arm. "I'm really good at this. And I can see you have this arranged pretty well. Why don't you let me plunge in here with my fresh eyes. You go somewhere and take a little rest."

"No, I can't—I shouldn't." He looked into her face and suddenly realized how lucky he was. She seemed so confident and self-assured. "Okay. Just for a little while. But if you have any questions, don't hesitate to ask."

She agreed. And reluctantly he withdrew, retreating to his side of his bed again. She plunged into Barclay's books. And while there came a time when she wanted to ask him questions about her task, she didn't.

* * *

During her first hour she located the mistake he had not been able to find—the one that prevented him from balancing his columns. And she'd started on that box full of expenses. It wasn't too long after she'd begun that task—with receipts stacked in piles around her on the floor—that she took her first break.

She just looked up. And her eye was drawn to a set of pictures hanging on the wall. On examining them she discovered they all were pen and ink line drawings with washes of color behind—or over them. Mountain scenes with rustic buildings, extremely well done. Then she noticed the signature—"By Bill."

All but two of the pictures in the office and living room were by him. Not only had he sketched those rustic scenes, he'd also painted large canvasses. The portrait must have been of his wife.

On her second break she ventured into the hallways and discovered his bedroom, a second bedroom and the bathroom. His paintings hung everywhere.

Midway through the morning she listened at his doorway—not daring to venture inside again. Good. He still was sleeping, the sound of his rhythmic breaths attesting not only his need for rest, but the quality of it as well.

It was shortly before noon that the phone rang.

She picked up the receiver. But before she could say anything, Bill did.

"Hello."

"Mason, this is Wayne Barclay. You got my books ready yet?" came the abrasive voice.

Silently, Carolyn stuck her tongue out at the phone.

"No, sir. Not just yet. But soon. Very soon."

The obsequious tone of Bill's voice disappointed Carolyn.

"How long you going to take?" Barclay pressed. "You promised them by noon."

"I know. I'm almost done."

"Okay. See that you're here no later than one."

And then he hung up. There wasn't a thank-you or a by-your-leave. The fury she once felt toward that man rekindled itself.

"How we coming?" Bill asked, staggering into the room.

"You don't need to take that from him," she said. "He's a jerk."

"I know," Bill admitted. How right she was. Janet had said the same thing. She had been right too. But somehow he'd never been able to deal with aggressive people—pushy people. He knew they took advantage of him. But no matter how hard he tried—no matter how many times he promised Janet—he always seemed to give in to the Barclays of the world. And it bothered him that he wasn't stronger—more in control.

He shrugged. "He's my biggest account."

"Still, you don't deserve to be treated that way. You shouldn't let him get away with that kind of thing."

"It's all right. When I'm done, he pays me in cash."

"Not nearly enough, I'll bet."

"Yeh. You're probably right. But business is business. And so how close are we to being done?"

"We're not close. It's all done."

"Really?" He sounded surprised as well as pleased. "How'd you do that?"

She shrugged. "Fresh eyes. Works every time."

"Great. I'll give him a call and let him know we're coming right over."

"Wait a minute. How about if you let me make that call?"

"You?"

Before he could object she'd twirled his Rolodex to the *B* section, located Barclay's card and had begun to dial the number.

"Hello, Mr. Barclay?"

"Yes? What do you want?" His voice had turned no sweeter in the past few minutes.

"This is Mr. Mason's assistant calling."

"Assistant? He doesn't have an assistant. Exactly who are you anyway?"

"No, Mr. Barclay. I *am* Mr. Mason's assistant. I'm calling you right now from his office."

"From his home, you mean. What is this? What's going on. Is Mason there? Let me talk to him."

"Yes, Mr. Barclay, Mr. Mason is here, but he's in a very important meeting and cannot be disturbed."

"Important meeting? What are you talking about? Why isn't he working on my account?"

"I'm afraid he's tied up, Mr. Barclay. He asked me to call you and tell you that he will deliver your books to you this afternoon—around three o'clock."

"*Three o'clock?*" His shout came with such force that Carolyn had to hold the receiver away from her ear.

Bill's eyes reacted to the sound by opening wide. His mouth gaped.

But Carolyn enjoyed the sound and winked at her boss.

"That's right, Mr. Barclay. Three o'clock is confirmed. Thank you very much."

She hung up and allowed herself to burst into a laugh.

"Are you sure I wanted to do that?" Bill asked, not quite reaching her level of ecstasy.

"Yes, you do. And you do have an important appointment."

"I do?"

"With me."

The phone rang.

She picked it up.

"Mason Accounting Service," she answered as if she'd been doing such a thing for years.

"Get me Mason on the line. This is Wayne Barclay."

"I'm sorry, Mr. Barclay, Mr. Mason is in a meeting at the moment and cannot be disturbed. Would you care to leave a message?"

"You'd better believe I want to leave a message. You tell that snivelling little bookkeeper if he wants to keep my account he'd better have my books over here before one o'clock, or I'm taking my business elsewhere."

"Thank you, Mr. Barclay. I'll give him your message. I'm sure he'll be happy to consider your ultimatum."

After she hung up she looked at his face. There still was color there, but she wasn't all that certain she could see much life.

"You've just lost my biggest account," he said quietly.

"No I haven't. Trust me. It's his game. He's played it for years and he's good at it. He's using you, Bill, like he used my husband. And he'll push you as far as you let him push."

Bill shook his head.

"And besides. What if he does look for another accountant? How many do you think would take his abuse? And for how long? Trust me. When you take these books over to him, he'll not say a word about all this. In fact, he just might try to get you to do something more for him."

Suddenly Bill realized how well she knew his client. That really was how Barclay dealt with people. And for the first time since waking up he allowed a smile to creep onto his face.

"You know, I do believe you might be right."

"Of course I'm right. So where are you taking me to lunch?"

* * *

Within a week thoughts began creeping into Bill's mind—he ought to marry this woman. He found himself creating excuses to see her, be with her. At first such ideas would dissolve in the presence of one of Janet's pictures or something special they'd shared. Then he found himself feeling guilty at night in their room, surrounded by all of Janet's things.

Then he found himself spending more and more time at Carolyn's place. And eventually, it didn't bother him to sleep in his own bed when he came home from a date with her.

The big shift came in the middle of the night after he'd been "working" with Carolyn for nearly five weeks. He began talking with Janet.

He'd not done that before. It seemed appropriate now.

"Sweetheart. All the time we were together you know how much I loved you. And I still do. You know we'll be together forever. But I'm still stuck down here on earth. And it's been so lonely—until I met Carolyn. I promise, you'll never be far from my thoughts. Even when I'm around Carolyn I can still feel you near me. But she's a nice person. I guess you know that. And we have so much in common. It's just so pleasant to be around her. I really don't know what I'd have done without her in the business. She's been a big help. Would you feel all right if I married her? Just for the little time we both have left here? I kind of need to be around her. It's terribly lonely here without somebody."

When he was finished he just lay there staring at the night-darkened ceiling. And he listened. But nothing came to him. And then he realized something had happened.

All the guilt was gone.

*   *   *

They decided they wanted a simple, quiet wedding. But when it took place there was nothing simple nor quiet about it. Oh, the ceremony was simple enough. Only they had to hold it in the largest sealing room in the Provo LDS Temple. And by the time all the adult members of both families—those who held temple recommends—crammed into the room it was standing room only.

In lieu of a reception they decided to have a family dinner. They kept adding names to the list and finally decided to hold the thing in a reception center. With the wide range of ages of all the children and grandchildren—and a few friends thrown in as well—the rest of their celebration was anything but quiet.

*   *   *

They decided on neutral territory for their first night together. And in that motel room—after such a long, busy day— he simply flopped onto one side of the bed. Carolyn would have done the same only she felt it best to sit beside him.

"You're tired," she told him, as if he didn't know.

He nodded, letting her get away with such a remark. It was worth it to feel her hand caressing his head.

"It's probably not going to be much of a wedding night for you."

She chuckled. "You think that matters to me?"

He smiled and shook his head. Then he raised himself so he was leaning on one elbow. He placed his arm around her.

"I really do love you, Carolyn."

"I know."

"And I'm still in love with Janet."

"I know."

"But I promise you. We're going to be happy together."

"I know."

And they kissed.

By the time they got back from their honeymoon they'd decided to live at her place and hold regular office hours at his. Barclay hit the roof. He wasn't allowed to call in the middle of the night anymore. It became the final straw. And he notified Bill he'd found another accountant. He demanded any and all papers and files Bill might have.

"When I walked out of his office," Bill told his wife that day, "I felt such a relief. I can't believe I took all that guff for all those years."

Within a week they had two new accounts. Each paid the same as Barclay. And they both took half the time Barclay's account took. It seemed like a new era to Bill. Carolyn began her campaign to get Bill painting again.

* * *

Every morning they walked together at the mall. They'd walked a lot on their honeymoon. But it was not exactly the same. They'd spent a lot of time gawking at the scenery. They chose Seattle because neither of them had been there before. There was a lot to see up there. All too soon it was over.

Now they were back and into a routine. It seemed fun to arrive at the mall at the same time, to finish and go home together. Carolyn even slowed down to Bill's pace. He never mentioned it but thought it was nice she'd want to stick with him rather than whiz past him as she once did.

Then one day he realized she wasn't pumping her arms with such vigor anymore. Still he didn't say anything. But within a month of their return he could sense something really was wrong.

"You feeling all right?" he asked her one day as they were about to leave for home.

"Of course. I'm just tired," she said with a smile. "Being a newlywed isn't as easy as it used to be."

He laughed with her and let her get away with her excuse. But that evening, when she fell asleep during her favorite television show he decided he'd have to say something to her.

He waited until after their walk the next morning.

"Honey, I think it would be good for you to see a doctor. Get a checkup, okay?"

She looked at him in defiance. But before she could speak out with her objections, she felt dizzy and had to grab hold of him.

"Whoow!" she exclaimed with a shake of her head.

He held her in his arms and felt her relaxing against him.

"Finally falling for me, are you?"

He could feel her respond.

"I don't know what happened. But I'm okay now."

"You can make the call—or I'll make it. But you're going to the doctor's office—today."

* * *

Doctor Tibbs looked back and forth along the six-foot-long sheet of paper on which he'd recorded Carolyn's EKG. He marked places where the strokes had shown similar patterns.

"There's something going on in there that I don't like, Carolyn."

"Do you have any idea what it might be?"

"Well, I'm not entirely certain, but I'd say we're looking at some blocked arteries around the heart. Just looking at this EKG is not conclusive. I'd feel more comfortable if we did an angiogram."

"Now tell me what that is again," she asked.

"Okay, we just run a tube up the artery from down in the groin area, on the leg right here," he explained. "We inject some dyes and take pictures of your heart."

"What if you find something?"

"Well, as long as we're in there anyway—and if we find a blockage in the arteries around your heart—we can try to dissolve them with some chemicals or we can do a procedure called angioplasty. That's a little balloon we slip in there. We blow it up until we expand the blood vessel so it can handle a normal flow. It works quite well in most cases."

"What if that doesn't fix it?" Bill asked.

"Well, in most cases it does a good job. But if it doesn't we're looking at open chest surgery and a bypass procedure."

They talked for a while about chances and percentages. And on the way out, Bill angled the doctor aside and asked about costs.

"That much?"

"I'm sorry. That's what it costs. I wish it were less. There's not much I can do. Let's see, you don't have insurance, do you?"

Bill shook his head.

"I've know people who put off this kind of operation until they were 65 and let the government pick up the tab. But I wouldn't recommend that for Carolyn. It's too long to wait. And it wouldn't be fair to her. I'll be happy to wait for my money. And you can even make arrangements at the hospital," Dr. Tibbs offered.

"Thank you," Bill said, shaking his hand.

* * *

"We can't afford it," Carolyn argued.

"We can't afford not to."

"But it'll take so much of our reserves."

"So what? I'll get another account. I'd even take Barclay's account back if it was the only way."

"Don't you dare."

He laughed. And he held her.

And she felt assured and safe. Still, it bothered her to think that she had married him to take care of him. Now he would have to take care of her.

* * *

Bill's great concern now was with their finances. He inventoried every possible resource. He could sell his house. They still had hers. Actually, it was larger than his place. And they didn't need both. On the other hand, if he got another account they could build up their reserves again. With both of them in reasonable health they could handle at least one more account with no trouble at all. The question was, how long would both of them be in reasonable health?

* * *

The procedure couldn't be scheduled for two weeks. Bill used it to scout around for another account. He circulated a letter and left his card with numerous businesses around town—friends and friends of friends.

Nothing happened until the day of her surgery.

"Mason," the voice over the phone forced into his ear.

"Yes?"

"This is Wayne Barclay calling. I see you've been scrounging around for new accounts. You must be hurting for money. Well, I've decided to let bygones be bygones and give you another chance." Without waiting for Bill to answer he continued. "You can pick up my books this afternoon. I won't need them until tomorrow around six."

"I'm sorry, Mr. Barclay. I'm just leaving right now to take my wife to the hospital."

"Wife? I thought your wife died."

"I've remarried. And my wife's going in for an operation. I couldn't possibly pick up your books today."

"Okay. That's reasonable. You can take the day off. And you can pick them up tomorrow. I'll even let you take until Wednesday to get them back to me—by noon."

"Mr. Barclay, thank you. But I'm not going to even think about business until we get home from the hospital."

"Call me."

"I don't know."

"Call me! I need to know if you're going to do them or not. I'm giving you first chance at them. I need to know if I have to find someone else."

"All right, I'll call you."

But in his heart and mind Bill wondered if he ever would. He'd taken the easy way out. It wasn't a good time to argue. They had to leave.

"Who was that?" Carolyn asked.

"Nobody," Bill answered.

And he meant it.

* * *

At the hospital Bill felt uncomfortable waiting in the very room where he'd spent so many hours when Janet had died. He looked at the tray of picked-over doughnuts and wondered if they were the same ones that had been there before. He knew they weren't. But thinking of it drew his mind from Carolyn for a few seconds.

They always took so long in there. How could they be so cruel to the patient's family?

He had faith in Dr. Tibbs. Janet had too. For her it had been too late. The massive damage inside the heart simply was too much for Dr. Tibbs and his team to cope with.

Funny, now that Bill thought of it, he'd never asked how Carolyn felt about Dr. Tibbs. It shocked him to learn how long it had been since Carolyn had seen a doctor. She should have known better. She claimed she'd felt so healthy, strong. Seeing a doctor was something she really didn't like to do. And judging from the way she felt, there didn't seem to be any reason for going in—just for a checkup.

Bill remembered how healthy she looked before they were married—hoofing around the mall the way she did, pumping her arms up and down. She certainly didn't look sick.

But she was.

And it was killing Bill to have to sit here and wait for the results of another heart procedure. Janet's had been far more serious. And even though angioplasty was commonly done these days, there was nothing easy about this one either.

He and Carolyn's oldest son had given her a blessing last night. That should have been enough for Bill to hang onto. But Bill reached out again. For the hundredth time he turned his thoughts toward the Lord and pleaded that Carolyn would be all right.

"Father," he said within his mind, his lips moving slightly. "I've grown to love that woman. And it would be real hard to lose her—like this."

*   *   *

But he didn't lose her. Dr. Tibbs came out of the operating area and reported that she was doing fine.

"We had a minor problem with the balloon. But it was a mechanical thing. Once we got it working right, everything went smoothly. She's doing fine. She's in recovery. They should be taking her back to her room in about 20 minutes or so."

*   *   *

It took Carolyn about three weeks to get her old stride back. She didn't walk as fast, but the stride was there. Her speed would come with a bit more time.

The pressure was off.

Except that Bill hadn't found another account.

And he hadn't called Barclay.

So Barclay called him.

"You promised you'd call. I've been waiting here. And I can't wait much longer. Are you coming over here to pick up my books or not?"

"Not."

"What?"

"Not, Mr. Barclay. I couldn't possibly do your books. I don't have the time nor the inclination to handle your account."

"What kind of talk is that? I'm offering you business, and you're turning me down?"

"I most certainly am."

There was a major pause in their conversation. After a time Bill wondered if they were still connected. Then he heard Barclay breathing.

Bill looked over at Carolyn. She'd heard Bill's side of the conversation and she was excited at the firmness in her husband's voice. She stepped into the kitchen and lifted the extension in there. The long cord allowed her to move to where she could watch Bill. It was hard for her to keep from giggling out loud.

"Okay. I'll play your game," Barclay finally said. "What is it going to take to get you to take my account?"

She looked at Bill and mouthed the words, "He can't find anybody else!" And then she doubled over trying to hold back her laugh.

"I don't know, Mr. Barclay. But I do know that if I do take it, it will be on my terms and not on yours."

"And what might those be?"

"Well, to start with, you will have to buy yourself a computer."

"A computer? Do you know how much those things cost?"

"Yes sir. And I also know how much money you have in the bank—or at least how much you had in the bank. Would that amount be more or less than what you had in the bank when I was doing the books before?"

After a long pause, the hopeful client admitted, "More."

"Okay, then not only can you afford to buy one, Mr. Barclay, I'll show you how to save money when you do."

"You will?" Barclay's voice brightened.

"Yes. And if I do take your account it will be on an hourly basis. No more flat rates."

"But that leaves me open for—" he stopped short of finishing.

Bill finished his thought for him. "For my controlling what you pay me?"

"Yes. How will I know I'm getting my money's worth?"

"How can you even think that? Barclay, I've saved you thousands of dollars in taxes and have worked at least four times longer on your account than any other account I've ever had. It's time you carried your own weight around here."

"Okay—okay. So when are you coming to pick up my books?"

"I'm not."

"What? I thought you said you would."

"I'm not coming over there anymore. I don't have time for all that nonsense. If you want me to do your account you're going to have to bring your work here—and pick it up when I'm finished. Office hours are from nine to five, Monday through Friday."

After another pause, Barclay accepted.

"I'll be right over."

* * *

Carolyn answered the door and discovered that time had not been kind to the man she once knew as Wayne Barclay. A man of medium height with a slight build, his face had weathered from stress. He stood on the porch holding a box filled with papers and ledgers. Also, in one hand he held his hat.

"Good morning," he said graciously, not giving any indication he recognized her. "Is Mr. Mason at home?"

"Yes he is. Won't you come in?"

"How do you do," the visitor said after setting his box on the sofa. "My name is Wayne Barclay. You must be Mrs. Mason."

"Yes. How do you do, Mr. Barclay." She held out her hand and felt a rather weak response in his handshake.

"You look familiar, Mrs. Mason."

"Yes. People tell me that a lot."

Bill came from the kitchen. He'd been in the basement for a minute. He greeted his new client and noted the box of papers and ledgers.

"I trust this will be the last time you'll bring your books in this form?"

"Oh, yes. And I'm certainly interested in the computer you mentioned."

Bill gave him the sheet he'd prepared with the specifications he wanted.

"Next time all you'll need to bring me is one of these," Bill said, holding up a micro-floppy disk.

Barclay smiled and nodded.

"Mr. Barclay, how is your wife?" Carolyn asked.

"My wife?" He hesitated. And then he looked a bit uncomfortable. "I don't have a wife. She died some years ago."

"I'm sorry." Carolyn felt embarrassed at having asked. "I didn't know. You must miss her. I know it's hard living alone. I hope I didn't offend you."

He nodded and moved his arms with a nervousness that made him look awkward.

"No. It's all right. I'm used to it now. And I do have my business to keep me occupied."

"Yes. Of course you do," Carolyn said warmly. She looked at Bill.

And he noticed something going on in her mind.

"Well, Mr. Barclay, we normally take new clients out to dinner. But in your case, I'll bet you'd just as soon have a home-cooked meal for a change."

Barclay's eyes brightened.

"Would you like to come over for dinner tomorrow night?"

He fumbled for words but found himself accepting and then falling over himself as he retreated out the door.

"Are you sure you want to do that?" Bill asked.

And then he caught on.

"Come to think about it, I wonder if that friend of Jeanette's happens to be free tomorrow night?"

More than Marks
on Paper

KATHLEEN DALTON-WOODBURY

When they pulled into the driveway (West Virginians called it a parking pad), Susan Taylor turned to her husband, Kevin. "Can I please call Mom? I really need to talk to her about this."

Kevin glanced at his watch. "It's almost time for the rates to change."

"I know. But I'll hurry if you'll take care of Lucy." She looked into the back seat, where their daughter had fallen asleep in her carseat. It was such a long drive from church, this was the only way she got her nap on Sunday. She turned back to Kevin. "Please?"

"But can't you talk to Aunt Margaret? She does genealogy, too, and she lives a lot closer."

Susan closed her eyes and took a deep breath. "I know that, Kevin. But that's *your* genealogy. I have to do this with *mine*. Besides, I haven't talked to her since Christmas."

Kevin looked at her for a moment and then shrugged. "Okay. I'll get Lucy."

As Susan opened her door to the heat and humidity of West Virginia, she heard him remind her again that it was almost time for the rates to go up. She hurried into the house, across the variegated orange shag carpet that must have been there for decades, and into the glaring yellow kitchen with its faded hens marching across the wallpaper.

As the phone began to ring in her mother's Utah home, eighteen hundred miles away from this West Virginia kitchen, Susan could feel the tears welling in her eyes. She blinked at them and swallowed. She would *not* cry on the phone this time.

"Hello?"

But the sound of her mother's voice speared through her like lightning and for a moment she couldn't speak. The "hello?" was repeated and Susan swallowed. "Mom?" And the tears overflowed.

"Susan? Is everything all right? Is Kevin okay, and Lucy? Are you all right?"

Susan turned away from the sounds Kevin and Lucy made as they came in the front door. She couldn't let Kevin see her crying again. "We're okay, Mom." She swallowed once more. "It's just that they sang 'Dear to the Heart of the Shepherd' in church today, and I feel so much like one of the lost sheep out in the wilderness."

Susan's mother gave a little sigh. "Is that why you called? Susan, you've got to stop feeling this way."

"I know, Mom. And no, it's not why I called. I'm sorry." She grabbed a tissue from the box on the kitchen counter and took an expensive moment to blow her nose. "Excuse me. No, the reason I called is that I've been called to teach the family history class."

"Well that's great. Your grandmother would be proud of you."

"But that's just it, Mom. *Gramma* did all that stuff. How am I going to teach a class like that to these . . . strangers, when I don't know anything about it? They're going to expect me to know everything since I'm from Salt Lake."

"Oh, Susan, of course they won't."

"Yes they will, Mom. Sister . . . oh, I don't remember her name, but anyway, one of the little old ladies came up to me after they sustained me and said that very thing. What am I going to do?"

There was a pause on the other end of the line, and Susan felt Lucy tugging on her skirt. "Mommy, who are you talking to?"

Susan leaned over, covering the mouthpiece, and whispered, "Nana."

"Can I talk to her?"

"Not right now, honey. Go change your clothes."

"Susan? How about if I send you your Book of Remembrance, and you can look through that?"

"How long will that take? They want me to start the class in a few weeks."

"Well, it's pretty big. I'll have to send it parcel post." Papers rustled. "Oh, wait a minute. Here's an idea. I can send you Major Crider's autobiography—it's only a few sheets—by first-class mail. He lived in Kentucky. Maybe you can find out something about him and then share your experiences with the class."

"Major Crider?"

"Oh, you remember. The so-many-greats uncle who lost an arm in the Civil War and married his nurse? She left her home near the battle and moved to the other end of Kentucky with him. It's a very romantic story and I think it would generate some interest."

"Where did he live?" Maybe it would be close enough that Kevin could go there and find out some historical stuff for her. He was always going off to visit historical places here in West Virginia. When he wasn't taking her and Lucy to visit relatives in neighboring states, that is.

"Let's see. It says here that he was born in Eddyville, Kentucky. And he was injured at Cynthiana. Oh, and he served in the state legislature in . . . Frankfort. Did you get that?"

Susan grabbed the pen and notepaper by the phone and wrote down the names. "Yes, I got it. I'll ask Kevin to look in his maps. Maybe we can go there." She sighed, suddenly feeling better. "Thanks, Mom. Yes, please send all that stuff, especially the autobiography. I think that will help. I sure appreciate you, Mom." The tears started welling again. She'd better hang up. "I love you, Mom."

"I love you, too, honey. I'll get these in the mail tomorrow. Give my love to Kevin and Lucy." And she was gone, eighteen hundred miles away once more. Susan hung up the phone and went to find Kevin.

*　*　*

Susan turned around to check on Lucy again as they pulled up next to the historical marker at the Cynthiana battleground. "She's still asleep, Kevin. Why don't you go ahead and look around? I'll stay here in the car with her."

"Just a minute. I want to get this on film. Could you read the marker for me while I tape it?" He got out of the car and walked around to the marker, aiming the camcorder. "Okay."

"Battle of Cynthiana. Here Colonel John Hunt Morgan defeated federal forces and captured the town July 18, 1862. On June 12, 1864, Morgan as Brigadier General was defeated by federal General Stephen Burbidge."

"Okay, thanks." Kevin stood for a moment, turning to make a panoramic record of the setting. The town sat across the river. To the left and on the other side of the stream squatted a low hill. To the right, across the river and along its curve, a high ridge rose from the town and extended a ways behind the car. Directly behind the car and on this side of the river spread a large flat area. Maybe Kevin knew where everything had happened—he'd visited enough battle sites—but Susan had no idea. Major Crider had been on a hillside somewhere after his injury, but which hillside, and where, was anyone's guess.

She watched her husband walk along the stream toward the river, stopping every so often to raise the camcorder to his eye. How she had ever let him talk her into coming along, she'd never know. Although she had to admit that the scenery from Charleston to Cynthiana had been lovely. She hadn't realized how green and lush "green and lush" could be. And she was surprised to find out that the East really wasn't wall-to-wall city. Even along the interstate the greenery simply loomed over the road. So different from the dry, brown sagebrush you'd see from the Utah highways. The gentle rolling hills and stone fences along the road from the interstate to Cynthiana with occasional glimpses of stately manors, and the many horse farms with their long-legged thoroughbreds, gave Susan a much better feel for the area than flying over it had ever done. It was rather pretty after all, even if it was so much more humid.

If it hadn't been for that man, that historian, she could have let Kevin go alone. But she'd called the public library at Eddy-ville, thinking they might have some kind of information about their local hero, and the librarian had said with some surprise that she'd just been speaking to a man who knew a lot about Major Crider. She gave Susan his name and address, and when Susan called him, he made her promise to stop by and see him. "I'll take you around and show you his old house—won't be standing much longer, no one's lived in it for years and it's falling apart—and his grave, and I'll introduce you to his grand-daughter."

"Oh, I don't want to impose."

"No such thing. Miss Lillian would love to meet some family. She hasn't any children of her own, her only living sister is in a nursing home, and she'd be thrilled to meet you. Besides, you'd like to see his books, wouldn't you? You come by and see me, and I'll take good care of you."

And so she'd come. Lucy had been wonderful, playing happily in her carseat and accepting the toasted cheese sandwich for her lunch without fussing.

Susan turned as, on cue, her daughter stirred and looked up. "Are we there yet?"

Susan smiled. "Well, we're at one of the places. Do you see Daddy?" She reached back to unfasten the seatbelt buckle on the carseat.

Lucy squirmed out of her seat, trying to see him, and then jumped up and down between the front bucket seats when she finally succeeded. "*There* he is! Daddy!"

"I don't think he can hear you. Shall we get out and walk over to him? There's a stream you can throw rocks into." Susan opened her door and pushed her seat out of the way so she could help her daughter out of the car.

* * *

Frankfort, state capital of Kentucky, was a surprise. They'd been driving along the rolling countryside when the road dipped and moved them down into a tight little river valley. Suddenly there were cliffs around them, hiding the afternoon sun. The new state capitol, looking very much like the one in Salt Lake, sprawled up a low hillside, but they were looking for the old state capitol, the one Major Crider had known. Small and not nearly so impressive, it had its own dignity.

The building was closed for the night, and Susan sighed her relief. Kevin would have liked to look around for a while, but Lucy was ready for bed, and so was she. So back up the road to the motel they'd seen on the way in. And then up early tomorrow.

Later, Kevin turned to her as they lay in bed, whispering so he wouldn't wake Lucy up. "You know, I'm so glad I was able to get a few days off. It really means a lot to me to be driving around Kentucky with my two best girls. My little historical trips get pretty lonely sometimes without you."

Susan didn't answer for a moment. Why hadn't he said anything before? Had she been so steeped in her own homesickness that she hadn't noticed his loneliness? She had to admit he'd tried very hard at first to get her to go with him, and he'd been so excited to have her come along this time that it had been embarrassing. "I've been selfish, haven't I?"

His pause told her that he didn't disagree. "Well, I've been pretty selfish, too, I guess. Expecting you to drop everything and come play with me in some strange new place. I should have been giving you more time to get used to living here in the East."

Susan thought there'd never be enough time for that. The humidity, the noisy little treefrogs, the smell from some of the refineries or whatever they were on the river, those nasty tent caterpillars she'd caught Lucy stomping the other day—in her bare feet! She suppressed a shudder.

"Well, maybe if I'd been more willing to come play, I wouldn't be feeling so guilty now. Will you forgive me, Kevin? I'll try to do better, I promise."

He rubbed his hand up and down her arm. "Of course I forgive you. I'll try to be better, too. I love you, you know?"

"I love you, too." She started to say more, but she could tell by his sudden snore that he'd already gone to sleep. She smiled to herself at his ability to shut off like that. He was done talking and so *zonk!* Well, they had a long day ahead, and she needed to get to sleep too, even if it took her longer.

* * *

The historian, Mr. Hammond, was a lean, dark man. Susan wondered if he had Indian blood in him. "Just call me Joe," he'd said when they first met. "After all, you're kin to Major Crider, so that makes you seem like family to me." He had her ride in his car while Kevin and Lucy followed in theirs so he could show her the way to Major Crider's house. Susan took the tape recorder and taped everything he told her about the countryside, the people who had come from the eastern seaboard to settle the area, Major Crider's people, and, she realized, hers as well.

The house was Victorian, just like all the houses she'd loved looking at in the Avenues section of Salt Lake City. As she got out of Mr. Hammond's car, she couldn't help but "ooh" at it.

Mr. Hammond chuckled. "You should have seen it when I was a boy. Major Crider grew up in it and then he brought Miss Sarah here all the way from Cynthiana after the war. Over two hundred and fifty miles on bad roads. This house must have been a fine sight to her."

To the left of the front door, a covered porch extended around the corner and beyond. To the right, a rounded tower rose above the second floor, topped by a cupola. Shattered window glass reflected bits and pieces of the surrounding countryside. Susan made her way toward it through a jungle of weeds. How could they have let it go to ruin like this? She turned back to look as Kevin, holding the camcorder, approached with Lucy. Good. At least they'll have some record of it when it's finally gone.

"That round room on the second floor was Miss Sarah's room. She liked to sit there and read, or so her granddaughter tells me."

Susan thought how lovely that would have been. "It's a good thing Miss Sarah can't see it now." She stepped closer, putting her hand on one of the porch posts, pushing at it lightly to make sure it was firm.

"Don't go stepping up onto the veranda like that, Miss Susan. Those boards are rotten."

"Can't I look inside?"

He grimaced and then nodded. "But you've got to be careful. Here, let me show you. See where the joists run along under the broken boards? If you stay near them until you get to the wall, you should be all right."

It was a good thing she'd worn her hiking boots. Their stiff soles supported her better on the slim joists than her sneakers would have. Finally she stood in the doorway.

"Now don't go in. Those floorboards are even worse than these out here."

Susan leaned against the doorjamb to see past what was left of the shattered door. A little to her right, a once-elegant stairway ascended to the second floor. Even if she could have entered the house, there was no way she could have gotten up the collapsed steps. And she would have loved to look out through the upper story windows. But Mr. Hammond was right. It looked like someone had taken a sledgehammer to the entry floor. What was the point of such destruction? They'd even hammered at the fireplace she could see in the room to her left.

"Is this the parlor opposite the stairs?"

"No, that's the dining room. The parlor is over there, below the Major's bedroom. If you look down the hall in front of you, you can see the door to Major Crider's library, behind the parlor."

Suddenly the words to "My Old Kentucky Home" came to her mind. She could remember her mother saying that as a young girl she'd seen Great-Grandpa Bennett cry when he heard that song. Chills crawled over her skin as she thought how this might be the very house he thought of at those times.

"Mommy! Look at these flowers I picked for you!"

Susan turned to see her daughter running toward the house. She'd better get off of the porch before Lucy decided to follow her. "Wait there, Lucy. I'm coming to look at them."

Mr. Hammond took her hand to help her down the loose boards on the steps. She smiled her thanks to him. And here she'd thought the Southern Gentleman was just a stereotype.

Every kind of weed and wildflower Susan could imagine seemed to cluster in Lucy's hand. It was a good thing she didn't have allergies. "Oh, how pretty. How about if we take them to Major Crider's grave?" She looked up at Mr. Hammond from where she squatted beside Lucy. "That is the next stop, right?"

"Sure enough, Miss Susan. And it isn't too far from here. See that building over there?"

Susan stood up to look across the fields of spring corn. She could see a small, house-sized building about a hundred yards away.

"Major Crider's daddy gave the land to the church, and that's where the whole family was buried."

Kevin had come up and was looking at the house. "Why'd the family let it go like this?"

Mr. Hammond looked back at the building. "Oh, the family hasn't owned it for years. Major Crider grew up in it, and then when his parents died, he inherited it—being the youngest and the others already having homes. But when his children were grown and married, he sold it to go live in Frankfort. That was when he was in the state legislature, you see. After he retired, they owned a hotel for a while, and after Miss Sarah died, he had a house down by where they flooded old Eddyville when they dammed the rivers.

"His only living descendant is Miss Lillian, and though I'm sure she'd like to do something about this house, she doesn't have the money. Come on. She'll be expecting you soon."

* * *

The church and cemetery were situated more like neighbors, on adjacent plots instead of on the same piece of land. Together, and yet not quite together. Mr. Hammond led them to the group of graves nearest the church, but he stayed back while they walked up to read the engravings. Two Washington-monument-like headstones stood in the middle of a cluster of ground-level stones. Susan walked up to the nearer and larger one. "In Memory of Our Beloved Father and Mother, George and Rebecca Crider." On one side of the monument were the words "George Crider March 15, 1800—October 24, 1868" and on the other side were the words "Rebecca Koon Crider May 21, 1798—April 10, 1870."

"Do you have the pedigree chart your mom sent you?" Kevin had come up beside her.

Susan showed him the papers she had brought from the car. "It's in here somewhere." When she found it she handed it to him.

"Okay, let's see. George Crider. Here he is."

Susan looked at the paper he held. Yes, the dates matched.

This was Major Crider's father, then, and her own third-great-grandfather. Once again chills spread across her skin.

She pointed to the name on the next generation. "That's Major Crider's sister, my great-great-grandmother. She was the oldest, and Major Crider was the youngest. My great-grandfather was actually a year or two older than Major Crider."

"So this granddaughter we're going to see is your . . . what cousin?"

Susan shrugged. "Maybe she knows. I certainly don't know how to figure it out."

They turned to the other monument. This one had the words "Major John Wesley Crider, Patriot, Statesman, Father" on it on one side, and the words "Sarah Jameson Crider, Beloved Wife and Mother" on the other side. Below, at the foot of the monument, the birth and death dates were carved. Susan looked around at the other stones. Some of the names were on the pedigree, but though others had the same last names, she didn't recognize the first names. These people were all related to her, and she didn't even know how. By the time her Book of Remembrance arrived, she wouldn't remember their names to know who was buried here, who she'd visited. She swallowed against the tightness in her throat.

"Do you have enough videotape to get these graves, Kevin?"

Kevin turned from reading an inscription and raised his eyebrows at her. "I've got plenty of tape, but I'm not sure there's enough time left on the batteries to get this and to get Miss Lillian. You did want to get her on video, didn't you?"

Susan nodded. "Yeah. That's right." She stood beside Sarah Crider's grave. This woman had left her home and family over a hundred years ago. And there were no phones in those days. She'd gone on a journey that had taken much longer than their flight from Salt Lake City had taken. She knew what it was like. In fact, she'd had it harder than Susan was having it. "Do you think we could come back here sometime, Kevin?" She blinked quickly before looking at him.

"Sure. If you want to. I think we can arrange it." He smiled, and the tightness in her throat went away as she smiled back. Then Susan turned to look for Lucy. The little girl had left a wildflower on each grave and was working her way through the cemetery. "How do you think she knows to do that?"

Kevin shrugged. "I guess she paid more attention than we thought last Memorial Day." He started through the graves to get her.

Susan felt the familiar twinge at the thought of home. But even though she couldn't go with the family to decorate the graves at Wasatch Lawn, there were graves here she could visit. Graves that belonged to her people, too.

Kevin and Lucy were walking toward where Mr. Hammond waited by the cars, and Susan had turned to follow them when she saw a long narrow headstone sticking up out of the ground to her left. There were two names, but only one had both dates: "Andrew Moses Larkin September 12, 1899—August 14, 1965" and "Lillian Jackson Larkin November 2, 1904—." Why was there no death date? And then she had an idea. She turned and beckoned to Mr. Hammond.

When he joined her, she pointed to the headstone. "Is that unfinished side for the Lillian we're going to go meet? For when she dies?"

"Why yes, Miss Susan. Miss Lillian and her husband bought that headstone after their little girl died." He pointed to the ground near her feet. "So they could all be together here."

Susan turned to look down at a small piece of granite she had taken for a footstone. "Suzanna Larkin July 4, 1931—March 6, 1937."

"Do they have any other children?"

Mr. Hammond shook his head. "Miss Suzanna was the only one."

Susan started walking toward the car. Miss Lillian had been a young mother once, had had a daughter like Lucy. The small grave didn't bear thinking about. "So after Miss Lillian is gone, there'll be no one?"

"Well, Miss Susan, I reckon that's right. Except for you, and your family, that is. And you'll be here to remember them. So it'll be all right."

Susan smiled at him. Yes, she would be here to remember them. Only think if she hadn't come, *then* who would there be?

* * *

Mr. Hammond insisted on going home before they went to Miss Lillian's house. "I'd only be in the way. She knows you're coming, so you don't need an introduction. This is a family thing. So you run along now. And thanks for letting me show you around." And he wouldn't accept anything but their thanks for his time and trouble.

So when the door opened, Susan didn't know what to expect. The little woman standing in the shadows beyond the door didn't look like anyone in her family, and she was probably thinking the same thing about Susan.

"Hello. Lillian Larkin? I'm Susan Taylor. And this is my husband Kevin, and my daughter Lucy. Mr. Joe Hammond said you'd be expecting us."

The woman came into the light that shone through the doorway. Her eyes were crinkled tight and Susan realized she was smiling. "Please call me Miss Lillian. How did you say you were related?"

Susan held out the pedigree chart and pointed to George Crider's name. "That's my third-great-grandfather, Miss Lillian."

The woman took the sheet from Susan's hand and walked further into the house. "Well, come on, come on."

They followed her into a large sitting room. In one corner stood a longer-than-full-length mirror and in another sat a waist-high cabinet of some sort. A loveseat and two chairs made a conversation area in the middle of the room. Miss Lillian took one of the chairs and Susan, Kevin and Lucy sat in the loveseat. There were so many little knickknacks on tables and shelves around the room that Susan regretted bringing Lucy along. It she were to break anything, Miss Lillian would surely never want to see them again.

Susan studied the little woman as she studied the pedigree. Her reddish brown hair was cut very short and had no grey in it, though the light wrinkling of her skin made it look like there should have been grey. Her figure was slender and almost boy-like. And yet, according to what Susan had heard, her grandfather had been quite a large man. She must take after her grandmother then.

Suddenly Miss Lillian looked up and smiled. "So this means we're what?" She looked up toward the ceiling as if for an answer, and then back at Susan again, still smiling. "Second cousins, twice removed, I believe." She handed back the pedigree. "Would you like to see your third-great-grandmother's family Bible?"

Susan felt her eyes widen. Once when she was a little girl, someone had shown her a family Bible with spaces in the center pages for marriages, births and deaths. She'd thought it was a wonderful thing to have, but most people she knew didn't use one. "Oh, yes, please."

Miss Lillian turned to a shabby book on the table next to her and handed it across to Susan. "The family information is on the middle pages."

Susan turned to find several pages of faded ink in several different hands, chronicling the lives of people long gone. Her throat tightened up and tears once again welled in her eyes. "Did Rebecca Crider write this?" She pointed at the first marriage date, "George Crider married Rebecca Koon on December 23rd, 1820."

Miss Lillian leaned forward to look. "Yes, she did. That book was given to her as a wedding present by her parents."

Susan turned the pages, reading the names and dates. "I have to teach a class on genealogy soon. Would you please tell me about these people?" And Miss Lillian did. She talked of the cousins and the aunts and uncles and grandparents. And as she talked, Susan began to see similarities between her and the relatives on her mother's side that she'd grown up with. Her words brought the names and dates on the pedigree chart to life and gave them personality. They weren't just marks on paper anymore.

Susan was grateful that Kevin had brought the tape player and plenty of tapes, because Miss Lillian wouldn't let them use the camcorder on her. Miss Lillian filled two tapes before Susan noticed that Lucy had fallen asleep in Kevin's arms.

"Oh, Miss Lillian, I'm sorry. I'm sure we've overstayed our welcome." Susan stood up, shutting off the tape recorder and putting it into the bag with the camcorder.

"No such thing." Miss Lillian joined her. Lucy moaned as Kevin stood up, but she kept sleeping. "It's meant a lot to me to be able to talk about my family. I'm the only one left, you know."

Kevin bounced Lucy to a more comfortable position against

his shoulder. "Will you let us take you to dinner tonight, Miss Lillian? We'd like to visit some more, but we don't want to impose on you if you have other plans."

Miss Lillian smiled and shook her head. "This old lady needs to get to bed early as much as that young one does. And you'll be wanting to start home early tomorrow, right? How about if you come back another time, and I'll take you to lunch? There's this lovely restaurant I like to go to. And since I'm saying no now, I won't take no for an answer later."

She ushered them toward the door. "That mirror there was from Major Crider's house. And you haven't seen his library yet, so you have to come back for that." She turned to the strange, waist-high cabinet. "And I need to play you something on my old-fashioned music box. It plays these metal plates." She opened the cabinet, and Susan caught a glimpse of something flat and round and bigger than a pizza pan. "And I haven't shown you the pictures yet, either." She turned and faced Susan, and her eyes were almost closed with the broadness of her smile. "When you've found family, you don't want to wear them out all at once. And you want to have reasons for them to come back."

The smile lessened for a moment. "You will come back, won't you?"

Susan looked into eyes as lonely as the ones she'd been seeing in the mirror lately. The tears welled up and over. "Oh, Miss Lillian, we'd love to come back. Do you have a piece of paper? Let me give you my address. And I'll write down yours. We can write letters until next time, okay?"

Miss Lillian turned to a desk behind her and brought back two little vellum visiting cards. "Here. Write it on here. Would you like me to send you a photocopy of the pages in the Bible? For your class?"

"Oh, I'd like that very much." Susan felt an urge to hug her newfound cousin, but wasn't sure how the woman would respond. So she took her hand instead. "Oh, thank you, Miss Lillian. I'm so glad we found you. Especially after thinking all this time that I was alone so far away from home." She tilted her head toward Kevin and Lucy. "Except for my husband and daughter, that is."

Miss Lillian squeezed Susan's hand and then pulled her into a hug. "Oh, me too, Susan. The dear Lord must have sent you." Then she pulled back and looked at the address Susan had given her. "You know, the Koons came from West Virginia. You might be able to find other cousins if you do some searching there. But if you do, promise you won't forget about me."

Susan laughed and shook her head. "I'll never forget about you, Miss Lillian. After all, you're family."

Flower Girl

HERBERT HARKER

Justin Mercer sat musing in what his family laughingly referred to as his study. Since early morning he hadn't had a moment to himself, and it was sweet now to reflect on the change that had so abruptly entered his life—a change whose course he knew he could not predict. He himself would have to change—the old path he had taken was not good enough any more.

He would probably be conducting many of his interviews in this very room. Would it be appropriate, he wondered, to order a new brass nameplate for his desk: "Bishop Justin Mercer." Technically, there'd be nothing wrong with it, of course, but it might cause certain people to smile up their sleeves. Well, he could think about it.

As his eye moved over the room he thought, This is where the changes begin. No more skateboards in here. No old magazines. Those carpet samples will have to go. How long had they been there? The "new" carpet was almost worn out.

He would need a new desk, of course, and a swivel chair. New pictures. One of those side-entry filing cabinets that look like wood paneling. . . . It was crazy, all the hours he had spent in this room and endured the sight of other people's discards stacked everywhere. Well, he'd put the family on notice: three days to retrieve their treasures, and everything left was marked for the trash.

The door moved slowly open, and his daughter's face appeared there. "Daddy . . . ?"

"Come in, honey." She must have come to congratulate him privately. But her expression was a little severe, and his stomach did a turn. It had been a perfect day so far; did this mean it couldn't end perfectly, as well?

Billie slipped into the room as if she were uncomfortable here, though that didn't make sense. She practically lived in here, talking on Justin's phone for hours at a time, and always leaving the desk littered with homework and gum wrappers and pieces of clothing. Sometimes one might think she had gone back to her bedroom naked, yet that too strained credulity. She was modest as a Quaker. Just look at her—dressed in that awful old blue warm-up suit. She sat in the little threadbare armchair in the corner and began to gnaw her thumb.

"Is something wrong?" Justin asked.

"Daddy . . ." She was looking into her lap. "Why didn't you tell me that you were going to be bishop?"

It surprised him; he could hardly think what to say. "I just found out myself last night. I told the family when I came home."

"But I was over at Sharon's."

"Exactly. Then this morning I had a seven o'clock meeting. There was no chance. . . . Honey, I wanted to tell you."

At last she raised her eyes, but still she didn't look at him. "I felt like such a fool. When President Bickford announced it I almost fell off the bench. And after church the kids were all laughing at me. 'Didn't you know?' " Now her eyes did meet his; it was his that looked away. "You could have told me if you wanted to."

He leaned forward in his chair and began to doodle on the blotter pad with his pen. "Billie. . . ."

"Sharon said, 'I thought your father told you everything.' "

"Billie, I'm sorry."

"You were just too full of it, weren't you? You couldn't think of anybody but yourself."

"That's not true."

"Grandma and Grandpa were there. You obviously had time to tell them."

"I guess I didn't know it meant so much to you."

She hesitated. "Will you please look at me? Will you quit scribbling?"

He put down his pen. "Billie. . . ."

"I thought it was going to be Brother Link."

"Yes, so did I. I think a lot of people were surprised."

"I don't know what to do."

"What do you mean?"

"You wouldn't understand."

"But. . . ." He felt completely baffled. She had never talked to him this way before. "You said a minute ago that you and I can always talk—you told Sharon that we tell each other everything."

"That's not what I said. . . ."

"You said. . . ."

"I said you told me everything. It was a lie. You never tell me anything, but do you think I want the kids to know that?"

"I don't understand. I thought. . . ."

"You thought! Of course. You think for all of us, as if you didn't deem us capable. But how could a brilliant man like yourself have kids that were morons? Did it ever occur to you that we can think, too?"

"Billie! I forbid you to talk to me that way."

"Yes. You're the bishop now. You deserve a little respect. Well, I respect you, Daddy. But I can't talk to you."

Her seriousness unnerved him. "You seem to be doing a pretty good job. I've never had a talking-to like this before."

"Big joke. Ha, ha. Well, you can't just laugh it off this time."

Justin reeled. He felt as if he were being whipsawed. "Time-out, okay?"

Now she did laugh. "You're the king of the time-outs, Daddy. But you never called a time-out for yourself before. Maybe there's hope after all."

Justin could not understand what was happening. Was he going to let this slip of a girl run him down, and then back over him? "I'd like to make a suggestion."

"Permission granted," she said.

He almost lost it there—his own daughter pretending he had come on bended knee; now, on the day when for the first time in his life he had felt the rush of real power in his bones; humbly, mind you, filled with self-abnegation. But it was useless to deny that with the mantle of spiritual responsibility for people, there came a swelling sense of power over them. (He'd have to be careful of that.) And as he watched his teary-eyed daughter he amended the thought—no power over Billie, not any more. A spasm of despair went through him. Where Billie was concerned, he suddenly felt weak as a breath. She had never given him any trouble; she had always done what he asked her to do. She had been the very light of his life. And now, all in a moment, she had moved out of his reach. The realization struck him like a cold hand on his heart. In a couple of years she'd be a legal adult. His last cord of influence would be cut, except, of course, the tenuous thread of moral suasion.

"I suggest . . ." he began, and stopped. He had to be more assertive; somehow he had to take charge of this conversation. If he didn't, what would she think of him? "I suggest that we start again."

"All right."

"I'm sorry that I didn't tell you about it. I should have stayed up last night until you got home. But I had a big day yesterday. Your mother and I went to bed early."

"Of course. You start to feel like Rambo, there's certain things you have to take care of."

"What's that supposed to mean?" He felt his ascendancy slipping away again.

"Oh, Daddy. I wasn't born yesterday. I know about guys."

Who was this? Where was his angel—his sweet little girl? He had to take the offensive before she walked all over him. "So I goofed. All right, it's over. And it's not the end of the world. What's the big deal, anyway, whether you knew I was going to be bishop? I don't get it."

"You never do, Daddy. The fact is, I didn't care whether you told me or not. But if you had told me I could have warned you not to accept."

"What? Why shouldn't I accept?"

"Because you can't be bishop."

"You don't think I'm worthy, is that it?"

"Of course you're worthy. There's not a black mark against you—you made sure of that. And what else matters, eh? No.

The reason you can't be bishop is because you have me for a daughter."

"That's nonsense."

"That's why I wanted Brother Link. I've been waiting for months."

"Waiting?"

"I have to talk to somebody, and you know I can never talk to Bishop Carver. He doesn't even listen to you. As soon as he sniffs some problem, he gives you his plastic lecture about chastity and shoots you out the door. I thought if Brother Link was bishop, maybe I could talk to him."

"What about? Can't you talk to me?"

"You don't listen either, Daddy."

This was more serious than he expected. Maybe it was really serious. He almost choked on the words. "Are you pregnant?"

"That's what I thought you'd ask."

Waves of anger kept rising in him—he couldn't seem to hold them back. "Don't be smart with me."

"Now you're talking like a father. I'm speaking to you as my bishop."

"Is this a confession?"

"Yes."

He couldn't imagine where this was leading.

She said, "You don't want to hear it, do you? Why don't you want to hear it? Because you'll have to resign your precious bishopric. You don't care what happens to me, do you?"

"Billie, I'm sorry. I'll listen. And you don't have to worry—whatever the trouble is, we can fix it."

"Are you sure?"

He spoke with all the earnestness of his soul. "Of course we can fix it. That's what repentance is."

"Who said anything about repentance?"

"Then, why talk to your bishop?"

"Because it's not that simple."

Justin said, "Billie. You know I have always thought of you as my little girl. I can't get used to the idea that you're growing up—that I shouldn't treat you as a child any more. But I want to be the person you need, whether it's as your father, or as your bishop."

"No. I'm not pregnant," she said.

Relief washed through him. Instantly he felt a great stone moved from his heart. It was true—they really could fix it. It would be all right. "Oh, Billie."

"And no, I'm not a fallen woman. Nobody has touched me."

"Then, what . . . ?"

"I wish they had!" she cried. "I wish I was. . . ."

"Stop it!"

"That shocks you, doesn't it?" But her sullen words carried no sting any more; they were spoken softly, with a sense of weariness, almost of defeat.

"I don't know what's happened," he insisted. "But you mustn't give up. You can be forgiven."

"Aren't you forgetting about the unforgivable sin?"

Mentally, he staggered. He couldn't imagine what she was talking about. What did Billie know of murder, or denying the Holy Ghost?

She said, "It's you that's still the child, Daddy."

The cold was creeping into his breast again. "You have to tell me," he said.

"Please don't demand anything more. I'll tell you."

He waited. She took a little time to compose herself. Presently she looked at him, meeting his eyes squarely. "You remember the 'Flower Girl'?"

"Yes, of course."

"Well, that's me. I'm the Flower Girl."

He choked. He actually ducked his head, and his eyes released a gush of tears onto his cheeks.

"It's true," she said, not boastfully, but with a quiet, understated certainty that left no room for doubt. "A bit of a blow for the great newspaper editor, isn't it?" she said. "The watchdog of the public welfare, the pursuer of truth, no matter where it leads. . . ."

It was impossible! Last winter there had been a car accident—a group of young people went over a bank; two of them killed, one died at the hospital. But there had been a fourth person, a girl, who walked away from the wreck. Where she crossed the fence, a rose corsage lay in the snow. Justin's reporter dubbed her the 'Flower Girl,' and described her as the only person who could tell what had happened, the only one who might have saved the injured girl's life. Though she had behaved so shamefully at the accident, he called on her to come forward now and tell her story. Wasn't that the least she could do to heal the common wound which the town had suffered? Justin himself had been outraged and had written an editorial demanding that the police find her. But the Flower Girl was never identified.

He said, "You couldn't be! You went to the dance with Eddie."

"Yes. Remember, I told you. Eddie and I had a fight. He went home without me."

Yes. He remembered. Billie came home late that night, cold and disheveled, her feet soaking wet. She had a fight with Eddie, she said. Some fight. But Justin had never suspected anything deeper. Looking back now, he wondered why. Even when his wife had noticed a change in Billie—a sobering; a melancholy, almost—he had thought little of it.

Billie explained. "I was so mad I started to walk home alone. But it was cold, and the snow kept getting in my shoes, and when this carload of kids stopped and offered me a ride, I took it. I knew them from school, but they weren't members of the Church, and. . . ."

"I'm mad all over again. Wait till I get my hands on that little freak, Eddie. . . ."

"Actually, they were drunk, and I wished I'd kept walking."

"But, what's the problem? They picked you up, and then they had an accident. Maybe you were the lucky one, but it certainly wasn't your fault. We can go down to the police station in the morning and straighten it out."

"How do you mean?"

"Well, tell them what happened. So they can close the book. . . ."

"What good would that do now? It's all over."

"We'd be doing our part. We're good citizens."

"I won't tell them, Daddy. And you can't."

"Oh? Why can't I? You didn't even swear me to silence."

"This is a confession, made in confidence to an authorized ecclesiastical authority, as they say. You can't tell it. I've seen movies, and I know."

"But why not let it be known? You didn't commit any crime."

"I left the scene of an accident."

"But, you're not involved. It wasn't your fault. You were like an innocent bystander. You're not in any trouble. Even if you were, it would be far more important to tell the truth."

"Are you sure?"

"Always tell the truth, Billie. It's your surest guide."

"I can't tell it."

"Of course you can."

"Are you sure? The truth that you're so keen about is that I was driving. They were all drunk, and Rich asked me to be the designated driver."

"Rich?"

"Remember? He was one that was killed in the accident."

"Well. I don't think you have to tell them who was driving."

"They know who it was. Your own paper published it—the Flower Girl was driving. They could tell by the way the bodies were lying in the car. Besides, that's part of your precious truth. Isn't that what you want? If you don't tell them that, why tell them anything?"

"Just a minute," Justin said. "Just quit talking for a minute, okay? Let me think."

Billie said, "How's that for a twist? I was supposed to be the good angel, I was driving. But I'm the only one that didn't get killed. Not a scratch. . . ."

"Your mother was worried about you that night. She prayed all night long."

"Maybe Jeannie's mother was praying, too."

"Don't be absurd."

"You don't think other people pray?"

"Well, of course. Sometimes."

"Maybe it just doesn't do them any good. God doesn't hear them."

"How can you associate prayer with a carload of drunks?"

"You forget, Daddy. I was in that car. But of course I wasn't drunk. So that makes it okay; all I did was kill a girl. If I'd reported it, Jeannie might still be alive." She shook herself. "I can't stand it. It just plays over and over in my head. I can still see the blood, and hear her scream. I knew she had to have help, but I was so scared. . . . I didn't think it would take them so long to find the car." Her eyes were streaming tears, and her face so contorted with anguish that he felt he couldn't bear it. She said, "We don't have to tell them, do we?"

He was completely undone. "I can't even think straight. You've got to give me some time."

"What difference does it make now? It's not going to help anybody."

"It'll help you. It's the only way you can get beyond this."

"That means you'll have to put it in the paper, and everybody will hate me. And I'll go to jail, won't I?"

"This is hardly murder, Billie."

"Jeannie's blood was innocent. Isn't that murder, when innocent blood is shed?"

"There are things we can do. We can fix it. I promise I'll do everything I can."

"Yes," she said. "Everything except forget I ever told you. God says that when he forgives you, he remembers it no more. What do I have to do? I've confessed to the Lord; I've confessed to my bishop. When do I get this forgiveness?"

"Billie, listen. . . ."

"That's why I hoped Brother Link would be our new bishop. I could talk to him. When he was our seminary teacher I talked to him all the time. He wasn't shocked at anything I said, and I know he'd never rat on me. If he was my bishop I'd be okay."

"Well, he's not your bishop. I am, and I can't make an exception, just because you're my daughter."

"An exception to what?"

Justin said, "To telling the truth; to facing up to what we've done."

"I knew this is what would happen. You want me to go to jail, don't you? You want to teach me a lesson so I won't humiliate you any more." She slowly drew away, and rose, and walked across the room. "Now what am I going to do?"

"Billie, you have to trust me."

"Because you always tell the truth, right?"

He was growing angry again. "When did I ever lie to you."

"All your life. You told me you loved me. What kind of love

is it that would send me to jail? You know what will happen if you tell them."

"I can't see any other way."

"It's not too hard. You and I are the only people who know. I'm never going to tell. And I'm not going to stay around here, waiting for them to come and get me."

"What do you mean?"

"I'm running away. Don't try to stop me."

"Are you blackmailing me?"

"Where's the hurt? I'm a liar already, and a murderer."

"You've got to finish school."

"Daddy! Can't you see how lame you are? Here you are looking at me for the last time, and all you can think about is whether I finish school."

"You have to give me time to think."

"Take all the time you need." She started out the door. "I'll stay at Sharon's tonight."

"Billie, wait. . . ."

She looked back at him and raised one eyebrow. It was a thing she did when she knew he was angry.

"Wait a minute." Of course, what she said was right. What difference did high school make when her eternal life hung in the balance? What difference did last winter's car accident make? What good was it to be bishop if he couldn't save his own daughter? Finally he asked, "What do you want me to do?"

"Promise me you'll never tell, that's all?"

All? That was all? Did she have any idea what she was asking? "You know I can't promise that, Billie."

She said, "Good night, Daddy."

"No! Wait. Just a minute. . . ."

"Good-bye." The door closed behind her.

Justin Mercer went to his knees. In recent years he had neglected his personal prayers, and he sensed that the Lord was far from him. From the depths of his soul his spirit called, but the cry seemed to be lost in the vast darkness outside the window. Could God really be out of hearing? He called again, ran after him, as it were, calling.

One part of him said that he was running after the wrong person—that he ought to be out there chasing Billie. But another part said, "No! That would only make her run faster." And while he struggled within himself, he remained on his knees—minutes, hours, he couldn't tell.

Eventually there came to him, as softly as sunlight pushing a shadow across the grass, a strange sense of peace, an almost hallowed serenity. This was incomprehensible. He had always considered himself to be a man of action; now he had no idea what it was he ought to do. He rose stiffly to his feet and walked out into the foyer.

His wife was looking down from the landing, dressed in her nightgown. "Justin. Aren't you ever coming to bed?"

"Yes, I just. . . ." He had no idea what time it was. "I'll be up in a few minutes. I just need a little air." He stepped out into a night so mellow that he stopped there on the porch and breathed it in like some life-restoring elixir. What was happening? Had he forgotten already the abject misery on his little girl's face? What kind of monster had he become?

He drifted down the sidewalk, rudderless, subject to every passing wave of fancy. Should he go down the street to Sharon's house, and wake the family and demand that they return his daughter to him? Should he walk across town to President Bickford's and resign his bishopric? That would require some explanation, and what explanation could he give? He could not discuss the situation with Billie until he had resolved the question between them. He felt uncertain what that question was, but while it remained he could not betray her confidence.

He stopped. Where was he going? What madness had seized him, that he could have felt that glowing euphoria when he stood in the shadow of destruction? The night wind rose, and drove the darkness in upon him. He didn't know which way to turn. As he walked through the park his soul seemed to struggle in waves of despair. He steadied himself against a low stone wall, and without even thinking, sank to his knees beside it. He prayed for Billie; he thought of nothing else, but that simple prayer he repeated again and again.

"Daddy. . . ."

He looked around. Stiffly he rose to his feet, shamefaced that he had been caught. "Billie!" She was standing a few feet away, her hands hanging at her sides, her hair stirred by the wind.

She said, "Don't you think it's time you were in bed? You need your sleep now, you know."

"Yes. I'm on my way. I was just saying my prayers."

"So was I."

"You didn't go to Sharon's?"

"No. I found out I didn't want to do that. I was sitting here in the park, wondering what to do, and I saw you come. . . ."

"You've been watching me?"

"I've been watching you all my life, Daddy. But you were too close; I couldn't really see you, not until tonight. When I watched you pray, I could see you."

"Yes. I'm not very good at it. We need some of your mother's prayers."

"You can't tell Mother."

"I know."

"Maybe our prayers will have to do."

While they talked, they had steadily moved closer together. Now he reached, and took her hand. "Let's try it." They knelt beside the wall, their shoulders touching. "Would you like to pray first?"

"And then you?"

"Back and forth, until we get an answer."

She said, "What are we praying for?"

"For wisdom, I guess. To know what to do? Praying to know what to pray for. What are you praying for?"

"For us, Daddy. For you and me."

"That I won't tell the police?"

"No. Not that."

"Yes, that would be a waste. I'm never going to tell anybody."

"What?"

"I realize now that's not for me to say."

"But you think I ought to tell them?"

"I really don't know. That's up to you."

She gasped, and then, still kneeling, she turned and threw her arms around him. They embraced each other, bent beside the wall. "I thought you didn't care about me."

How could he have been so blind?

"It's all right," she said. "I don't know what's going to happen, but it's all right now."

"Now?"

"You see, you do love me. And I'll bet you didn't even know it before."

He thought, Yes. Yes, I knew. Wasn't there some way I could have shown you?

"And this wasn't just an exercise," she said. "I wasn't testing you. I didn't know what I was doing, any more than you did. But see? Now I'm going to get rid of this. I'm going to face people, and I'm going to sleep nights. And if it means I have to go to jail, I'll do that, too."

"Oh, no, Billie. I'd die."

"Even dying, I don't care about any more."

They remained kneeling, her arms still tight around him. Then she started to disengage herself, and rise. But he wouldn't let her go. "Don't you think we ought to thank him?" Justin's soul was singing, full of light.

"My knees hurt," she said.

"Yes, I know. That will help us keep awake."

She came back into the circle of his arms.

He said, "A prayer of thanks won't take long."

He heard her whisper, "And my other prayer is answered already."

Hanauma Bay

MARGARET BLAIR YOUNG

It could well be that God showed Moses Hanauma Bay in a
vision, to help him understand just how hard it would get to
keep the Sabbath holy. "Temptations like this," etcetera. I
wouldn't doubt that for a second.

Because Hanauma Bay is glorious: clear, warm water, white
sand, submerged lava banks—pocketed, tunneled, walled with
coral and full of fish—always waiting, Sabbath or no.

At the time God was maybe showing that vision to his
prophet, Pele's lava was pouring into the sea like red hot brains,
infiltrating water, fisting bulbous roots of magma across the
ocean floor, blowing muddy red bubbles, then cooling to stone,
At the time, Hanauma Bay was a nervous crater. But after its
lava was spent and the hot spot had moved on, an unhurried
sea paid it back, worked at it, claimed it piece by piece, wore
down its outer curve, and then pooled inside.

That's where we swam, my husband, three kids, and I. In
the crater.

I carried my six-year-old son, Dabby, and tried to walk him
out to the fish. But you can't walk—the spread of coral over the
lava is uneven and unpredictable, and you can't see it from
above water—so you have swim over it. Which we did, both in
our face masks, our snorkels up for air, both of us kicking, my
arm supporting my happy boy from underneath. We saw maybe

fifteen tropical fish varieties: white carp, zebra-striped angels, yellow tang, butterfly fish.

My oldest, Shelly, was on her own, just a yellow-green snorkel twenty feet away, though she'd call back sometimes, "I just saw a _____" and fill in the blank with an exotic fish name, including *Humu-humu-nuku-nuku-a-pua'a*. She was so proud she could say it, I pretended to believe her.

I took four-year-old Junie out too, but not for long. She took a breath of air that turned out to be water and panicked. Before I could stop her she was above water, gasping, and the mask and snorkel were off her head and in the ocean.

Dabby's mask and snorkel. I saw them sinking, first the snorkel—straight and quick—then the mask, slowly, gracefully, dancing down. Disappearing.

"Junie," I said, "honey, why did you take the stuff off you?" She cried and clung to me. "Don't let me go!" she sobbed. "Hold me tight or I will drowned!" I tried to see down but was blind above water, and Junie wouldn't let me duck my head back in. And wouldn't let me swim back, she was so scared, so I moonwalked over the coral with her in my arms, trying to feel with my toes for ledges and hills, nearly breaking my leg two times, and scratching my knee so badly I started imagining sharks.

Dabby, ready to fish-look again, was livid when he saw her without his things.

"Where's my mask?"

Still clinging, she pointed out to sea.

"You lost it?" he shouted. "My snorkel too?"

"Honey, she was scared," I explained, putting her down.

"You *lost them*? You total dumbhead! You stupid little chicken! You wimp! You total wimp!" Dab is a redhead, like me. His face goes pink when he's mad. It was a deep, deep pink now, but white around his lips.

Junie's quivery breaths metamorphosed to a whine. "Not even! Dabby stink-talked me! Dabby called me wimp!" She's a redhead too. Her cheeks go rosy when she cries—which is often. My little ones both looked furiously sunburned, leaning into each other with clenched fists and wide-open mouths.

"She didn't mean to lose anything, Dab," I said, mentally

reviewing how much the equipment had cost. Still encroaching on his sister's space, he paid no attention, so I repeated it, then yelled myself between them: "We'll find your dang stuff!"

They stopped and looked at me. We must have been a sight: three red-faced redheads in a mad huddle.

"We'll find it," I assured us all more softly, glancing around to see who was watching. "Of course we'll find it."

We didn't.

We had an extra snorkel, but the fish are a blur without that underwater urim and thummim, the face mask. Dab couldn't wear mine or my husband's, since ours are prescription, and Shell wasn't seeming to hear when we called her. So Dab was beached.

"Go make a sand castle," I suggested to my redheads. But when Junie started to, Dab kicked it down and said, "Serves you right, wimp."

That bought him five minutes of time out, up against a palm tree. He frowned and snarled the whole time, which bought him another five. When that was up, Junie had two wet hills ready to mold into castles. Dab appraised them with terrible, familiar words: "Totally incompetent."

I couldn't believe he would say that. It wasn't just that they were big words for a six-year-old, but those particular words. I could feel them in the air, pushing me, moving me, stinging my cheeks. "Totally incompetent." It was the phrase my ex-husband, Shelly's "other dad," had often described me with. Where would Dab have heard? How would those words have found their way to his mouth?

David, my present (my eternal) husband, held my hand—maybe to keep me from hitting our boy. Because he knew those sounds were rousing me. He talked in his controlled, bishoply voice: "Dab, I understand you're upset. I hate losing things too; you know I do. But you've got to forgive your sister. She was frightened out there, and she certainly didn't mean for it to happen. Anyway, it's much more important to forgive her than to see a bunch of fish. Isn't it."

"But I wanted to go back out," Dab said, face primed for a good cry.

Dave bowed his sunburned, bald head. "Mom and I will

look for the stuff, son. And we'll come back here another time—remember, we live in Hawaii now. But you'll have your sister forever. You can't afford to stay mad at her. I know it's hard to control that temper, but you've got to try. Remember what we talked about yesterday. What would Jesus say?"

"Jesus made this place too, duh! You think he liked what she did?"

"There's no mask in the world more important than your sister's heart."

"Well, what about if it had diamonds? What about then?" he demanded.

"Even if it had diamonds. There's nothing more important than love in an eternal family."

"Yeah, right." He punched the *T*.

"Can you forgive her?"

"If you find my stuff, maybe."

"Even if we don't. Can you forgive? What would Jesus do?"

No answer to that one. Dabby sulked and let Junie finish her castle. And before long, he was making one of his own.

Shelly was still out there, floating. By the time she came back, it was dusk. She let Dab take a quick turn with her mask, but he didn't see any fish. Apparently the critters know when night's coming. They curl up against the lava walls, or disappear into mysterious pockets, or hide themselves in places we don't suspect, and wait for light.

Shell's "other dad" is named Gus. He visited us three weeks after that trip to Hanauma Bay so he could have some time with his daughter—who is the one good thing in his life, the one person who loves him. He brought his girlfriend, but they were fighting, so he visited our house alone, and gave Shell a Minnie Mouse nightshirt for her present. She oohed and aahed and told him she totally adored it. When he left for the night (off to work on some resolution with the girlfriend), I said, "Does he remember you're fourteen, Shell?"

"Of course he does." She gave me a teenaged look.

"Minnie Mouse? Isn't that a little weird? Why would he buy you something like that? He's always buying you nighties and you never wear one of them. Why does he keep doing it?"

"I don't know. Because he loves me, I guess. He said he couldn't resist it. Said it jumped out at him."

"So he's bribing you with Minnie Mouse?" I held the nightie up like a flag.

"Could be worse."

"You think he'll ever let you grow up?"

She knife-eyed me and moaned "Mom" like a sick ghost.

"Well?"

"I don't know, okay? You think you'll ever let me love him?"

There was a sudden, stunned space between us. Shelly watched me from her side of it. This was not the first time she had hung a pocket in the air.

"Let you?" I repeated thinly. "Honey, I'm thrilled you love him. I'm thrilled." I folded Minnie Mouse and returned it to her. The space was still there, like a misplaced comma.

"I know you hate him. You'll never forgive him. Ever."

"Shelly, that's just not true."

"Oh. Sorry, then." She looks just like him: blonde and brown-eyed, slim, a toothy, mocking smile.

"Where would Dab have picked up words like that?" I said to Dave, curling against him in bed as his arms came around my waist from behind. We could hear the ocean outside, the rhythmic, steady, patient waves.

"What words?"

"Remember? At Hanauma Bay? He told Junie she was 'totally incompetent.' "

"Oh." He stroked my neck. "What's making you think of that? Having Gus around?"

"Shell thinks I'm harboring resentment."

He considered it with a vague "hum."

"If I were harboring resentment, would I have offered Gus a place to stay while he visits? I'm not harboring resentment; I'm harboring him, for crying out loud. Some ex-wives won't even let their kids read letters from the other parent. Now that's harboring resentment."

"Mm-hm. That is."

"Far as I'm concerned, Shell could be God's gift to Gus, the one way he can be saved, and that would be fine with me.

Maybe she'll get called on a mission to Oklahoma and tract him out, baptize him up, you never know. If I resented him—"

"Honey, you're a good person." He kissed the back of my head. "Don't worry. Shell knows how to get you, that's all. And as far as 'totally incompetent' goes, I suspect Dab got it from Shelly. I've heard her say it once or twice."

"Have you?" I turned to him.

"Oh yeah."

"Dab's got a temper problem." I resumed my former position.

He pulled me to him, teasing. "Really? I'm amazed."

"Honey, I'm serious." I reached behind and stroked his sweet, bald head. "It worries me. What if he can't control it? If a man can't control his temper—"

"Dab will be fine."

"If he says things like that to his wife—"

"He won't."

"But what if he does? What if? I love him so much!"

On Sunday, Gus took Shelly. She said she'd pack a couple of shirts, in case one got dirty, but I knew she was packing her swimsuit. Like I said, Hanauma Bay would tempt anyone to Sabbath-break—and Gus doesn't keep our standards; it wouldn't matter to him. In fact, he'd adore it if she shared his sins. That would be a sign of love. And he's a sign-seeker, clinging to her soul. She's all he's got.

"She took her swimsuit," I told Dave after Gus and Shell were gone.

"Did she?"

"I can understand her wanting to please him, even if it means breaking our rules. I can understand that. It's the deception I hate."

"You're sure she's going swimming?"

"I'm sure." I could picture her perfectly, doing jumping jacks in the ocean like a cheerleader for the waves, dancing in the water, swim-walking away.

"So what did you do all day?" I asked her when they returned and Gus went to his room downstairs. (It's not a bedroom really, more a storage area—the windowless place where I sort laundry—but we've put a bunk in it and I don't mind him sleeping there.)

"Oh, just looked around the island. Just drove around, you know. Actually, it was kind of boring."

"Let me help you unpack."

"I can do it, Mom."

But I had the bag, and then the yellow swimsuit in my hand. "It's damp," I observed evenly.

"Is it?"

"Sure is."

"Well, I guess that's from yesterday, then."

"Why is it in your—"

"I don't know, Mom. I guess I accidentally left it there, duh. Look, I wouldn't lie to you. We just drove around. I was bored as heck." She glanced away, then defiantly faced me again.

I nodded. "You've never given me any cause not to trust you, Shelly. So I'll believe you now."

"Well, okay." And she was gone, off to watch *The Empire Strikes Back* with the redheads.

I put on my nightgown as Darth Vader said, "Luke, your destiny lies with me, for I am your father." It's Dab's favorite movie, and we've all seen it way too many times. He could turn it off and we could give the rest of the script verbatim. "Join me. Together we will rule the galaxy. . . ." Tonight the lines sounded like a bad joke, like somebody thought I needed some sympathetic vibration.

I should say, I don't hate my ex.

Living with him was hell. Fire and brimstone, and me two-stepping over the hot spots. But I don't hate him.

I do not hate him.

But.

"Mom?" Shelly was at my door, teary. "Mom, I feel really bad."

"Oh?" I sat on the bed, and she joined me.

"I lied."

"Did you?"

"Yeah. We didn't drive around the island. We went to Hanauma Bay."

"Uh-huh." I brushed my hair.

"I thought you'd be mad if I told you. Thought you'd yell at me."

"Why would I yell?" I kept it quiet.

"Oh, you know."

"Do I ever yell at you?"

"Yeah. Sometimes you do."

"I wouldn't yell. I understand your wanting to be with your dad. And I know he has different standards than we do, and that makes things awkward. I understand all of that. It's the deception I don't like."

"I feel really bad."

I put the brush down and took her hand. "Well, that reassures me. You've got a working conscience, at least." I gave her a brave smile and a hug. "Did you look for Dab's stuff while you were there?"

"Yeah, but I didn't see anything."

"So did you see some good fish?"

"No good fish, Mom. They were all Sabbath breakers."

"Aw, no they weren't. They were in their Sunday schools."

She laughed, and we were friends again.

Later, in my husband's arms, I could hear Gus downstairs, moving around; could hear the bed creak as he climbed into it; could imagine him in the dark, curled up like a comma, a lonely, angry man. Hiding in places I'd never suspect.

That My Soul
Might See

RICHARD H. CRACROFT

I

Thomas B. White Jr. gazed absently at the bleak Salt Lake City skyline stretching away from room 411 of LDS Hospital. Even the leaden drab of Zion in the clutch of the January thaw was more appealing to Tom than the pathetic scene that continued to unfold behind him in the hospital bed, as it had for the past thirty minutes, since Dr. Paul Holton had confirmed the sentence: Thomas B. White Sr. was blind. The second surgery to reattach the retina on his left eye had failed.

Tom Jr. felt as if they were all caught up in a nightmarish reenactment of his father's loss of sight in his right eye a year earlier. Again, the two tedious, motionless months in bed had been for nothing. Again, the blessings, the fasting, Tom Sr.'s name placed each morning in the Salt Lake Temple, the promises and confident utterings of holy men—all for naught. But this time the loss was final. For Thomas B. White Sr., age fifty-three, prosperous businessman, beloved former bishop of the Twenty-First Ward, immediate past president of the Ensign Stake, devoted Latter-day Saint, loving husband, kindly father, life was over—or so it seemed to Tom Jr.

Tom focused his attention on the diverting little drama which suddenly unfolded before his window vista: Hailing the driver with her cane, an old woman hobbled toward the yellow and white city bus idling on Eleventh Avenue. Apparently confident that the driver had seen her, the woman planted her cane firmly on the sidewalk and moved with a rhythmic awkwardness toward the bus door, shut against the cold. Tom's attention drifted toward the adjacent parking lot and a workman vigorously engaged in chipping away with his shovel at acres of thawing ice. Suddenly a puff of black exhaust from the bus caught Tom's eye, and he watched the bus pull away from the curb, with the old woman still a yard from the door.

The woman stopped, her whole body visibly registering dismay, and she shouted something at the departing bus. She raised her cane, shook it at the apparently oblivious driver, then stomped her foot on the sidewalk, twirled around twice, and threw her cane at the diminishing bus. It was a feeble toss, but the cane bounced off the curb and into a puddle of ice-melt. Tom laughed, and at once felt ashamed. He was laughing less at the woman's very human predicament, he rationalized, than at her vigorous dance of anger, her feeble throw, and the futility of it all—which had done little more than attract the attention of the ice-chipper in the parking lot. Registering the woman's plight, the workman leaned his shovel against a "Physicians Only" signpost and strode across the lot to retrieve the old lady's cane, now afloat in the puddle. Pointing and gesticulating, he took her by the arm, assisted her to the City Lines waiting bench, and returned to his own exercise in futility.

Tom shrugged at the irony of the simple drama, amazed that such inconsequential events continued in the face of his father's tragedy, which was taking place just a few dozen yards above them, in room 411—a scene now fixed indelibly in Tom's soul: Thomas B. White Sr. had lain on his back in the darkened room, his head fixed between two rigid forms, his hand stroked by his wife, Grace, and awaited what he had dubbed "The Unveiling."

After Dr. Holton had cut and peeled away the bandages, and the nurse, Afton Blackham, had carefully cleansed two months' accumulation of matter from Tom Sr.'s eyes, Dr. Holton had asked him to open his eyes. He had done so, and his look of anticipation went blank, his mouth went rigid, and Dr. Holton's question, "What do you see, Tom?" became superfluous as Tom

Jr.'s father slowly murmured, as if hoping he were wrong, "Nothing. Absolutely nothing."

The nurse, her professional demeanor gentled by the familiarity and friendship of two months, had stifled sobs and quickly left the room. And Dr. Holton, after a cursory examination, stammered a half-broken, "Tom, I'm sorry. It didn't work. I'm afraid I've done all I can do." Then he slid behind his professional mask and briskly told Tom Sr. he would arrange for some physical therapy and some adjustment counseling, would write orders for his release tomorrow morning, and would see him at his office on Monday morning. Then, his face again contorting in emotion, Dr. Paul Holton had emitted an uncharacteristically subdued, "I'm truly sorry, . . . God bless you," and left the room.

The dynamic lull had been broken suddenly by Grace's sobs. She had embraced Tom's sobbing dad, and then the two of them had wept wordlessly in each other's arms for a long time.

Standing before the window, Tom had wept with them. He felt betrayed. Amidst his struggles to keep his faith intact over the past two years in college, he had kept on teaching Course 15 in Sunday School, and he had kept on praying. And as his father's health problems had crescendoed into one, final, see-or-be-blind retinal surgery, Tom had seen his opportunity clear: If God was listening, if He really rewarded the good and the faithful, if He really wanted to reveal Himself to one who sought Him, He would restore vision to a man altogether worthy of a blessing from the Lord. Tom had performed his first priesthood administration just prior to the surgery and had promised his father that the surgery would be successful; he would see again. That comforting blessing had been reinforced by the Fast Days observed, first by the ward and then by the entire stake—"hedging their bets," his dad had called it.

Pondering these matters as he drove to and from his daily hospital visits, Tom confidently bargained with the Lord, promising in his prayers, "If Thou wilt heal my Father, and grant him vision that he may continue to serve Thee, I will see this as a sign and know that Thou art, and I will serve Thee and proclaim Thee wheresoever Thou wouldst send me."

So much for all that, Tom thought, and watched as the ice-breaking workman hailed the driver of a late-model Plymouth, leaned into the window of the car, then waved goodbye. The car exited the lot, turned right, and stopped in front of the old lady on the bench. The door on the passenger side opened, the woman on the bench stirred, hobbled to the open door, leaned forward, then slid into the seat, the door closed, and the car drove off. The workman leaned on his shovel, watched the car turn down "D" Street, then returned to his chipping.

"Eb! . . . Dear, it's Eb," Tom's mother said, and Tom turned to see his mother rise from her bedside chair to greet the old man with the shock of beautiful white hair who stood, hesitantly and inquiringly, behind the half-opened door.

"Welcome, Eb." Tom's father smiled from his high-recline position at where he supposed Bishop Ebenezer A. Childs stood. "You just missed The Unveiling."

"I know, Tom," said the eighty-four-year-old stake patriarch. "I talked to Paul Holton downstairs."

"The Bishop," who had been released after twenty-five years of service as bishop of the Twenty-First Ward only on being called as stake patriarch, shook hands with all three of them, and, on seeing the red and swollen eyes, apologized for coming at an awkward moment.

"Not 'awkward,' Bishop—you're family," Tom's mother had clarified. "But *hard*."

Eb Childs nodded, walked to the bed, put his arms around his former clerk, counselor and successor, and wept—and the three Whites joined him once more.

"I wish I knew what to say, Tom," he said, blowing his nose on a red bandanna handkerchief.

Tom Sr. laughed, and broke the mood. "That's a first for you, Eb." He inquired about Sister Nora, Eb's invalid wife.

Forgetting Tom Sr. could not see, Eb smiled and nodded his thanks for the inquiry, looked for a moment at the three of them, and said, patting Tom Sr.'s hand, "I was wrong; I know exactly what the Lord wants me to say to you."

Quietly, simply, powerfully, Patriarch Ebenezer A. Childs rehearsed for them the Plan of Salvation; and they listened as if hearing it for the first time. He reminded them of their heavenly home and spoke of the tests to be endured before returning home. "So buck up, m'boy," he chuckled, "and remember, you're over halfway there. Keep an eternal perspective, even if it looks very dark at the moment. Remember the Lord's words to the Prophet Joseph in Liberty Jail: 'All these things shall give thee experience, and shall be for thy good.' You just jumped headfirst into a big pond of Experience."

Suddenly Tom blurted out the thoughts which overwhelmed him, even in the face of the Bishop's words: "But why Dad? Why blindness? Why does God ignore our prayers, our blessings?" He stopped, embarrassed by his outburst but relieved that his father's look was not one of the reproach but of interest in the Bishop's answer.

Unruffled, the Bishop nodded, looked unperturbedly at the corner of the room as if seeking his words, and said to all of them, "You know, we all lead custom-made lives. Our Heavenly Father reaches into our lives to allow the kind of experience which will refine us for His presence. It seems," he directed his words to Tom Jr., "your dad needs the refining experience of being sightless. I don't know why, nor does Tom, nor do you. But, believe me, the Lord knows. I mean, maybe your mother here needs to learn whatever it takes to be the wife of a blind man; maybe you and your two big sisters and their families need to learn what it takes to be the children and grandkids of a blind father."

He turned to Tom's father. "Oh, you don't know exactly *why* this thing has happened to you, Tom, but I just got a brief peek into your future a moment ago, and I can promise you that someday you'll say, with Brigham Young—I read this to Nora just last night—'We have our losses, our crosses, our sorrows, our disappointments; but the day will come in eternity when we will look back on all those things and say, "What of all that? It was but for a small moment and now we are here with our Lord and Savior."' Just wait, Tom White"—Bishop Childs patted Tom Sr.'s arm—"someday you'll find yourself saying of your blindness, 'What of all that? It was but for a small moment, but oh, what I learned from it all!'" He paused, obviously moved by what he was seeing and feeling, then said, in a voice suddenly made thick by emotion, "I prophesy, Tom, in the name of the

Lord, that one day soon, while you are still right here on this earth, you will publicly thank God for your affliction; you will witness before the saints that God 'took away [your] eyes,' as the song goes, 'that [your] soul might see'; thank God that, as He did with Alma the Younger, He has allowed you to plunge into darkness so that you would become enlightened." He stopped speaking.

"Amen," Tom's mother had said, deeply moved. And Tom had echoed the word in his mind.

"So be it," his father had added. "God bless you, Eb. Thank you."

And Ebenezer Child, cutting off conversation, returned to his ailing wife, and to his own death some months later; Tom's mother went downtown to apply for a job (her first in thirty-two years) in the Presiding Bishop's Office; Tom Sr. got out of bed, put on a robe, and began to hobble up and down the corridors on the arms of chatty Pink Ladies (learning his new dependency and defining his independence); and Tom Jr. barely made it to his 11:10 A.M. Anthropology 245 class.

II

Looking out at the Vorarlberg Alps moving by the train window in stately panorama, it seemed to Elder Thomas B. White Jr. that all that had happened in another life. And now his mission was over, and the train was rushing toward Zurich, where he would transfer to the 16:23 train to Basel and the Swiss-Austrian Mission Home at Leimenstrasse 49, where he would be joined in two days by four other released missionaries. Together they would head, via Paris, for Southhampton, the S.S. *United States,* and home.

He felt very good about his mission. He had worked hard, absorbed the gospel by sustained study and teaching, learned how the Spirit of the Lord worked with him, and been successful in making a goodly number of good people in Austria and Switzerland acquainted with the transforming truths of the Restoration. But he stood most amazed at the changes that the Lord had brought about in the essential Tom White, while Tom White was eagerly bringing about essential changes in others.

And he wondered at the chain of events, now so apparent, which had worked those changes in that callow, frightened young man who had stood so tentatively, some thirty months earlier, on the brink of total immersion in missionary work.

The lights in the cabin flickered on and off as the train clattered into the Vorarlberg Tunnel, and Tom gave up attempting to read the newspaper he had purchased from the train window during the stop in Innsbrück. This happy journey home as a seasoned missionary of God had its origins, he mused, in questions raised in his soul by his father's plunge into blindness. Or had it? At any rate, it was his dad's blindness that had led Tom to frame the questions, and it had been the Spirit of the Lord that had led him to the answers—that had prepared him to answer the questions he would encounter again and again in war-ravaged Austria. Widows and grieving mothers would ask him and his companions, "Why would God, if there were such a being, allow such suffering and misery among his children? To what purpose suffering? To what purpose this human crucible?"

Similar questions had hung in the air, unanswered, during those difficult first months of his father's adjustment to the dark. For his part, Tom Sr. had seemed oblivious to such questions. Within months of his release from the hospital he had learned to walk with a white cane, to work with his hands, to read and write Braille. He had founded a frozen foods brokerage business with money advanced by State Vocational Rehabilitation and staffed primarily by visually impaired men and women, and the firm was prospering modestly, making a living for all hands. His father continued to be active in Kiwanis, in serving on city boards, in presiding over the State Association for the Blind, and in serving as a member of the Presiding Bishop's Committee for the Sightless. His adjustment to blindness seemed phenomenal and inspirational; he was sought after as a speaker by civic and church groups throughout the state.

Tom Jr., approaching the Mormon missionary age of twenty, impressed by his father's adjustment and by his apparent trust in a guiding providence, had felt hesitant to discuss the Big Question with his father. He remained a closet Doubting Thomas, awed by the wisdom of his professors and the complex of Truths he was learning at the university, yet attracted by the faith of the lives of men and women who trusted in God. Torn, Tom vacillated between the poles and remained uncertain about preaching Mormonism for thirty months.

Though Tom and his father avoided discussions about religion, they had become even closer after his father's blindness. His mom, sensitive to the changes occurring in her family, had urged young Tom to set aside the usual manly restraints on father-son emotion and touch both of them at times of greeting and departure—"Yes, I know you always kiss me, son, but now you need to hug and kiss your dad, too. Give him the chance to 'see' you with his hands—it's the only way he'll ever have to 'see' you anymore."

It made sense to young Tom. So he kissed and hugged Tom Sr., and so opened opportunities to say and hear the unusually tender word, to open occasional moments of real communication with his father.

One Saturday afternoon in mid-April, after returning from the library, Tom entered the dining room and found his father seated at the table, reading his Braille edition of the Book of Mormon. Tom gave his dad a shoulder squeeze and a perfunctory, "How's it going?"

"I feel very *badly* today," Tom Sr. said, rubbing his reading finger and thumb together and reminding his son of the old grammar lesson about "feeling bad" and "badly" and "good" and "well" which his grammatically exacting father had taught him. Then, abruptly closing the volume, he said, "I must admit, Tommy, that I'm also feeling *bad*."

Tom dropped his books on the table, pulled out a dining room chair, and sat down with a "What's wrong?"

"Son, I don't think I can stand the dark any longer." His face grimly supported his expression. "I don't think I'm going to make it. I can't go on like this."

Stunned by his father's naked despair, Tom stammered lamely, "Well . . . what's the matter, Dad?"

"The Alpha and Omega of the whole thing is this . . ." His father hesitated, wanting to get it just right for a son he sensed was stunned by this revelation of his father's clay feet. "I suppose I'm having my own version of Joseph's Liberty Jail 'O God, where art thou' experience, Tommy. I'm standing in Alma Jr.'s sandals, awash 'in the gall of bitterness.'"

He looked off into the dark that was really the china cabinet, and said, oblivious of Tom, "If a wise and all-knowing Heavenly Father is really in charge, if He really does direct our lives and has to use blindness, or polio, or whatever damnable curse to shape us up, then," he paused, groping, "then He ought to give us a blueprint, some direction, some assurance, like any good building contractor or architect. Then we could understand where we're heading, how we fit in the pattern. He ought to allow us the dignity of knowing the meaning and purpose of our suffering." Tom Sr. stopped, clearly feeling guilt at having revealed so much of his dark side to a son who he sensed was undergoing some spiritual turmoil of his own, and on the verge of making a decision about a mission.

Tom Jr. sat silent, confused. His father, in honoring him with his confidence, had just restated the Big Question that had troubled Tom all these months, the question which seemed to be the hinge on which his own door to the future hung. He groped with how to express his shared doubts with his dad.

"Dad . . ." He had taken the floor, without any idea as to what he would say. Suddenly he saw Bishop Childs in his mind's eye; he felt his words of prophecy rise in his soul and fill him with peace and harmony, and he was overwhelmed by a vision of the plan of God which the Bishop, now a few months dead, had rehearsed that January morning.

He looked up at his father, who was waiting, as open and vulnerable as on the morning he had first ventured to walk, escorted by only his slender white cane, to priesthood meeting, and had become totally confused and had stood helpless in the middle of the road, awaiting assistance—which a frantic Grace, tearfully watching from their porch, had soon sent in a hurried-up young Tom.

Now Tom ventured to the rescue again, assisted by unexpected succor: "You already know the answer to your question, Dad." He hesitated a moment, aware that this was not the tack his father had expected. "You've always taught Mary and Sue and me that Heavenly Father is in charge; that He's running the ship." Conscious of a thrill across his back, a chill across his forehead, he continued: "But it's true. It's no bedside story. He really is in charge. He's the manager. It's like the Bishop said, for some good reason Heavenly Father has allowed nature to take its course, to blind you. Bishop Childs said the reasons would become clear to you in this life. Maybe. But, regardless, Heavenly Father wants you to have faith in Him and to trust Him.

"Hey, as soon as Alma turned on faith in Jesus, the light came on in his darkness. And remember, Dad, that the Lord answered the Prophet Joseph's 'O God, where art thou' with peace and the promise that his afflictions would be 'but a small moment,' after which—hurrah! Whatever happens will be because God directs our course. It's all in His hands."

Listening intently, his father opened the volume he had shut earlier, felt along the tops of the pages, and then, settling on a page, said, "I just read, before you came in, where Nephi said . . . ," his finger moved down the page, "that 'Adam fell that men might be,' but just before that he says . . . ," and his finger moved along the page, 'But behold, all things have been done in the wisdom of him who knoweth all things.'"

Excited, Tom broke in, "That's it, Dad—that's the answer."

"'All things have been done in the wisdom of him who knoweth all things,'" his father repeated. Tom swallowed hard, surprised at how strongly he felt about what he was hearing and saying, conscious again of that gentle shudder up the spine, the flash of light, the chill across his forehead.

"That's the way it is . . . isn't it?" his father said. And then, firmly and sincerely, "And I know that. I forgot it for a moment; I got lost in the dark." He added, "Thanks for turning me around, Tom. I think I can see the light around the next bend." He looked at where he thought Tom's face was, smiled his "I'm all right" smile, and confessed, "I guess I've been struggling with a case of creeping spiritual cataracts." The tears began to flow freely down his face.

"Me, too," said Tom. He pulled his father to his feet, embraced him, and whispered, "There has been more than one blind guy in this room today."

On that April afternoon, soon four years past, Tom's stupor of thought lifted. The Plan of Salvation, with the Lord at its center, focused his life, located him, and gave direction to his prayers, his thoughts, his scripture reading, his studies at the university, his whole life.

The next day, Tom interviewed with his bishop and took the first steps leading to his call to the Swiss-Austrian Mission a few weeks later. And at the May stake conference, Thomas B. White Sr. was called as patriarch of the Ensign Stake of Zion.

The train suddenly burst from the long Vorarlberg Tunnel into blinding light, which filled the cabin. Tom chuckled at the timely—and overt—symbolism.

III

The light continued to grow from that central experience, as Elder Thomas B. White Jr. discovered the next evening at dinner. President Jesse R. Curtis had put Tom to editing the new mission proselyting plan, which Tom and others had been field-testing for some months. The task had engrossed him all day long, until 18:30, when he finally put the red-marked manuscript on the mission secretary's desk and walked, famished, into the deserted dining room, only to discover the dinner was long over, the dishes done, the lock on the refrigerator in place.

"Fasting is good for the soul, Elder," said a voice behind him in a strong German accent. Tom turned to see the face of another elder grinning at him through the doorway.

"But when one is in danger of being translated, as I am," Tom retorted, "a little *Wienerschnitzel* and *pommes frites* helps to keep a body firmly in the world so I can go on being an example to you lesser creatures." Tom smiled and reached out his hand in introduction to Elder Reinhold Berndt, who was being transferred to Interlaken as branch president and was to be instructed about his duties in the morning. He had just arrived, Berndt explained further, and was desperately in need of a companion to track down a stray *Wienerschnitzel* and some *pommes frites,* and perhaps share a piece of *Schwarzwäldertorte.*

"This is clearly to be interpreted as a call from the Lord," Elder White said, looking beatific, "and who am I, about to be translated correctly, to turn down the Lord? I will brave with you the heavy mist settling along the Rhein, and together we will find a hospitable *Gasthaus.*"

As they ate, the two elders exchanged mission shoptalk, established mutual acquaintances, and Tom responded at length to Berndt's request to tell him what he'd learned during his mission, how he had changed, how he felt now it was over. Then, uncomfortable that he had dominated the conversation, Tom asked Elder Berndt how, after just over a year in the field, he had become a legend among the missionaries for his hard work and phenomenal success among saint and sinner.

Berndt, waving off the compliment, said simply and soberly in his accented English, "I love this work, Elder White—I mean, it is the most important thing any of us can do." He rearranged the utensils on his empty plate, seemed to consider whether he wanted to confide his feelings, and then launched: "I didn't want to come on a mission." He looked for Tom's reaction. "A year and a half ago I would have given anything not to have to come here." His voice grew hoarse with emotion. "I wanted to be home, married to Joan, starting a family, entering my profession—certainly not here in Austria or Switzerland, eight thousand miles from everything I love." Elder Berndt spoke almost wearily, as if rehearsing an old grief.

"What kept you out here, then, Elder Berndt?" Tom asked.

"I told you on the way here that my family and I left Düsseldorf as soon as we could after the war. My two older brothers and my father were killed in the war; I was separated from my mother and sisters at the *Zusammenbruch*—'the collapse'—but found them when I went to a sacrament meeting called by a few Mormon survivors. We began making plans, even then, to emigrate to Utah. We finally made it over in 1950; I got a job as a custodian and worked my way through the University of Utah. I graduated in 1957, about the time that Joan and I met at a stake M-Men and Gleaner fireside. I had just started working on my master's degree in accounting—I finished the degree at the end of fall quarter—a year and a half ago. We were planning to get married that January.

"In September my bishop called me in and talked with me about a mission. I told him that I was nearly twenty-seven years old, engaged to be married, and waiting for news about a full-time position with Texaco. I told him that the time for me to go on a mission had passed.

"Good old Bishop Russon." He laughed with affection. "He reminded me of all the Lord had done to spare my life and bring me safely out of the war. He asked if I didn't owe the Lord a little debt of gratitude.

"I told him that I knew all of that but felt I could pay my debt to the Lord in other ways. Maybe someday Joanie and I would go on a mission together. He said, 'That's okay by me, Reinhold, but you had better be sure it's okay with the Lord.' As I left his office, he said, 'Do me one favor, Brother Berndt— pray about this decision, will you? And let the Lord respond in His own way. Don't you dictate His response.'"

"I wasn't quite sure what the bishop meant, but I talked it over with Joanie, and—yes, we prayed about it and decided to go ahead and get married, even though she said she would be glad—well, at least *willing*—to wait for me while I served a mission. Everything was fine until one Sunday evening in October, when we went to sacrament meeting in a friend's ward. The speaker was really good, a blind man. He stood up there and told how much the Lord had blessed him. I began to squirm. He told a lot of stories about the unexpected blessings of being blind, about how much he had learned. Then he said that he wouldn't have chosen blindness as a schoolmaster, but it had been the means to open his eyes, to teach him to trust the Lord, to understand Nephi's words in 2 Nephi. I looked it up and memorized it: 'All things have been done in the wisdom of him who knoweth all things.'"

He stopped speaking, leaned back in his chair, and said, very carefully, "Right there in sacrament meeting I understood why I had been spared in the war, why I had been permitted to come to America. I knew that God had a work for me to do, and that the beginnings of that work lay in serving a mission. Listening to a blind man tell me he was grateful for his blindness, I knew I had been ungrateful; I knew that I had bowed to my own will and not the Lord's; I had been blinder than that speaker; I had been just like those lepers who didn't return to thank Jesus for healing them.

"I suddenly knew what the bishop meant. I knew that Heavenly Father had used that blind man to answer my prayers—not the way I wanted—to open my eyes, so I could really see. Elder White, that man changed the course of my life. My fiancée and I walked from the meeting knowing that I must go on a mission. We went at once to my bishop's office; he was still there. We talked; we wept; we filled out papers. I was called to the Swiss-Austrian Mission. I am here because the Lord wants me to be here."

Tom, thrilling with the now-familiar assertions of the Holy Spirit, said, "And the Spirit affirms, Elder. You chose the better part."

"I often wish I could thank that blind man. I don't even know his name," Berndt mused.

"His name is White, Thomas B. White Sr." Tom grinned. "I know him well. He's my father."

Berndt gasped, then stared at Tom. *"Nein. Unmöglich"*— "impossible"—he said, reverting in his surprise to his native tongue. Then he stammered, *"Reiner Zufall . . .* pure coincidence!"

"Coincidence?" laughed Tom. "Sure, just like our meeting in Basel tonight is *Zufall!* Are you kidding? Uh-uh. After all, 'all things have been done in the wisdom of—'"

" '—him who knoweth all things,'" Elder Berndt completed.

The elders walked silently out into the cold night. The mist on the Rhein had lifted and dispersed, and the eddies around the Wettsteinbrücke reflected not only the brilliance of the moonrise but even suggested the brightness of the stars.

Your Own People

JACK WEYLAND

Twelve-year-old Tamu Brown looked in the refrigerator for another Diet Pepsi, just in case one had somehow gotten separated from the three she'd already had that afternoon. If Mama had been feeling good, she'd have never gotten away with three in a day; it wouldn't matter to her that this was the hottest day of the year.

But Mama wasn't feeling good. Last year she spent three months in the hospital for blood clots. The doctor told her there wasn't much he could do and she might die if the blood clots ever made their way to her heart.

Mama wasn't Tamu's mother; she was her grandmother, but everyone called her Mama. She was raising Tamu because her real mom was away.

Tamu found an orange way back in the fridge. It was so old the peel had started to shrivel but deep inside it was cold and juicy. Tamu was on her way from the kitchen to the living room concentrating on separating the orange into sections when she looked out the window and saw them.

It was the second time they'd come. Tamu always left the house when they showed up. They looked like visitors from an awkward planet. She wondered if they tried to look totally out of place or if it was something that just came natural to them. First of all, they were white in an all-black neighborhood. The only white people who ever came knocking around her neighborhood were cops. These boys were wearing white shirts and ties, and they rode bicycles even though this was the hottest day of the year.

Mama was sitting in the living room right next to the fan. She was a big woman and she needed a lot of breeze to keep cool.

"The white boys are back again," Tamu complained.

"On a day like this?" Mama said.

"The heat must not bother 'em none, 'cause they're on their bikes."

There was a knock on the door.

"Answer it, girl," Mama said.

"What'll I tell 'em?"

"Tell 'em we're not interested."

Tamu opened the door. "We're not interested." She closed the door.

Mama caught sight of them at the door. They looked like they were about to have heat stroke. "Tell 'em they can come in."

Tamu opened the door again. "You can come in."

"But only for a glass of water," Mama added.

"But only for a glass of water," Tamu repeated.

She opened the door and they came in.

"Have 'em sit down," Mama said.

"Sit down," Tamu echoed.

They sat down. Tamu stared at them. They were so soaked with sweat it looked like somebody had taken a hose to them. Even so they had more clothes on than anybody she'd ever seen. She could see an undershirt under their white shirts. The only other people she'd ever seen in undershirts were people in Sears ads but they were paid to do that.

One of them was tall with thin wisps of light brown hair. When he talked he looked like he'd swallowed a mouse that was still fighting to get out. The other one was short, with a quick smile and a soft big belly and a pair of glasses that kept sliding down his nose.

"Kind of hot out today, isn't it?" the short one said.

White folks aren't too smart, Tamu thought, if they had to

go around asking if it's hot out. "This isn't hot," she said. "You should see it when it's *really* hot."

"Shush, girl," Mama said.

The taller more awkward one with the Adam's apple smiled at Tamu and asked, "What's your name?"

"Tamu," she said.

"Tamera?" he asked.

She rolled her eyes. "TAMU I SAID!"

"Tamu, mind your manners," Mama said.

"That's a nice name," the taller one said.

"Get the boys a glass of water," Mama said.

Tamu went into the kitchen.

"AND HOW ARE YOU TODAY?" one of them said so loud and cheerful it was like when a TV commercial suddenly jumps out at you.

"I'm afraid I'm doing poorly today," Mama said.

In the kitchen, Tamu filled two glasses with water from the tap and carried them out to the boys.

"WOULD YOU LIKE US TO PRAY FOR YOU?"

"Here's your water," she said, thrusting the glasses out at the boys. "And you don't have to shout you know. She's not deaf."

"Tamu, mind your manners," Mama said and then asked the white boys, "Tell me again what church you're from?"

"We're from the Church of Jesus Christ of Latter-day Saints."

That was the longest name for a church Tamu had ever heard. And what did ladders have to do with it? She imagined their minister climbing a ladder to give the sermon. She pictured a choir where women with voices so strong they could stun a cat at a hundred yards sang "Oh Bright Mansions Above." Except in her mind the choir in these boys' church would all be standing on stepladders. She could believe these boys came from a church with ladders.

"Is that a Christian church?" Mama asked.

"Yes, ma'am, it is."

"I'd like you to pray for me then."

"We have a special kind of prayer we do," the one with the Adam's apple said. "Would you like us to do that?"

"Yes, if you'd like."

Tamu was all set to laugh inside but there was something about the gentle way the short one asked Mama what her full name was and then put a drop of oil on her head and talked softly with his eyes closed, and then after that another prayer with both their hands on her head. There was something about the way it made her feel inside that made her think that maybe she shouldn't make fun of these boys so much.

When they were done, it was quiet. "You'll be okay now," the one with the Adam's apple said.

It didn't work that way though. A few minutes later just as they were about to leave, Mama moaned with pain. "Oh, merciful heaven," Mama groaned. "This is the worst it's ever been."

"I thought you said it was going to get better," Tamu challenged.

"She will get better," the one with the Adam's apple said.

"Oh, my," Mama moaned.

"Do you want us to call an ambulance?" the short one asked.

"Yes, please, I think I'd better get to the hospital. Tamu, come here. Run to the shop and tell Frank what's happening. Make sure he lets everyone know."

Tamu ran to the auto shop a block away where her uncle Frank worked. By the time she told him and rode back with him in his car, the ambulance had already arrived. They were rolling her grandmother out on a stretcher and lifting her up into the back when she and Frank pulled up. He was a big man with a well-kept mustache and beard. Some people said he was the best mechanic in California.

The two white boys were standing there looking even more confused and out of place.

"Who are they?" Frank asked.

"Boys from the church."

"What church?"

Tamu shrugged her shoulders. "Don't know. It's got a long name though. Longest name for a church I ever heard. And they got ladders."

"What are they doing coming around bothering people?" Frank asked.

"Don't know. They've come before. Today Mama had me let 'em in and give 'em a glass of water."

"You can't let them kind in. Once you do you never get rid of 'em."

"They said a prayer for her."

"Didn't do much good if you ask me," Frank said.

"Is she going to die?"

He patted her arm. "Nobody knows what's going to happen. We just have to wait and see."

Not long after they got to the hospital, the doctor came out from examining Mama. "I'm afraid she's not going to make it through the night."

By eight-thirty the family was all gathered at the hospital in Mama's room. Tamu was the only child there. They let her stay because Mama was raising her and so it was more like she was one of them, one of Mama's children. Her uncle Robert put his hand on her shoulder and said, "She's lived a long life." Somehow that was supposed to make it all right, but it didn't.

Tamu overheard her uncle Frank and his wife Latasha talking. "Who's going to take Tamu if Mama dies?" Frank said.

"If you ask me, her own mother is the one who should take her."

"You know we can't ever let her go back there," Frank said.

"You want us to take her, don't you, even though we're just barely getting by as it is. And where would she sleep? You know we don't have the room for her."

"We'd make room. Somebody's got to take her. That's for sure."

"We can't take everybody."

"She's not everybody. She's part of our family and you know she's no trouble."

"That's right but nobody is ever any trouble until they come. Why does it have to be us, Frank? Just once why can't it be somebody else?"

Frank turned and saw Tamu listening to them. Latasha glared at Tamu and walked out. Frank came over and put his workingman's hand on Tamu's shoulder. "She don't mean nothing by it. It's just that things are hard now for us but don't you worry. We'll make sure you've got a place to stay."

Tamu went in the hall because it was too dreary in the room with the lights down low and everybody talking soft and Mama looking like she was just waiting to die. She made her way to the candy machine. Her uncle Baxter saw her there and gave her a dollar. She bought a candy bar and walked to the end of the hall to a waiting room where she could look down at the parking lot. Near the edge of the lot, she saw the two white boys on their bikes pedaling their way to the hospital. Tamu laughed at the sight of them. They'd ridden their bikes all the way and it must be ten or so miles and this was the hottest night of the year.

Tamu watched them lock their bikes four floors below from where she stood. She hurried back to the room because she didn't want to miss any of this. She stood so she was just to the side of Mama facing the door to the room. On both sides of the bed tall dark faces poked into and out of the dim light.

The two came in. At first they didn't realize there were others in the room. Since it was dark, the one with the Adam's apple turned on the light.

"Turn off the light," Latasha ordered.

You didn't argue with Latasha. The boy turned off the light. "Sorry, it was so dark I didn't know anybody was in here."

"That's cause we're dark," Tamu said, purposely trying to embarrass them.

"I didn't mean that," the one with the Adam's apple stammered. Tamu nearly laughed out loud. Didn't they know they weren't wanted? Why didn't they just let well enough alone and go back where they came from?

"We're missionaries from the Church of Jesus Christ of Latter-day Saints."

Nobody reached out to shake their hands. Everyone was hoping they'd pick up on the fact they weren't welcome and just leave.

"We visited with this woman earlier today," the tall one explained. "We said a special prayer for her, and then, when she got worse, we called the ambulance."

Everyone was waiting for Frank. He was the oldest and it was his place to get rid of them. "Ordinarily," Frank began, "we'd invite you to stay but this is a hard time for the family.

The doctor told us our mama's not going to make it through the night." The two missionaries looked confused. Frank decided he had to make it as plain as possible. "Our mama's dying."

The taller one got a big smile on his face. "Don't be silly, she's not dying. She's going to be just fine. You people just need a little more faith."

Tamu broke out in a big grin. This was better than she thought it'd be. The only question in her mind now was how badly Frank was going to hurt the two white boys. And if it wasn't Frank then it would be Baxter, and if it wasn't Baxter, then it would be Robert, and if it wasn't Robert, then it would be Esther Mae, which would be even worse because she out-weighed Robert anyway.

Frank cleared his throat. "I'm afraid I'm going to have to ask you both to leave now. This is a family gathering and you're not in our family."

The tall one nodded his head. "All right, we'll be going now, but there's something I got to tell you—she's not going to die."

"What gives you the right to come in here uninvited and tell us something like that?" Esther Mae railed. "You should both be ashamed of yourself—going around trying to give people false hope. Now you two get yourself out of here and don't ever come back, you hear me? We don't need your kind around here and that's a fact."

"You don't understand. We gave a special prayer for your mother this afternoon."

"Well you can special prayer yourselves out of here. Who do you think you are, anyway?" Like an unstoppable army Esther Mae was advancing.

They were smart enough to get out of her way. "She's not going to die," the one with the Adam's apple said. He looked for someone who would understand what he was trying to say. His eyes darted around the room and then finally rested on Tamu.

Esther Mae, with her hands on her hips, wanted action. "Frank, either you get rid of 'em or I will."

Frank stepped forward. "You'd both better go now."

The two boys didn't need to be told again.

The aftershock from the boys' visit rattled around the room, each one saying why they were insulted by the visit. Tamu left the room, ran down the hall to the end of the building, and looked down to the parking area. She saw the two white boys come out of the building, unlock their bikes, and ride off into a city that didn't want them around. More than anything now, she felt sorry for them. They were doing their best but their best just wasn't very good. And what did they expect would happen anyway? Why didn't they just give up? What made them keep going day after day? Didn't they know it was hopeless? They were selling something that nobody she knew wanted.

The family waited for Mama to die but she hung on. Finally at eleven-thirty there had to be some tactical decisions made. Latasha took charge. She said that there was no telling how long this might drag on and they had to work it out 'cause some of them had work in the morning and there was no use all of them staying there all night. She volunteered to stay with Mama that night and Robert would come spell her in the morning. When he had to go to work, then Esther Mae would come and Frank would show up after work and stay until midnight, and then Latasha would come back and stay the rest of the night. Baxter would come whenever he could.

Tamu went home with Frank and slept on the couch. They all slept in. The first thing she heard in the morning was Latasha coming through the door and calling out, "Mama's okay! They examined her this morning and they can't find any blood clots. They all went away overnight. He let me bring her home."

Tamu jumped out of bed and threw on her jeans and forced on her shoes and ran to Mama's to see if it was true. If it was true, then it was a miracle. And if it was a miracle, then it was because of those two white boys. And if it was because of them, then she knew they'd come back again and for some reason she couldn't explain, that made her happy.

*   *   *

The next Sunday Frank was grumpy about having to take Mama and Tamu to church. "We must've passed a hundred churches since we been on this road. What's so wrong with them that you can't go there to worship?"

"You know why," Mama said.

"It didn't have anything to do with them two. You would've got better anyway."

"I don't think so."

Since Mama had come home from the hospital, the two white boys came almost every day. They brought videos and lessons and pamphlets. At first Tamu listened from the kitchen but then finally she just gave up and came in and sat on the floor next to Mama and listened too.

They had three lessons in a week and now they were going to church for the first time.

By now Tamu had names to go with the white boys. The tall one was Elder Northrup. He was from Bountiful, Utah. The short one was Elder Foster. He was from Enumclaw, Washington.

They had exited the freeway and were entering a neighborhood with lawns and an occasional swimming pool in the backyard. "The only black folks you're going to find around here will be cleaning ladies," Frank said.

"Just keep driving and keep your thoughts to yourself," Mama said.

"I'm serious," Frank said. "This is crazy. What makes you think these folks are gonna want you coming to their church?"

"The elders said it wouldn't matter."

"And you believed that?" Frank asked.

"God loves all people," Mama said.

"Well, maybe so, but looking around these places, it looks like maybe he loves some folks more than others."

"You're a good boy, Frank, to bring us here. You've always been a good boy."

"My biggest problem, Mama, is that I can never say no to you," he said.

She smiled. "That's the way it's supposed to be."

Frank pulled up in front of the church. It was big and brick and beautiful.

"You want me to go in with you?" he said.

"No, we'll be fine. Just come back and get us at noon."

"Noon? That's almost four hours away."

"The elders said that church is three hours."

"Mama, listen to me, it's not fair for you to tie up my whole day, running you back and forth. Do you understand what I'm saying? Besides, an hour of church ought to be enough for anybody. I thought I'd run out to Wal-Mart, get a few things and then come back for you. I'll be ready to head back about ten. Don't make me wait around until noon."

"All right, we'll be ready about ten," Mama said.

Mama had to walk slow up the sidewalk. By the time they made it to the front door, she was breathing hard and her face was beaded with sweat. Tamu opened the door and they went in. The building seemed deserted.

"There's nobody here, Mama," Tamu said.

"That's 'cause we're early. It doesn't start for half an hour. I didn't know how long it would take. Let's just go in and take our seats and think about God."

They sat down on a side bench three rows from the back. The only sound was Mama's breathing as she tried to recover from the walk into the building. It was deliciously cool and quiet and clean.

Tamu hoped everybody would know how much trouble Mama went to to get ready for church. She'd done her nails and fussed over her hair and fretted if she should wear the gold-colored choke necklace she loved so much or if it would be too much for church. In the end she decided not to wear it.

Tamu felt something happening. She couldn't explain it exactly except it was the feeling that she had come home. It was something she had never experienced and it made her wonder if it was what the elders talked about. She closed her eyes and let the feeling wash over her and wiped her tears with one of the tissues that Mama always had plenty of. "I feel real good, Mama, do you?"

Mama put her big arm around Tamu's shoulder and pulled her in to her. "I feel good being here with you in church. You're a good child—always have been."

"I want to be good, Mama."

"That's all I ever want is for my children to be good."

"Was my mama ever good?"

"Of course she was. Every child is good—and then, I don't know, things change."

"I want to be good all the time, Mama. I don't ever want to be bad." She knew it was the feeling in the church that was making her say these things.

"That'd make me so proud if you'd stay good. I know I made some mistakes with your mama, but sometimes I think I'm getting a second chance with you. All I ever pray for, girl, is for you to be good."

"I will, Mama, I will. I'm going to join this church and be good forever."

"I'll join too and we'll come here every Sunday."

"Oh, Mama, I'm so happy." It felt good to be hugged by Mama.

A boy about Tamu's age came in, took one look, and ran back into the hall. "Come here. You got to see this!"

A woman came in next. She took one look, stopped, and came over. "Is this your first time? I'm so glad you came today. Do either one of you sing?"

Mama smiled. "I used to sing in a church choir."

"Well, I hope you'll sing with us. I'm the choir leader, and we practice after church. Can you come today?"

"Yes, we'd love to," Mama said, and then her smile faded. "Well maybe we'd better not today. My son is picking us up early."

"Where do you live? Maybe I could take you home after choir."

Mama told her where they lived. It was a place where, two summers ago, there had been race riots. The woman's face turned red. "Well, that is kind of far for me. Maybe next time you could ask your son to pick you up at one."

"Yes, we'll surely do that," Mama said.

Tamu watched the people as they came in. Some went out of their way to avoid Mama and Tamu, while others came over and shook their hands and welcomed them to church. Once the elders showed up, everything was better. Elder Foster sat by them while Elder Northrup went and asked people to come over and say hello.

By the time they left at ten, Mama and Tamu had told the elders they wanted to be baptized.

* * *

The week after Tamu was baptized was the happiest time she'd ever had. She felt totally clean and forgiven. Every night she and Mama read the scriptures. The elders came every day and sometimes they stayed and ate with them. Tamu took down all her pictures of rock stars and put up pictures of temples the elders brought her. Every morning she knelt down and said her prayers.

Everything was good until the meeting they called fast and testimony meeting. It started out the same as the other times but then the man said he was turning the meeting over to the bearing of testimonies.

A woman got up and said, "Lice have just entered the church and so everyone needs to get a special kind of shampoo. I can give you the name of it after the meeting. And then I think we all need to be careful who we let our children play with."

Some people turned around to look at Tamu and Mama. Elder Northrup leaned over to Mama and whispered, "Don't pay any attention to her."

Tamu wasn't at all upset because she knew the woman wasn't talking about her because she'd never had lice and Mama had never had lice and nobody in her family ever had lice. She must be talking about someone else because if she didn't have lice she couldn't give 'em to anyone.

Beads of sweat were forming on Mama's forehead. "What's wrong, Mama?"

"We're never coming back here."

"She wasn't talking about us, Mama."

"She was so, girl."

"We don't have lice, Mama."

"She thinks we do."

"I'll go tell her then after the meeting."

"You'll do no such thing."

"But we have to come back so we can sing with 'em."

"We're not singing with these people. You stay here. Keep looking back at me. I'll let you know when Frank comes."

The missionaries left the meeting to go talk to Mama. Tamu couldn't tell what they said but it must not have done any good because Mama didn't come back into the chapel.

A few minutes later Mama nodded her head from the hall and Tamu got up and walked out of the chapel.

*   *   *

The missionaries tried but Mama could not be persuaded to return to church. The bishop and his wife came by and brought them some cookies and pleaded with Mama to give it another try but it did no good. She couldn't let it go. "None of my children ever had lice. That woman had no call to talk like that about something she don't know nothing about."

"I talked to her about what she said. Her kids did pick up lice from somewhere."

"Not from us."

"I tried to tell her that. I guess it was the way she was raised."

"I'm not ever going back," Mama said.

"I think that's a mistake." A short time later the bishop asked Tamu if she wanted to keep going to church.

Mama didn't like Tamu to be pressured into something she didn't want. "She and I'll talk about it. If she comes, she comes. We're not promising you anything."

After the bishop and his wife left, Mama said, "What are you going to do, girl?"

"I might go back."

"Why on earth would you go back?"

"Remember how it was when we first got there, before anybody came, how peaceful it was, and the feeling we got?"

"What feeling you talking about?"

"A good feeling. It was like I'd come home."

"What are you saying, girl? That everything was fine until people came? What good is it to belong to a church where you only feel good when there's nobody there?"

Tamu knew that what she'd felt was real. "I'm going back, Mama."

"You'll be the only black there."

"I don't care. I'm going back."

"You'll have to talk to Frank about that. He may not want to take you, you know. Sunday is his only day to sleep in."

The next Sunday, though, Frank did take her to church. "This is the last time I'm going to do this. The only reason I'm doing it today is I need to pick up a few more things at Wal-

Mart. From now on, you're on your own. There's plenty of churches by us you can walk to. It don't make sense to travel this far just to say a prayer or two." Just before dropping her off, Frank asked, "You sure you're going to be okay?"

"I'll be okay."

"There's nobody here yet."

"That's 'cause we're early."

"When does it start?"

"In half an hour."

"How come we're so early?"

"That's the best time."

"The best time for what?"

"For the feeling."

"What feeling?"

"Don't know for sure."

Frank shook his head. "You are the craziest child I ever did see."

Tamu got out and ran up the sidewalk to the front door as Frank was driving away.

The door was locked. They're not even going to let me in this time, she thought. They got to. They got the feeling in there. They can't keep me out. If they don't want me around, I'll leave once they all get there. Just let me sit there by myself until they start coming, that's all I ask. She went around the building to the back door. There were four cars parked in back. She tried the door. It wasn't locked. It wasn't me, she thought. It was just because they all drove here and nobody goes in the front, that's all.

She went into the chapel and sat down. She closed her eyes and said a prayer for the feeling to come. It was there but not like the first time. She kept thinking about what Mama had said. "What good is it to belong to a church where you only feel good there when nobody's there?"

She worried about what it would be like once the people came. She'd be all alone this time. Elder Northrup was going home next week and Elder Foster thought he was about to be transferred soon so before very long *they* wouldn't even be there for her to sit with.

She wondered if the woman would get up and talk about

lice again and about her special kind of shampoo and telling
people they shouldn't let their children play with just anyone.
She wondered if people would turn around and look at her
again. Maybe Mama had been right all along and it was a mistake for her to come back again all by herself.

People started to come in. A man came by and shook her
hand and asked her name. He told her he was the steak president. He told her he was glad she'd come.

A girl came up to her. She was blonde and fragile looking
and was wearing a long peach colored dress with lace. "You're a
beehive," she said.

Tamu knew she wasn't a beehive. "And if I am, what does
that make you?"

"I'm a beehive too. You got baptized didn't you?"

"Yeah."

"So now you have to go to beehive class."

"When's that?"

"It's the last hour. You gonna come today?"

"I can't."

"You got to."

"Why?"

"We need more beehives. We had five but when they turned
fourteen they all became my maids."

Tamu's mouth dropped open. "You got five maids?"

The girl looked at her for a long time before she said anything. "I don't have any maids. I said they're my-a maids."

Tamu had no idea what this silly girl was talking about—
either they were her maids or they weren't.

Once she'd done a report on Mayan Indians. Maybe that
was what it was all about. She didn't remember very much
about the report. Maybe for now it was best just to play along
like she understood it all. "Well, isn't that something?"

"You all alone today?" the girl asked.

"Yeah, mostly."

"What's your name?"

"Tamu."

"Do they call you Tammy?"

"No," she said emphatically. "They call me Tamu because
that's my name. What's your name?"

"Jennifer. You want to sit with me and my family during church?"

"You'd better aks your mama if that'd be all right."

"You mean ask."

"That's what I said," Tamu said.

"No, you said 'axe your mama.'"

"Yeah, well you said Mayan maids." They both smiled at each other.

"Do you have lice?" Jennifer asked.

"No."

"I didn't think so. My mom and dad said that was mean what that woman said. Come sit with us. We always sit in the same place. Near the back. Everybody wants to sit there but we come early because my mom has to put the hymn numbers on the board."

Tamu looked up at the woman putting the numbers on the board. The woman looked back at her and smiled. "Hello," she called out.

"Hello," Tamu echoed.

"You got one of these yet?" Jennifer asked, showing her a small white booklet.

"No. I don't got anything yet."

"You can have that one. It's an extra. This tells how you got to live when you're a member."

Tamu read the cover—*For the Strength of Youth.*

A two-year-old came tottering up the aisle toward them. "That's my brother Travis," said Jennifer. "You might need to help me take care of him if that's all right."

"I don't mind."

"If you get hungry, we got Cheerios. It's mostly for Travis though."

It was better being with someone. Travis was fascinated with Tamu, and near the end of the meeting he ended up asleep in her lap.

At ten-fifteen Tamu went out to talk to Frank. "I'm going to stay."

"What are you talking about? You can't stay. How would you get home?"

"I don't know. Walk I guess."

"You can't go walking around a neighborhood like this. They'd have you arrested and in jail in ten minutes."

"I got to stay," she pleaded.

"Why do you got to stay?"

"They need me."

"What are you talking about? They've gotten by just fine without you all this time. What makes you think they suddenly need you now?"

"They need more beehives."

"What are you talking about, girl?"

"I'm not sure but I think beehives are girls my age."

"I swear I don't know what's gotten into you. Why can't you just be with your own people?"

"Let me stay, Frank, please."

"No sir, you get in the car right now. I've spent most of the only day I've got off driving you around and what good is it doing? You think you're better?"

"No, I don't."

"Well I'm not so sure. You got to learn to accept who you are and be proud of it. Now get in the car. I mean it, girl. I'm your uncle and I got responsibilities when it comes to you."

She cried all the way home. She knew she'd never be allowed to go back to the church again and she'd never see Jennifer again and she'd never hold Travis on her lap and she'd never find out all what it meant to be a beehive.

"There's no call for you to carry on so," Frank said.

"You don't know what it's like in there. You don't know the way it feels. And I'll never have it again."

"What feeling you talking about?"

"I don't know what it's called."

"I'm doing what I thinks best. Next Sunday you can go to one of the churches around where we live."

When he let her off, she ran inside to her room and fell down on the bed and cried some more. Mama did her best to make her feel better. She made a cake and borrowed her favorite movie. Tamu still felt bad but she let Mama talk her into having a piece of cake and some milk and she did watch the movie with Mama.

At nine that night Frank came over. He sat down right next to her and put his hand on her knee. "How you doing, child?" he asked.

"Okay I guess," she said dully.

"You left this in the car," he said, handing her the *For the Strength of Youth* booklet.

"I guess I won't need that anymore," she said, tossing it into a wastepaper basket.

"I read it just to see what they were teaching you. You really think you could live the way it says in here?"

"I think I could."

"They got some pretty tough things in there. No drinking, no smoking, no carrying on. Looks to me like it'd be almost impossible to live the way they say."

"I could do it."

"How do you know that?"

"Because I know how I feel when I'm there."

"I don't think you can live like it says you're supposed to." He paused. "But if you could, then . . . then you'd escape a lot of grief. I see it every day around here."

"I could do it, Frank. I know I could."

"Well, maybe we should see if you can. From now on I'm going to be watching to see how you do. You understand what I'm saying?"

She nodded. But there was a question she was almost afraid to ask. "Are you going to take me to church?"

"I will, girl. I'll take you there and I'll pick you up."

"You'll pick me up at noon?" she asked.

"That's right, at noon." He smiled at her. "Looks like I'm going to end up being Wal-Mart's best customer, doesn't it?"

"Why are you doing this, Frank?" she asked.

"I guess that's my business."

As she thought on it later that night, she wondered if maybe the reason Frank changed his mind about taking her to church was that in two years he'd have a daughter who'd be a beehive too.

By that time, Tamu thought, Jennifer and I will be Mayan maids.

Still Dancing

SUSAN DEAN STRANGE

Deanna shut the front door behind her and almost dropped her books on the hall table as she usually did, but caught herself. A date with Todd was worth it. She stacked her books neatly and even hung up her jacket.

She took a deep breath and called, "Mom, where are you?"

"I'm in the kitchen," her mother, Joan, said, "where I've been the last ten years you've been coming home from school."

Deanna walked into the kitchen and kissed her mother on the cheek as she always did, then decided to add a hug and still another kiss.

"My, Deanna," Joan said, "you're in a good mood today." She handed Deanna a bag of Oreos. "Here, your favorite kind."

Deanna sat down at the table and grabbed a handful. Thank goodness they were her mother's favorite too. She'd really be in a good mood after she ate a few. "Have a cookie, Mom," she said. "Have two or three or four."

"No thanks. I'm on a diet. A serious one." She sat down across from Deanna with a diet drink.

Oreos out. Maybe flattery. "You sure look nice today, Mom. Is that a new blouse?"

"You gave it to me two years ago. How was your history test?"

"I think I did okay. Did you go to the beauty shop?"

Her mother looked a little suspicious, but just answered no.

"Then it must be your makeup. Did your Mary Kay order come today?" She bit off a cookie and tried to look as innocent as she could, ignoring the hard stare her mother was giving her.

"What do you want, Deanna?"

"Oh, Mom," Deanna said, then went in for the kill. "You're the best mother in the world, and I know you'll be thrilled that Todd got his driver's license and asked me to go to the dance next week with him. I told him that I had to ask you but that I knew it would be okay. Okay?"

Without a moment's hesitation, Joan said, "No."

Deanna had expected that at first. She was prepared. "Is it because I'm not quite sixteen yet?" she asked. "You know you've always told everyone that I was mature for my age. And I'll be sixteen in just ten short months."

"You know the rule. You can't date until you're sixteen. It worked fine for your sisters."

"But Eve's mother is letting her go. We could even double-date." Deanna knew she was losing. And she knew just what her mother was going to say.

"I'm not Eve's mother."

Deanna had been right.

"But how can I disappoint Todd? He got a hundred on his driving test, and he's even looked at tuxedos."

"Give me the phone and I'll explain it to him." Joan stood up and poured a glass of orange juice. "Let's not argue, Deanna. We've always agreed on this before."

"Mother!" Deanna was beginning to get mad. Usually her mother was great. Had she forgotten what it was like to be in love? "I've waited forever to date Todd. We've liked each other since fourth grade." She really wanted to say *loved*, but she didn't want to use such a strong word with her mother.

"No, Deanna."

"Just this one little date and I won't ask again until I'm sixteen?"

"Deanna, don't beg. You usually get just about anything you want, but on this I will stand firm."

One last try. "Don't you want to ask Dad about this?"

"No," her mother said. "He came home from work early

feeling a little under the weather, and I don't want you to bother him. I'm going to take him some juice."

Deanna noticed then that Mom had put some juice and cookies on the tray that was reserved for sick people. So that was it, then—her worry about Dad was clouding her reason. She just needed some time to reconsider.

"Here, Mom," she said, taking the tray. "I'll give the tray to Dad, and you can rest a few minutes before supper. I'll set the table and even make the salad."

"Thank you, Deanna." Then, as Deanna walked out of the kitchen, she said, "Deanna?"

"Yes, Mom?"

"The answer is still no."

Deanna knocked quietly on her parents' bedroom door and walked in. Her father was lying in bed, and he did look pale.

"Hi, Dad," she said. "I brought you some cookies and juice. Mom said you weren't feeling well."

"Thanks, sweetheart," he said. He propped himself up on the pillows and took the tray from her. "How was school today?"

"Fine."

"Did I hear you and your mother arguing?"

She stood before him and wondered if she should tell him the whole story. He could probably get Mom to change her mind. But he did look pale.

He decided for her, though. "Whatever it was, Deanna, mind your mother," he said. "Even if you don't agree."

"Yes, Dad," she said miserably. She hadn't felt so persecuted since she had wanted to get her ears pierced again.

While her dad ate his cookies, Deanna picked up the wedding picture of her parents that her mother kept on the dresser. She liked to look at it and try to imagine them when they were both younger and thinner. In the picture they were obviously in love, gazing into each other's eyes. If only they could remember what it was like.

Dad was finished now and was lying back against the pillows. She put the picture down and took the tray from him. "Do you need anything else?" she asked.

"No, I don't think so. I just don't want you arguing with your mother again."

"But what if she's wrong?" Deanna asked hopefully. Maybe it wasn't too late.

"Even if she is, which I doubt," he said, "changing her mind would take more strength than I have tonight."

The next morning at breakfast she gave her mother the silent treatment, but Mom was even more silent that she was because her father hadn't slept well. Deanna tried to look depressed, but even that was wasted. Mom looked more depressed.

She finally gave up and peeked in at her father, but he was asleep and she didn't bother him. Her last hope had been that her parents had discussed the problem last night and Dad had convinced Mom to change her mind, but evidently that hadn't happened.

* * *

Deanna usually didn't see Todd until third period, so she and Eve had two classes to plan how she was going to break Todd's heart and convince him not to ask anyone else to the dance.

"He wouldn't do that to you," Eve said. "He loves you."

"I know," Deanna said. "But he's so excited about being able to drive. Why did my mom have to do this to me?"

"She's usually so nice," Eve said. "Like the time she let us have that barbecue for the yearbook staff and I set the picnic umbrella on fire cooking the hamburgers. She gave all the firemen a cupcake."

"Yeah," Deanna agreed. "But she and Dad have been acting so old lately. About the most exciting thing they've done is to get double cheeseburgers instead of regular ones the other night. And that was just because we had coupons."

"Well, they've been married so long, what do they remember about being in love?"

By third period they had decided that Deanna would assure Todd that they could have just as good a time if they met at the dance. And that if he didn't drive any other girl anyplace for the next ten months, Deanna could still be the first girl that he drove.

She never got to third period, though, because her mother called the school office to say that her dad was having chest pains and was on his way to the hospital. Deanna, frightened and quiet, was driven to the hospital by her guidance counselor.

Hospitals had terrified her since she'd had appendicitis, and she was afraid she'd faint as she walked down the long hallway. When she reached the right room she took a deep breath before she pushed open the door.

The room was full of white coats and machines. As the people moved around she could see her father on the bed, looking small and even paler. He was alternately answering questions and closing his eyes, so he didn't see her. A nurse did, though, and walked over to her.

"Are you his daughter?" she asked.

"Yes," Deanna said. "Is . . . is he going to be okay?"

"He's getting the best care possible," the nurse said gently. "Your mother is down in the waiting room. We'll come and get you when you can come back in."

She walked down to the waiting room and saw her mom standing in front of the window. She looked tense and alone. Deanna walked over to her. "Mom?"

Joan turned around. "Deanna, I'm glad you're here." She put her arms around her daughter. "Did you see your father?"

"They wouldn't let me," she said. She hugged her mom back and felt a little less afraid. "Will he be okay?"

"I hope so, honey. I've never seen him in so much pain in all the years we've been together. It scared me to death." Joan's voice broke.

Deanna put her arms around her mother's shoulders, a little awkwardly since she was not used to doing the comforting. "Don't cry, Mom. He'll be all right." But she wondered if she could believe her own words.

"I'm sorry, Deanna." She wiped her eyes. "It's just that nothing has ever been seriously wrong with Dad before."

Deanna remembered back two years ago when Grandpa had died and Mom had looked as solemn as she did now. But then, Dad had been with her, and she hadn't looked so alone. "He'll be okay," she said again.

They sat down on the green vinyl couch. Mom became calmer as she told Deanna about how her father had had chest pains and about how she had called for an ambulance. As she finished, a nurse came to tell them that they were taking her father downstairs for some more tests, and he wanted Joan to go with him.

"Will you be all right?" her mother asked.

"Sure. I'll wait here, and maybe they'll let me see him when he gets back."

Joan gave her a hug and started to leave, but turned back. "Will you do me a favor, honey? I was supposed to give a report at the Booster Club meeting tonight. Can you look in my wallet and find Mrs. Sterns' number and tell her I can't make it?"

"Sure, Mom."

She looked out of the window for a few minutes, wondering how her mother could stand being around her father with all those tubes and needles stuck in him. They made her feel faint.

Then she sat down and started looking through Mom's purse for the notebook she kept for addresses and phone numbers. She usually didn't snoop around in her mother's things. After all, she didn't want Mom reading her diary. But when she opened up the notebook a piece of paper fell to the floor, and she thought that it might be the number she needed. She opened it up and began to read.

In her father's handwriting was written:

> If I could choose from every woman who breathes on this earth the face I would most love, the smile, the touch, the voice, the heart, the laugh, the soul itself, every detail and feature to the smallest strand of hair, they would all be Joan's.

Deanna smiled, because her father was very unpoetic. If it wasn't in *Newsweek* or the *Wall Street Journal*, he couldn't remember it. She recognized the passage from Mom's favorite movie, *Camelot*. It was King Arthur's speech about Guinevere. Dad must have given it to her way back in college.

Then she felt a shiver of excitement, because that poem proved that they were once madly in love. If she showed this to her mother and reminded her how romantic Dad used to be, surely she would change her mind about the dance.

She fingered the note, trying to imagine her father giving it to her mother and how long her mother had kept it. But as she turned the paper over to put it back into the notebook, she saw a date written on it. And it didn't take a calculator to figure out that Dad had given Mom the gift of that beautiful poem exactly twenty-three days ago.

It was unbelievable. Her father giving her mother a poem like this? Todd was in advanced English, and he'd never given *her* a poem.

Her parents? Her father was a man who snored through the evening news every night. Her mother was a person whose favorite food was tapioca pudding. Boring.

But then as she thought about it, she remembered that Mom never ran the dishwasher during the news so she wouldn't wake Dad up. And Dad always made sure he bought tapioca pudding mix when he went grocery shopping.

She was so immersed in this revelation that she didn't hear her mother come in until she was beside her. "Deanna, your father is going to be okay. It's not his heart. They think it's something wrong with his esophagus that medicine can take care of."

"Oh, Mom," Deanna said with relief. "I'm so glad." She grabbed her mother in a big hug.

They talked for a few minutes about Dad's tests, and then Deanna decided there was no time like the present for what she wanted to say.

"Mom," she began, "about the dance—"

"Deanna, let's not get into that now."

"But I think you'll like this, Mom," Deanna said. "I've decided not to date until I'm sixteen. And I won't even fuss about it."

Joan looked at her a few seconds. "That's all?"

"That's all."

"But I don't understand," her mother said.

"You're wrong, Mom." She handed her mother back her pocketbook. "You do understand. You really do."

Dad and
the Studebaker

RICHARD M. SIDDOWAY

When we were growing up in the fifties, the Forbush family reunion ranked just above having a root canal without anesthetic. We technically belonged to the family, but since we lived in Salt Lake and the rest of the family lived in Parkerville, a three-hour drive away, the only time we saw our cousins was at the annual family reunion.

We would come in corduroys and shirts with buttons. Our cousins would wear coveralls and no shirts or shoes. There were the three of us: my oldest brother, Earl; then Bob; then me—Carl, the runt. Our thirty-odd cousins viewed us with distrust and disdain. The picnic in the Parkerville City Park was always a disaster. As we tried to juggle flimsy paper plates full of food, our cousins would jostle us and potato salad would join Jell-O on our shirt fronts and laps. We, of course, took the scolding from our parents. And as I raised a paper cup of homemade root beer to my lips, one of my cousins invariably would bump my elbow, sending a cascade of foaming brew into my face. These were not happy times.

The one bright spot at the family reunion was Uncle Heber. My mother's younger brother by two years, Heber was the peacemaker of the family. He smoothed over the squabbles, wiped up the spills, and organized the relay races. As we left for home, he always slipped a silver dollar into each of our pockets.

As much as I disliked the family reunions, I looked forward to seeing Uncle Heber.

My father and Uncle Heber first met, so I am told, at my parents' wedding. Uncle Heber told my father he'd better take good care of my mother. My father took offense at Uncle Heber's "meddling" and developed a dislike for him. Dad was like that—quick to take offense, and slow to forgive. I think, too, he was jealous of Heber's hair. Dad was nearly bald by the age of thirty. All that was left was a narrow fringe, which he let grow until it was nearly shoulder-length. He then combed the right side across the top of his head to the left side and vice versa. Until the invention of hair spray, he held his hair in place with a generous application of Vaseline. Heber never lost a hair, as far as I could tell.

"Heber will never amount to anything," my father frequently said to my mother, "unless he gets away from that hick town he lives in." My mother, of course, had been born in that same town.

Uncle Heber began working for the Parkerville State Bank right after he got home from the mission he served for The Church of Jesus Christ of Latter-day Saints. At first he was a teller, which meant he swept the floors and emptied the trash cans as well. One of the frequent bank customers was Cora Mae Wheelwright. When Heber became a teller, she became an even more frequent customer. After a year of courting, they married.

Aunt Cora Mae used to chuckle, "When we were dating Heber always wanted to take me to the bank so he could get me a loan." I was nearly thirteen years old before I understood the joke.

By the time I graduated from high school and our family quit going to the reunions, Uncle Heber had become chief teller, then loan officer, then vice president of the bank. Each time Uncle Heber was promoted, Aunt Cora Mae wrote a letter to my mother with the news. My mother learned not to tell my father about Heber's success.

There are pessimists, and then there are pessimists. My father was the high priest of the Church of Eternal Pessimism. Some people look at a glass that is half full and see it as half empty. My father always noticed that the glass needed washing, too. Mother called him "the leprechaun" because he was always searching for a pot of gold. Dad was a great salesman. He had the gift of gab, and he always believed in the product he was selling. Unfortunately, he also always believed his boss was cheating him. After a year or two of working for a company, my father and his boss would have a "confrontation." Dad would then start looking for a job with another company. The new company, he believed, would provide the road to the pot of gold. It always proved elusive, however.

A new job always meant a new car. My father was a car freak. Some people believe that you are judged by the clothing you wear or the size of your house, but not my father. He believed that your automobile was your statement to the world. Not that we ever had a *new* car—I mean, one right out of the automobile dealer's showroom—but we always had cars that were new to us. Every Saturday, rain or shine, my father washed and polished his car. Twice a year he waxed it. We were forbidden to eat anything in the car. Most men's homes are their castles, but my father's castle was his car.

When Mother read Aunt Cora Mae's letter nearly forty years ago about Uncle Heber's promotion, she exclaimed to my father, "Well, Heber's got a car like yours—a Studebaker." My father was reading the newspaper. As a six year old, I watched the paper slide downward until his eyes appeared over the top of it.

"What year?" he growled ominously.

Mother scanned the letter. "Cora Mae doesn't say. All she says is that Heber liked your Studebaker so much last year at the reunion that he went out and bought one for himself."

"Two-door or four-door?" rasped my father between clenched teeth. His eyebrows knit together above the newspaper.

My mother shrugged her shoulders. "Doesn't say." She also neglected to tell my father that the reason for the new car was another promotion Heber had been given. "Do you want me to write Cora Mae and find out?"

"Up to you," gruffed Father. Mother smiled and wrote a letter to Cora Mae.

A week later my father was adjusting the controls on our television set. He was working for an appliance store at the time and had brought home a Hoffman with a deep yellow screen. He had developed a passion for playing with the knobs on the back of the television set in an attempt to get a better picture. The result was often no picture at all.

My mother said, "Got a letter from Cora Mae today. Heber's Studebaker is a '51 tan two-door. She says he got a good buy on it."

My father let out a yelp of excitement. "A '51! We've got a '53, and ours is a four-door. I can't wait to go to the reunion! His is tan—ours is yellow!"

The only thing Heber's car had that ours didn't was a little plastic propeller attached to the cone on the grill. But even that didn't dampen Dad's enthusiasm over owning a car two years newer than Heber's. Dad kept his Studebaker until he was certain Heber had sold his. Although the Studebaker was replaced by a Buick, it became the focus of conversation whenever Uncle Heber's name was mentioned.

My brother Earl graduated from high school and wanted to enroll in college. Dad wanted to help with tuition, but he was looking for another job at the time. Earl had just about given up hope when the letter came. The return address was from Parkerville. "Dear Earl," it began. "Your Aunt Cora Mae and I are very proud of you. We'd like to help our favorite nephew with his college pursuits. Enclosed is a check for $200." Two hundred dollars! Tuition for a quarter. Each quarter another letter arrived for Earl.

When Bob, my middle-button brother, graduated, Dad was between jobs. A letter arrived from Parkerville. "Dear Bob, your Aunt Cora Mae and I are very proud of you. We'd like to help our favorite nephew with his college pursuits. Enclosed is a check for $225." Uncle Heber apparently knew that tuition had gone up twenty-five dollars.

When I graduated a similar letter from Parkerville arrived. It appeared that I was now the favorite nephew. "It's a shame Heber and Cora Mae never had any children of their own," said my mother. "I think it's wonderful they think so highly of you three boys."

Our contact with the Forbush side of our family shrank as the years sailed by. We didn't see much of our immediate family, either. Earl became involved in insurance sales. Over the years he worked for a number of companies and was so busy that our contact was minimal. While Bob was in college he worked for an automobile dealership in Salt Lake. Although he had a degree in plant physiology, he eventually opened his own automobile repair shop. My own medical practice required fourteen-hour days. The family drifted apart.

Then Mom died. She and Dad had spent fifty of her seventy years together. At the cemetery after the dedication of the grave, Uncle Heber and Aunt Cora Mae hugged Dad before leaving for Parkerville. They climbed into their new Cadillac and waved as they drove away. "Show-offs," said Dad. "He's never forgiven me for owning that yellow Studebaker."

A few days later the phone rang at my office. "Doctor, it's your brother Earl." Earl never called unless there was a crisis.

"Earl, what's wrong?" I exclaimed into the phone.

"Nothing. I just had a great idea. I was driving down from Twin Falls the other day and I saw this car and—well, I had an idea."

"What car?"

"An old Studebaker. It's out in a field beside a barn. On impulse I stopped and asked the farmer if he'd sell it. He will for five hundred dollars."

"Why do you want it?" I asked.

"For Dad. Didn't you hear him at the funeral? He's never forgotten that Studebaker. I thought maybe you and Bob and I could get this old car restored and give it to him for his birthday next spring. It wouldn't cost much. I mean, Bob could do all the work on it, and the two of us could help with the costs. What do you think? Should I go get it?"

"How does Bob feel about it? I think he's going to end up doing most of the work."

"He says it's okay with him if it's okay with you. What do you say? Want to help me go get it?" I hadn't heard as much excitement in Earl's voice in years.

"Sure, Earl. When do you want to go?"

"Thursday's your day off, isn't it? If you can pass up your golf game, maybe we could take my truck up and haul it back. Okay?"

"Sure, Earl." I paused. "Do you want me to bring the five hundred dollars?"

"That would be great! I'm a little short right now, but—"

"Thursday's great, Earl."

After paying five hundred dollars for the car, it took only two hundred more to put tires on the rims before we were able to tow it back to Salt Lake. Bob took a look at the engine and declared it would have to be totally replaced, as would most of the car. At least the grill was in good shape. "I don't know," said Bob. "This is going to be a major job."

Earl jumped right in. "I'll come over every night and work on it, if you tell me what to do. I'm sure Carl can help supply money for parts—he's pretty busy being a doctor and all, but if you and I do the labor . . ." He shrugged his shoulders.

Bob was right. It was a major restoration. In all fairness, Earl did offer to help, but Bob found it easier to do the work himself instead of having to train Earl. I spent a few hours on it, but generally just supplied the money. One week before Dad's seventy-second birthday, Bob gave the car its final coat of yellow paint.

"She's a beauty," exclaimed Earl. "A fully restored 1953 four-door Studebaker. Just like Dad used to have. We have done a truly magnificent job!" He clapped Bob on the shoulder. Bob *had* done a great job. The car looked brand-new and ran like a top.

"I want to add one thing," I said. "Can you drill me a little hole in the nose cone, Bob?" I took a little plastic propeller from my pocket.

The three of us met at Dad's house for his birthday. Bob parked the Studebaker in front of the house.

"Not much to celebrate this year, boys," Dad said as we sat in the kitchen eating birthday cake. "I never knew how much I'd miss your mother. . . ." His voice trailed off.

"Dad," said Earl, "we, the three of us—well, you remember that Studebaker you used to own?"

"How could I forget it?" said Dad. "Biggest lemon I ever owned. Right color, too—yellow. I only kept the darn thing because Heber had one."

Bob's mouth dropped open. "You never liked it, Dad?"

"Never ran right." He shook his head.

"Dad, look out the front window, will you?" Earl gulped. Dad made his way from the kitchen into the front room. He looked out the window at the gleaming yellow Studebaker.

"You boys?" he pointed his finger at each of us. "You boys did this for me?" The tears formed in his eyes. He patted the strands of white hair across his bald head. "Let me get my hair combed, and let's take a drive to Parkerville!"

Sandwich Filling

SHARON DOWNING JARVIS

Through the scuffling and chatter that accompanied the twenty-nine third graders' return from lunch recess, JoEllen barely heard the tone that always prefaced an announcement over the intercom.

"Mrs. Burchard?" It was the voice of Mrs. Hilliard, the school secretary.

"Yes?" JoEllen responded, glancing toward Barbara Flindt, the children's teacher.

"There's another telephone call for you. The caller says it's important."

JoEllen didn't miss the implied criticism in the "another."

"All right, thanks. I'll be right there."

Barbara Flindt's eyebrows rose, but she didn't look at her aide. She moved smoothly to the front of the classroom and directed the students to take out their math books.

"Excuse me," JoEllen murmured, and escaped down the long hall. Part of her mind noted the buffed gloss of the floor tiles, a sure reminder that it was Friday, with the scuffed evidence of a week's worth of children's passage polished away. The other part of her mind was busily scanning a list of possible callers: the hospital, calling to tell her that Curtis or one of their three children was injured or dying; Curtis or one of their three children calling to say they were ill and needed her. Her nine-year-old already called to ask where JoEllen had put the math homework he'd needed help with last night. She hoped it wasn't the fire department, informing her that her house had just gone up in flames, or one of Mama-dee's neighbors, reporting that she had broken a hip or suffered a stroke. The list was endless.

She reached for the phone on the office countertop and pushed the blinking button. "Hello?"

"JoEllen? Is that you?"

JoEllen sagged against the wall. "Yes, Mama-dee. What's going on?"

"I wanted to be sure and catch you before you got away. When you come today, I need some more of that fried chicken you got last time, and you'd better bring me some of those 22-by-24 plastic bags, and some heavy-duty drawstring trash bags. And I think I'd fancy a lemon pie from Duffey's, if you've got time to pick one up. What time will you be here?"

JoEllen brought the receiver back from the ten-inch distance that made Mama-dee's phone voice comfortable to listen to. "Now, remember, Mama-dee? I wasn't planning on coming out today."

"You weren't? Oh." There was a moment of silence. "But I haven't seen you in three days."

"Um, no—no, I was there last night. We talked about Granddaddy's war experiences, remember?"

"Was that just last night? It seems so long ago."

"It was last night, hon. And I said I'd be out again Sunday afternoon, because on Saturday, Curtis wants me to ride over to Dothan with him on business, and then we thought we'd stop by and visit his mama and daddy, and make a day of it. And today, I need to get ready—do some stuff around the house, be with the kids—you know."

Mama-dee's sigh was barely perceptible. "I realize you have other responsibilities, JoEllen, but I need you, too. You just don't know how long the days are, when I don't see you."

"I know you get lonesome. Why don't you call up Mrs. Hastings and ask her over to visit?"

"If Gladys Hastings wants to see me, she knows where I live. And I s'pose it's the same for you, for that matter. Seems to me, though, that you and me ought to spend every minute we can, together, while we can. I won't be around forever, you know—and you're all I've got, JoEllen. *All I've got,*" she repeated, her voice quavering.

JoEllen closed her eyes. Here's a ticket, JoEllen, to go on another guilt trip. You choose—either drive down to see me, whether you can spare the time or not, or hop on that old Guilt Express, boarding now. "Well, maybe I can run down for just a little bit," she heard her voice saying. "I'll pick Katy up from school and bring her with me."

"Oh. Well . . . do as you please, JoEllen. I know a little girl doesn't like listening to an old woman's complaints, but maybe she can play outside while we talk."

"I'll see, Mama-dee. Right now, I need to get back to work, but I'll see you about three-thirty, okay?"

"All right, dear."

JoEllen replaced the receiver with a sigh of her own. "I'm sorry," she said to Mrs. Hilliard, who observed her over her reading glasses. "I've told my family they're not to call here except for emergencies, but I'm afraid we all have our own notions of what consitutes an emergency."

"I understand, but would you please ask Mrs. Flindt to go to Mr. Catmull's office as soon as possible? He's waiting," she added significantly.

"Of course. I'll hurry."

She set off at a near-jog, her sneakers making squishing sounds on the polished floor. She loved the purposeful, peaceful feeling of the school during classroom hours—the sudden laughter from one room, a teacher's animated story-telling voice from another, the rustle of turning pages from a third.

The children in Mrs. Flindt's third grade class had been given their math assignment and were settling in with much slapping open of books and zipping of pencil bags. JoEllen relayed Mrs. Hilliard's message and agreed to keep an eye on the class. She sat down at her table in the back of the room to grade spelling papers.

"Who called you?" asked Jerome, turning around. He was an irrepressible little boy with an interesting haircut and skin the color of Mama-dee's mahogany bureau.

"Bet it was her boyfriend," ventured Sally, a cheeky little blonde across the aisle.

"If ya'll must know, it was my grandmother," JoEllen whispered. "Now get busy on your math."

"Grandmother!" Jerome echoed, wide-eyed. "You got a *grandmother?* Whoo-ee, she must be old! I mean, I got a grandma, and she's old. She's *fifty.*"

"Fifty's not very old, Jerome. In fact, it's looking younger all the time. My grandmother's eighty-six."

Jerome was rendered speechless, but not Sally. "What'd she call you for?"

"She wants me to go see her this afternoon."

Sally wrinkled her nose. "Bor-ing."

JoEllen smiled. "Do your math."

Two hours later, her own daughter, Katy, echoed Sally's opinion. "Mom, do I gotta go to Gramma-dee's with you? There's nothing to *do,* there."

JoEllen glanced at the six-year-old slumping as low as the buckled seat belt would allow. Even in this sullen and rebellious mood, Katy was beautiful. Unlike the boys, who had both inherited JoEllen's straight brown hair, Katy had received her father's nearly black crop of gentle waves, which contrasted strikingly with her storm-cloud blue eyes and fair skin.

"Well, honey, what would you rather do? Do you want to stay home with Rick?"

"No, I want to be with you."

"Well, then, you'll have to go to Gramma-dee's, because that's where I'm going."

"I thought you went there last night."

JoEllen nodded. "I did, but she needs a few things from the store, and she gets lonesome for us."

"Not for me," Katy said, with an unchildlike certainty that caused JoEllen to glance at her again. "She doesn't like me."

"Of course she does, angel—she loves you. It's just that she's old, and not quite herself these days. I wish you could have known her when she was younger. She was different, then."

"Old people are stupid."

Whoops, JoEllen thought. *That wasn't what I meant to convey.*

"Older people are all different, Katy, just like young people. Some are happy and nice to be around, and glad to see people. Others are not well, and may seem grumpy or sad. They aren't as much fun to be around, but they need visits and help as much as the pleasant ones."

Katy pondered this in silence, then asked, "Where's Benjy?"

"Benjy has Cub Scouts at three-thirty, and his piano lesson at 4:45, so he can't come today."

"Wish I could just stay at Carol Anne's house."

"I know, but you'll be at Carol Anne's all day tomorrow, and I want some time with you, too. I miss you when you're gone too much."

"Yeah. I miss you, too, Mommy, when you're gone too much. I like it lots better when you're home."

"So do I, baby. So do I."

They stopped at a supermarket to buy Mama-dee's plastic bags, and JoEllen purchased a coloring book and a box of crayons for Katy, resisting the impulse to give in to her daughter's pleadings for a new Barbie she had spotted on a high shelf.

"Mommy, please—I *need* her!"

"Sweetheart, you *need* things like food and clothes and shoes and medicine. You just *want* another Barbie. Mommy doesn't always have money for things we just want. You already have—what? Five Barbies?"

"Yeah, and see? I've got three Kens and two Barbies. That means one of my Ken dolls doesn't have a girlfriend. He's sad. He's in love with *her.*" A nod of Katy's dark head indicated the upper shelf. "Besides, Carol Anne has her, and she won't let me play with her."

"Ahh. I see. Well, I'm afraid your lonesome Ken will just have to see her at Carol Anne's house, and love her from afar."

"Mo-om! Mom, listen. If you get her for me, I won't be bored at Gramma-dee's!"

"That's what the coloring book is for—and besides, we're not staying long."

"That's what you always say, but you stay *forever.*"

"I won't. I promise." Gently, JoEllen turned her child away from temptation.

"I hate coloring. All we do all day in school is color."

"You'll be the best in the whole state of Alabama."

"I don't care. It's dumb."

Katy was mutinous and subdued for the rest of the eleven-mile drive to Mama-dee's house, a white frame bungalow set under ancient shade trees on a pleasant street in the town of Opp. It was the house where JoEllen had grown up, beginning when she had been just a little older than Katy. She and Brian, her older brother, had gone to live with Mama-dee when their widowed mother died of cancer at age thirty-one.

After the air-conditioning in the car, even the deep shade of the trees around the house did little to ease the heat of the May afternoon.

"It's hot here," Katy complained. "Inside and out."

"I know, honey. Why don't you come inside and say hey to Gramma-dee, and then I'll give you a cold drink to bring out on the porch while you color."

JoEllen shifted her shopping bags to one hand and knocked with the other, calling through the screened door, "Mama-dee? We're here."

She watched through the screen as Mama-dee slowly made her way forward, holding on to pieces of furniture to steady herself.

"Well, at last! I'm so glad you're finally here. What took you so long?"

JoEllen glanced at the wall clock as she leaned to hug Mama-dee's bent frame. "Why, we're early, Mama-dee!" she said cheerfully. "I said it'd be around three-thirty, and it's only three-seventeen."

"Oh. Well, I forget these things. It seemed a long time to me. Hey there, Mary Katherine—have you got some sugar for an old lady?"

"Yeah," Katy said, putting up her arms for a hug, but Mama-dee drew back.

"'*Yeah*'? Whatever happened to 'Yes, ma'am'?"

"Yes, ma'am," Katy echoed resignedly, and was rewarded with her hug.

JoEllen unpacked and put away her purchases, and found a can of fruit punch for Katy.

"I believe I'm going to have me a piece of that pie right now, JoEllen. Cut yourself some, too. What about Mary Katherine—will she eat some?"

"I hate lemon pie," Katy said, her nose wrinkled. "It's sour."

"Just say, 'No, thank you, Gramma-dee,'" JoEllen corrected, and with an expressive roll of her blue eyes, Katy complied.

With Katy settled on the front porch, JoEllen glanced through Mama-dee's mail, then set about filling the empty compartments of Mama-dee's weekly pill dispenser—three yellow diuretics, one peach-colored blood thinner, and one bright pink circulation aid for each day. Then she counted the foil-wrapped strips of soluble potassium tablets—and counted again.

"Mama-dee? You been getting all the potassium you should? Three a day?"

"My body doesn't require that much. It's more than I need, so I cut back on it."

"Oh—did Dr. Griffin change your dosage?"

"Dr. Griffin is a *young* man. There's no way he can understand how an old woman feels! In fact, I believe I'd like to switch doctors. I'd like a more mature man—somebody closer to my age."

JoEllen hid her smile. "Now, Dr. Griffin's not all that young, is he? I'll bet he's fifty-four at least."

"Well, I'm eighty-nine!"

"Um—eighty-six, actually. And I don't think there are any doctors your age practicing around here, are there? Dr. Elliott retired, didn't he?"

"Died of a heart attack six years ago. He was a no-good doctor, anyhow. But Dr. Griffin doesn't understand my condition, either. I have a very complicated condition."

"Well, he's a well-respected internist, and he does a lot of work with older people."

"He's an *internist*? Well, no wonder, JoEllen—he's not even a full-fledged doctor, yet! How come you're taking me to him?"

"No, no, honey—that means he's a specialist in internal medicine—the things that go on *inside* a body. You're thinking of an *intern*. That's different."

"Are you sure?"

"Positive."

Mama-dee leaned back in her chair, arthritic fingers pressed to her chest. "Law, that did give me a turn, to think you'd been taking me to a—what? An intern?"

"I wouldn't do that. Dr. Griffin's the best around. Tell you what—let's give him a call and check on how much potassium he wants you to have."

"You can call, if you want. But I know how much I need."

JoEllen used the phone. "He's at the hospital right now," she reported. "His nurse took the message, and he'll call you back after hours."

"All right, dear," Mama-dee said meekly. "I don't know what in the world I'd do without you, JoEllen, to keep me straight. What would I do? If something happened to you, I'd just be lost! What would happen to me?"

"Don't fret, Mama-dee. I'm here, and likely to be around as long as you need me. But if I couldn't get to you, I'm sure your neighbors and the folks from church'd pitch in and help."

"Oh, you can't count on other people. Not like family. And nobody else knows how I like things done. JoEllen, what is that child doing out there?"

JoEllen peeked out at Kay, who was coloring peacefully. "She's just coloring."

"Oh, I surely hope she doesn't break her color crayons and smash them into the floorboards of that porch! I'd never get them up."

"She doesn't do that, Mama-dee. She just takes one color at a time, and puts it back in the box."

"All right, if you say so. Maybe I'll have a piece of that chicken, now, and that'll be my supper."

JoEllen surveyed the contents of the refrigerator. "How about if I slice up some tomatoes and cucumbers to go with it? You haven't touched any of these nice vegetables I brought you."

"No, dear, just the chicken. It seems to be all my body requires, these days—that and a little sweet."

"You know, there's an awful lot of salt in this kind of chicken, and I hate to see you eat too much salt—it'll make you retain fluid." She peered under the table. "Your ankles are already swollen."

"Well, a body needs a little salt in this weather, to make sweat. I understand my body, JoEllen. My appetite lets me know what it requires."

JoEllen gritted her teeth. It was a source of frustration to her, these little binges dictated by Mama-dee's appetite. For six solid weeks, she had eaten little other than canned ravioli, then she had turned to mustard greens and cornbread, and now it was the fried chicken and lemon pie. Taken over a year's time, she supposed, Mama-dee got a fairly balanced diet.

"Mommy?" came Katy's plaintive voice at the door. "I broke my red point off. Will you peel the paper back?"

"What does she want, now?"

"It's okay, Mama-dee." JoEllen set a chicken breast and a napkin before Mama-dee, then stepped onto the porch. She found the broken point, tossed it into the shrubbery, then peeled the paper from the end of the crayon and handed it back to Katy.

"When are we going, Mommy? I'm tired of coloring. See? I did four pages."

"You are so fast! They're beautiful, too. Why don't you walk around Gramma-dee's yard and look at her flowers? But don't pick any. I'll just be a minute longer."

Katy made a pouty face, but cleared the front step in a leap and started around the corner of the house.

"Don't leave the yard," JoEllen cautioned, and Katy answered with a wave.

Mama-dee stood at the door, frowning. "You know, JoEllen, it's high time you taught your children some manners. Why, by the time you were three, you knew how to say 'ma'am' and 'sir' and 'thank you' and 'please.' You were such a perfect little lady—all my friends used to remark on it."

"You sure you're not thinking of my mother, Mama-dee?"

"No . . . well, maybe it was. It all runs together in my memory, sometimes. Anyway, children today are just not as polite and well trained as they used to be, and I hate to say it, JoEllen, but that includes yours."

JoEllen sighed. "I'm sure that's true," she agreed. "But times change, you know? Most of Katy's friends don't say 'ma'am' and 'sir' all the time, either."

"Some things never change, and good manners and respect for one's elders is one of them. Now, JoEllen, before you rush off, will you help me get my trash ready to go out?"

"Yes, ma'am. Happy to."

"You know how I like it done up, don't you? Keep the bathroom trash strictly separate from the kitchen trash, and tie it up in one of those 22-by-24 plastic bags, then put that into a brown paper sack, then tie it up tight in one of those heavy-duty trash bags—the black ones—and put it out in the can. I just can't bear to think of my bathroom trash spilling all over the road, and the rough way those men handle it, it could happen. Do up the kitchen trash the same way, and then wash your hands with that pink soap."

"All right," Joellen said, smiling to herself as she remembered what Curtis had said a while back: "Mama-dee's trash is immortal, do you realize that? It'll never have the oportunity to biodegrade. Centuries from now, anthropologists will use it to study twentieth-century man. Heaven only knows what conclusions they'll come to—'Twentieth-century Homo sapiens consumed a very restricted diet, consisting primarily of the flesh of a fowl cooked in very hot oil. He also apparently consumed huge quantities of something called a Pink Beauty Bar. It is unclear whether this was a staple of his diet, or a dessert confection, but—'"

"Stop it, Curtis," JoEllen had scolded, giggling. "Don't make fun of Mama-dee."

"I kid you not, JoEllen—that woman could use her own private landfill project."

"JoEllen," Mama-dee was saying, "you'd better eat you a piece of this chicken. You must be hungry, by now."

"Oh, no thanks, Mama-dee. I've got to hurry home and get supper for the family."

"Well, I surely hope you children have a safe and pleasant outing, tomorrow. I know you need a break from catering to this old lady."

JoEllen gave a final turn to the twist tie on the kitchen sack. "I do need a break, from school and the kids and everything," she said, agreeing without seeming to. "And Curtis, bless his heart, deserves a little undivided bit of my attention. We haven't gone anywhere together for the longest time."

"Mm-hmm. You know, JoEllen, you've been looking tired and peaked, lately, and I got to wondering about Curtis. Does he really treat you right? Are you sure you're happy with him? Because if you're not, you know you always have a home, here with me."

JoEllen shook her head, trying not to show her annoyance. "After all these years, Mama-dee, are you still worried about our marriage? Curtis is the most wonderful man in the world! He's patient and good and works hard, and he's a good daddy to the kids. Of course we're happy. I'm just tired sometimes because it seems like I never stop."

"Well, I hope you're telling me the straight of it. But I mean what I said—you always have a home, here."

"Thank you for that. But seriously, hon—I think you've been watching too many talk shows. Now, I'll see you Sunday, okay?"

JoEllen collected Katy and her coloring book with a sense of relief, but the tension that had begun building in her neck and shoulders when she was called to the phone at school was still burning between her shoulder blades, and by the time she reached home, it had developed into a full-blown headache.

Rick, her eldest at age fourteen, met her in the driveway and put both hands on the car door to prevent her getting out. "Mom!" he yelled through the closed window. "Where the heck have you been? Don't you remember we're s'posed to sign me up for Little League by five, today, or I can't play! We've only got ten minutes!"

JoEllen rested her aching head against her hands on the steering wheel. "That's right," she said, remembering. "Well, hop in, slugger, and let's boogie. We'll make it."

"Okay. Move, twerpette," he added to Katy. "I don't want anybody to see me riding in the back seat, like a little kid."

"No-o!" Katy objected, predictably. "I had it first!"

"Take turns, Katy," JoEllen admonished. "You've had twenty-two miles up front, and this seems to be vital to Ricky's ego."

Complaining, Katy climbed over the seat, and they were off again.

On the way home, they picked up burgers and fries for everyone, which nobody minded except JoEllen, who gave up her plans for a good, home-cooked family meal with salad and vegetables and real whipped potatoes. Maybe for Sunday dinner—she didn't feel up to cooking tonight, anyway.

She awoke the next morning in a much better mood. A night's sleep had erased her headache, and she had the rare treat of a whole spring day ahead to spend alone with Curtis. She turned her head on the pillow to look at him, then reached over to trace the slightly receding line of his wavy black hair. He stirred, and with a contented chuckle moved closer to her.

Even when the phone rang while they were eating breakfast with the kids, JoEllen had no premonition that her perfect day was about to be altered. Ricky answered, and held up the receiver with a significantly doleful look at his mother. JoEllen frowned a "Who is it?" look at him.

"Gramma-dee," he whispered. "She sounds freaked." JoEllen caught Curtis's gesture of lifted palms that he let fall to the table. It clearly said, "Why am I not surprised?"

"Hello, Mama-dee? What is it?"

"JoEllen, I need to talk to you." Her voice did indeed sound agitated and quavery.

"All right, go ahead. I'm listening."

"No, I can't talk over the phone. They might be listening."

"It's okay, hon, we don't have party lines anymore. Nobody's listening."

"I still need to talk to you privately. How soon can you get here?"

"Well, I—don't know. Curtis and I are just getting ready to leave for Dothan, and—"

"You have the rest of your life to spend with Curtis. I need you right now. This is an urgent matter."

"Can't you even tell me what kind of problem you have? Are you sick, or hurt?"

"Not yet, but I hope I'm still alive when you get here. There are things going on that are just not right."

"What kind of things?"

"I can't say. But bad things—things that are a danger to me."

"Mama-dee, if somebody's prowling around or trying to break in, you need to call 911."

"They're *in* the house, JoEllen. They're in the walls."

"*What?*"

Mama-dee's voice dropped to a ragged whisper. "They're in the walls, and they're slipping out at night and watching me while I sleep. They have some secret way of getting in that I don't know about, and I want you and Curtis to find it and brick it up. It's not right, for them to do that!"

"Dear heaven," JoEllen breathed, and sat down hard on the nearest chair.

"What's the matter?" Curtis asked. Speechless, JoEllen shook her head, her hands lying limp in her lap.

"Well, what does she want?"

JoEllen blinked, and managed to lift the receiver to her mouth. "Uh—just a minute, Mama-dee." She covered the receiver with one hand. "She's talking crazy, Curtis—she's all upset about somebody hiding in her walls and coming out at night to watch her. I think we'd best go see about her. I'm scared."

"Man, Gramma-dee's flipped out, for sure!" said Benjy in awe.

"I coulda told you that, a long time ago," Rick put in, and for the first time, JoEllen was aware of all three children staring wide-eyed from the breakfast table.

"You kids finish eating and put your dishes in the sink," she told them sternly. "Katy, have you got all your Barbie gear ready to go to Carol Anne's?"

"Tell Mama-dee we'll be there soon as we can get away," Curtis said, adding for the children's sake, "Sounds to me like she must be coming down with a fever or something."

They were halfway out the door when the phone rang again. JoEllen, the closest, stared at it, sorely tempted to ignore it, but a deeply ingrained sense of responsibility took over, and she answered. A few minutes later, she tossed her purse into the front seat of the van and climbed in.

"Who was the phone for?" asked Rick. "Was it Gramma-dee, again, wanting to know why you're not there yet?"

"It was Carol Anne's mother," she said slowly. "It seems Carol Anne's been diagnosed with strep throat, and they can't have Katy over today, after all. Sorry, Katy-babe."

"Mo-om!" Katy wailed, breaking into tears. "We had everything all planned out!"

"I know," JoEllen said dryly. "I know exactly how you feel."

Curtis tossed his sunglasses on top of the dash and rubbed his hands vigorously over his face. "So, what now?"

JoEllen saw their beautiful day, their time together, draining away like iridescent bubbles down a pipe. "I just don't know," she said miserably, wishing she could wail like Katy. "Ricky? What if we had you stay home today and keep an eye on Katy? We'd pay you."

"No way, Mom! Brad and I have gotta have today to finish our biology project and work on our go-cart design. The project's due Monday, and he has to go out of town tomorrow."

"Well, normally I don't like people coming over when we're gone, but maybe we could make an exception this time, and Brad could come here. If I called his mom, do you—"

"No, Mommy!" Katy's voice was an explosion of rage and fresh tears. "No, Mommy, no—I don't want to stay home with Ricky and Brad! They won't be nice to me. Please, Mommy— *please* don't make me!"

"Katy, hush that racket!" her father commanded. "We're trying to make a rational decision, here, for the best good of ever'-body."

"It's not the best good of me! No, Mommy, please no . . ."

"Hush, honey," JoEllen said, trying to make her voice soothing. "We'll think of a plan."

In the end, the only plan that proved workable was to drop the boys at their appointed friends' houses and take Katy along with them. She subsided, sniffling, into a corner of the back seat.

Curtis was silent on the drive to Mama-dee's.

"I'm sorry, honey," JoEllen said once. "I didn't want today to turn out this way."

"I know," he answered. His voice was mild enough, but he didn't look at her or offer any consolation. They rode in uneasy silence. Katy fell asleep in the back seat.

Mama-dee was waiting in a rocking chair on her front porch when they arrived. JoEllen's heart melted at the sight of her. She looked suddenly fragile and vulnerable, her wispy white hair on end, her faded blue eyes wide with apprehension. She clutched a sweater around her shoulders, and a thready purple artery was beating under the papery skin at her temple.

JoEllen knelt at her side. "Now, Mama-dee, tell us exactly what happened."

"Well, I woke up about three-thirty, just in time to see him slip out of the closet. I think that must be where they have their entrance, Curtis, and I want you to brick it up for me. I'll pay for the bricks and mortar."

"Who was it?" JoEllen pressed gently. "What did he do?"

"He took two great big steps and sat down beside my bed and just looked at me."

"Did he say anything?" JoEllen felt a sense of unreality, even to be discussing the subject here in the bright morning sunshine.

"He never said a word. He just sat there and stared."

"So—what'd you do? Did you scream, or ask him what he wanted?"

"No—no, I didn't scream or anything. I just laid there and looked at him, and I guess I finally fell back asleep."

Curtis cleared his throat. "You lay there and went back to *sleep,* with an intruder sitting by your bed? With all due respect, Mama-dee, I believe you must have been dreaming."

"I was not dreaming, Curtis! I'm not a child—I know the difference between waking and dreaming. I heard them talking in the walls before he ever came out of the closet. So I know there's at least two of the rascals."

JoEllen sent a pleading look at Curtis. "Let's all go look things over together," she suggested, and helped Mama-dee to her feet.

The closet in Mama-dee's front bedroom was stuffed to capacity with dresses, coats and sweaters. On the floor, Mama-dee's collection of shoes stood neatly in pairs. The seldom-used ones in the back sported a greenish coating of dust and mildew.

"Is this how everything was when you got up this morning?" Curtis asked. "Nothing looks disturbed."

"I haven't touched a thing, except to make my bed, of course. But you go ahead, Curtis, and move things aside if you need to. That secret entrance has got to be there."

Curtis raised his eyebrows at JoEllen, but obediently got down on his knees and began to thump on the closet walls. Joellen looked around the familiar bedroom, unchanged in all the years of her memory.

"Um . . . Mama-dee, where did he sit, when he was looking at you?"

"Right there. Right by the bed."

"Well, what did he sit on? There's no chair or anything, in here."

"I don't know. He must've brought something with him."

Curtis stood up and brushed at his knees. "Sound as a dollar—no secret doors that I can see. Now, Mama-dee, you've gotta realize that this was a dream. Nothing's disturbed, there's no place for anybody to sit, and honestly, why would anybody sneak into your bedroom and just sit and watch you? What'd he look like?"

"He was young, and not anybody I recognized. He had blondish hair and he was kind of ruddy-complected, and he had on one of those knit shirts with a couple of buttons at the neck—light blue. And he wasn't a dream, Curtis Burchard, I know that much!"

Curtis winked at JoEllen over Mama-dee's head. "Well, maybe he was just—you know, a guardian angel or something."

Mama-dee sat down on her white chenille spread and stared at him. "Oh, goodness, that must be it! It must mean I'm going to die soon. He came to prepare me, and here I've been angry with him!"

"Now, Mama-dee, I was more or less kidding about that. I truly feel it must have been some kind of dream or hallucination. I understand they can be awfully real, sometimes."

Mama-dee's eyes suddenly snapped pale blue fire. "In other words, you think I'm loony! Ya'll both think I've lost my reason, don't you? I don't know why I ever thought I could confide in you—"

"Mama-dee!" JoEllen interrupted suddenly. "Did you leave your bedroom light on last night?"

"No, I never do. I can't go to sleep unless it's dark. I even pull my shades against the moonlight."

"Well, you said it was about three-thirty when you woke up, and it's still pitch-black then—so did you turn your light on when you woke up?"

"No—no, I just opened my eyes and saw him jump out of the closet and sit there. I didn't move. I was too scared, and too mesmerized to do anything."

"Then how'd you know he had a ruddy complexion and a light blue shirt?"

For the first time, Mama-dee looked uncertain—even pitiful, JoEllen thought, and disliked herself for having to force her grandmother to acknowledge reality. Mama-dee's head began to wobble slightly on her thin neck. "I don't know, JoEllen—I just know I saw what I saw."

"Come on, dear, let's all go sit in the front room. We're not going to find anything here." JoEllen edged through the narrow hallway with Mama-dee clinging to her arm. "You know what I think? I suspect you've got some kind of chemical imbalance in your body, Mama-dee. That can cause a person to be confused, and even see and hear things. I'm going to call Dr. Griffin and see if we can bring you in for a blood test this morning, before the lab closes."

"Well, I don't know of anything I've eaten to cause that."

"Don't worry about it, hon. Did Dr. Griffin ever call you back yesterday evening about your potassium?"

"He may have done—the phone rang, but I couldn't get to it in time. People these days can't wait a minute."

JoEllen made arrangements with Dr. Griffin, who heard her story, had them bring Mama-dee in to be examined, and recommended hospitalizing her for tests. He also suggested to JoEllen that it might be time she considered not allowing her grandmother to live alone any longer.

"If he knew Mama-dee as well as I do, he'd know what he suggests is easier said than done," JoEllen remarked to Curtis as they finally pulled away from the hospital, leaving Mama-dee sleeping peacefully under the influence of a mild sedative.

Curtis turned the car, belatedly, toward Dothan. Katy played quietly in the back seat with her Barbies.

"I know it's hard, hon," Curtis agreed. "But the man is right. Mama-dee needs somebody with her, and it can't always be you. She's been running you ragged."

"But who could we get that she'd accept? She can't afford a live-in nurse or companion, and neither can we. She already has home-health aides from community services, and you know how she complains about them—if they wash dishes, she does them all over again as soon as they leave, and if they try to prepare a meal for her she says she'll eat it later, then throws it out because she's just sure they weren't sanitary enough about fixing it."

Curtis shook his head. "It's a wonder to me that she'll eat food you bring in from restaurants and bakeries. Well, it seems to me, hon, that she has a few limited choices. She could come live with us—"

"You know she won't hear of that," JoEllen interrupted. "She freezes at our house, winter or summer, and we only have one bathroom, which with three kids using it, isn't always going to be spotlessly clean. Plus, we don't have a bedroom for her— we'd have to move Katy in with us—and you know how she is whenever she visits. She's always shushing the kids and their friends and sending them outside to play, and turning off the music or the TV. Says she has to have perfect peace and quiet."

"That's pretty hard to come by at our house," Curtis agreed. "And to tell the truth, I think it'd drive me nuts, too, if I thought I had to creep around my own house in perfect peace and quiet all the time. Maybe if we could afford to add on a bedroom and bath for her, but the way our house is designed, I sure don't know where that would go, even if we could afford it. And I hate to think of moving to a bigger place."

"I don't want to move, either—and I don't think we could handle higher payments. We maybe could sell her house, or rent it—but it's getting really old, and the way things are set up, half the proceeds would go to Brian."

"What about Brian? Mama-dee raised him, too, and he has plenty of room, and no kids to disturb her."

JoEllen wrinkled her nose. "I know. But remember, I talked to Brian about having her over last Christmas, when we wanted to go to Disney World? He seemed agreeable, but then he called back and said Lorraine wouldn't hear of it. She has her career and her fancy entertaining, and anyway, Mama-dee'd still be alone most of the time if she went there."

"Well, I guess you know what the other alternative is—some kind of care facility. She'd have twenty-four-hour care, balanced meals, somebody to make sure she's getting her medicines, nurses to fuss at . . ."

JoEllen managed a small laugh. "But I bet they wouldn't separate their trash into categories and triple-bag it."

"And I'll bet she wouldn't know the difference."

"Oh, honey, haven't you ever heard Mama-dee hold forth

on the subject of rest homes?" JoEllen ticked off the objections
on her fingers. "Forgotten and left alone to die, neglected for
hours at a time on urine-soaked mattresses, a haven for roaches
and mice, unsanitary kitchens and bathrooms, bossy and cruel
attendants, patients screaming for attention, people stealing all
your money—you know she made me solemnly promise, years
ago, that I'd never put her in a place like that."

"I'm not suggesting a 'place like that'! Surely there must be
some nice, clean places with staff who care about old folks,
don't you think?"

"Not to hear her tell it. She says that whatever comes, she'll
always be better off in her own home."

"Maybe so—but at what cost to her safety and to your peace
of mind and time and freedom? Because it's you she wants,
JoEllen. She's way too dependent on you, physically and emotionally. Nobody else caters to her whims the way you do. You're
the nurse and companion she wants, twenty-four hours a day."

"She knows I can't do that."

"She may know, but it won't prevent her trying. Look at it
clearly, hon—think of the old litany she chants to you, over and
over—'You're all I've got. What would I do without you? We
should spend every possible minute together. I need you to be
here today—and tomorrow—and the next day . . .'"

"I know," JoEllen admitted, staring at her hands. "But she
raised me, Curtis, when I was orphaned. Took me in, and Brian,
too, of course—loved us and brought us up the best she could. I
love her for that. I owe her."

"Course you do, honey. You love her and you owe her the
best available care in her old age. She's more than a grandmother to you, I realize that. I'm fond of her, too. But what
you've got to decide is what form that love and care is going to
take. Personally, I don't think leaving your husband and kids
and going to live with her is the answer."

"Don't be silly. I'd never do that."

"JoEllen, look back on the last few months. Think about
them. Day by day, bit by bit, you've been doing just that. You
just haven't packed your bags yet."

JoEllen felt tears crowding her throat. "I've tried not to ne-
glect things at home. I'm sorry if you think I have."

Curtis shook his head. "It's not in you to be neglectful. That's why you're up at midnight doing the laundry or mopping the kitchen floor or ironing my shirts. You're trying to hold three full-time jobs, hon! You've got school, home and kids, and Mama-dee. Not to mention the PTA and your Sunday School class. But lately, Mama-dee's needs have increased, and she's been crowding everything, and everybody else out."

"Well, school will be out for summer vacation, soon. I'll have more time, then."

"Will you? Mama-dee'll *think* you have more time—to spend with her. But what you'll really have is three kids, also out of school and in need of close supervision and being taken around to their swimming lessons and ball games and such. Believe me when I say they're not gonna want to spend all summer waiting around for you on Mama-dee's front porch!"

"No, I don't!" chimed in Katy from the back seat. "I'm already sick of going there."

JoEllen put her face in her hands. "I feel like—like the filling in a grilled cheese sandwich—just stuck in the middle with plenty of heat and pressure from all sides! Whatever I do, somebody's mad at me. And I feel so *guilty* all the time. If I'm home, I feel guilty because Mama-dee might need me, and I'm not there. When I'm at her house, I feel guilty because the kids might need me at home! I'm just so—inadequate!"

Curtis reached to touch her knee. "Honey, the only thing inadequate about you is that you don't seem to be able to clone yourself. If you could just manage to be three or four people instead of one, ever'thing'd run a lot smoother."

JoEllen tried to laugh, but it came out more like a whimper.

"Tell you what," Curtis continued. "Tomorrow afternoon, let's go look at a few care facilities and see what we think."

"Oh, boy—I don't look forward to all this."

"I know. It won't be easy. Change never is, even when it's needed."

But strangely, as JoEllen watched the green countryside flow past, she began to feel a little better. It was such a relief to know that for now, at least, Mama-dee was not alone—that she was being watched over and cared for—that she, JoEllen, was free to enjoy the present moment with her husband and daughter, guilt-free. She glanced into the back seat, where Katy was murmuring Barbie doll conversations to herself.

"Hey, Katy-bug. What're you playing?"

"Boyfriend and girlfriend."

"Oh?" JoEllen stretched to see the dolls. "Um . . . how come they're not dressed?"

" 'Cause they're on a date."

"Curtis, she's got the boy doll lying on top of the girl doll. Where'd you learn to play that way, Katy? Is that how Carol Anne plays?"

"No."

"Probably off of the TV," Curtis said darkly. "I knew we shouldn't've got cable."

"Was it from the TV, Katy?"

Katy was silent.

"Katy? Where?"

"From Brad." Katy's voice was very small. "Only, I wasn't s'posed to tell you."

"Brad *who*?"

"Brad, Ricky's friend."

"Brad Hixon?"

"Yeah."

"Oh my—what else did he teach you?"

"Nothing. 'Cept he said sometime he'd play boyfriend and girlfriend with me, for reals. But I didn't want to. That's why I didn't want you to leave me with them today, Mommy—'cause he keeps saying let's play."

"I'm gonna kill him," Curtis said under his breath.

JoEllen was trembling inside. "When—when does Brad talk to you about this?"

"He always comes over. Ricky always calls him when you go to Gramma-dee's, 'cause he knows there's plenty of time. Ricky says he'll get even with me or Benjy if we tell."

JoEllen had to ask. "Has Brad ever touched you, Katy?"

"No. But I think he wants to."

"Is Ricky in on this boyfriend-girlfriend game?"

"I don't think so. 'Cause Brad said me and him could just meet in the bathroom and it'd be like a secret date—nobody'd know."

"What about Benjy?"

"Benjy doesn't know. He's always over at Kevin's or playing dumb computer games."

"I see. Well, Mommy and Daddy are sure glad you didn't want to play with Brad. And we're real proud of you for telling us. Now, why don't you dress your dolls up real cute and play like they're . . . um . . . going roller skating."

"Okay."

JoEllen faced the front again, and sat with her eyes closed.

"Sounds like we might have dodged a bullet, this time," Curtis said, his voice sounding as shaky as she felt.

"I hope so," she whispered. Tears formed and ran warmly down her cheeks. She didn't need to look at her husband to know that his mouth was set in a straight line, and that his knuckles were white as he gripped the steering wheel. Curtis was kind; he wouldn't rage at her, wouldn't say, "I told you so!" or "This is what happens, JoEllen, when you're not home enough." But she knew.

Mama-dee, I'm sorry. I'm sorry if it'll make you sad or angry that I can't be with you all the time, or that you can't keep living alone. I'll do the best I can for you, and I'm sorry if it's not enough. But I can't trade my children's happiness and well-being for yours. What kind of mother would I be if I did that? Not the kind you were, to two generations of us! If you're able to think clearly enough, you'll understand. It's all a matter of . . .

"Priorities," she said aloud, and opened her eyes. Curtis covered her hand with his and squeezed.

"Priorities," she repeated, clinging to the word like a lifeline.

Now Let's Dance

ZINA PETERSEN

Provo to Liza was always a real teenager of a town. Ugly, gawky, bad complexion, confidence undermined by instability, obsessed with self-image and trying to be big. Only the parts still child were beautiful, and how much does a teenager want to keep the child of himself?

They were getting out of Provo. They decided this and ached to find themselves still there. One night when they were so tired of the whole thing, they walked for two miles, streets they knew too well, and Jay put his arm around Liza, warmer than cotton. They looked at a place where earlier there had been a house and now there was a pile of dust and rubble, and Liza said she would let Jay take her away from all this. They both knew about the awful wound that change makes, but they wanted it for themselves, their own choice, not someone else's.

They saw Jay's parents up in Edgemont, and so much there was the same as always. His parents' confidence was undermined a long time ago, and what was left was Geneva Steel Mill, which finally collapsed financially, right on top of Liza's father-in-law. In the confusion of the smalltown factory in the wake of reorganization, he was left without a job. For a day, he talked about getting another job. Then for three months, he talked about getting a plot at the cemetery, and still Jay's mother would ask them, after a night of watching Dad watch TV, "You're going home so soon?"

When Geneva changed hands, Jay worried to hear his father—his own father—talking about death. Jay took up the *Daily Herald* and found an ad. He said, "Let's go," and he and Liza got in their bug the day before Christmas and drove to Orem. Jay said, "I have no idea how he'll take this."

Liza said, "He'll love it."

Jay said, "We'll see."

There was only one puppy left unclaimed: red-haired, with a white Florida on its chest. The kid offered to keep it until that night, but it smelled so they said they'd take it now to give it a bath. Jay talked about how his father had bought him a pair of puppies when he was just two years old, and since two-year-olds can't really appreciate puppies, they must have really been for Dad, so he must really like dogs, so . . . And then Jay stopped and said, "I don't know about this."

When Liza made Christmas cookies, the puppy, clean now, slept across her stocking feet under the table. With her toe she could feel the puppy's heart tapping inside the little chest.

They went to Liza's parents' house first, and they gave Liza's father a sweater. He accepted.

Jay's father, though, looked at the big red box they offered him and said, "It has airholes; take it away." He would not accept the dog and left the room. Jay's mother took the dog and said, "Give him time." But Jay said, "I don't believe this," and got so angry at the pain and his father's incurable despair that he wanted never to go back.

But in a month his mother had a birthday. Liza put her arms around him from behind his back as he made dinner, and she said quietly, "We don't have to be like them to still love them. Please, Jay."

At his mother's house, the puppy sat nameless in the kennel built long ago for Jay's childhood dog, shivering and crying while they all sang "Happy Birthday."

* * *

On the Fourth of July, they started to think about getting a better car. From the top of the ferris wheel, both a little breathless, they saw over the trees, down past First South to where there was a Ford dealership. They bought a cotton candy, and took it with them when they went to the lot. There was a dark blue car with stickers on all the windows. Jay said he wanted a big trunk for all their stuff; Liza nodded. When a dealer asked, "What do you expect in standard equipment?" she said, "Escape, a way out, an exit."

"And options?" said the dealer. The dealer had large pale hands, and he bounced his fingertips together as he spoke.

"Blessings," said Liza. She was mostly talking to Jay.

All the cars had flags of many colors on the antennae, antennae to make any insect jealous. They were there to make the cars festive; it was the Fourth of July. The salesman said, "What can I do to get you to commit today?" and Jay said, "Give it to us."

They put aside money every paycheck for half a year; near Christmas they came with two thousand dollars for a down payment and traded the bug over, and signed and signed and signed their names. Liza hoped Jay would have confidence in making the purchase, but his eyes showed the same guardedness to her that they showed the salesman. But it was done. The bug wouldn't have made it to the East coast, and if they were going to be serious about leaving, they said, they ought to be serious about leaving.

* * *

They came east to the East. In the East, they saw only one season at once; they could not see the weather just past lingering on mountains. March was not spring and winter, but merely winter. Cold and too long.

They found a place to live, twice and a half what they had paid in Provo, less than a third what the going rate was for the area. It was a basement apartment beneath a man and his wife, a wife whose job was to die of cancer. She would die and die and she never would be gone, and her pain wrenched her, and through the heating vents, the cries wrenched Liza. The woman called to Liza, for help not from Liza but from her own husband. He would get angry and not respond; he wanted his wife to be as frustrated with him as he was with living with the almost empty, clenched, horrible container of his wife. As she called to Liza (forever saying it Leeza, Leeza, until Liza told her no, it's Lie-za. Then she called for Leeba), the woman choked and gasped, making Liza cringe and cower under covers too thin to block out the casualties of age and cigarettes and having been born.

In the East Jay and Liza were poor, with more money and more places for it. Though it was not what they escaped for, they worked very hard at their jobs. Liza thought always of how they would rather not work so hard, come home so tired, be so at each other, irritable, angry—please. "Liza," Jay said, "this isn't why we're here. To fight. Don't." And Liza would seethe and think he was just saying that to get out of facing things.

Liza found an ad, "Volunteers Needed For Counseling." It would cost nothing, she could talk to someone objective. She planned what she would say: "I expected to be sad, to miss people. I did not expect for it to hurt in my teeth and my face and the palms of my hands. I did not expect to be so stretched out and desperate-feeling." She planned to say, "I feel like I am someone in the background of a grocery store commercial. I consume. All I do is buy things and find a use for them and use them up and buy some more. And if I weren't there it would not distract from the message any." She planned to say, "My husband, Jay, feels this way too. His father rejected a gift, once."

She found the building; it was white brick with dirty ice cracking on the sidewalk beneath her feet, and she went in and found the right room. There was no one there. She waited with her hands in her lap until a man came in. He was tall with white eyebrows and almost white eyes. He made tea.

After he asked all the questions about her age and her background he said "Why'd you come?"

Liza had planned to say, "I'm just really homesick, but I don't think I like my home that much either. Does that make sense?"

"What seems to be the issue prompting your coming here?" he asked again. Liza put her hands over her face and did not answer.

* * *

The phone rang, and when it did, Liza's first thought was that it was a friend from home, or her mother, or Jay's mother. Since they moved in, most of their calls had been for the Schwartz family, though, not for them. One time, Jay had spent ten minutes convincing a caller that his name really was Jay. They joked about changing their names to Solomon and Emily Schwartz, so that they could get a phone call once in a while. This time it was the landlord: "Mrs. is out of prescription, could you listen for her till I get back from the druggist?"

Liza couldn't say no, and she knew he meant for his wife to have company. Upstairs. "I'll be up in a second."

"Thank you so much. She's out of prescription."

"I'll be up."

"Thank you. Lovely of you."

Liza sat beside the joint of the hospital bed that had been moved into position for watching the television that was never turned off. Mrs. looked at the television and over to Liza again, and said, "Went to school over at State, long time ago."

"Oh?"

"Mm-hm. Long time ago." She dragged on her cigarette one last time, and then as she put it out in the ashtray near her head, smoke slid off the end of it, up toward the ceiling, bumping and curving around a lampshade, soft and silent.

"Sheeba?"

Liza said, "Yes?"

"I'm sorry about all the noise. Sorry, because I know it bothers you, I know you hear it. The pain gets so bad, I just can't . . . and then he gets mad at me, too. I don't see how you stand it, must be horrible, all that noise." Mrs. put her hand up to her face. "Sometimes . . ."

Liza put her hand out and held the woman's pale fingers, completely awed by her own reaction.

* * *

The next week Liza waited in the counselor's room again, and read a quote on his wall: "'We're all mad here,' said the

Cat. 'I'm mad. You're mad.' 'How do you know I'm mad?' said Alice. 'You must be,' said the Cat, 'or you wouldn't have come here.'" She read it over and over. It was a piece of cloth, with the felt letters painstakingly glued on beneath a striped Cheshire Cat.

This time the man smoked a pipe, and he spoke coarse words in an evenly soft voice. Liza didn't understand him always. He made a comment and his voice went up, so Liza knew it was a question. She looked at him. She said, "Once more, in English?" and he smiled.

* * *

Liza told Jay about the counselor's white eyebrows. She told him about his pipe. "I think it's bamboo. And he wears a leather hat, all stitched up with twine, and a sheepskin coat, very he-man. I think he thinks he's Crocodile Dundee."

Jay smiled. "And he smokes?"

"A pipe. Not bad at all. Not like—" and Liza pointed at the ceiling. The landlord's wife smoked rancid-smelling cigarettes, smoked them when she was not coughing. "And he makes tea. He always comes in late and then takes his teakettle down the hall to the drinking fountain to fill it and then he comes back and does this little tea-making ordeal, and he clonks his pipe on the ashtray and goes through his desk for the right type of tobacco—takes forever."

"It sounds kind of nice," said Jay. "Like something steady and predictable."

Liza thought about this. "You're right. He does it on purpose. To give us less-stables something to rely on. His vices, instead of our pain. Hmm."

"Hmm," said Jay.

* * *

Usually in the morning Liza and Jay woke to shouting: "Ow! Ow, it hurts."

The day of her appointment, Liza drove Jay to his bus stop and didn't want to go back to the apartment. She drove until the gas gauge was exactly halfway between one quarter and empty, and then remembered she needed to lock the door back at the apartment. A courtesy to their landlord, who could never leave his wife alone for her fear of dying without him. When she reached the house, she saw that the private entrance she and Jay used was propped open, and an ambulance was in the driveway. Her landlord met her, and said, "Had a little scare. She's all right, though, now."

A bit unsteady, Liza smiled and said, "Well, that's good." She got back in her car and drove to the parking lot of the building where her appointment was, and she waited in the parking lot for it to be time.

* * *

"Do you feel like," the man paused and sucked on his pipe. His cheeks went from sunken to hollow, and back out again. "Do you feel like, there is anything different in the way you view the world, than the way other people do? Than the way your husband does, for instance?"

Liza put her feet up on the seat of her chair, hugged her legs to her chest. "Yes."

The eyebrows went up.

Liza didn't elaborate, so he asked. "How?"

She looked at the smoke looping relaxed and gray to the ceiling from the bowl of the pipe. Smoke, stuff so light gravity lost to heat. Would those particles fall, ever? "I see it smaller. Tiny."

"Explain that."

"I don't see it that way always. Not always. It's just, when something big happens, I see it small. I mean, big happy or big sad, or just, I don't know. When something happens that involves a lot."

It still wouldn't do for him; he would not help her.

"Okay," said Liza. "What I mean is, I have this image in my mind. I see something happen, like a death, or a disaster, with earthquakes, or fires, or something really, really, significantly—changing—for a person or a bunch of people . . . something in the news, or if one of my friends, I don't know, has a baby, big things. I see this scene of the event really happening, and then, it's like a camera pulls out, really, really fast, I mean really fast, so that, I see the thing happen in sort of long, long distance, and at cartoon speed—too fast, and very far away; it's like I see the whole planet, and how tiny it is, and yet I can still see things happen on it."

Liza stopped. But the man still didn't respond; he looked at her as if she would catch her breath and explain herself.

"And that's yes, that's different. I think. From how my husband—other people—see things. I guess."

Now he moved his eyes to meet hers. "Do the people still hurt? Do you think it's maybe an attempt to reduce the pain of human suffering? Pain and fear is less threatening if it is tiny?"

Liza winced. "No! No not at all, no. No. It doesn't reduce anything. I just see it small. And it isn't something I do, it just happens."

"So you produce this image for yourself spontaneously—it just happens—when something signals imminent emotional change for you or someone you know or hear about?"

Liza didn't want to tell him about it anymore. He was getting it wrong. "Nothing is reduced except time and size. That doesn't reduce pain. It doesn't reduce—I mean, my friend still has a baby, right? And the experience of having it still changed her, you see, but it all happens so fast, and she recovers, so fast."

"So it's almost an attempt to speed the healing process, so that you can get away from the pain, both ways, as you said. Time, and size."

Liza wanted to say, not attempt. Not mine; it just happens. And not get away. She rocked back and forth on her chair.

He noticed. "Are you cold?"

"Yes."

He got out of his chair and turned a knob on the wall.

"Thanks."

"Damn thermostat's broken." He tapped his pipe on the ashtray and sat down again. "How old did you say you were when you were married?"

"Nineteen. I know, too young. I knew it then, too." Liza smiled.

"How old was he?"

"Twenty-two."

"And it's been—?"

"Almost four years. Four years. I count ahead because our engagement was so long. Feels like I've been with him for a long time, long long time." She laughed.

"Too long, perhaps?"

"What?"

"Are there any patterns—I remember you said something about 'the same old fight' last week—are there any cyclical, repetitive things that go on with—"

"Well, yes. I still feel scared of conflict. Still hate to have stress between us. That's why the move has been so hard, I think. Stress comes from outside places and we still don't—we still take it out wrong sometimes."

"What does that feel like?"

"Um. What? What does what feel like?"

"Being scared of conflict."

"It hurts; it screws up my stomach. Adrenaline, too; my heart starts beating really fast, and, I just mostly I feel sick to my stomach. It starts as soon as I can tell there's tension that will lead that way. I hate it a lot. I wish it would stop. It scares me."

"Any other physical symptoms? Palms sweat, knees shake?"

"Mostly just my stomach."

He looked at her intently. "It sounds to me as if there is a certain amount of disgust."

"What?"

"Stomach. Usually the human animal associates stomach problems with disgust, feelings of rejection, of rejecting. Nausea?"

"No. No nausea. What do you mean?"

"Are there feelings of disgust associated with your fights? On your part?"

"No; I told you. Fear. Maybe I am a little bothered by the fact that it doesn't seem to change fast enough for me, but."

"So what is it fear of?"

"Fear that." Liza stopped. But she was here to tell him. She told him. "I'm afraid. When we fight he accuses me of—and he's right, that I don't think enough, that I react to immediate things too fast. I'm afraid because I say, 'Let's not fight; I love you,' and he says . . ."

The man's face had no expression.

"He says, 'Why should I believe that, when—'" She stopped again, her throat tightening around the words. "I'm afraid of finding out I don't really love him. I'm afraid of that, oh, I'm scared of that!"

The man let Liza cry for a moment before he said anything.

"So. When those moments get tense, part of the tenseness is your fear of what might be revealed emotionally to you?"

Liza nodded.

"And you're afraid that yours might be a marriage of uneven affection? One of you feeling more than the other?"

She nodded again.

"This—disgust, in your stomach. Have you ever thought that maybe the responsibility for that lies outside yourself?"

Liza didn't nod this time. She looked at him and said, "You mean that maybe what I'm afraid of is not that I don't love him?"

The man said, "Your fear of making that discovery is enough evidence of your own love, don't you think?"

". . . But that he doesn't love me?"

The man didn't say anything. He looked satisfied.

Liza lost all her breath. She began to shake, and felt her jaw go slack, too frightened to cry again. She closed her eyes and thought for a long time, slowing herself down as much as she could.

Finally she said, "That's the dumbest thing I ever heard. Jay's crazy about me; Jay would do anything for me. That's the dumbest thing I ever heard. You only know what I've told you, how can I—I feel bad, I'm sorry; I haven't been fair to you as a counselor, because you only know what I complain about. That's not fair. You don't know him, he's—you only know what I've told you."

The man opened his desk drawer and rummaged in it for a moment, stabbing things aside with an index finger. "I think," he said, "we may need to get to the point where your definition of selfhood doesn't involve him so much. Where you can be a self independent of the fact of who you're married to—or even that you're married. Not that I see you needing, necessarily, to separate—"

"What?"

"But that we get to a point where the courage to separate comes as part of the emotional independence. Where you can make such a decision free of fear for either consequence. Make the decision one that involves all the pluses and minuses." He found a dirty bag of tobacco and plucked it out of the drawer.

"Courage?" asked Liza.

"Mm." He nodded.

"I thought. I thought." Liza looked at him. "I thought courage was more like, risking the damage. John Wayne; courage, you know, being willing to do something—stupidly—dangerous. Walking through minefields. He was courageous because he walked through a minefield. There were big minuses, but it was courage. I thought."

He laughed. "Well, John Wayne is a little bit different situation than your marriage."

She wanted to say, My marriage is fine, sort of. It hurts, but so does being alone. She looked at the wall hanging.

"'How do you know I'm mad?' asked Alice.

"'You must be, or you would not have come here.'"

"So you mean leaving is courage?"

"Takes courage."

"But it's also cowardice. I mean, not if he really does . . . not love me, but that's the dumbest thing I ever heard, so."

The hanging said, "'We're all mad here.'"

"You're probably right," Liza said.

In her mind Liza's camera pulled away from a tiny planet where tiny brave men were doing tiny courageous things. She did not tell the counselor. The frantic little people killed and died for each other, fought with each other, for each other, clung to each other, desperately refusing to hate, or be indifferent, even for an infinitesimal fraction of their split-second lives. No. Courage is different. She thought of Jay, their first year of marriage, during a fight. Her tears did not touch him at all, but her bare feet in the snow tore him away from the car door, already open. He finally gave up neither his escape nor his frustration: still furious, he scooped her into the car ahead of him, and drove away from her, with her.

"I guess to me courage is doing all of it," she said. "Not just one scary part. Both scary parts. All the scary parts. It's all frightening. I just don't know how to be selective with fear."

"That is what I can help you with, I think. Coming to see just what that fear is comprised of. If it is something you feel you want to work on. The courage to recognize . . . all of your valid options as valid options." Liza watched as he pushed his white hair over the top of his head, skillfully glancing at his watch. She took the cue before he gave it.

"Well, maybe I could work on being selective. Maybe, next week. That's something I could work on." The little planet got slower and larger and closer until it was lost in her awareness of changing, coming back into herself, away from her imaginary outerspace.

*   *   *

That night in bed she told Jay she had decided not to go back. "I'm bored with him. You shouldn't be bored by someone who is supposed to be there to talk all about you. It's usually my favorite topic. Jay?" Liza looked at him in the glow from the reading lamp.

"Hm?"

"I wanted. I want. I can't figure out some things. I want to figure out some things, instead of being told what to figure."

Liza looked at her fingernails, studied them as if she had scraped up something to say, the right way to say it, and it was crinkled and bunched underneath them.

"He told me he'd help me have the courage to leave you. It didn't sit right, at all. And, tell me something." She twisted around in his arms to see his face directly.

"What?" Jay looked at her with his brow knit, but smiling underneath—an expression she never could have described to the man with white eyebrows.

"I'm serious."

"I know."

"Well, then be serious. Jay."

"I am; I just have to use my thinking-about-things face when I think about things."

"You're impossible. I'm serious here."

"I know. Really, Liza. Go ahead."

She looked at his face, his eyes, his mouth, trying to find something she could be objective about. "Jay. Have you ever wanted to . . . wanted *me* to . . . leave you? Seriously?"

Jay kept his thinking-about-things face. "I hope not. Not seriously. I used to think it would have been easier for you if we weren't married. But no, not seriously. Have you?"

It was an easy answer. Nothing else could ever be as easy or as difficult, or as right.

Liza said, "No."

"Well then that's settled." Jay kissed Liza and tightened his arms around her, drawing her in to him, and they stayed that way for a long time.

From upstairs came a rasp of coughing and then shouting: "Ow! Ow! Don't touch me, don't touch me it hurts!"

Liza tensed.

"Wait," said Jay. "Listen to this, instead." And he reached up above them on the bedstead and turned on the radio. "Listen! Music, okay? Liza?"

Liza was confused; she was hearing pain and music, and something about the music was so . . . odd, and then she figured it out. It was comic. Ridiculous. A comic opera, but not stopping the death upstairs, going on anyway: shouting and singing.

Liza stopped thinking the same way, as if the needle that ran along the grooves in her brain to play out thoughts had suddenly become a dragonfly, and light as smoke, refusing to play out the confusion of such a combination; so many pains and hurts and such pleasure in love and in Jay. She thought, How can I be aroused when someone is dying? She thought, I am happy, shaky, anxious, sad, horrified. She thought, Jay! Loves me! There is opera in this tiny little world, and there is sex, and death, and men with bamboo pipes who want you to have courage.

And with that, what could she do but laugh, laugh? And Jay laughed with her, they laughed together, in their ancient embrace, the opera and the shouting—they laughed at all of it, through it, because of it, with it. Jay laughed, and Liza laughed, and the world all around them laughed, strange and breathless, inexhaustible, glorious.

The Door on
Wickham Street

ROBERT ENGLAND LEE

Grandma's hand was warm to the touch. And a tangible purity emanated from deep within her which could be sensed as one touched her hands and face. Her bedclothing, with lace ruffles about the hems, exposed only her head and hands.

Grandma's room was in Aunt Julie and Uncle Philip's house on Wickham Street. On Thursdays I would walk the mile and a half from my office to Aunt Julie's home. The walk was always invigorating—fresh air, the noise of little children playing, shadows of flowering trees and the scent of flowering plants in abundance, people working in their yards, and birds communicating in a language they alone understood, but many not of their species appreciated.

From this fresh, alive, vibrant world I would walk with a steady rhythm into a world where death was very near. A small table lamp was the only light in Grandma's room. The window blinds were closed, the curtains drawn, so that virtually no light passed through them. Aunt Julie would leave the house when I came, only to take a break from watching over Grandma or do some shopping or visit friends, pretending there was some other thing that justified her existence at this moment in time.

I held Grandma's pure hand in my own for an hour or so as I had done every Thursday afternoon for many months. But on this visit the reality of her mortality was sure. The end was very near. It wouldn't be today or even next week, but the fight for life, once clearly manifested by the tension in her hand, had clearly gone, and she seemed to submit to the inevitable in peace.

Her hand, limp in my own, was wrinkled with age and the work of raising ten children in poverty. As I held it, I remembered that another once held this same hand. In the later years of their marriage, she and Grandpa seemed surgically joined at the hand. One might find the two of them seated before the picture window, which offered a splendid view of a mountain range and a field of corn. As summer progressed the corn overtook the mountain range, obscuring it completely for several days, until harvest. An uneasiness prevailed in their home when they could not see the mountain.

There was little conversation in these moments on the couch in front of the picture window. They would sit for hours in comfortable silence, clinging confidently to each other and to the hope that death would not bring an end to their relationship. But in the event that this was all there was they held on.

When it came time to move to some chore or greet someone at the door or retire for the evening, Grandma would raise her sacred hand to the rough cheek of her beloved and say, "I've loved you from the first day I saw you."

Grandpa would shuffle off, his feet brushing against the carpet, to do whatever needed to be done and when the task was completed, and not before, he would return again, seek out that part of him he had left behind and sit awhile.

The love they felt for one another was rarely communicated in words, only when Grandpa had to leave for chores, and then only Grandma would speak. Grandpa spoke with his hands. His fingers were long and gnarled with age and labor. Homes, gardens, automobile engines, and little boys' hands had come to know these giant Grandpa hands and all were better for having known that touch.

With Grandpa gone the duty of holding the hand of "Mother," as he used to call her, fell to others. And Thursday afternoon belonged to me. We had a little ritual, she and I. When I was seated I would run my hand along her cheek. It was our special signal, or so I thought. Feeling the rough skin along the corners of her eyes and the dimples near the corners of her mouth, which always broke into a smile whenever I did this, caused her to laugh, though lately it had been more a quiet giggle.

It was this laugh that distinguished her from every other soul on earth when I was a toddler. And now that I was in my mid-thirties it became my own private way of verifying that this was indeed Grandma.

Near the end Grandma could not remember who I was. Oh, I was somewhere in that part of her mind where all her children, grandchildren, great-grandchildren, friends, brothers and sisters were stored. But I was lost as an individual. All the experiences she had shared with all those she had ever known had become wrapped together to form a conglomerate person which never really existed. And when she spoke of one she spoke of all. There was a quiet joy which came to my heart whenever, in her memoirizing, she would stumble upon me. There was quiet anxiety whenever the unmarked road led to moments of disappointment or despair which I had caused her to suffer.

Even as the end approached, there were events which remained removed, sequestered from the memory the rest of us had entered. She began to wrest these memories on Thursday afternoons with her pure hand in mine.

Perhaps it was the familiarity of my hand in hers or the regularity of my visits, or the soft brush across the cheek, but now, after nearly a year, she trusted me with something she had not trusted to others. "When I close my eyes, when I die, I will open them again and see the face of Satan."

She was speaking from memory now, not a memory of conversation but a memory of thought which, without the controls that normally keep such thoughts repressed, came forward spontaneously when the conditions were right. When my hand was in hers those conditions seemed to exist and on a spring afternoon, where not a breeze stirred the air I was introduced to the private hell she had had to overcome and suppress for all her adult life.

"Whatever makes you think such a thing, Grandma?"

"Well, I just know he'll be there."

"Grandma, this is foolishness. You're joking with me again.

How can you believe such a terrible thing? Is it something you read? Something you heard? What is it that makes you say such a silly thing?"

"It's not a silly thing. It's true."

With that the conversation would stop awhile.

Grandma was at peace. She was well prepared for this eternal torment. My instincts told me that if I waited patiently she would reveal the source of her expectation. And one Thursday afternoon, without coercion, without request, she told me why her soul would wake in hell.

She began, "When I was younger . . ." I thought of her as younger. I thought of this mother who delivered four children before she reached her twenty-sixth year. I heard the wind whipping her plain, handmade calico dress and the snapping of the skirt against the eternal breeze which blew without mercy across the land she and her auto mechanic sweetheart had chosen for their home. She spent a great deal of time in the garden, in the dirt the man she loved cultivated. The days it was her destiny to live within required a garden, a successful garden, and that garden meant the difference between living through the winter barely on the edge of survival and not living through the winter at all.

So she and her babies would be out in the garden in the wind and dirt while her husband worked at odd jobs in exchange for food or clothing.

"When I was younger, I found out I was going to have another baby." This would be the fifth in seven years. "And I was so happy. I couldn't wait to tell Dad. And when I told him he cried and held me in his arms and we both cried. It was such a sweet day. We went to Dr. Evans's place and told him. He checked me over and told me he didn't think it would be wise for me to have another little one so soon.

"Well," Grandma said with a slight laugh, no doubt duplicating the conversation held sixty years earlier, "the little baby is here, so *he* must think I am ready."

Dr. Evans was . . . well, he was a doctor. He was inspired in all that he said and could not make errors in judgment or be even slightly misinformed. The community depended on that constant because they could neither see nor touch God but they could see and touch Dr. Evans. So Grandma, with her eighth-grade education, and Grandpa, who left school after the third grade, trusted the god they could see and feel.

"He said I would die if I didn't have this little procedure, this little thing like an operation. What if I were to die and leave my little babies and Dad alone?" She spoke with the innocence of a five-year-old. Yet, one could not escape the inevitable conclusion that innocence fled from Grandma's soul that day sixty years ago. But, as she continued, one could not conclude that the departure had not been permanent.

"Oh, Heavenly Father," she whispered, without convulsions, without sobbing, without bitterness, "how could I have known? Who was there to tell me? Dad and I wanted to do what was right. But when that little soul was ripped from mine I knew I had done wrong. I felt dark and wicked and dirty, the kind of dirty that doesn't wash away. It was like a little light inside me had gone out and I couldn't find the string to pull to make it come on again.

"Oh, Heavenly Father, why did you leave me?"

I spontaneously brushed her cheek with my hand. A tear had emerged and had slipped down this wrinkled cheek, a cheek upon which I had sobbed as a little boy, a cheek which had never known rouge, not because of religious principle but because of economic reality squarely faced.

"I learned to turn to God in such moments. I learned to do a little prayer when a thing like this came up, a thing that might take you away from God unexpectedly. I didn't learn it right away. But whenever the light went out I would eventually get around to doing this and as time went on I found that I came back to it more quickly." She giggled a little. "God taught me in His own way how to turn the light on. And He also taught me that I had done wrong and I would have to pay.

"I prayed to be forgiven. I prayed that God would give me a chance to make things right with Him. And it wasn't long before little Margaret, little black-eyed Margaret, came from God to our home."

* * *

In 1932, Grandpa bought a car. It wasn't a new car. It would never be a new car. But this was the first. This was the last thing that separated Grandpa from equality with the rest of the little community which was his world. He was told he could have the car when it came time for his boss to buy a new one. Grandpa paid for it by setting aside a portion of each check and handing it to his boss for ten years. He treated the car with dignity and respect and serviced it with patience whenever there was any part to be replaced or bolt to be tightened. When the hood was raised his children would gather in reverent awe and be placed in positions about the infected area holding wrenches and screwdrivers and wires, like nurses holding scalpels and sutures, and Grandpa would call for the right piece of equipment and place it where it was supposed to go.

In later years this ritual would be repeated as his sons drove home for family reunions. Each would park his car on the rolling lawn in front of the house. A semicircle of shining power would form, and all the hoods would be raised skyward in reverent salute to the man who had taught all the boys how to treat their cars with reverence.

Grandpa taught his children how to listen to the messages an automobile engine sends. "When it's healthy it hums. When it's sick it coughs." All would lean forward as the long, gnarled, permanently grease-stained fingers made their way into the bowels of the car to do some procedure that would make the car well again. With some experimentation the remedy would be stumbled upon and all would be happy—the greasy doctor, the consortium of infant nurses, and the Ford. The tools would be replaced, the hood wiped clean, and the vehicle, with a healthy hum, would begin its return to the cement slab sheltered by cinderblock. Then Grandpa would put the car in reverse and ease it backwards into the shelter until he saw the top of the garage door in his front window. No surgeon operated with more precision.

Two months after Grandpa took possession of the automobile, the Ford took sick. Two boys lifted the hood, the side that needed to be lifted to effect a cure, and two daughters stood in their appointed places on either side of Grandpa. The procedure was new to Grandpa and much experimentation was required. Vital organs were placed carefully on a rubber mat near Grandpa's feet. Many would be returned before the procedure ended. Those forgotten on the mat would be returned when they were discovered. But on this night, this late night in the 1930s, Grandpa would not prepare to enter the cinderblock garage until all was dark.

Grandma continued, "Late one night, I heard this cry from the front of the house and thought Dad had hurt himself. But his voice came again more clearly. 'It's Margaret,' he said. 'I've killed her.' "

Little Margaret, little three-year-old Margaret, grown weary with things mechanical, had toddled into the garage, fallen asleep and become forgotten. When Grandpa backed the car toward the garage door he felt an unexpected bump and shuffled out to see what it was.

"When he saw the body," Grandma whispered, "he let out a cry and went to the back of the car. When I arrived he was holding the back of the car above the ground and he cried for me to pull her out from under the wheels. By the time Doc Evans arrived little Margaret was dead.

"Dad picked up the car," she said. "You'll be all right Margaret. Don't you worry now my baby." The bed swayed slightly as she moved her body from side to side as if the baby had been in her arms again.

When Dr. Evans pronounced the baby dead Grandma went to her room and knelt at the side of her bed, as she had many times before, and spoke to the God she had come to worship fully and completely, the one she could neither see nor touch. On knees made rough by work and prayer she spoke.

"Heavenly Father, this is Sarah.

"Heavenly Father, I know I'm not much compared to you and the other things you've made. I know I'm not worthy to ask much from you. And I haven't come to ask for anything really. I've come more to tell. I've come to say that if you want to send me more children I'll take as many as you send me. I won't complain. And I won't do that awful thing I did before.

"But, Father, please, please don't take any more babies away from me."

Grandma was sobbing now. She had taken herself back

through that horrid lane of memory which led to death and to the deal she made with God.

She pressed on, "And then I said, 'Father, I ask nothing for myself except little ones to hold in my arms. You can take away anything else from me and let the devil have my soul when I die. But please don't take any more babies.'"

In her little-girl, innocent mind God had accepted this arrangement. And in her little-girl, innocent heart she knew the devil would welcome her in hell after she closed her eyes in death.

She would be quiet, for a while at least. It required all her concentration to stay alive one more day. For she knew if her eyes closed she would die and the rest of the scenario she had formulated over sixty years would follow: Satan, hell, eternal torment. She had read it all in the scriptures from her youth and she knew it all applied to her.

While she strained at life another hour I dozed off.

With her hand in mine I slipped quietly into a numbing, tingling, coming-going realm in which a semi-reality was taking shape. I was transported to a moment shared with Grandma not many years before, when I came with a group of carolers to her home. We were made up of friends and family, going to homes which had been chosen by the group, homes which would welcome a visit from this little community of sometimes-on-key performers.

I knocked three times as I always did and proceeded to walk into the house. Grandpa shuffled to the door.

"We've come to sing to you," I said. And he shuffled back to the chair where Grandma sat, and called, "Mother, the whole town's out on the front lawn."

The carolers were singing "Joy to the World" as Grandpa escorted his bride to the front door. He walked behind her like a giant guardian angel. Both took little shuffling steps toward the chorus of middle-aged parents and children of all ages.

While in this state of mind I became aware that the chorus was seated on folding chairs on the front lawn. This was strange to me. For it had not happened this way. There were no chairs in the experience I came to call reality, but in this little dream sequence, this semi-consciousness, there were folding chairs.

As Grandma came through the front door to the assembled choir, the chorus spontaneously rose to its feet. And as they rose I heard the muffled sound of their rising. That sound like the flick of a giant bird's wings. That sound when all stand at once to honor another. This rush of wind was so real that when I reentered the conscious world I sought to discover what device had caused the noise. But Grandma and I were alone. I arose and brushed my hand along her cheek as I left.

The week passed without incident: chauffeur service, doctor's appointments, interviews with prospective clients, lectures on proper behavior for the children, leaking faucets, and one bill which did not get paid.

It was Thursday again, and I heard the metal in my shoes snap against the cement sidewalks that led to Aunt Julie's house and the hardwood floors that led to Grandma's room. "It's a good thing you married Louise," she said as I entered the room. "She's taught you to be on time." I smiled, knowing that she had no notion of my true identity, but also knowing that Uncle Ed *was* better off for having married Aunt Louise.

* * *

Grandma continued with the memory games, which kept me interested for several minutes, and then we came to the devil again. Her hand tensed. She held my own as tightly as her nine decades would allow.

There was no television, no radio. There was no other way to pass the time except to sit with her hand in my own.

The nurse examined a chart and Grandma's vital signs and politely left the room. I felt Grandma's hand. The veins bulged through the layers of skin. The palm was rough and the skin at the base of the fingers was wrinkled and folded unnaturally because Grandma had lost so much weight recently. The tips of the first two fingers of her right hand were rock hard and the wrist was stocky, without elegance or grace. This was a seamstress, this was a woman who picked potatoes and berries. This was a woman who made her own diapers and cleaned them by hand. This was a woman who bore ten children, and caressed them with her own hands.

I found myself remembering a Founders Day celebration that took place years before, when Grandpa and Grandma were honored as pioneers of the community. Grandpa drove the car he had lifted by himself forty years earlier, and Grandma sat by his side, waving to the crowd. A celebration was held at the church, and when Grandma and Grandpa walked in the crowd stood and when they did the noise I had heard the previous week came into my mind again and I was awake.

The noise was so real, so tangible, and yet the room was void of any instrument that could make such a sound, the great winged bird sound.

Grandma was now asleep. How strange it was to feel peace emanating from such a troubled spirit. She had strained so long and hard to keep hold of life that she had nearly exhausted what little energy remained in her delicate frame.

I would be back in a week.

During that week I asked my daughter Sarah, named after Grandmother, to rummage through the papers handed down to me that represented my connection with the past. Certificates, statements, charts and notes were all jammed into a drawer. Sarah took each document, one by one, until she stopped at the one she felt I might enjoy. It was Grandma's statement of her life, an attempt at an autobiography, in her own handwriting, on an 81/2-by-11 piece of yellowing paper. It read as follows:

Was born on December 1, 1899, in a log cabin in Etna.

I had been to Etna and seen the cabin. By the time I arrived on the scene a tree had fallen during a storm, and a large tree limb was now occupying the front room.

That year there was fever and sickness about and Mother feared that her little Sarah would die.

Fell into tub of water prepared for bath when two years old. Mother feared her little Sarah had drowned.

Survived the fever and moved on to whooping cough at age 7. Seemed that everyone else had the cough so they didn't close the school.

I pictured a one-room school full of kids from 7 to 19, coughing that relentless, exhausting cough that never gives up until your body is too tired to cough and then it keeps going until your ribs begin to separate.

Snowed so bad in 1912 that we walked to school along the top of the fence.

The "we" here consisted of six older brothers and sisters.

That same year we moved into the house Dad built. Seven rooms. There were 70 cases of small pox that year. No school. No church. No deaths. Had red measles when school started up again. Not expected to live.

Invited to capital city to participate in dance instruction in 1914. Came home to Etna and taught the other young folks how to do the steps. Returned to capital city in 1916 to work for Aunt Bess at the record store. Came home to Etna for good after that.

Always a large crowd at the house. Nine brothers and sisters and their friends. Meant that we always had 15 to 20 folks around the table. Doing dishes was a time to laugh and talk and get to know one another. Hannah Bell took off with a boy one night after supper and before dishes were done. Mother told everyone that was helping with dishes and clean-up to stop what they were doing and leave the dishes to Hannah Bell and the boy. The two of them were up till midnight washing, but there was no laughing or talking or getting to know one another. Saw them from around the corner. Watched the boy till he was done washing. Married him two years later, December 19, 1919.

Went to Phoenix, Arizona for our honeymoon and stayed there two years. Our first child, Thomas, was born there in 1921. Then we moved to Malta, to work with Calvin's brother and had George in 1922. Henry was born in 1924, the year we moved to Springfield. Moved back to Etna in 1925 where Calvin worked for the railroad and where Eliza was born. Proved up on a homestead while living in Marion in 1926. Came back to Etna in 1928 where we had Margaret, Calvin, Jr., Arthur, June, and Philip. Little Margaret was killed in a car accident when she was three years old.

Sang in the choir at church. Taught Sunday School for forty years and loved the little ones. Taught the teenaged girls during our weekday meeting for thirty years. And was president of the young women's group for two years.

There it was, the summary of nine decades of living. Someone at Church had said a person should write his life history. So Grandma had gone home and scratched it out. She gave all her children a copy and they made copies and gave them to their children. Though they had the handwritten story generations not yet born would never connect this written history to the woman with the perpetual smile. They would never know that she handled the stem of a raspberry plant the same way she handled a newborn child. They would never know that she made every meal for sixty years as if God Himself were coming to dinner. They would never know the laugh, the spontaneous laugh, that sprang from an innocent soul, while canning a thousand jars of fruit and preserves every year for most of her adult life.

What they would know is that she never used the word *I* when she wrote her life story. They would know that when she came to their homes she wanted to be in the room where the children were playing. They would know that she couldn't remember their names and that she smelled funny.

*   *   *

It was time to go to Aunt Julie and Uncle Philip's house to visit Grandma. I walked along the sidewalk, placed there sixty years earlier by Grandpa and his brothers. I walked in the shade of trees planted by that same crew. I walked to Julie's house, the one Grandpa built with his own hands. Back to the office-turned-bedroom I came. The nurse, a middle-aged lady who had come regularly for many months, touched me in a strange way that suggested all was not well. Everything seemed the same to me, the same feeling of purity pouring from the hand. But the nurse said, "I think we're very close to the end."

I held Grandma's hand.

"You were gone a long time," she whispered. "I thought you might be lost." She gave a little laugh. We were alone. She raised her feeble hand to my cheek and said, "I've loved you from the first day I saw you."

I placed my hand under her feeble body and pulled her close and bathed her face with my tears. I knew she wasn't really talking to me when she said those words. But I loved her the more for loving Grandpa in this state of unconscious-consciousness.

Her hand was in mine again and after a moment of calm a rustling came from the opposite end of the room. I turned toward the noise and saw a strip of light forming from nothing.

Then, like a door opening before my eyes, there appeared a glorious room full of people I did not recognize. They sat in an orderly fashion, as if anticipating a command. And, responding to a signal from some unseen hand, this assembly, dressed in white and glowing as if on fire, simultaneously rose to their feet. The noise they made was the noise of a giant bird's wings, flicking against the wind, the sound a giant flag makes when it first catches the morning breeze. It was the noise I had heard before and now I knew its source. And from the midst of this flaming assemblage there came a little child, about three years old, stretching her hand out to take "Mother."

"Grandma, the whole family is here!" I shouted as I came to understand what was happening. I held her body up to see what I was seeing. She was gone. I turned quickly to see the fiery room and saw the little one leap into her mother's arms and a tall man with wavy hair shuffle to her side. . . .

The nurse entered the room, responding to my shout. The wooden door flew open and the door of fire quickly closed.

"She's gone," I said.

The nurse spoke in reverential terms about Grandma and left us to be alone. The word spread throughout the house and soon the room was filled with quiet reverence springing from the generations which were still here.

Three days later the funeral was held in the nearby church. The chapel section was reserved for the family. Friends had to sit in the overflow section where the cultural hall began. Humble people, who knew quite a lot about automobiles, came shuffling in quietly. Children and grandchildren and great-grandchildren who loved God made their way to their places in reverent awe.

All this, I thought, from a woman who never had a dime to her name. All this from a woman who spent the better part of her life knowing she would be in hell perpetually. How can it be that one so great could have lived with such a thing?

The memorial service continued with the eulogies and crying and singing and stories about cars. And once again I was transported, once more a door opened before my eyes, not a blinding door, like the ones I had previously seen, but a simple one, barely visible.

I saw a woman sitting in a wheelchair, surrounded by little girls, one of which grew up to be Grandma. They listened intently as the aged one told them of her journey through a great struggle.

"There I was," she said, "seven months pregnant and pushing a wagon up a hill. It took all of us pushing to get over the ridge." To my view came the image of a young woman in her late teens pushing a covered wagon up a hill. Her face still had the vigor of youth but her body was malnourished as were the bodies of those beside her. They pushed with all their might while others cracked whips over the heads of the oxen, also near death, which drew the wagon upward.

"I shall always believe that the Lord gave me special strength to climb that mountain. I couldn't eat the fat salt bacon, so I settled for bread and water, which was all the food that was left. The next day, while we were camped between two mountains, I gave birth to my first child."

She pulled the afghan which draped her legs a little closer, pointed a gentle finger at each of the girls and said, "You have no idea how I suffered during that day. And the next was spent riding over rough ground to the next camp. We had to keep moving cause of the weather. However, I was not the only one to have this experience, as there were two other babies born during the journey."

Then this old woman, with her hair pulled back in a tight bun behind her head began to sing in a sort of shrill voice, which once had been sweet but could no longer carry a tune:

> May peace come to thy troubled soul;
> There is no need for fear.
> He who is thy great Provider
> Is by thy side quite near.
> He it is who fed thee last;
> He'll feed thee yet again.

Thy troubles shall be in the past,
And thou in His arms fore'er remain.

Someone said, "All rise." And the rising sound, the giant bird sound, the flag-catching-the-breeze sound returned. The gray door of this vision closed. And three generations rose to pay homage to "Mother." As I stood I reflected upon the marvels I had seen in the little snippets of light granted to me by Divine Providence. In my state of gratitude Aunt Julie came to me, took my arm and led me from the stand.

"If only you could have seen her," she said. "You and she seemed so close. It was as if you were not really blind when you were with her. I saw the way you held her hand and stroked her cheek so carefully each time you came and went. If only you could have seen her face."

I had seen her face and more, and when the time is right I will sit with my grandchildren and talk about the times I saw her. And I will sing to them a hymn in a strange off-key, a hymn of deliverance.

Worthy to Be
One of Us

ORSON SCOTT CARD

When the children moved out of the house and started their own families, Joseph and Rachel couldn't decide whether to be relieved or depressed about it. On the one hand, they would have their own lives back. No more racing home to have a car available for somebody's date. No more sorting through the clean clothes to pick out items that somebody slipped into a batch of the parents' laundry. No more taking endless messages or giving endless reminders. Rachel could actually go with Joseph on any of his lectures or conferences that she wanted. Joseph could probably do some of his work at home instead of having to flee the house to get peace and quiet in his office up at the university.

On the other hand, the children were in the most exciting phase of life, and for many years their activities had been much more important to Joseph and Rachel, emotionally at least, than their own. The house felt empty. "It's too big now," Joseph said, several times. And then the suggestion: "A condo closer to campus."

But Rachel didn't want to leave the ward. Joseph's life was focused on campus. Rachel's life was centered in the Primary and the ward choir. Joseph could leave the ward and still have his friendships at work. For Rachel it would be starting over. She had twenty-five years invested in the Lakeview Third Ward and she wasn't going to throw that all away. One thing about having your career be in the Church: you never vested. There was no pension that you could take with you, eking out long friendships and favorite callings during the lonely years of old age. When Joseph finally repeated his remark about moving nearer to campus often enough that Rachel realized he was serious, she answered as clearly as possible. "I'm not going anywhere. When I'm old and decrepit, coming to church with a walker, I intend to be surrounded by children I taught in Primary."

"All the children you taught in Primary will have grown up and moved away, like our kids," said Joseph.

"By then I'll be senile and I'll *think* they're the same children," said Rachel. "Don't expect me to be rational about this. If you move, you move alone."

"I can't keep up the yard anymore, not with the boys all gone."

"Hire a kid from the neighborhood," said Rachel.

"And then pay for another sprinkler head every week when it gets chopped up in the lawn mower," said Joseph.

"If you keep grumbling I'll make another no-salt dinner."

"If you make another no-salt dinner I'll eat out."

"If you eat out I'll buy a whole new wardrobe for fall."

"If you buy a whole new wardrobe I'll buy a boat and go fishing."

"If you buy a boat and go fishing I'll go out and buy a ten-pound salmon so that we can add it to what you catch and have ten pounds of fish for dinner."

"All right, let's skip all the expensive stuff and have salmon for dinner." Joseph laughed and kissed her and went up to the office. He never mentioned the condo idea again.

But they were wrong about having an empty house. They were wrong about needing less space. Because Joseph's father died on Halloween, and with him gone there was no one to care for Hazel, Joseph's mother, who was severely limited because of her arthritis. "I don't want to be a burden on my daughters-in-law," said Hazel.

"Your daughters live in New Jersey and Rio de Janeiro," said Rachel. "You can't deal with the humidity and pollution in either place. And I liked you even before I decided to fall in love with your little boy. I think we can get along." Inwardly Rachel knew that it would be a severe trial for both of them. But she also knew that there was no better choice. Someday I may need someone to care for me, she thought. I'll treat Mother Hazel exactly as I hope to be treated—plenty of independence, plenty of opportunities for her to help out, and zero tolerance for any interference in the running of the household, not that Mother Hazel has ever tried to meddle.

"I'll do it as long as you understand that I have got to be allowed to help out even if it drives you crazy, because I can't stand to be idle," said Hazel.

"You can help out as long as you fit into the way I do things in my kitchen," said Rachel, "even if you think it's completely boneheaded."

They presented Joseph with a fait accompli. "Your mother is taking the girls' bedroom and she's getting exclusive use of the second-floor bathroom," said Rachel.

"How nice," said Joseph. "Especially because all the rest homes I've looked into are either resorts or prisons, and none of us can afford the former and I would rather die than put you in the latter."

"You've been looking into rest homes?" asked Hazel darkly.

"I didn't know that Rachel would be willing to let you live here," said Joseph. "And you always said that you'd rather be in a rest home than burden any of your children."

"I was lying," said Hazel. "Besides, I refuse to be a burden. An albatross, maybe, but not a burden."

So it was set. By Thanksgiving, Hazel would be in residence, and the house would not be so empty.

In all the busyness of getting things ready for Hazel—they even priced home elevators and stair climbers, until Hazel informed them that she could still climb stairs—it took a while for Rachel to realize that Joseph really wasn't taking the death of his father in stride.

"I'm doing fine," said Joseph. He had a puzzled look on his face.

"I know you are," said Rachel. "But you get this lost look sometimes. You just stand there, in the middle of some action."

"I'm an absentminded professor. I usually *am* lost."

"Just now, you stood there looking in the mirror, your tie half-tied, for five minutes."

"I forgot how to do a double windsor."

"You don't have to talk about it if you don't want to. But I think it has to do with your father."

"Maybe it does."

"Maybe you need to cry. You didn't, you know."

"He was old. He was in terrible health. Pain all the time. Death came to him as a relief. He was a good man and the Lord will honor him in the next life. What's to cry about?"

"You tell me."

"I still have my mother," said Joseph.

"Is that an answer?"

"No," said Joseph. "I think it's a question." He laughed mirthlessly. "I'm not sure how to deal with her without Dad."

"Excuse me if I sound judgmental, but I'm not aware of your father ever 'dealing' with her."

"But he did," said Joseph. "Quietly, alone, later, patiently, he dealt with her."

"And that's it? That's what you miss about your father? That he won't be here to help with Hazel?"

Joseph seemed to be thinking about her question. But then he finished adjusting his clothing and left the room without saying another word. Rachel wrote this up on her mental chalkboard and drew a big thick square around it: Joseph is having a very hard time dealing with his father's death. She had no idea what to do about this, or even if she should do anything at all. But she would watch.

At Thanksgiving, everything went perfectly. Hazel had been in residence for two days and had already shed any hint of being a guest. Thanksgiving dinner could have been a nightmare—two women in the kitchen!—but Hazel did only what she was asked, except that she made a batch of candied yams, which Joseph and Rachel both loathed but which Hazel needed in order for it to be really Thanksgiving. "My mother made them," she explained. "When I eat them, I see her again. Silly, isn't it? Conjuring the dead with candied yams." It made Rachel think about what she would always carry of her mother, when the time came that she couldn't just fly down to Phoenix to see her. That whipped-cream-and-jello dessert they called "Gone with the Wind"? "All foods have to have a name," Rachel's father had said. "Calling it 'That Green Dessert' could describe half the food in the fridge." So Rachel's younger sister, who was an absolute *Gone with the Wind* groupie, had named it for the *sine qua non* of American literature. But did that dessert really stand for Rachel's mother, or was it just a family thing? Joseph hated it anyway, so Rachel only made it when her parents or a sibling came to visit. Or when Joseph was traveling. Maybe it was one of the last remnants of her single life. Who could guess what any of these things really meant? Everybody had their own private mythology, with inexplicably powerful icons arising from the most commonplace things. Candied yams. Gone with the Wind. A double windsor knot.

Three of their kids lived in Utah, but Lettie (who had finally forgiven them for naming her Letitia after a great-grandmother) and her husband had taken the family to New York to visit his parents. That left Will and his wife Sarah—whom he called, for reasons that probably did not bear examination, "Streak"—and Dawn and her husband Buck. They were all coming to Thanksgiving dinner, with three children among them.

Dawn and Buck only had their three-month-old daughter Pearl, who was, literally, no trouble. Buck bragged that if he looked at her and said, "Sleep now, Pearl," she dropped off immediately. Will and Sarah, however, had the twins, Vanya and Valiant, and at three years old they regarded it as their mission in life to take apart anything that had ever been in an unassembled state. To Will's credit, he did his best to keep them under control, but Sarah was about eleven months pregnant and her idea of discipline consisted of languidly calling out, "Please don't be such naughty-nasters, boys."

Rachel could hardly criticize her for not leaping to her feet and bounding after them, not with her belly that was large enough that Joseph was talking about helping them build a stable for the foal she was apparently going to have. But Rachel and Hazel had spent half an hour removing everything breakable from the main floor of the house before they got down to the serious business of fixing Thanksgiving dinner. Thinking of having the twins in the house made Rachel glad that she wasn't starting a new family right now. She just didn't have the energy.

Neither did Sarah, of course. The name "Streak" had to be ironic.

The twins burst into the house screaming "Gamma Ray! Gamma Ray!" at the top of their lungs. Rachel wasn't sure she'd ever forgive Joseph for coming up with that grandma nickname for her, but all her grandchildren called her that now, and Rachel had finally decided to regard it as a genial tribute to Joseph's career in nuclear physics, even if she *had* always loathed "Ray" as a nickname for Rachel. Then they caught sight of Hazel and screamed—even louder, which Rachel would not have thought possible—"Hazie-Ma! Hazie-Ma!"

"I truly hate that nickname," murmured Hazel as she patted the heads of the two little boys who had attached themselves, remora-like, to her thighs.

"I haven't really forgiven Joseph yet for coming up with Gamma Ray," said Rachel.

"He came up with Hazie-Ma, too. That's why I cut him out of my will."

They watched through the open front door as Sarah came up the steps, rocking from side to side like an elephant trying to free its feet from clinging mud. "Streak," murmured Hazel. Rachel smiled and patted her mother-in-law's shoulder. For all of Hazel's cantankerousness, for all that she sometimes had to be "handled," she and Rachel had always seen the world through the same amused-but-affectionate eyes. Hazel had been ward drama leader when Rachel was going through Young Women, and Rachel had become like another daughter to her. A kindred spirit. This all happened while Joseph was on his mission, and Hazel had written to him in his last month that he'd better not date Rachel when he got home "because I don't want to lose her as a daughter when you decide to break up with her." Naturally, this guaranteed that Rachel was the first person Joseph dated when he got home. As Hazel had predicted, they did break up—three times, before they finally got married—but Rachel had made a point of staying close to Hazel through the ups and downs. It drove poor Joseph crazy, since, as he often complained, he could never gripe to his mother about the wretched way his ex-girlfriend had treated him. "She was always on your side, Rachel," he told her. "If we ever got a divorce, I'm afraid you'd probably go home to *my* mother."

Since those Young Women days and the courting days that followed, Rachel had come to know Hazel much better, and knew more about her difficulties than she had ever suspected before. But it never dimmed her love for Hazel, which was quite independent of her love for Hazel's son.

Now, looking at Sarah coming up the stairs, Rachel wondered if any of her daughters-in-law felt toward her anything like the bond of affection that she felt toward Hazel. Hazel had cast her as Fiona in a ward production of *Brigadoon*. What role did Rachel's daughters-in-law feel that she had cast *them* in? Rachel studied Sarah's face and tried to determine how the girl might feel about her husband's family. As far as Rachel could tell, all Sarah felt was tired.

The twins were already out of the room; poor Will was chasing after them, calling out the words that struck fear into Rachel's heart: "Vanya, Val, put that down! You'll break it!" I will not think of this, Rachel told herself. Possessions are not as important as family, and Will is doing his best.

Hazel pointedly looked Sarah up and down. "Well, is it large twins or small triplets?"

"God, I hope not," Sarah blurted. Then she covered her mouth with her hand and the look of dismay on her face was almost comical. "I'm so sorry," she said.

"For what?" said Hazel. "Sounded like a prayer to me."

Sarah laughed in relief, and so did Rachel. Hazel could do that, put people at ease in a moment. When she wanted to.

Still, it bothered Rachel that taking the name of the Lord in vain came so easily to Sarah's lips. She just hadn't been raised like Rachel's other daughters-in-law. She grew up Mormon, but in a rural family in Draper where the farmers still used the same one-syllable word for manure that the ancient Anglo-Saxons had used. There were junker cars parked on her family's lawn— the back lawn, though, which was probably a mark of the upper class in Draper—and even though Joseph used words like "salt of the earth" to describe Sarah and her family, Rachel had often asked herself how a son of hers could even be attracted to people like that, let alone *like* them, which Will seemed to do. Will was a brilliant young lawyer. He would move in elevated circles all his life. He might run for office someday. And this was the woman he would take with him to the Senate or the governor's mansion?

Even as she had these thoughts, Rachel stifled them. She knew it was a flaw in her, not in Sarah. I'm a snob, she realized. I never knew it till Will married Sarah, but I truly am a snob. All those sermonettes I've given about how the Lord is no respecter of persons and how the poor and uneducated are more likely to be in tune with the Spirit of God than the rich and "wise"—I meant every word of them, until my son brought home a farm girl who knew what a carburetor was for and how to fix one, "except it's a pretty useless skill these days," Sarah had explained, "what with computerized fuel injection." Rachel had only been able to smile and nod, having no concept what these things were except words in advertisements.

Ever since then, though, it had always been Sarah who had that polite smile on her face, pretending to understand what was going on as Will and Joseph launched into long esoteric discussions of arcane Church doctrines or issues in law and ethics or scientific and academic questions. It was the way Joseph had always talked to all his children, assuming that as long as you had reasoning behind it you could have an opinion on any subject, but Rachel was pretty sure Sarah felt completely excluded. Rachel had even pointed out to her that she was perfectly welcome to speak up. "I would," Sarah said, smiling. "If I could ever understand what they're talking about."

Poor child! Poor child!

Well, she and Will would be married for a long time—if the twins didn't drive them both into the loony bin. Plenty of chances for Sarah to learn to take part in Will's intellectual life. Rachel had had it easy—she was a professor's daughter and had learned all the social graces from her mother, who was the consummate unaffected hostess, so that without an ounce of pretense she could make anybody feel welcome in her home. Sarah simply hadn't grown up with this—but she would learn. And she was trying to learn, too. Rachel could see how Sarah's eyes were upon her, studying her whenever she came to visit, watching how Rachel did things, learning, learning. Despite all Rachel's misgivings, Sarah was trying to be a good wife and she would become just what Will needed. And one thing was certain: Sarah was already what Will *wanted*.

A couple of times it had occurred to Rachel that perhaps what Will loved about Sarah was precisely that she was nothing at all like Will's mother. But Rachel dismissed that thought from her mind as quickly as possible. She and Will had always gotten along quite well. He couldn't possibly have disliked her enough to try to marry her opposite.

Hunger tamed the twins as no amount of discipline could: When mealtime came, they were perched in duplicate high chairs, cloaked in huge, smocklike bibs that didn't bode well for the condition of the floor after dinner. Oh well, it's only carpet, Rachel told herself. Dawn and Buck arrived at the last minute, depositing Pearl in a babycatcher on the dining room floor. Joseph called on his mother to say the blessing, and to everyone's surprise, she said nothing more than the standard blessing, plus one sentence: "For all thy gracious gifts to us during this year, we give special thanks today." That was it. When everyone looked at her in surprise after the amens, Hazel only laughed and winked. "One of the things I like to be thankful for at Thanksgiving is hot food!"

I hope I get old like her, thought Rachel, not for the first time.

And then she wondered: Was the short blessing really in order to let them eat while the food was still hot, or rather because a mere month after her husband died Hazel wasn't feeling all that grateful? Unlike Joseph, Hazel had wept copiously at her husband's funeral. Still, since that cathartic day Hazel had hardly spoken of her husband. It struck Rachel that she and Joseph might well be coping with their loss the same way— by avoiding thinking or feeling anything about it at all. Rachel resolved to watch more carefully.

Will was telling everybody about how only a few days ago he had accepted the offer of a law firm in Los Angeles. Dawn and Buck were teasing him about being part of the recently cancelled TV show. "Will you be Arnie Becker?" Dawn asked.

"No divorces," said Will. "And no love affairs."

Everybody laughed. Even Sarah, who then piped up with her own jest: "I'm sorry they cancelled that show. I was watching it so I could understand what Will's life was going to be like. But except for the ones who were lawyers themselves, I can't remember ever seeing any of their wives." She laughed, and so did everyone else, but Rachel didn't have to be a genius to detect the fear that lay under the joke.

"Anyway we went to a realtor to see about putting our house on the market," said Will. "And it happened that one of the agents in the firm was looking to buy a . . . how did they put it? . . . a *starter* home . . ."

"A cheap little rental property," said Sarah. "I think those were the exact words."

"Yes, that's it—Streak here always remembers the *exact* words, it's why I don't dare argue with her," said Will. "I can face *anybody* in court, but that's because none of the other lawyers have Streak's steeltrap mind." He laughed, and so did everyone else, but it seemed to Rachel that she wasn't the only one who was unsure whether Will was sincerely complimenting his wife and laughing at the other lawyers, or ironically teasing his wife by praising her for attributes she didn't have. Steeltrap mind? Sarah managed to keep it hidden under her cowlike docility.

"So they already made you an offer on the house?" Buck asked. "Because it really *would* be a good rental, being so close to the university."

"If anyone can ever repair the damage the twins have done," said Sarah, laughing. Again, everyone joined in, but with uncertainty about how much truth lay behind the joke.

"They didn't just offer," said Will. "They bought. The only drawback is we have to be out of the house by December first."

"But your job won't even start in L.A. until March!" cried Dawn.

Rachel looked up into Joseph's eyes. They could both see the handwriting on the wall. Will was planning to move back in with them.

"Will, for a smart guy you are sure dumb," said Dawn, in her patronizing sister voice. "You could have sold it five times over, if you'd just waited, and to somebody who wouldn't take occupancy until after you left. You're going to make Sarah have the baby while you're camping out in some makeshift apartment!"

Dawn was the only one who ever talked to Will as if he were an idiot child. Will didn't seem to mind. "We were hoping," he said mildly, "that all that empty space in the basement here might be available for a few fledglings to return to the nest. It's only till March, but it will save us a lot of money—I think the exact amount is 'oodles'—if we don't have to move twice. We can just have the moving company pack everything up—at my new firm's expense, I might add—and store it until March. And it would be a great help to us when the baby's born, to be living here where Streak can get plenty of help from Mom. If you don't mind, Mom."

"Fine," said Rachel. "If I get the new baby."

Will looked her in the eye. "You get the twins, Mom. But you raised me. You're tough. And as my work winds down, I'll have more and more time at home. The worst of it would be between now and New Year's. It's a terrible imposition, but where are we going to find a rental for these three months? Nobody in their right mind is moving out between now and New Year's."

"Exactly what I was going to say," Joseph said. "You know that with Mother living with us, we—"

"With Mother living with you," said Hazel, "things couldn't be better. I can help with the twins."

"No, Mother," said Joseph. "That's too much for somebody your . . ."

"My age?" asked Hazel. "That's rich. I may not be fast, but I'm mean. Nothing wrong with these twins that can't be cured by smacking them around a little." There was a momentary pause. "That was a joke, you beastly children. I never raised a hand to *you*, Joseph. You should have leapt to my defense."

Now everyone laughed. But Joseph was still reluctant. "Will, you should have asked us before you went ahead and sold your house."

"If you can't do it, we'll work something out," said Will.

"What about Sarah's family?" asked Joseph.

It was Sarah who answered. Firmly, loudly. "No."

Everyone looked at her.

"You mean your parents really wouldn't help?" asked Rachel, surprised. "I know they're all alone in that big old farmhouse, and there's plenty of land . . ."

"I mean my children aren't going to have any memories of living *there*," Sarah said firmly.

"It's really not an option," said Will, his face reddening. He was going to back his wife up on this one, clearly, and he also wasn't going to brook any questions.

"Of course you can stay here," said Rachel. "Your father was only reluctant because he's trying to protect me from overwork. But Mother Hazel's right, she'll be a great help to me. Between the three of us, Sarah, we womenfolk will have those two monsters outnumbered. Just do us a favor and don't have another boy. Smart as the twins are, a solo would probably be born running."

"It's a girl," said Sarah.

This was the first they had heard of the sex of the child. "Ultrasound?" asked Dawn.

Sarah shook her head. "I've known all along."

Another silence.

Will finally spoke up. "Sarah . . . dreams. Sometimes. She knew about the twins before the doctor did."

Rachel had a strange feeling in the pit of her stomach. Why did this bother her? She had always known that some women had visions, true dreams, intuitions that turned out to be true. It was one of the gifts of the Spirit. And it was certain that Sarah didn't boast about it, since this was the first they had heard about her being a visionary woman. Still, there was something faintly awkward about the way Will phrased it. He didn't just say she had a dream about this baby. He said that she dreams "sometimes." He wasn't telling about one experience— he was saying that this sort of thing happens a lot. A very different claim. It made Rachel wonder who really had the upper hand in their marriage. If anyone does, she reminded herself quickly. After all, Rachel and Joseph had a perfect balance. There *was* no upper hand.

Even reminding herself of how good her own marriage was didn't make her bad feeling go away. She wondered: Do I feel uncomfortable because I don't really believe in people who regularly get visions? Or do I feel uncomfortable because my son married a woman who is much more closely in touch with spiritual things than I am?

"Well," said Hazel, "that's a *useful* talent, I'd say! Is the baby going to be all right?"

Sarah smiled faintly. "We're going to love her very much."

"We don't talk about this stuff much," said Will. "It's . . . sacred, I'm sure you understand. I don't know why I mentioned it today. I guess if we're going to live here I thought . . . I don't know what I thought. Just till March, can you handle it?"

"What are you going to name her?" asked Hazel.

"We have some ideas," said Sarah. "But nothing is set."

"Just don't name her Hazel. I've always resented my father for giving me that name. It's even more old-fashioned now. She would be teased mercilessly in school."

Buck hooted in laughter. "You can say that again! My parents didn't even have the decency to name me 'Norman,' which would have been bad enough. No, every school year the teacher had to read out my name." He put on an exaggeratedly high teacher's voice: "'Normal'? Is that right? Is that a name, or an evaluation?"

"I've always wondered that myself," said Will.

Dawn answered. "It's *not* a description," she assured him. "At least not an accurate one."

"What *I've* always wondered," said Joseph, "is how you came up with the nickname 'Buck.' I mean, are your folks deer hunters or something?"

"Simple enough story," said Buck. "They call me Buck so they can tell me apart from my little brother."

"Oh, what's *his* name?" asked Hazel.

"Buck," said Buck. Then he took a bite of turkey.

It took a moment for everyone to realize that he was joking. Dawn jabbed him with her elbow. "You didn't have to pull that old joke on my family!"

He shied away from her. "Don't touch me when I'm eating unless you're giving me the Heimlich maneuver."

She started tickling him. "I don't use Heimlich, I just tickle."

"Tickle and *jab!*" Buck cried, holding her hands away from him.

"Children," said Joseph sternly. "Try to behave at least as well as the twins."

Well, thought Rachel, that was that. Somehow they had agreed to let Will and Sarah and the twins move into their basement. And Hazel, somehow, was going to help with them. The house was going to be full again. It was just bad luck that it happened to be Rachel's least-favorite grandchildren who were going to be tearing her house apart. Actually, it was bound to be a good thing. When Rachel had a chance to know them better, no doubt she'd find and appreciate the twins' better qualities. The same might even happen with Sarah. Sarah who took the name of the Lord in vain. Sarah whose parents kept dead cars on the lawn. Sarah who had visions.

Strange and mysterious are the ways of God.

The twins weren't as much of a problem as Rachel had feared, in large measure because Sarah went over the house with them, her expert eye spotting everything that the twins might be able to break. For a while, Rachel feared that there'd be nothing left, but as she boxed up every bit of ceramic and her entire clock collection, she reminded herself that it would only be a few months. Apparently Sarah spotted everything. The twins quickly learned that there was nothing to destroy inside the house and so they went outside and worked over the garden. Well, that was all right. A few passes with the rototiller in the spring and there'd be no trace of their massive construction projects in the dirt. The only drawback was having to bundle them up for the cold weather every time they went out. But having them out of the house for hours on end was worth the work. Thank heaven the weather was staying dry.

And when the twins were inside the house, Hazel *was* a help. She had infinite patience as a performer, apparently, telling stories to the twins whenever they wanted, which was often. And always with different voices for all the characters and a lot of silliness and wit so the boys were laughing all the time. They actually preferred Hazel to the television. But after a few stories, Rachel could tell that Hazel was exhausted and so she'd bundle the twins into their jackets and herd them outside. In the meantime, Sarah would lie miserably on the couch in the family room and call out, "I can take them in here! Please don't wear yourselves out!" They cheerfully ignored her, except when Hazel went in and plumped up her pillow and gave her hot chocolate or lemonade or milk or whatever Sarah could finally be bullied into expressing a preference for that day. "You are the most *un*demanding, *un*particular pregnant woman I've ever known," Hazel told the girl. "I swear if the baby said, 'Well, Mom, shall I come on my due date?' you'd answer, 'Oh, you just come when you want. This month. Next month. Whatever.'"

"I just don't *have* that much in the way of a preference," said Sarah.

Whereupon Hazel would turn to Rachel. "I swear if Sarah's head was on fire, she'd just say, 'Now, if you're going into the kitchen anyway, and it's not too much trouble, would you mind bringing me back a glass of water to put this pesky fire out? But only if you're already going to the kitchen, don't make a special trip on my account!'" Rachel noticed that Sarah laughed at these jokes, but at the same time she could see that the girl had some kind of pain behind her eyes.

Sarah's due date came and went. December 8th. December 9th. December 10th. "I'm going to start jumping off the bottom step," Sarah told them miserably. "If that doesn't work, I'll try the second step."

"No such thing," said Hazel. "If that baby needs a few extra days to get ripe, don't worry. Besides, the doctors never really know when the true due date is. For all you know, this little girl was conceived late in the cycle."

On the 11th, there was a little false alarm—a sharp pain that Sarah was *sure* wasn't a contraction but she still had to go check. Hazel bravely stayed with the boys while Rachel took Sarah to the doctor's office for an unscheduled checkup. All the way there, Rachel kept assuring Sarah that the doctor would probably make them go right to the hospital and call Will from there. Sarah said little, and her tacit disagreement turned out to be correct. The doctor was as frustrated, it seemed, as Sarah was. "You're not dilated at *all*," he said. "I really don't want to induce until there's some sign that your body is in birth mode."

"That's all right," Sarah said miserably.

On the ride home, Rachel finally let her curiosity get the better of her manners. "Can I ask you something personal, Sarah?"

"I would hope so," said Sarah. "And I'd also hope that if I don't want to answer, I won't have to."

"Of course," said Rachel. "And it's rude of me even to ask, but the curiosity is killing me. How did Will come to start calling you 'Streak'?"

Sarah laughed sharply and looked out the window for a long time. Just as Rachel was about to say never mind, she spoke. "I'm very shy about my body," she explained. "The first time we went swimming, he dived under the water and snapped my swimsuit. I was mortified, but he assured me that I had run from the poolhouse into the water so fast that he wasn't sure I was *wearing* a suit. Actually, it was when he did that and I found that I could forgive him for touching me like that, well, that was when I realized that maybe I *could* marry somebody." Sarah laughed nervously. She had said more than she planned to, but less, it seemed, than she wanted to.

Immediately Rachel remembered how, at Thanksgiving, Sarah had been so adamant about her children never having memories of the house she grew up in. "You were molested as a child, weren't you?" Rachel asked.

Sarah nodded. "I knew you guessed when I reacted like I did to living in my parents' house. It wasn't my father, though, I don't want you ever to think that. My father's youngest brother lived with them for a while because of some trouble he was in out in Star Valley, Wyoming. He stayed for a year. I turned eleven that year. He made me do things."

"You don't have to tell me more than that, Sarah, if you don't want to," said Rachel.

"I have some pretty bad memories of that time. Because I felt for the longest time that I was partly at fault. I mean, at first it was almost exciting. I was curious."

"You were a child."

"I know that as a Primary president you have all sorts of training in dealing with this."

"Less than I should," said Rachel. "And more than I was ever required to have."

"Well, they *say* that the child is never at fault. But I was over eight years old and I wasn't stupid. I know that it was mostly him, even though he really was a child himself, only fifteen. But it was partly me, and I couldn't feel right about anything until I was seventeen and I decided that maybe other people could do what the therapist said, but *I* had to repent. Like Enos, you know? I prayed for two days. In the summer. My mother understood a little and she refused to let anyone go searching for me. Out in the far corner of the orchard. It works, you know. I was forgiven."

Rachel had tears in her eyes, but when she glanced over at Sarah she could see that the girl was dry-eyed.

"I don't get emotional about it now," said Sarah. "It's at the very center of my life. Not the molesting, but the forgiveness. That was when I first had a, you know, dream. I don't have a lot of them, if that's what worries you. It's more like going to a movie with a friend who's seen it before, and right before the scary parts she says, 'Don't worry about this, it turns out all right.' "

"But you still can't go home."

"Bad memories."

Rachel had a sudden insight and had to blurt it out. "Did your parents know what kind of trouble this uncle of yours had been in back in Wyoming?"

"They knew it was trouble with a girl. Father told me that it never crossed his mind that it was somebody as young as me, that his brother was messing with *children*. Afterward, Father wanted to get his brother put in jail for what he did to me, but I refused to let him. I knew that Ammaw and Old Man—my grandparents—I knew they'd blame me the way they blamed that evil girl back in Star Valley. *She* was *twelve*. So the way they saw things, I must be even more wicked. It was really ugly. I love my parents, but they come visit us, I don't go visit them. If I was a better Saint I'd forgive them, and I have, in my head. It's just my heart that doesn't know it, when I go home."

"You poor thing," said Rachel.

"Oh, I'm fine. I just wanted you to understand that it's not because my parents wouldn't help me. And I'm not really insane or hateful. I'm still going to be a good mother to your grandchildren."

"Well of course you are," said Rachel. "I never for a moment thought otherwise."

"But you were worried when I reacted like I did about going home."

"I was just afraid that there was some kind of rift in your family. I was worried about *you*. I know you're a great mother."

"Not lately," said Sarah. "I'm just a mountain of flesh piled up on beds and couches made of stone."

"Is that furniture uncomfortable?"

"Air pressure is uncomfortable when you're this far along. I have no navel. But where it used to be, I have this patch of incredibly sensitive skin. And lately it feels like it's spreading. Pretty soon my whole body will be nothing but one huge extruded navel. Touch me and I'll scream."

"I'll remember not to slap you around so much."

They laughed.

As they pulled into the garage, Rachel said, "Don't you worry about what you told me. I won't tell anybody."

"Well, I hope you *will* tell your husband. I was hoping you would. So I won't have to explain it."

"But no one else."

"That's very kind of you."

"Hey, I was going to the kitchen anyway."

That night, when Joseph got home from a late night of grading finals with his grad students, Rachel told him about the conversation. She cried in telling it, all the more because Sarah hadn't shed a tear. "Well, it explains one thing that I'd wondered about," said Joseph.

"What?" asked Rachel.

"Why Will was drawn to her in the first place."

"Oh, Joseph, he couldn't possibly have known about . . ."

"I know that he fell in love with her because she's a great person and all that. But there's a kind of frailty about her. She needs protecting. And Will needs to be a protector."

That was true. They both knew that about Will. Unusual in a youngest child. He should have been the spoiled one. Instead he was always looking out for other people. All through Primary, he was the one who would never let anybody tease or pick on anybody else. What Sarah needed, Will was; what Will needed, Sarah was.

"But it's more than that now," Rachel said.

"I know that," said Joseph. "I mean, Will can't be *too* protective if he calls her Streak."

So they figured they knew everything, understood everything.

Except Rachel still had a nagging doubt. There was still something wrong. Something in Sarah that made Rachel worry. Was
it her spirituality? Hardly that. Rachel was always more, not
less, comfortable around spiritual people. No, there was just an
awkwardness. Sarah had told Rachel about the most terrible,
intimate secret of her life, surely—and yet Sarah still seemed
reticent and shy. Something was wrong, still.

On the 16th of December they had their traditional Christmas party for friends in the ward and stake, mostly people who
had worked with Rachel in the Primary over the years, plus
some special neighbors. Everyone made much of Sarah and
Will and their kids, and Hazel of course, but then it was time to
put the twins to bed and Sarah insisted on doing that herself.
"You go help her, Mother Hazel," said Rachel after she was
gone. "You know how tired she gets, and she wouldn't ask for
help if . . ."

"If her head was on fire, I know," said Hazel with a smile.
"Consider it done."

About fifteen minutes later, Rachel realized that she hadn't
brought the candy up from the cold room in the basement. She
tiptoed down the stairs in case the boys weren't soundly asleep
yet. Nobody could possibly have heard her come down. Which
was why Hazel didn't stop talking to Sarah when Rachel came
within earshot. Surely she would have stopped if she had
thought that anyone could overhear her.

"Of course you know that Will's a special boy. They're all
special. All of Joseph's and Rachel's children. Absolutely brilliant, every one of them. I'm in awe myself. But there's a special
burden to being the wife of a man like Will. He's going to be a
great man, like his father. The best of a good lot, really. And a
woman in your situation really has to keep on her toes just to
avoid getting in the way."

Rachel could hardly believe what she was hearing. Surely
Hazel wasn't trying to tell Will's wife that she wasn't up to snuff,
was she? If she listened just a moment longer, Hazel would say
something that would clarify everything and Rachel would see
she had been silly to jump to such an awful conclusion.

Suddenly there were hands on her shoulders, sliding down
her arms, wrapping around her body from behind. Rachel
jumped—but such were her eavesdropping skills that she didn't

make a sound. She just turned around and faced Joseph and touched her fingers to his lips. "Listen," she whispered.

He seemed to notice his mother's voice for the first time.

"It's a special burden to take this family's name on you," Hazel was saying. "I know it—I wasn't born with it, either. Rachel is a natural, she really was born to be married to a man like Joseph, but I wasn't that sort and neither are you. It's just a fact of life."

Sarah murmured something.

"Oh, don't even *think* that you can ever measure up. No matter what you do, Sarah, people are going to look at you with Will and they're going to say, 'What does he see in *her*.' The thing you have to worry about—the *only* thing—is making sure that *Will* never wonders that. I hope you're using this time that you're in Rachel's house to study everything she does and learn from her. She is the perfect wife for a prominent man. But then, she has a real education herself, and she's a professor's daughter."

"I'm going to stop this," whispered Joseph. But still he didn't move. This was his mother, after all. One doesn't just interrupt one's mother. Or rather, Joseph didn't. Actually, nobody did. Not Hazel. Hazel wasn't good at taking anything that seemed like criticism.

"You just have to cling to your children," said Hazel. "*They* will never know that you aren't really part of this family. For them, you're the heart, even as Will is the head. So you mustn't worry about a thing. When you have one of those awful times when you think everybody must think you're a complete idiot, you just hold these little ones close to you because *they* won't judge you and find you unworthy the way everyone else does."

That was just too much for Joseph. He strode into the bedroom where they were talking, and in a fierce whisper he said, "Let's come out of this room right now."

Hazel and Sarah followed him out and he closed the door behind him. "I didn't want to wake the twins," he said.

There were tears in Sarah's eyes. Tears on her cheeks. She didn't cry when she told Rachel about her awful childhood experiences, but she cried listening to Hazel tell her she would never be worthy of her husband. Rachel wanted to slap her mother-in-law. She had never slapped anyone since she grew past the phase in her quarrels with her brother, but apparently she still could conjure up a real lashing-out rage even after all these years as a Primary leader with a permanent smile plastered on her face.

"What's the emergency?" asked Hazel.

"You, Mother," said Joseph softly. "You're the emergency. I overheard what you were saying in there, and—"

"You were *eavesdropping?*"

"Yes, Mother, I was. I'll be made a son of perdition for it, I know. Me, Cain, and the devil. But yes, I heard what you were saying to Sarah and I couldn't believe those words were coming out of your mouth."

"I was only reassuring her that—"

"Reassuring her! 'Oh, don't even *think* that you can measure up.' That must have been a real comfort."

"Sarah understood what I meant," said Hazel.

"Is that why she's crying?"

"Watch the way you talk to me, young man," said Hazel. "I may only be an old woman who's good for nothing at all anymore, but I'm still your mother."

"Yes, you *are* my mother. The very same woman who used to weep for days before her mother-in-law came to visit and then weep again for days afterward. And why? Because dear old Mattie was always judging you and you never measured up. That brought you so much joy, of *course* you had to plunge Sarah into—"

"Please," said Sarah. "She didn't make me cry. I was already crying when—"

"No, there's something you have to understand," Joseph answered. "You have to know that when I was seven I came in and found my mother sobbing her heart out and I said, 'Why are you crying, Mother?' and she said, 'Because Mattie's right, I should never have married your father, I've ruined his life.' And I knew then and there that this was wrong, it was evil, *no* woman should *ever* make another woman feel unworthy of her place in her own home."

"Are you suggesting that I am anything like my mother-in-law!" Hazel was furious now.

"I'm suggesting that what you were doing in that bedroom was *exactly* what Mattie Maw did to you when you first married

Dad. Remember the story you told me? How Mattie called you in and sat you down and explained to you that there was a special burden placed on women who married into that family? Mattie's father, after all, was an Apostle, and her husband's father was a great colonizer and his mother was famous in the Church as the general president of the Relief Society—"

"The YWMIA," said Hazel coldly.

"*And,*" said Joseph pointedly, "she had always thought that her sons would marry within their social class. Daughters of General Authorities, presumably, or people with enough money to move in those lofty circles. Of course that was the 1930s, I'm sure things are different now, but she was full of stories about how her marriage to Grandpa was *the* event of the season in Salt Lake City, and her oldest boy had married the daughter of another Apostle but it was beyond her how Dad—she said Alma, of course—could have lost his senses to such a degree as to pick up with a girl whose father was—well, no one even knew *where* he was, and there was certainly no money and less breeding and I think the exact phrase she used was, 'Try as you may, Hazel, you will never be one of us. All you can do is just stay out of Alma's way.' That was a terrible thing for Mattie Maw to say and it caused you more pain than anything else in your marriage and now here you are saying it to Sarah and it—"

"Yes, it caused me pain," said Hazel. "But as you condemn me you're forgetting one tiny little fact." Suddenly she burst into tears. "Every word she said was true!"

"No it wasn't," said Joseph.

"Oh, even *you* know it's true. Look at you, Mr. Professor with all the brains, pointing out to the poor daughter of a scrubwoman that once again she's . . . *blown* it!"

"It was never true, Mother. I can't believe you still believe it!"

"I knew it before she ever said it. And so did Sarah! We're just alike, Sarah and I. We both married up. Too far up, and it made us sad all the time. I dragged my husband down. I wanted to help Sarah do better than I did! And she wants to. She asked *me* for advice!"

"She asked *you*?"

"Oh, is that so incredible? Is Mr. Genius-with-Atoms really

so stunned that someone might actually ask his poor ignorant non-college-graduate mother for some advice about something besides the best way to get a stain out of wool?"

Rachel could see Joseph retreat from his mother's onslaught. Rachel had only caught glimpses of this side of Hazel before. But she was beginning to understand why it was that people had always been careful to "handle" Hazel. "Mother, don't do this," said Joseph quietly.

"Oh, is this something *I'm* doing? Is crazy old Hazel having another fit, is that it? You come in here and accuse me of something truly awful, but if I dare to express the tiniest objection suddenly *I'm* doing something bad? Oh, we must calm Mother down. We mustn't let other people see how badly Mother behaves when somebody *hurts* her, when one of her children *stabs* her in the heart in front of her daughter-in-law and her granddaughter-in-law—"

"Mother, listen to me—"

"Oh, I know, I'm busy not measuring up right *now*, aren't I? I'm proving Mattie was right once again, aren't I? Now poor Rachel has to face the fact that she's taken a screaming fishwife into the house with her and—"

Rachel spoke up. "Mother Hazel, I don't think—"

"I'll have you know something, Rachel," Hazel lashed out at her. "I *hate* hearing anyone but my own children call me Mother. He can call me Mother because his body came out of my body, but you came out of someone else and she's the *only* person on God's green earth who should ever hear the name 'Mother' from your lips. And do you know the worst thing about it? It's knowing that since you call me 'Mother Hazel,' *he* must call *your* mother 'Mother Amy.' Or no, it's probably 'Mom Amy,' isn't it? And she has no *right* to hear him call her Mother because she didn't bear him and she didn't raise him and cook his meals and clean up his sheets for all those years he was a bedwetter and—"

"Mother!" Joseph said.

"Oh, haven't you told her you were a bedwetter?"

"Mother, of course I did, the tendency is hereditary and I told her and all my sons who were bedwetters after me. It's one of many family traditions that we have proudly passed along."

Perhaps they were both aching for release, because this was enough to set them both to laughing. Uncontrollably, for several minutes, while Rachel and Sarah looked on. Rachel had no idea what Sarah was making of all this. For that matter, Rachel had no idea what *she* was making of it. She had heard from Joseph about some of the legendary quarrels he had with his mother, but in all their umpty-four years of marriage she had never seen anything like this. Now, at last, she understood what the great secret of Joseph's family had been. Hazel had seemed to be the sweetest, most kind and understanding woman in the world when Rachel was growing up. But behind closed doors, she had a temper that must surely be listed in the *Guinness Book of World Records,* at least in the top five.

They stopped laughing. Joseph spoke again, more softly. The moment he opened his mouth, Hazel started to speak, but Joseph laid his hand on her shoulder and she stopped. The gesture looked familiar. Then Rachel realized: It was the same thing Joseph's father had always done, when things were getting tense. A hand on the shoulder, as if there was a button there that when you pressed it, Hazel became calm and quiet, at least for a moment, at least long enough to speak a few words of conciliation.

"Mother," Joseph said, "Mattie Maw was wrong. She may have been right about her feeling that you never truly belonged—she was a snob—and she was maybe right about *you* never feeling that you belonged because you're a reverse snob, you've spent your whole life knowing that you were never worthy of associating with the only people that you thought were worth associating with . . ."

Hazel started to interrupt—apparently the hand on the shoulder was only good for a few sentences—but now Joseph raised his other hand to signal her to wait. Stage two? How many gestures does he have left, Rachel wondered.

"But I wish you would look at reality. The reality is that Dad's brother who married the Apostle's daughter hasn't been in church for thirty years and my cousins are all suntanned men of the world who drive Porsches and have divorces and marry younger women who get older after all but you'd never know it because their faces are stretched so tight you could use them as trampolines . . . but *you,* the one who wasn't worthy to marry the grandson of an Apostle and of the general president of whatever, not to *mention* the non-General Authority colonizer, *you* were the one who kept your family in the Church and every single one of your children is now a temple-attending Latter-day Saint and frankly I think that counts for something. I think it counts for a hell of a lot more than whose marriage might have been the social event of the season in Salt Lake in 1935."

"I can't have done too well," said Hazel, "because I raised a son who says 'hell' to his mother."

Joseph was furious. "You mean that out of all I said, that's the only thing you heard?"

"Joseph," said Rachel, patting his arm—*her* calming gesture. "Joseph, she was joking."

He looked more closely at his mother, who, despite the tears running down her cheeks, wore a kind of smile.

"Oh. I guess it was funny, then. I missed the point."

"Well, I got the point," said Hazel. "And yes, having worthy children *is* more important. But in case you didn't notice, that's exactly what I was telling Sarah. That the children make up for everything. You live in the children. You might get in your husband's way, but if the children make him proud, then it's all worth it." She started to cry again. "When your father was lying there in that hospital bed having all those heart attacks in a row, do you know what he said to me? He said, You made us some good children, Hazie. That was the last coherent thing he said to me. Talking about *you,* Joseph. And your brothers and sisters, of course, but you. And that was my career, my children. You married somebody who could do it all, children *and* being a good public wife. But all I could do was the children, and what I was telling Sarah, before I got interrupted, what I was telling her was that the children are *enough.* Only *you* had to burst in and demonstrate to her that even when you succeed in raising children who are every bit worthy to be part of this *distinguished* lineage, some of those children will still look you in the eye and tell you that you're too stupid to live."

"I didn't say that you were—"

"I may not be college-educated, I may not have graduate degrees and your magma-come-louder—and *yes* I know it's

Latin and it's *magna cum laude* but I also don't care—because I still know when someone has called me stupid and that's what you called me tonight, and I . . . don't . . . have . . . to . . . stand . . . for . . . that."

Hazel pulled away from him and hobbled to the stairs, starting the long climb up two flights to her bedroom.

Rachel started after her. Joseph put his hand on her arm and mouthed, barely whispering, "Let her have her dramatic exit."

"I heard that, you smart-alecky brat," said Hazel from the stairs.

"No you didn't, Mother. You always say you heard us, but you never do."

"I should never have come to live here," said Hazel.

"But at least it wasn't your daughter-in-law you fought with," said Joseph. "It was your son."

"Don't rub it in," she said. And, as she finally, arthritically, disappeared up the last few steps, she continued to recite, "How sharper than a serpent's tooth it is to have a thankless child."

"Joseph, you have to let me go to her," said Rachel. "She's going to move out."

"I'll go to her," said Joseph. "But I've got to give her time to start packing. It'll never work if she hasn't got a bag open on her bed."

"Are you serious? Are you taking this so lightly?"

"You forget that I grew up with this," said Joseph. "I was always the one she'd listen to. The fact is that she's still acting mad but it's over. She doesn't say 'smart-alecky brat' until the fever's broken." He turned to Sarah. "My mother meant well, Sarah, but she's wrong. You're not just like her."

"Yes I am," said Sarah. "I've known it all along. If you'd only listened to me you wouldn't have had to quarrel with your mother because *I'm* the one who told *her* that I'm not worthy to be part of this family and I've always known it, I knew it when Will asked me to marry him and I should have turned him down and now I have the two brattiest children in the family and I know that everybody looks at me and pities me because I can't produce *good* children like Dawn the writer and Buck the historian or—"

"Sarah," said Joseph.

"I'm just so tired all the time and so I started crying as I was putting the boys to bed and Hazel asked me what was wrong and so I told her, I couldn't help it, I've kept it to myself but I finally had to admit it to somebody that I know I'm failing at this and *that's* why she was telling me the things she—"

"Sarah," said Joseph, "you're not failing."

"Of course you're going to try to comfort me now and tell me that I'm doing just fine but we both know that it's a—"

"Sarah," said Joseph softly, "do I have to fight with you the way I fought with my mother before you shut up and let me talk to you?"

She fell silent.

"I grew up with my mother. I grew up knowing how Mattie Maw judged my mother and how my mother judged herself, and you know something? I actually *learned* from the experience. And Rachel was born with a good set of values or else her parents did something right but anyway, we both feel the same about this. Absolutely the same. I'm going to say it this once. And then I'm going to say it again every time you seem to need to hear it, until you finally hear these words echoing in your head when you go to sleep and when you wake up. Are you ready to hear this?"

"Yes, *sir*," said Sarah, only a little bit snottily. Only pretending to be rebellious.

"All that matters to Rachel and me is that our children be good. That they stay firm in their faith and love the Lord and do good to everyone around them. You know what I'm talking about? It's called the gospel. That's what we care about. And all these years as we've watched our kids growing up, we've been so afraid, what if they find someone who won't keep them strong in the Church? Especially Will. Because he's so brilliant, he relies on his mind for everything, his concept of the gospel was always completely intellectual and he never realized it, he didn't see that anything was missing. So I worried about him. And then he found you, and I thought, well, the boy has his head on straight after all. He didn't go for one of his law school groupies or some high-powered on-the-make colleague. He didn't go for a trophy wife. He married a good woman who is filled with love—so much love that the Lord even trusts her with two impossible children and she's doing *splendidly* with them I might add—and then at Thanksgiving comes the clincher. It turns out that Will, my intellectual son, has chosen a woman who completely fills the hole in his life. He married a woman who has visions sometimes. And he believes in those visions, and honors the goodness in his wife that keeps her that close to the Spirit. Are you listening to me, Sarah?"

"Yes," she murmured.

"What I'm explaining to you is that I'm not an idiot and I wish you wouldn't be one either. I'm smart enough to know that Will found the wife who is the answer to our prayers. I wish you would realize that, too."

She burst into tears again and fell into Joseph's arms and hung there, weeping into his shirt. Rachel reached over and patted Sarah's shoulder. "Me too, Sarah," she murmured. "What he said." Then she looked up at Joseph and air-kissed him. "I'm going upstairs before our guests form a search party. And you need to get up and talk to your mother before she calls a cab."

As Rachel left, she could hear Joseph saying to Sarah, "Will you be all right? Have we settled this nonsense, for the next couple of days at least?"

"Yes," said Sarah.

"All right, repeat after me, Will is very lucky to have me. And his father and grandmother are *not* strange."

Laughing, she started to repeat it and then cried again and then laughed and then Rachel was upstairs circulating among the guests.

*   *   *

Later that night she watched as Joseph undressed wearily. "We have too many friends," he said. "I'm getting too old to host these parties."

"Don't worry," said Rachel. "Our friends are getting older, too. They'll start dying off and then our parties will be smaller and more manageable."

"I can't believe you'd say something so heartless and morbid."

"Joseph, it's about time you knew how heartless and morbid I am."

He must have detected from her voice that she wasn't joking now. He turned to face her, gave her his whole attention.

"You gave me too much credit tonight, down there with Sarah. Maybe *you* valued her for what she means in Will's life, but never once did I think of it that way. In fact I always sort of thought that Will married beneath him."

"Do you think that now?" Joseph asked seriously.

"Are you kidding? No, I don't think that at all, now. In my heart I always knew better, anyway. Thanksgiving, when she and Will told about her having a dream that their baby was a girl and they both obviously believed it was from the Lord, that dream, I got this really uncomfortable feeling and for days and days I thought it was because there was something wrong with Sarah for having visions. But you know what I realized tonight? It was something wrong with *me*. Because her spirituality, it's something wonderful, just like you said, it's what Will needs. Only *I* was being a snob, I was looking down at her family and their cars on the lawn and—"

"You *are* a dreadful disappointment to me," said Joseph. "But you know what? I've decided to overlook this flaw in you and—"

"I'm not joking, you know. That was a very serious confession."

He immediately dropped his teasing manner. "I know you had misgivings about Sarah, and I know you didn't like her having visions. I kind of hoped that when she bared her soul to you about being molested as a child it would break down the barrier but it didn't, not completely. Not till tonight."

"So when you said what you did about how I was born with enough sense not to misjudge Sarah—you were lying?"

"It was future truth," said Joseph. "I knew that the moment I said it, it would become true. And it did, didn't it?"

She pulled him down onto the bed beside her.

"I'm really, really tired, Rachel, even though you are still the most beautiful woman in the known universe. At least the most beautiful one with arms and a head—I've always had a soft place in my heart for the *Venus de Milo*."

"I just want you to hold me for a minute."

"I can do that," he said.

"Your mother and Sarah both think I'm perfect, don't they?"

"So do I," said Joseph.

"I'm not, though," said Rachel.

"Close enough."

"But while you're busy understanding everything about me, I understand something about *you.*"

"What?" asked Joseph.

"Tonight something happened. You're not hung up tonight the way you have been ever since your father died."

"Oh, really?"

"I finally understood it," she said. "You felt the burden of dealing with your mother fall onto your shoulders. And until tonight you weren't sure you could handle it."

Joseph chuckled. "Well, actually, no," he said. "I've *always* been the one who could jolly Mom out of these moods better than anybody else, which isn't to say I was actually good at it. But what you said about my father—something *did* happen tonight."

"What?" asked Rachel.

"When I was telling Mom that she did a good job and that Mattie Maw was wrong about her? And then when I told Sarah she was just right for Will? All my life, it was my dad who said things like that to me. Good job. You did well. I'm proud of you, son. Not that Mom didn't say those things—she said them ten times more, in fact, but I needed it from my dad, you know?"

"Mothers give milk, fathers give approval," said Rachel.

"That's what had me upset. I know Dad was ready to go. His body was so ravaged. But I still needed him. Who would tell me that I was doing a good job? Only tonight I realized—I don't need that anymore. My job now is to tell *other* people they did OK. I'm the father now. I'm the patriarch. I'm the one whose job it is to bless other people. Even my own mother. That's what happened tonight."

Rachel held him close. "Did I do OK?" she asked.

And now, without a trace of jesting in his tone, he said, "Rachel, you are the greatest blessing in my life and in the lives of everyone you touch. When you meet the Lord face to face he will say to you, Well done, my good and faithful servant."

Tears sprang from her eyes and flowed down onto his shoulder.

"Are you crying or drooling?" he asked.

"I'm just happy," she said. "Like you said, you really do have the power to bless now."

* * *

It was the week before Christmas when Sarah's baby finally came, ten days overdue. It was actually a rather leisurely process, with plenty of time for Will to get home to take his wife to the hospital. With their mother gone, the twins got so hyper that Hazel and Rachel remarked several times that they would *much* rather be going through labor right now. Of course, they both knew that this was so false that it wasn't even worth saying, "Just kidding." They had just got the boys settled into bed when the phone rang and, against their own better judgment, they told Vanya and Val that they had a new baby sister.

Because Sarah had been so ambiguous about her vision of her daughter—"We'll love her very much"—Rachel had been half-afraid that the baby would be born retarded or crippled. But she was fine, a sturdy, healthy baby. Rachel wondered then if the problems would come later; she wondered what piquant burden of foreknowledge Sarah and Will silently bore. But whatever it was the Lord had shown her, it was certainly true that they loved the baby very much.

They blessed the baby in Joseph's and Rachel's ward on the first Sunday in February. They named the baby after her great-grandmother Hazel, and in spite of all her protests, they knew the old soul was thrilled. In March Will and Sarah and the twins and little Hazy moved to Los Angeles. They didn't come back until Hazie-Ma's funeral the next autumn, a year almost to the day after she had been widowed. Her last words were, "Alma, what kept you?" Sarah gave Rachel a copy of the four-generation picture they had taken: Hazel holding baby Hazy, with Sarah and Will, Joseph and Rachel gathered around. "She won't remember her great-grandma," said Sarah. "But she'll have this picture."

"And the stories you tell her," said Rachel.

"I have parties at the house now, you know," said Sarah. "I pretend that I'm you and then I act it out and everything goes fine."

"That's awful. You don't have to pretend to be me or anybody else."

"Well, actually, I don't really have the figure to be you *all* the time," said Sarah. "I just don't rebound to my girlish figure after pregnancy. So when I choose my wardrobe, I pretend to be Barbara Bush."

"That's all right, then," said Rachel. "I can handle the role-model business as long as Barbara Bush is carrying half the load."

Family Stories and Family Relationships

DAVID DOLLAHITE

Families and stories are intertwined. From birth to death we are surrounded and nurtured by family members and the stories they live and tell. When children insist that their parents tell them bedtime stories, they demonstrate that they do not live by bread alone.

My field, family sciences, shares many of the assumptions and methods of the other social sciences. In the past, family scholars have relied mainly on traditional social scientific information such as *statistics* (about marriage, fertility, family structure, etc.), *theories* (about why families act the way they do), *survey information* (self-reports of attitudes, behaviors, and feelings), *observation* (of family interaction under laboratory conditions), and *interviews* (detailed answers to questions about family life). These methods are especially appropriate if one's basic purpose is description, classification, explanation, and prediction of external and aggregate behavior.

But family scholars also want to understand better the internal dynamics of families in order to help strengthen them. Personal narrative accounts of lived experience provide important information about the inner structures and processes of individuals and families. And stories usually involve some kind of change, so they provide information about transformation in families. Thus, an increasing number of family professionals are using narrative in their research, teaching, and counseling. For instance, my colleagues and I who are studying fatherhood at BYU want not just to understand the father-child relationship, but also to help turn the hearts of living fathers and children to one another (see Malachi 4:6). Because we believe in the power of personal narrative to turn hearts, we have begun to ask fathers and children to tell us about their most meaningful experiences with each other. These stories allow us a glimpse into their lived and shared experiences. And we believe that these stories will be more effective than the traditional products of social science research in helping us strengthen father-child relationships.

Few people would question the power of personal accounts to touch hearts and provide meaningful information about personal and family life. But what value does *fiction* have in helping people in the real world improve their family relationships? Friends and colleagues, learning that I was involved in editing a book of stories about family life, often asked, "Will they be true stories?" Even though nearly everyone has personally experienced the pleasure and power of fiction in books, television, or film, they still assume that "true" stories are better than fiction and that fiction stories are "not true." Of course, fiction does contain truth insofar as authors draw on their own and others' experiences. But even made-up portions of a story can still be true in the sense of teaching true principles or demonstrating true ways of living. I doubt that the parables that Jesus told to teach and change his hearers actually happened. He told these stories to illustrate principles of life, not to report on actual people and events. His stories are not thereby any less true or powerful.

No doubt fiction provides good entertainment and can illustrate moral lessons. But can fiction also help us better *understand, teach about,* and *strengthen* families? In some ways fiction may actually provide us with more honest, meaningful, and "true" accounts of family life than even personal narrative. Fiction can often provide more open and frank accounts of family life than autobiographical accounts; some things are too personal, painful, or costly to tell in first person. Fiction can consolidate months' or years' worth of experience into a short story (focusing on the central message) or can expand hours or days into a long story (providing detailed exploration of a single event or situation).

Fiction can give us well-crafted descriptions of family interactions, conflicts, and resolutions, while at the same time providing us with profoundly moving accounts of people's inner thoughts, feelings, needs, desires, hopes, fears, and prayers relating to their families. Fiction can give students of the family memorable, meaningful, and "true to life" examples of internal family dynamics. Family scholars can teach about families as well from fiction as from facts—perhaps better.

Let me illustrate with stories from this anthology. Scholars who study grief have found that men grieve differently than women. When compared to women's, men's grief is often: (a) less openly expressive, (b) more cognitive and internal, (c) experienced in isolation, (d) left unresolved until middle age, and (e) often forced into the open by some traumatic event, such as death or serious illness. Two of the stories herein deal mainly with unresolved grief in fathers. "Birthday Gift" by Carroll Morris beautifully illustrates a father's grief over the loss of a childhood pet, his distance from his own father, his love for his children, and his relationship with his wife. My story, "Possum Funeral," also addresses this issue. Many of my clients lacked close or positive relationships with their fathers; some had had no relationship at all, because their fathers had died or abandoned them when they were children. I wrote "Possum Funeral" to reflect and honor the pain and loneliness that accompanies father absence and distance, and to suggest that healing is possible with the help of a caring family and spiritual blessings from the Lord. I also wrote the story to teach that grief is a deeply personal and unique experience.

Some of these stories focus primarily on the marital relationship. These stories illustrate, among other things, the importance of marital trust ("Father, Forgive Us"), the need for appreciation of a spouse's work ("Me and the Big Apple"), the gentle, caring courtship and early married life of a couple who meet in their later years ("Mallwalker"), and the emotional struggles of a young wife ("Now Let's Dance"). "Still Dancing" shows an adolescent daughter learning a critical lesson: her middle-aged parents can be stable, responsible, limit-setting people and *still* have a loving, romantic marriage.

All family relationships are important and in some ways problematic. But my clinical experience has taught me that relationships across generations are especially critical and have high potential for joy or pain. Intergenerational relationships are often more complex, ambivalent, and conflict laden than marital relationships. This rich complexity is well portrayed in a number of stories. "That My Soul Might See" and "The Door on Wickham Street" show close intergenerational family ties where one of the people is physically blind but spiritually insightful. "More than Marks on Paper" highlights the power of family ties—however "distant" relatives may be on a pedigree chart, or however far away they may live, when human contact is made family ties bind people together. The emotional richness, depth, and practical complexity of an adult daughter-aging mother relationship is finely portrayed in "The Color-Blind Bull." This touching tale also demonstrates the ability of an older, wiser family member to teach. "Worthy to Be One of Us" weaves a tapestry of marital and intergenerational relationships that illustrates relationships among adult family members, secret shame, and the power of a father to bless. "Tim" shows a happy, generous family reaching out and literally saving the soul of a troubled young man. "Your Own People" shows a young woman's heart turning toward the gospel and depicts her caring extended family helping her along the way. "Dad and the Studebaker" depicts an extended family rivalry and three sons' willingness to use their time, talents, and resources to give their father something meaningful.

In our society, people get to choose their spouses. There is less choice in intergenerational relationships. Although people choose whether to have children, they do not choose the personality, temperament, gender, or degree of spiritual receptivity those children will have. Another difference between intergenerational and marital relationships is that while marriages usually occur between people who are about the same age, intergenerational ties are generally between people who are at least

20 years apart in age and experience levels; thus, they have different values, experiences, expectations, goals, and hopes. This is well illustrated by the story "Flower Girl," where a father and an extremely bright and strong-willed daughter must overcome differences in perspective and experience (as well as beliefs about a bishop's obligations) to deal with a tragedy. "Sandwich Filling" depicts the stress that people (especially women) experience in the middle years when caring for a spouse, children, and aging parents or grandparents.

Intergenerational relationships are permanent, whereas, in modern society, the marital relationship is temporary for many couples. Many people feel that they can simply end a marriage that leaves them dissatisfied. But even when a marriage dissolves, parents and children almost always maintain some degree of contact with an expectation of permanence. The potential problems of this for adults and children are illustrated in "Hanauma Bay," where differences in the values and standards of the divorced, biological parents of a child cause family conflict.

The stories in this anthology provide insightful, touching, and sometimes profound glimpses into contemporary family life. They reflect the diversity of contemporary family situations, including families at different stages (young married, child-rearing, middle years, aging family members), different structures (first marriage, remarriage, stepfamily, single-parent family, extended family), and families in various cultural settings. Each story also relates some way in which family members choose to turn their hearts toward one another.

Few, if any, of the families depicted in this anthology are dysfunctional to the extent that family therapy would be necessary. However, when intergenerational relationships are distant, abusive, oppressive, hostile, or otherwise problematic, family members experience anxiety, pain, confusion, guilt, and sorrow. Thus, in a fulfillment of the Lord's words to the prophet Malachi, when the hearts of family members in different generations are not turned to one another, there can be a "curse" in the sense that their lives are unhappy, insecure, and painful (Malachi 4:5–6).

This curse can be avoided by the creation or regeneration of good family relationships—by a turning or returning to one another. Healthy family relationships, especially intergenerational ones, can be deeply satisfying and spiritually rewarding. They can be the foundation for a widening of love and unity with all people. The scriptures show that the Lord wants our hearts to be willingly turned to him (see Matthew 22:37), our spouses (see D&C 42:22), our parents and children (see Malachi 4:5–6), and our brothers and sisters in the gospel (see 1 Peter 1:22; Moses 7:18). The gospel is about drawing on the power and example of our elder brother, Jesus Christ, to turn our hearts to our Father in Heaven and to all of his children, to create a vast, eternal family. To do this, we begin at home, by creating eternal marital, sibling, and intergenerational family relationships. And the term *eternal* refers to quality, not simply duration (see D&C 19:6–12). We are still seeking that ideal and need to change and grow in significant, often difficult and painful ways to reduce distance and misunderstanding in our family relationships. That in turn requires that we experience what the scriptures call a "change of heart" (see Alma 5:26).

An old Hasidic teaching states, "Give people a fact and you enlighten their minds; tell them a story and you touch their souls." It is the purpose of these stories to touch souls and turn hearts. I hope that in reading these stories you have found your heart softened and therefore will choose to draw closer to your loved ones in thought, word, and deed. Share those stories that prove meaningful to you with others who may be struggling with something in their own families; help them see they are not alone in their difficulties and that there are solutions to most family problems. Especially, I hope these stories might direct your heart toward the Father of us all, who has the desire and the power to bless us, if we are willing, binding us to him and to one another in bonds of eternal love and joy.

Finally, because my colleagues and I use narrative accounts of people's personal experiences in our efforts to help turn the hearts of fathers and children to one another, I invite you to send me a written or tape-recorded account of an actual meaningful family experience, if it involves a father in some way. It need not be what you consider a dramatic or profound experience, for often "out of small things proceedeth that which is great" (D&C 64:33).

David Dollahite, Ph.D.
Department of Family Sciences
1074 Kimball Tower
Brigham Young University
Provo, Utah 84602
(801) 378-4179

About the Authors

Orson Scott Card, currently Young Men's president in his ward in Greensboro, North Carolina, is married to the ward's early-morning seminary teacher, Kristine Allen Card. Together they are the parents of Geoffrey, Emily, Charlie Ben, and Zina Margaret. Card is the author of several dozen books and publisher of Hatrack River Publications. On the America Online computer network, he created and supervises the private Mormon community called Nauvoo.

Richard H. Cracroft, chair of American Studies at BYU and director of the Center for American Values in Literature, has been a major figure in Mormon literature for many years, as author, teacher, critic, reviewer, and editor. He has served as chairman of the English department and dean of the College of Humanities at BYU and as president of the Association of Mormon Letters (1991). He also served as president of the Zurich Switzerland mission from 1986 through 1989.

Kathleen Dalton-Woodbury has for many years been the director of the Science Fiction and Fantasy Workshop, in which new and aspiring writers learn from each other by correspondence. A native of Salt Lake City, she has a bachelor's degree in math education and a master's degree in mechanical engineering. She currently teaches a writing class at East High Community School, and two of her science fiction stories have been published. She and her husband, an engineer with Questar Corporation, are the parents of three girls. She serves as ward librarian and family history consultant, and he is ward executive secretary.

David Dollahite, originally from Fairfax, California, joined the LDS Church at 19, then served a mission in New England. Now on the BYU Family Sciences faculty, his teaching and scholarship center on strengthening families and turning the hearts of fathers and children to one another. He and his wife, Mary Kimball Dollahite, and their four daughters live in Orem, where he serves in a bishopric and does some marriage and family therapy and a little storytelling. Aside from the bedtime stories he makes up for Rachel, Erica, Camilla, and Kathryn, "Possum Funeral" is his first try at fiction.

Jaroldeen Edwards was born and raised in Canada. A graduate of BYU, she has lived most of her life in the environs of New York City, though now she resides in Laguna Niguel, California. She is the mother of twelve children and the author of seven published novels. She has served in all the auxiliary organizations of the Church and has taught seminary; at present she is Young Women's president. She is a frequent lecturer at women's conferences and youth events.

Randall L. Hall was born in Logan, Utah, and claims Mantua as his hometown. He and his wife, Lloya, now live in Orem and are the parents of ten children. Currently director of seminary teacher training at BYU, he has served as a bishop, high councilor, and a member of the Church Curriculum Writing Committee. His previous publications include a novel (*Cory Davidson*), a book of poetry (*Mosaic*), and poems and stories in various periodicals.

Herbert Harker was born in Cardston, Alberta, and grew up on a farm near Glenwood, about twenty miles away. Besides many stories and essays, he is the author of four novels: *Goldenrod,*

Turn Again Home, Circle of Fire, and *Hostage.* Today his children are grown, and with children of their own have scattered themselves from Kuala Lumpur to New York City. He lives in Santa Barbara, California, with his wife, Myrna, and spends the first half of every day, Monday through Saturday, at his lapboard, writing.

Sharon Downing Jarvis grew up in Florida and Virginia, graduated from Florida State, and taught English in the Florida public schools for six years before returning to school (BYU), where she met her husband, Wayne. Now the parents of a son and daughter, they reside in Orem, where Sharon edits her ward newspaper, teaches in Relief Society, researches her Southern roots, and continues to write. She is the author of two novels, *The Kaleidoscope Season* and *The Healing Place.*

Robert England Lee was born and raised in Pocatello, Idaho. He is married to the former Peggy Furniss, also of Pocatello, and they have eight children. He serves as coordinator of seminaries and institutes in the Raleigh, North Carolina, area.

Freelance writer *Jean Liebenthal,* a native of Idaho, has seen her stories published in a number of publications, including *Redbook,* the *Ensign,* and *This People.* She is also the author of three short novels, *Up on the Housetop, Cottonwood Summer,* and *Feathers and Rings.* Teaching cultural refinement and singing in choir are Church activities she has particularly enjoyed. She and her husband, Jack, have four children and eight grandchildren.

Carroll Morris holds a BA in German from BYU and an MA in German from the University of Oklahoma. She is the author of four novels focusing on issues of Mormon culture: *The Broken Covenant, The Bonsai, Saddle Shoe Blues,* and *The Merry-Go-Round.* Her most recent publication is the nonfiction book *If the Gospel Is True, Why Do I Hurt So Much?* Currently a Relief Society homemaking teacher, she and her husband, Gary, are the parents of four college-age children—which is why she is currently employed as a copywriter!

Zina Petersen and her husband, Boyd, have two children, Mary Rose and Christian Degn. Having spent far too long among the grownups in her ward, Zina currently serves as the nursery leader, a calling she was stunned to find she likes. She is a graduate student in medieval English at the Catholic University of America—she hopes not permanently. The Petersens live near Washington DC.

Kristen D. Randle lives on the banks of the Provo River with her husband, their four wild children, and a brindled, brainless collie. A BYU graduate, she fills her days with algebra, church-stuff, quilting, refereeing the children, and managing the business and moral deportment of a phalanx of musicians who frequent the family recording studio. She also writes. She has a firm belief that light is better than darkness, and that every soul knows it, at some level.

Richard M. Siddoway was born and raised in Salt Lake City and Bountiful, Utah. He and his wife, Janice, are the parents of eight children. A former bishop, he is currently a counselor in a stake presidency. After years of teaching in junior high and high schools and as a high school assistant principal, he is now the supervisor of instructional technology for the Davis County school district. He is the author of *Twelve Tales of Christmas* and *Mom—and Other Great Women I've Known.*

Susan Dean Strange, an army brat, was born in Chincoteague, Virginia, and raised in such diverse places as Hawaii, Germany, and Kansas. She joined the Church in college. She settled in Danville, Virginia, where her seven children range in age from six to twenty. After a long interruption, she earned her bachelor's degree *summa cum laude* in 1992. Besides her two novels, *You're a Rock, Sister Lewis* and *True Rings the Heart,* she authors a column for her local paper. She says, "At the present, I enjoy life as a newlywed with my husband, Tommy, and driving children all over the place. In my spare time, I write in hopes of becoming rich and famous. If not both, then rich."

Jack Weyland has written seventeen books for LDS youth. For the most part these books are written between six and seven-thirty in the morning. During the rest of the day he teaches college physics. He is currently a faculty member at Ricks College. Jack and his wife, Sherry, have five children.

Jerry M. Young started his writing career as a reporter and then city editor for the Provo *Daily Herald.* After helping in Howard Nielson's campaign for Congress, Jerry became his press secretary, and since then has served as press secretary for numerous candidates as well as several companies. He has written two novels—*Eleña* and *Through the Mists of Darkness*—and is working on a third. He and his wife, the former Suzanne Cannon, have four daughters and fourteen grandchildren.

Margaret Blair Young is the author of two novels and two short story collections. She teaches critical and creative writing at BYU. She and her husband, Bruce, are the parents of four children.